BLEED
THROUGH

AYIN WEAVER

NovelWeaver Press

ISBN 978-0-9742339-3-2
Library of Congress Control Number: 2013949215

Cover Art & Design by NovelWeaver Press; info@novelweaver.com
Photography by Blake Webster, www.blakewebster.com
Interior Design: Val Sherer, Personalized Publishing Services

Source Notes:
*Native American/Lakota creation story of White Buffalo Calf
Woman compiled from these sources: www.sioux.org;
www.barefootsworld.net; www.nativeweb.org and are not under the
auspices of this book's copyright.

Bleed Through is a work of fiction; names, characters, events and
locales are the product of the author's imagination and/or are used
fictitiously; resemblance to actual persons (living or dead), events
or locales is coincidental.

NovelWeaver Press
Sebastopol, California

1st edition, 2013
Printed in The United States of America

To my mother who loved to write
To my father who loved to tell stories
To my family and all my relations
To the ones who remember

Acknowledgments

My debut novel, *Bleed Through,* could not have been completed without the support and encouragement of many friends, relatives, and colleagues. First, I want to thank my dedicated editors: Kemari Howell, Cris Wanzer, and Annie O'Flaherty for their expertise and enthusiasm; their keen vision made all the difference. I am especially appreciative of the guidance and wisdom offered to me by friends who read drafts of my book at different stages of development: novelist, Theresa Dintino; storyteller, Olive Hackett-Shaughnessy; author, Jan Phillips; intuitive artist, Leiah Bowden; musician, Amber Gaia; historian, J. Longfellow; teacher, Barbara Goodman. For the excellent professional advice, inspiration and encouragement I have received during the writing of this book, I wish to thank author/artist, Luisah Teish; authors, Mariel Masque, Uzuri Amini and Nancy Rose; special thanks for the mentorship from authors/workshop leaders: Kathleen Spivack, Alice Orr, Eunice Scarf, Jan Lawry, Dorothy Randall Gray, Rainelle Burton, and Pat Carr, and soulful guidance from Shelley Ackerman, Paula Scardamalia, Judy Hancox, Anne Schneider, Hilda Ward, and many others I met at the International Women's Writing Guild, including director and founder, Hannelore Hahn.

I am very grateful to many other friends and talented professionals who encouraged me along the way: Marilyn Greenberg, Paula Feinstein, Stephen Becker, Diana Fuerza, Lucy Whitworth, Rhea Schnurman, Linda Haering, Corrine Wick, Kristine Carey, Claire Etienne, Susan Hester, Sheridan Gold, Nita Platt, Penelope Starr, and more. Thanks also to Redwood Writers friends especially Jan Boddie, Dianna Grayer, Persia Woolley, and Jan Ogren. Much thanks also to the many friends who contributed to my book project's crowd-funding campaign. Additionally, much appreciation to book designer, Val Sherer, and photographer, Blake Webster.

Last, but certainly not least, I wish to acknowledge the ever-present love and devotion of my family, who checked on my progress regularly, who supported me through thick and thin, and from whom a story-telling tradition was born—and lives on.

The Families

RITA KERNER, Born 1947
Grandmother: Pearl
Mother: Lillian
Father: David
Sisters: Irene and Tina
Rita's son: Noah
Irene's husband and son: Gregory, Julian
Friends/Relationships: Marla, Arnie, Beth, Andrea,
Janice, Susan, Joel, Toby, Jane, Mrs. McCarthy, Cleo

CLARA DOYLE, Born 1842
Mother: Sarah
Father: Peter
Uncle : Kyle
Adopted family: Mrs. Riley and Anna
Anna's husband: Thomas
Inn Keepers: Matt and Sam
Friends: Ellie, Betsy, Rebecca, Stacy, Alice,
Miss Martha, Mrs. Landers, Doc and Preacher

BERTHA (ABRAHAM) WASHINGTON, Born 1894
Mother; Mayella
Father: Nathan
Sister: Dorothy
Adopted family: Ben, Beatrice, and Louisa Jackson
Bertha's husband: James Washington
Daughters: Belinda, Lucille, Michelle, Daniella, Denise
Belinda's husband: Jeremiah Williams
Sons : Arnie and James Jr.
Arnie's wife: Bernadette (+3 sons)
James Jr.'s wife: Olivia
Daughters/Sons: Nakisha, Jay Jay, Camilla, baby

CHASKE (First Son)/WAMBLEESKA (White Eagle), Born 1789
Father: Chetan Lootah (Red Hawk)
Mother: Takchawee (Dove)
Sister: Chumani (Dew Drops)
Wife: Dowanhowee (Singing Voice)
Daughter: Kimimela (Butterfly)
Uncles: Matoskah (White Bear), Wachinsapa (Wisdom)
Cousin: Napayshni (Courageous)
Other husband: Kangee (Raven),
Family members: Kimimela's mother, husband and son

BLEED

THROUGH

CHAPTER 1

Rita Kerner

BOSTON, MASSACHUSETTS, 1986

"Your name is Rita?" The doctor appeared suddenly in the doorway of the small, windowless room where Rita had been waiting. He glanced at her medical chart.

"Yes," she answered. She bit one of her nails, wondering why she had made such a stupid decision. Why had she been so gullible, agreed to sign those papers the intake social worker put in front of her? How had she fallen for that fake "let us help you" smile?

The doctor sat down in the office chair facing Rita. He was a balding old man about the same age as her father, she surmised. His suit and tie were old, out of date. His yellowing white shirt was tucked into his pants over a protruding belly. Rita folded her hands in her lap to conceal her anxiety.

"I'm Dr. Vagner." He spoke with a thick accent, one that matched a stereotypical gray mustache and beard.

Rita noticed an ID badge attached to the lapel of his suit jacket. Dr. Wilhelm Wagner. The hair on the back of her neck bristled. Just great, Rita thought, a German psychiatrist, probably a freaking Freudian. Worse yet, given his age, maybe a former Nazi. Where had this old man been during the war—the same war her father had fought in against Germany? The same war where her mother's cousins had been exterminated. Would he know she was Jewish by her looks, her last name?

1

Rita struggled to contain her over-active imagination. She didn't want a diagnosis of paranoia, an accusation with which she was familiar. She was an overprotective mother, sometimes possessive, even obsessive at times. But paranoid she was not. That word gave her reality no validity, just a negative connotation. Uneasy, Rita sat up straight, changing her demeanor.

The doctor pulled a pad from the desk drawer with hands that had a slight tremor. He scribbled something on it and placed it on her chart.

"So, *vhat* seems to be the problem?" he asked, looking in Rita's direction, but not making eye contact with her.

"I can't sleep. I haven't slept well in weeks," Rita answered, adding the word "well" to hide the severity of her problem.

"Weeks?" he said, raising his eyebrows.

"Yes, it's been several weeks," she repeated, wary of his disbelieving expression. "I tried some over-the-counter sleep medication," Rita continued, struggling to maintain a casual monotone. "I went to a clinic near my job and got some other pills after that, but they only help sometimes."

Dr. Wagner thumbed through papers inside a folder on the desk. "Yes, I see. Do you have nightmares?"

"Yes, but I am very stressed because…"

"What about voices? Do you hear voices? You told the intake therapist you hear things." The doctor's face was more animated now, his accent more guttural, pronounced.

"Yes, no…I mean, there are lists of words, like a radio is on in my apartment. I think it's haunted. My apartment, that is." Rita knew she sounded paranoid, maybe delusional. She was swimming into deep water. It wasn't good to say such things to a psychiatrist, especially during a mental health evaluation—and in a hospital, no less.

"You mean you hear voices? Who do you think is in your apartment?"

Dr. Wagner finally peered directly at Rita over his wire-rimmed glasses. Although bloodshot, his piercing blue eyes pressed her for the right answer—the answer he wanted to hear. He licked his lips. His cheeks flushed. Rita squirmed in her chair.

"Do the voices talk to you, tell you to do things? Do you see people?"

"No, no." Rita felt acid in her throat. She broke into a sweat. "No," she said adamantly. "It's just lists of words, like *window, pot, desk, cow*—just things. They make no sense. They keep me up at night."

"I see," he said.

Rita doubted that, but she could not prevent his assumptions. Nor could she stop his questions from steamrolling over her long enough to tell him of the recent loss of her second job, without which she could barely afford the basics for herself and her child. She could not explain about her health, the excessive loss of blood during her cycle—the real issues, things any doctor might see as normal causes of her stress.

But this psychiatrist was not any doctor. Rita could not tell him she was a lesbian and had just lost her new lover. She could not think about discussing the daily harassment from her child's father, Joel, or her ex-partner, Susan. How could she explain the complicated web of relationships? And no, she would not mention her dreams of a new war, tidal waves, or the bloodcurdling screams coming from her child's room, even though when she ran hysterically to check on him, he'd be sleeping peacefully. No—Dr. Wagner would certainly think she was hallucinating.

"What does the saying *birds of a feather flock together* mean to you?" Dr. Wagner asked.

"What?" Rita's eyes widened. Is he really asking me about birds? "Birds of a feather?" she said aloud. "Uh…it means stick with your own kind, I guess. Why?"

"What do you think *people who live in glass houses shouldn't throw stones* means?" Dr. Wagner waited for Rita's answer while he scribbled again on his pad.

Are you kidding? Rita almost said. Was this the *Theater of the Absurd? The Twilight Zone?* Was this a trick question, like the mathematical ones in school about trains traveling from different points that she could never understand?

"Do you have an answer?" he asked. She caught a glimpse of Dr.

Wagner's serious expression.

"I don't know," Rita whispered, feeling like a deer caught in the headlights. Throwing stones in a glass house couldn't be good, she thought. What was the right answer? What would happen if she said the wrong thing? Why was he asking these strange questions? Rita felt trapped. Triggered by her inability to comprehend, Rita found herself adrift in a long-forgotten childhood memory.

* * * * *

The inviting smell of oatmeal and toast permeated the Kerners' small Brooklyn apartment, offering warmth on a cold winter day. "Rita, it's time to eat breakfast and get ready for nursery school," said Rita's mother, Lillian. She helped her four year-old daughter into snug snow pants, under the child's wool jumper.

"Mommy, why am I Rita?"

"What? Not again," Lillian replied, annoyance creeping into her tone. "Because that's what your father and I named you when you were born. I've told you before." Lillian sighed. "We named you after my mother, Rhea, a name with the letter R. Just like R for Rita." Lillian looked at her strange child. "Can you say your ABC's, Rita?"

"A, B, C…my name is Bertha, Mommy."

Rita's father, David, sat at the small table where the family ate their meals, directly across from the living room couch. He looked up from his morning coffee and newspaper. "Don't you like your name?" David asked.

"Yes, Daddy, but I'm Bertha."

Lillian gave David a sideways glance. "She's a regular Sarah Bernhardt," Lillian said. But she knew the child was no actress. Something was wrong. Their doctor had warned them about possible brain damage resulting from the seizures Rita had suffered as a baby.

Rita didn't like to be called Sarah. It didn't sound right. She tiptoed over to the table and sat down in front of her hot oatmeal. She tore bits of toast into it. Then she reached for the sugar bowl on the table.

"What are you doing to your cereal, Rita?" David asked.

"I'm making bread pudding," Rita said without hesitation.

David sighed. "What the hell is bread pudding?" he thought. "You're going to eat that, not just play with your food, right?"

Lillian joined them at the table. "We don't waste food," she reminded her daughter. "Children in China are starving."

Rita nodded. Her mother often worried about those children, Rita thought as she mixed up the bread, cereal, and sugar with her spoon. She took a big mouthful. The sweet taste reminded her of something. "Oh," she burst out. "I remember, Mommy. I'm not Sarah, I am Clara!"

"For goodness sakes!" Lillian snapped. "You can change your name when you grow up if you don't like it." Exasperation laced Lillian's voice. "We are not going to call you Bertha or Clara or anything else. Your name is Rita," Lillian said, impatient with her daughter's odd conversations. "Now, say goodbye to your father."

David was putting on his winter coat. He bent down and gave Rita a hug. "Be a good girl." Then he kissed Lillian on the cheek and left for work.

"Now I don't want to hear anymore nonsense from you. It's time to go to school." Lillian had Rita's hairbrush in her hand. "Sit here while I brush your hair. And no talking!"

Grandmother Pearl came out of the kitchen holding Rita's one-year-old sister, Irene. *"Kain ein horeh*, protect us from evil," she grumbled under her breath with a disparaging look in Lillian's direction. *"Shena madala*, sweet little girl," she said gently, looking at Rita.

"Oy veh, another party heard from," Lillian sighed. She took Irene from her mother-in-law's arms.

Rita waited for the two women to yell at each other. Even though they lived together, there was no love lost between them. From different generations and worlds apart, they were all crowded into the tiny apartment. Pearl slept on a roll-out cot in the living room. Rita's bed and Irene's crib were crammed into the small room next to their parents' bedroom. The only other room was the kitchen where Grandmother Pearl cooked their meals. On winter days, Pearl sat in the warm kitchen looking out the third-story window at the snow-covered playground and benches that lined the sidewalk below. She tried to avoid her uppity, American-born daughter-in-law whenever she could.

Grandmother Pearl shook her head and walked back into the kitchen to wash the breakfast dishes. Lillian put Irene in her highchair and finished combing Rita's hair. "Can you be a nice little girl today?" Lillian asked Rita.

"I'm not a nice little girl?" Rita looked up at her mother.

"Just do as you're told, Rita. No more making up silly names."

"But you called me Sarah, Mommy. My name was Clara before."

"Before? Before what? Rita, I'm warning you, now. Enough! What is the matter with you?" Lillian yelled.

Pearl came out of the kitchen and yelled at Lillian. Once the shouting escalated, they spoke only Yiddish. Rita understood their tone, even though she could not understand all the words. If Father were home, the yelling would be worse, she thought. She was glad he had left for work.

* * * * *

"Rita? Are you close to your father?" Dr. Wagner asked.

Rita snapped out of her trance. She just looked at Dr. Wagner, but did not answer.

"How about your mother?" he said.

"My mother died last year," Rita sighed, feeling worn out. She was ready to leave.

"I see." The doctor wrote on his pad again.

"You know," Rita interrupted the interrogation. "I'm really tired. I just need something to help me sleep. I should get home. I need to get back to my kid, get back to work." Rita got up.

"I'm afraid that won't be possible," the doctor replied. "You will have to be here for forty-eight hours, for observation." Dr. Wagner stood up. Without another word, he gathered his papers and walked out of the room.

"Forty-eight hours? Observation? Does he think I'm…psychotic?" Rita murmured incredulously. Could they do that? Could they keep her here against her will? Why didn't she read those papers she signed? Where were her sleeping pills? She needed to get them back and get away. Didn't they understand she was a single parent with a job?

Rita took a few steps to the door. She peered in both directions down a long, empty hallway. Adrenalin pumping, Rita walked toward the nurses' desk directly across from the elevator. Out of nowhere, a pale, middle-aged nurse in a crisp white uniform intercepted her. She had Dr. Wagner's pad and Rita's chart tucked in the crook of her arm.

"Come with me, Rita," she quipped.

Rita hated when people she didn't know called her by her first name. Had no one learned any manners? I am thirty-nine, not a child—it's Ms. Kerner to you, she fumed. But she knew the condescension was intentional, part of the protocol. Protesting might have consequences. She followed the nurse to the nurses' station in silence.

"Wait here," the nurse ordered. She left Rita in the hall and walked to her desk behind a high counter.

A tall black man, young and clean-cut, stood nearby. Rita noticed he had an employee badge attached to his white uniform.

"I need my medication back," Rita said to him, loud enough for the nurse to hear. She clutched her purse. It had been rifled through for contraband—drugs in particular, even prescribed ones. At least they didn't take my money, Rita thought, relieved to find her wallet intact.

"You can't have those pills back," the nurse responded without looking up from her desk. Her voice reverberated in the hallway. "Dr. Wagner will prescribe the correct medication for your hallucinations." Then, in a sweet falsetto, she added, "You want to be rid of those voices so you can sleep, now don't you?" She rummaged through Rita's chart. "You can call someone. Your chart lists the phone number of your son's father. He can bring a change of clothes as soon as we get you into a room." The nurse got up from her desk. She looked in Rita's direction not making eye contact. "You can have your toothbrush, comb, but no razors or nail clippers." She turned away and picked up the phone.

Rita's heart pounded. Shit! I am in big trouble here, she thought.

She had automatically listed Joel's number in case of emergency, for the sake of her son, Noah. "Crap, if Joel finds out…" she said under her breath, her body revving into fight-or-flight mode.

She glanced at the young man, the hospital attendant. He waited in silence, standing close to the nurses' station. His eyes met Rita's. His lips mouthed silent words. Rita moved closer. The young man moved his head, motioning toward the elevator directly across from them. He stepped a few feet and pushed the elevator button with a magician's sleight of hand. The light above the elevator door indicated its imminent arrival.

"Get in the elevator," he whispered. "Get out of here."

Rita looked around. The nurse was busy, talking on the phone. The elevator door opened. In one swift motion, Rita turned, slipped inside, and pressed the ground floor button. Before the door slid shut, she saw the glimmer of white teeth against ebony skin—the smile of an angel.

When the elevator door opened again at the lobby, Rita controlled her impulse to bolt. She walked at a normal pace, so she would not draw attention to herself. There were only a few people in the lobby. No one seemed to notice her. It was dark already when she stepped out into the cold night air. She wished she had dressed in warmer clothes. Suddenly, a vision of Grandma Pearl appeared, an apparition holding a sweater. Rita could almost hear her melodic voice. She remembered how Pearl had kept her warm on chilly days.

* * * * *

"Can I keep my wool snow pants on, Grandma?"

"Yes, *Bubala*." Pearl walked to the hall closet and pulled a small cardigan sweater from a hanger. "Okay, *Bubala*. Here, stay warm. It's a cold day." She helped Rita put on the sweater.

Rita hugged her grandmother, feeling the soft cotton fabric of Pearl's apron. Grandmother smelled like soap and starch and chicken soup.

"Why don't you and Mommy wear pants, Grandma?" Rita asked. "I don't like it when I have to wear a dress. How come only boys wear pants?"

Grandma smoothed the child's hair. She did not always understand her grandchild, but the old woman never yelled at her.

"I want to be a boy again," Rita said, twirling in circles around the living room. "I want a horse. I am going to live in the country and ride my horse and wear pants all the time!"

"*Kum essen,* come eat. I have chicken soup, *Bubbie,*" Grandmother Pearl spoke in her broken English.

Rita sat down at the table next to Irene's highchair. Irene played with some noodles and cooked carrots on her tray. Rita picked up a noodle and fed it to her baby sister. *"Ess Bubbie,"* Rita said, mimicking her grandmother.

Pearl put a warm bowl of savory-smelling soup in front of Rita. She smiled, watching Rita eat the rich chicken broth filled with carrots, noodles, and parsnips made by her loving hands.

* * * * *

In spite of the warm memory, the bone-chilling cold shocked Rita back to reality. The icy wind whipped against her skin as she approached the corner, a block from the hospital. Still, the lingering thought of soup made her hungry. When was the last time she had eaten? She couldn't remember. Rita picked up her pace, hurrying toward Cambridge Street. Then pretending she was a normal person, she hailed a cab.

"Where to, lady?"

Rita was relieved that the cab driver acted like she was just a regular customer. She would be home in fifteen minutes. As soon as I get home, she thought, I'll get into my favorite sweatshirt and jeans, open a can of chicken noodle soup. She could almost taste it, feel it calming her nerves.

When she got to her apartment, Rita did not reach for canned soup. Instead, she scoured through the contents of a lower kitchen cabinet until she found an old bottle of vodka she'd bought for special occasions.

"This is a freaking occasion," she said aloud, pouring what remained of the vodka into a juice glass. Her hand shook when she brought it to her lips. She didn't care. She was alone. Eight-year-old Noah was at Susan's and the dog boarded for the weekend. She had planned it out, she thought, even if the best of intentions to get help had turned nightmarish.

How did things get so complicated? Rita sipped her drink. She should have been more careful, especially in choosing relationships. Early on, there had been plenty of signs. Had she just ignored the red flags, though, falling in lust with Susan? She had attributed Susan's drinking to the bar scene. But the self-centered drama and dependency had been too much. Rita shrugged. Why had she stayed with her so long? And why had she been so naïve, planning her pregnancy with only a verbal commitment from her friend Joel, who provided the necessary chromosomes—agreed to keep it to that. Rita shook her head in disgust, but couldn't dispel the heavy blanket of regret.

Walking into the living room, she sat down on the sofa and lit a cigarette. She looked at the full ashtray on the coffee table. One more thing to berate herself for—not quitting. She took a deep drag. "At least I dodged a bullet, more or less, getting away from that hospital," she said to herself. On second thought, maybe less. Without any medication and no more vodka, would sleep find her? She took a few more drags of her cigarette, then snuffed it out.

Rita got into pajamas and crawled into bed. Would the now lonely apartment leave her in peace? Would the voices start again or give her a reprieve? Wishing for the key to a restful night, she reached for her journal. Reading sometimes made her sleepy. She opened the journal to a random page and read the entry.

It was an ordinary spring day, but with no rain for a change. The weather was mild and sunny, the air fragrant. Wildflowers bloomed from the warm earth. Clara's long dark braids danced along the back of her cotton frock. She wandered down the hill from her house, past the horse pasture and chicken coops...

Rita read the passage twice, fascinated. She had no recollection of writing it, even though the words were clearly in her own handwriting. The date on the page was recent. What was the story about? she wondered, turning the page to yet another surprise—a pencil sketch of a light-eyed girl with dark braids. Under the picture, the word *Clara* was printed. The name was familiar—one Rita had liked when she was very young. But like a mirage, the more she focused, the more the memory eluded her.

On the next page were smaller sketches of two other children drawn in great detail. One was a picture of a darker-skinned girl with the words, *Bertha at 10 years old*, printed below it in Rita's handwriting. Another was a picture of a bare-chested young boy with waist-length black hair sitting on a pony. Not recognizing the entry or the pictures made Rita uncomfortable. She closed the journal.

Maybe, I *am* losing my mind, she thought. Maybe, I'm developing dementia, like Grandma Pearl. God, what if I'm having seizures when I sleep, like when I was young?

Rita went into the bathroom and took two aspirin. She turned on the television. *The Tonight Show* was just ending. Rita half-watched the *Late Night Movie.* She fell into a fitful sleep just before dawn crept along the windowsill. The alarm clock, preset for her weekday work schedule, woke her an hour later. She slammed the snooze button. The phone rang seconds later. Rita struggled to get out of bed.

"Hello?" she said, just above a whisper.

"When are you coming to get Noah?" Susan's voice whined.

"I'll come in a little while. What time is it? I thought you were keeping him, today." Rita's throat felt like sandpaper.

"I was, but I have to study. You sound lousy." Susan's said.

You woke me, you friggin' ass... Rita wanted to say, but held her tongue. It was too early to get into a fight with her ex again. Susan had stopped drinking after her car accident, but her nasty streak remained.

Rita still felt badly for Susan, a woman with an abuse-filled childhood. But she was done being protective, making excuses for Susan's lousy attitude, her selfish behavior.

Rita obsessed over her mistakes, while she made coffee. I should have moved out of state with Noah after we broke-up, Rita thought. Now it was really time to get away—take Noah and run. But how? Where?

Rita decided not to answer the phone for the rest of the day. She would pull herself together, she thought. She would go pick up Noah and get the dog. They would go for a walk at the Commons.

Rita opened the blinds on the east-facing windows. The sun peaked out from behind winter clouds, casting long morning shadows on frosty sidewalks. If it gets too cold, we can stop for hot chocolate, maybe go to the Children's Museum, she planned.

She showered and dressed, then checked her wallet. There was enough cash to shop at the market, later. She scribbled a little shopping list on the back of an old envelope. She would make Grandma Pearl's chicken soup for Noah with fresh chicken, noodles, carrots, and parsnips. It was his favorite, too.

Rita put her knit scarf around her neck and zipped her jacket, glancing at herself in the hall mirror before leaving. The dark circles under her eyes looked worse in the harsh morning light. *"Kain ein horeh.* May no evil befall us," Rita prayed. Then she locked the apartment door behind her and left.

CHAPTER 2

Clare Doyle

NEAR COOS BAY, OREGON TERRITORY, 1852

It was an ordinary spring day, but with no rain for a change. The weather was mild and sunny, the air fragrant. Wildflowers bloomed from the warm earth. Clara breathed in the fresh afternoon air as she walked toward the edge of the meadow, her long dark braids dancing along the back of her cotton frock. She wandered down the hill from her house, past the horse pasture and chicken coops on the far side of the neighbor's house, Mrs. Riley's place. She wanted to talk to Anna, Mrs. Riley's only child. Almost three years older than Clara, Anna was like a big sister.

Mrs. Riley, a widow, liked to have company, especially Clara's. She had always wanted more children, but Anna's father had died of pneumonia when Anna was only a year old. "The good Lord took my dear husband so young," Mrs. Riley sighed. "God must have needed him for something mighty important to take him from us," she had confided during one of Clara's previous visits.

"Hello, child!" Mrs. Riley now greeted Clara with a big smile that made her eyes squint. "How are you and that fine family of yours? You are a mighty lucky child," she chirped. "Such a nice house your father built." She peered out the window at the house on the hill. "How's that girl Ellie doing? Your daddy's sure a good man to get your mother some help with your new baby sister—fine thing." Mrs. Riley liked Clara's parents. She called the Doyle family well-mannered Eastern folk.

13

"Thank you, Mrs. Riley. Everyone's good at my house," Clara answered.

Peter and Sarah Doyle had come by wagon train across the Oregon Trail to the Territory in 1842. They had arrived on the coast two years ago looking for a homestead, after the gold find in Rogue River Valley. Mrs. Riley had sold them a bit of her land to build their house, but they would never be country folk like Mrs. Riley. Her family had lived in the far Northwest for generations. A hint of Mrs. Riley's Indian ancestry remained in her high cheekbones and almond-shaped eyes.

Clara was mesmerized when Mrs. Riley told them stories of long ago. "*Wakashan* was the language of my great-grandmother," Mrs. Riley usually began. "My great-grandfather, Irish he was, sailed with Captain James Cook some seventy years before I was born. They came to Nootka Sound at Vancouver Island," she motioned, "far north of this Territory. Married a Nootka girl," she said proudly. "That's where I got the Indian in me."

Mrs. Riley continued. "And the Irish came down from him and his kin, my grandfather and father. Married Irish too—my husband, James Mitchell Riley." Her blue eyes and light skin belied her Irish ancestry, but Mrs. Riley never forgot the Nootka stories told to her between the Bible stories in her youth.

"My grandfather knew the holy man from my great-grandmother's tribe," she would sometimes tell a story to Anna and Clara. "He was the keeper of a sacred abalone box filled with supernatural spirits," Mrs. Riley said, waving her arms as she spoke. "He could change into an eagle and fly into the clouds, bring spirits to heal the sick. He could peer into the future…"

Today though, Clara didn't have time for stories. She had promised her mother that she would be back for dinner before sundown, when her father would be returning from a business trip to San Francisco. Clara planned to tell Mrs. Riley, so she would not be disappointed or tempt her with delicious soup or pudding. Clara stood at the kitchen door.

"Well, come in, child! You're just in time for bread pudding, hot

out of the oven, sugar," Mrs. Riley offered.

Clara's resolve wavered. The sweet aroma of bread and cinnamon filled the air. "Oh, it smells really good! But, uh…no thank you, Mrs. Riley. I can't. We're having dinner early tonight, because my father is returning from a trip."

Clara didn't tell Mrs. Riley how they had gotten all dressed up just a few weeks ago. Her father had invited some important men to the house—something about a railroad, she'd heard him say. Her father's younger brother, Kyle, whom Clara had never met before, had arrived by what seemed a coincidence that same day. Company from California, more than two weeks' travel, was a rare event. Clara didn't mention how she had helped her mother and Ellie clean and cook, and polish the banister, the silver, and Father's gold pocket watch that morning. Nor did she say how fine they all looked. Even the baby was dressed in her Sunday best.

Clara had fixed ribbons in her hair by herself. When she came into the parlor, Mother had given her a big hug, smiling to see her girl blossoming into such a well-groomed young lady. Mother had looked beautiful and smelled like rose water. Father had been preoccupied, pulling his well-polished gold watch out of his pocket to check the time every few minutes. But today, Clara did not give Mrs. Riley all these details. She did not tell her anything about Kyle, her handsome and most charming uncle. She would tell Anna about him, though.

"Oh, all right, dearie, if you're sure you're not hungry," said Mrs. Riley. She put up the bread pudding to cool by the window. "Anna is upstairs. Run along, then." She smiled half-heartedly.

Clara dashed up the stairs. Anna was happy to see her friend. "I'm going to marry that Thomas Desell, Jr. one day. You wait and see," Anna said while she finished tying back her light brown hair. Anna liked Thomas, Mr. Desell's son. Father and son came every Wednesday to plow, chop wood, clean out the stalls, or do whatever jobs Mrs. Riley needed done.

Almost thirteen, Anna was very interested in what men and women did behind closed doors. Her budding interest was fascinating to Clara. Anna unbuttoned her dress and showed Clara her blossoming breasts, her soft, pink nipples. Clara had only seen her own mother's bigger breasts when she nursed the baby.

"They're not just for feeding the baby," Anna had told her. "They feel tingly. Well, you'll see," she giggled, covering up quickly. Clara touched her own chest. She felt a bit of tenderness, but nothing more.

"Men like to give you babies," Anna continued, teaching Clara. "When you get bigger, they climb on top of you, like a stallion does a mare."

Clara wasn't sure she understood, but she didn't like the idea, anyway. Maybe, she wouldn't have babies. She wondered how Anna knew about men making babies. Did someone tell her that, or did she just know it when she got breasts? Clara pondered.

"I'm going to marry Thomas. You know, he kissed me." Anna blushed.

"He did? What was it like?"

"Oh, it was just a little kiss, sort of wet and warm. He is very shy, you know."

Anna could not stop talking about Thomas. Clara listened, soaking up Anna's experience. "One day, you'll meet someone you like, too," she finally told Clara.

"I have," Clara blurted out.

Anna looked at her with wide eyes. "You? You met a boy? Where? When? How could you?"

"Well, no. I mean I met someone who is nice. I like him. I mean, not a boy, exactly." Clara's cheeks reddened. "I met my father's brother, Kyle."

"Your father's brother is your uncle. You can't like your uncle!" Anna laughed.

Clara felt confused. "But I do like him. He is very funny. We had a good time. He liked me, too. He told me so."

"But you can't marry your uncle! Besides, he's a man, isn't he? How old is he?" Anna asked, putting her hands on her hips.

"I don't know for sure. Twenty-two, I think."

"Ugh! He's a grown man, Clara. He can't marry you. You're ten!"

"I'll be eleven next month. Besides, I didn't say marry, but he likes me and I like him, too," Clara lifted her head higher. "He said he would come back to see me one day soon, even though he lives far away."

Anna looked at Clara. There was a glimmer in Clara's eyes. "That is nice, Clara, having an uncle like Kyle. But one day you'll meet a boy like Thomas, who you can marry and have babies with." Anna wore a dreamy-eyed smile.

Clara thought about it, but only Kyle's image appeared in her mind. She could almost hear him calling her name.

"Clara? Clara? Don't you want to get home to see your father? The sun's near setting over the hill." Mrs. Riley's voice interrupted her daydream.

"Oh!" Clara jumped to her feet. "Anna, I've got to go. Mother will be angry if I'm late for dinner." Clara ran down the stairs, waving goodbye to Mrs. Riley as she ran out the door.

Clara was out of breath by the time she saw her house. When she reached the top of the hill, she noticed the barn door was open. She peeked inside to see if her father was unbridling the mare. The mare was not there. Clara breathed a sigh of relief. She had made it back before her father returned home.

She went around to the front of the house. The front door was open. It swung back and forth in the breeze, hinges creaking. It was unusual for her mother not to close it securely. Clara went into the foyer, glanced into the parlor and through the doors leading to the kitchen. She knew her mother, Ellie, and the baby would be there. Bread, beans, and venison would be simmering over the hearth. She thought she smelled a faint aroma of sweet stew, but she saw no one. "Mama?" she called and waited. "Mama!" she shouted louder.

Clara stood motionless. A terrible chill grabbed her. Her teeth started chattering. The wind was blowing into the house through the still open front door. She walked back to the door and closed it. She looked at the staircase that led up to the bedrooms on the second floor. Something was wrong, very wrong. Where was everyone? Holding on to the banister, Clara started to climb the stairs. "Mama? Mama, where are you? Ellie? Father? Father, are you home?"

Back at the Riley's, the pan of bread pudding on the windowsill had cooled. Mrs. Riley picked it up and glanced briefly outside at the wisps of pink clouds, spread thin against the darkening turquoise sky. She looked just long enough for her eye to catch a glimpse of something on the hill at the Doyle's place. Her vision was no longer sharp in the twilight. She looked harder, squinting. There was a small figure walking with arms outstretched. Mrs. Riley saw it stumble, then fall into the tall grass. Her heart pounded as she lost sight of it.

"Anna!" Mrs. Riley shouted. "Anna, come here. Hurry!"

Anna was still in her room when she heard her mother yelling. Anna ran to the kitchen quickly. Her mother was leaning close to the window. "I saw something out there, Anna, up the hill at the Doyles' place. Something fell in the field and hasn't gotten up. Put your coat on, child," she ordered, grabbing her own shawl. "Come with me, Anna. I want to make sure Clara got home safely."

Mrs. Riley took the shotgun from the closet.

"But the wolves, Mama. Should we?"

"C'mon, Anna, there's still a bit of light. Hurry!" Mrs. Riley was out the door before Anna had her wrap on.

Anna had to run to keep up with her mother. She knew better than to keep talking. Mrs. Riley was not one to put up with complaints once she determined a course of action.

"It was over here, I think. Look around there, Anna." Mrs. Riley pointed to her left as they reached the hilltop. She held her shotgun in both hands with a finger on the trigger. She was prepared. Wolves and coyotes would be out at dusk. Mrs. Riley stepped slowly through the tall grass, searching for whatever she had seen from her window.

"Oh God! Ma! Oh, No! No! MAAAA!"

Mrs. Riley looked up to see Anna falling to her knees. Lifting her long dress, she ran toward her daughter as fast as her legs would go. She threw down her shotgun when she reached Anna. Anna was kneeling next to something, shaking and sobbing uncontrollably.

"Oh, God!" Mrs. Riley gasped in horror.

Clara lay motionless in the tall grass. Even in the dim light, Mrs. Riley could see the child was covered with blood. Clara's eyes were open, staring up vacantly.

For a long time afterward, all Clara could remember was having been at Anna's house that afternoon. In her dreams, she saw herself carried from the field. She remembered Uncle Kyle coming days later, lifting her from Anna's bed, then riding in a black coach down a road near a stormy gray sea to a cemetery. She remembered her uncle's soft voice whispering in her ear that he would return for her soon. He promised to take her away from this place.

CHAPTER 3

Rita Kerner

QUEENS, NEW YORK, 1957-1958

"*Bubala, kum,* come it's time. *Gey Schluffen*—go to sleep."

Pearl walked into the living room where Rita was drawing with her crayons while her parents listened to the radio.

"*House Un-American Activities Committee convicted several writers for un-American activities today in its ongoing...*"

Lillian and David had settled into their new living-room sofa to hear the day's news report. Lillian had already put Irene and Rita's new baby sister, Tina, to bed.

"*...Governor Orval Faubus sent National Guard troops to prevent nine Negro students from entering Central High School in Little Rock, Arkansas, today...speaking out, Martin Luther King, Jr. announced a nationwide resistance to segregation...*"

Rita's parents listened intently. Pearl shook her head, giving her son, David, a disapproving glance. "Rita, *Bubala, kum ahar*—come here," she urged her oldest grandchild. "*Gey Schluffen*—go to sleep." She pointed to the clock next to the radio. Reluctantly, Rita left her drawing of a boy on a horse.

"Goodnight, dear," Lillian said, kissing Rita's cheek.

"Goodnight, honey." David winked.

It was already nine o'clock, later than the usual time for Rita and Grandmother Pearl's evening ritual. Nevertheless, they went to Grandma's new room, a room all her own in their new attached

20

three-bedroom house where they had moved after Tina was born, two years ago.

Pearl sat down at the edge of her bed, so Rita could begin the nightly routine. The child took the tortoise shell brush from atop Pearl's dresser. Carefully, she removed the combs and hairpins that held Grandmother's hair up in a bun. The hair cascaded down Pearl's back. Rita let the brush glide gently through the long, silver strands, from the top of her head to the ends that nearly touched the floor while Pearl sat patiently. Holding one section of hair at a time in her child-size hands, Rita brushed gently to remove any knots. Usually there were none.

When Rita was satisfied with its luxurious smoothness, she separated three equal sections and started to braid it, not too loose or too tight. This beautiful hair, her grandmother's prized possession, was almost as long as ten-year-old Rita was tall. Silky and thick, the night braid needed no fastening.

As Rita held the three sections, overlapping each in turn, she listened to Grandmother's stories about her childhood in a far away land. Pearl grew up in a *shtetl,* a poor Jewish village in Russia. She was a girl with long, jet-black hair—her hair, a product of her family's Mongolian ancestry. Her family and neighbors in her village admired her hair for the money such locks brought. Each time her hair grew to waist-length, it would be cut and sold for wigs. There were tears, but no questions, no disobedience, no discussion. Being the youngest of seven children and motherless since her birth, Pearl was the chosen one. She would go to America to be cared for by the oldest brother, already in the "land paved with gold." Each small bit of money from the sale of her hair brought her closer to safe passage, out of harm's way to freedom. She would escape the fate that awaited those left behind. Rita never tired of listening to the tale.

"It was 1903. I was twelve. I came by myself on a big boat. My brother, I'd never met him, came for me at Ellis Island," Grandma Pearl told Rita in broken English. "I worked in a sewing factory until he arranged marriage for me." Her voice softened, "A year later, your father was born." Pearl smiled a rare smile.

Rita knew her grandmother had never learned to read or write. Married at eighteen, a mother at nineteen, Pearl and her husband, the grandfather Rita never met, worked at a deli on the Lower East Side. During the Great Depression, Rita's grandfather died. Left alone, Pearl and young David moved back in with Pearl's brother and his wife. Rita knew the story by heart.

Rita's father was Grandmother Pearl's whole life after that. David mastered English, like many first-generation Americans, but Pearl never did. Rita thought she knew how Grandmother felt. Even at ten, Rita had not yet learned to read.

For Rita, not being able to read made the first years of elementary school particularly hard. She did not understand schoolwork. Now in fourth grade, she was aware of how different she and her particular classmates were from most of the other children in school.

There was Henry, a huge boy with a big dent in his head, and Maryanne, who twitched a lot from Cerebral Palsy. Jimmy habitually pulled his pants down when the teacher wasn't looking. Fat George picked at his skin and shook his arms out in front of himself. Squeaky Patty always smelled funny, and Freddy talked nonstop to his imaginary friends. Then there was Rita.

The "normal" kids picked on them. They called them *retards*. They called Rita "Horse." She always found the nickname a strange one. She knew it was an insult, like being called *fat*, but she loved horses. She found herself pretending to be one. Sometimes, she would run home on her imaginary four legs as fast as the wind. In winter, when other kids built snowmen in the park, Rita built horses. She drew them over and over in her notebook, until they were perfect images. In her drawings, a young boy on horseback sometimes appeared.

It didn't matter what name she was called, though. Rita knew she was dumb, just like the other kids in her class who could not read. She usually stayed quiet at school, so no one would hear her say something stupid. But just the other day things had changed.

Mr. Kelly, Rita's fourth grade teacher, had caught Jimmy in action, pulling his underpants down. He hit the boy over the head with a book so hard that Rita could hear a crack. Jimmy's face turned red and he cried. The teacher just kept calling him names. That was the last day Rita stayed quiet. She got up. "Mr. Kelly, stop hitting him," Rita spoke up bravely.

"You better sit down or you'll get some of this!" the teacher boomed.

Rita sat down. But when the children lined up for lunch with their lunch boxes, Mr. Kelly tricked them. He made the children wait a very long time before dismissal. Maryanne had to go to the bathroom. She was squirming and twitching, waiting in line. The teacher walked toward her yelling. Suddenly, a big puddle appeared under Maryanne's feet.

"Look, her lunch box is leaking!" Mr. Kelly laughed nastily, pointing at miserable little Maryanne. All the kids looked at her.

Maryanne shuddered, dropping her lunch box, its contents slipping onto the wet floor. She looked up desperately, then hung her head and cried. She just stood in her urine, her white socks wet, stained.

Rita could not believe someone could be so mean. She turned and grimaced at the children near her, who stared and snickered. It would be the last time Rita was afraid of Mr. Kelly. She glared at him. "You are a very bad, mean person!" she shouted. Rita grabbed Maryanne's wrist, dragging her out of the line and up to the door of the classroom.

Mr. Kelly intercepted them. He towered over them, standing in their way.

"I'm taking her to the bathroom," Rita growled. She mustered her courage, feeling compelled to protect her classmate from Mr. Kelly's cruelty. In her most threatening voice she yelled at him, "I will tell my mother what you did if you don't let us go!" Unafraid, Rita stood her ground, Maryanne trembling beside her.

Mr. Kelly glared at Rita, but moved just enough for the two girls to flee. He resumed tormenting the rest of the children when the door slammed behind them.

That night, Rita told her mother what had happened.

"You're exaggerating, Rita," Lillian said. "A teacher wouldn't do something like that. Maybe you didn't understand what he meant, dear."

However, later that evening, Lillian made a phone call to one of her friends in the Parent Teacher Association. After David got home from work, Rita could hear her parents' muffled voices behind closed doors.

The next day, Rita was called into the principal's office. To her surprise, Lillian was there. Rita had to repeat what she had seen.

"Mr. Kelly hit Jimmy. He hits all the boys," Rita reported. "He made poor Maryanne pee in her pants and made the kids look. He is a mean, bad teacher," Rita complained. "He calls on us to read aloud, and when we make mistakes he laughs at us and calls us stupid. No one can read in my class." Rita began to cry.

She wasn't crying for Maryanne or her classmates. She wasn't crying because she couldn't read or had a mean teacher. She wasn't crying because she didn't understand things, or because she heard voices in her head, or because she had strange dreams. Rita cried because she felt better. It was the first time her mother believed her.

Grandmother Pearl always believed Rita. She knew her Grandmother listened even when she didn't always understand all the words. Rita wondered what it would be like if she, like Pearl, never learned to read. Would she always be in dumb classes? Would she be able to transcend language, time, and space whenever she wanted to, like she did listening to her grandmother's stories? Maybe, if I learn to read soon, I could teach Grandma too, Rita thought.

Every evening Rita helped Grandma Pearl with her nightclothes. And every evening Grandma Pearl told Rita a story. Then Rita put on her own pajamas and snuggled under the covers in Grandmother's big bed. Pearl sang a lullaby. Like always, she said, *"Gey schluffen, Babuska,* go to sleep, little grandma." Pearl gave Rita a hug before she turned out the light.

Though they still shared loving nightly rituals, Rita felt sad. Grandma was getting old. Rita missed the grandmother she had once known, the person Pearl had been. She missed sitting on park benches with Pearl and Aunt Esther outside their stuffy Brooklyn apartment on warm summer days, eating ice-cream Dixie cups with little wooden spoons. The endless hours at the meat grinder preparing stuffed cabbage, peeling potatoes for potato pancakes, grating beets for borscht, making chicken soup—those days had come and gone. Long summer afternoons sunning on beach chairs with white-creamed noses, standing ankle-deep in cold, salty water at Coney Island Beach splashing themselves, walking down the narrow path of clapboard bungalows at sunset to Grandma's room at Mrs. Goldberg's summer rooming house—were all just memories now.

The family had needed a bigger place after Tina was born. At first, Pearl enjoyed the novelty of having a bedroom of her own. As time went by though, the reality that her way of life had vanished took its toll. She lost the daily contact with her brother, sister-in-law and friends. Pearl didn't know anyone in Queens, no one her own age or background in this strange new place. Sometimes, Rita would find Grandmother Pearl in her room crying. Rita wondered if it reminded Pearl of coming to America and leaving everything she knew. The stress of moving away from her small family in Brooklyn not only brought sadness, but illness too.

* * * * *

Not long after Rita turned eleven, Pearl's dementia transported her back to the time before the boat. Rita came home from school one day and found Pearl hiding butter, salt, and sugar in her dresser drawers. "Grandma, what are you doing?' Rita yelled. She began to remove the food. But Pearl screamed.

"No, no, don't take our food!" Pearl cried.

"Grandma, it's me—Rita! We have to put the food back in the kitchen. The butter will spoil, get bugs. You can't keep this stuff here!"

Rita could not comprehend the horror of Grandmother's waking nightmares. She was embarrassed that Pearl was taking food from the refrigerator, squirreling away nickels and dimes from the family's coat pockets.

Perhaps because they were in America, no one had yet thought to explain the word *pogrom*. Perhaps it was just easier to forget.

Grandmother's family in the old country were all dead now. Someone had killed them in a war, Rita thought. So Rita was ill-equipped to convince her grandmother that no one was going to come into the house to steal food. Hard as she tried, Rita could not console Grandma Pearl. Nor could she hide her frustration at her grandmother's refusal to take her word on the matter.

"Grandma, I'm telling you the truth. Why don't you believe me? No one is taking our food!" Rita reprimanded as she took a stick of melting butter, slices of bread and a salt shaker from Pearl's dresser. Rita pushed Grandma Pearl away when she tried to stop her.

The old woman grew increasingly distant and hostile after that. She said Rita was her mother's daughter. In the old woman's eyes, Rita's mother was a thief who had stolen her only child. She had never approved of the marriage. In Pearl's opinion, Lillian was a bad influence with her educated words and lack of religious training. "It is your mother's fault that has forced us to move to this terrible place," she lamented. It was a place where Grandmother felt herself a prisoner. Even her only son, on whom she was now financially dependent, had changed. He had stopped listening to her.

In time, Grandmother turned to Irene to find solace. She found a younger, protective confidant, one who was less impatient with her. Pearl let Irene comb and braid her hair. She would tell her stories and pour out her heart to her younger grandchild.

It wasn't long though, before Grandmother Pearl's lucidity abandoned her more regularly. Her health deteriorated. "Her heart beat is erratic," the doctor told David. Rita overheard her parents discussing Pearl's condition.

"We'll need to find a nurse to give her the medication while we're at work. I think we should take the doctor's advice and call the agency that he recommended."

The following week, Mrs. Belinda Williams, a woman about Lillian's age, came to care for Pearl. She was a private care nurse from the visiting nurse agency. She made lunch for Pearl and administered the proper medication.

At first, Grandmother Pearl didn't like Mrs. Williams. "*A Schwartza*—a black?" Pearl complained resentfully to David.

Lillian said that Pearl was just ignorant and superstitious. Lillian was adamant that Rita not sympathize with Pearl about Mrs. Williams. "Not that long ago, Negro women couldn't get into a profession like nursing. It's important to give people a chance. Lots of people don't like Jews, either," Lillian explained to Rita. "It's just prejudice. Discrimination is wrong. This is America."

"I know, Mom. Grandma's old. She doesn't know any better." Rita didn't need an explanation. There were Negro kids at her school who got called names. Rita herself had been spit at and called "*dirty kike*" by some Catholic kids on the block, more than once. She understood the words *discrimination* and *prejudice,* even if she couldn't spell them. Rita had heard about civil rights on the news programs her parents listened to and discussions they had among their union friends when they visited. She'd heard about Negro children being prevented from going to white schools and about Martin Luther King's bus boycott in Alabama. "Maybe it will just take time for Grandma to understand," Rita said.

Regardless of Pearl's fear, Mrs. Williams was patient and kind. After a few weeks Grandma Pearl relaxed. She began to enjoy Belinda's visits. "What time is Mrs. Williams coming?" Pearl asked one morning. Rita smiled.

It was not only Pearl who looked forward to Mrs. Williams' arrival. Rita did, too. When she came home from school, Mrs. Williams would be finishing her own lunch while Grandmother napped. Sometimes, she let Rita taste the spicy pork chops or chicken that she brought from home. Rita had never eaten pork and loved its salty, sweet taste.

Even with good care, Pearl's health took a turn for the worse the following year. "It's her kidneys," the doctor told them. "Her blood pressure and blood sugar are also seriously elevated. It's just age," he said sympathetically. "There's really nothing more we can do."

Rita's parents were in turmoil. "Now what should we do?' Lillian asked David.

The next day, Rita eavesdropped on the hushed voices of her parents and Mrs. Williams. To Rita's disappointment, Mrs. Williams came for only one more week to care for Pearl. After that, over Grandmother's loud protests and Rita's pleas, Lillian and David reluctantly moved Pearl to Lawn View Manor, a nursing home forty miles away.

Chapter 4

Clara Doyle

Near Coos Bay, Oregon, 1859

Clara Doyle stopped at the edge of the road. Her dilapidated house stood empty on the long steep hill behind her, a dark ghost silhouetted by the setting sun. With her back to the grim reminder, she faced the sloping hill beyond the dirt road where the thick forest of cypress trees was her only view. In this direction, Clara's long black hair caught the wind and glistened in the waning rays of light.

Now seventeen years old, she wore her favorite dress, black and white checkered muslin with a white collar. The dress she received last winter hugged her voluptuous figure snugly. Clara put it on almost every day at this time, when the sun turned the sky a misty pink. When the weather was mild, she would come to this spot to wait as she had for a long time. Weeks had become months, then years. In a few days, it would be spring again. Clara would mark seven years of waiting for her Uncle Kyle to return.

Last Christmas had brought the dress and a note from Kyle, hand delivered by Doc Farley on his way to Coos Bay. Clara had received it with great joy and renewed hope.

Clara sat down in the tall grass. Her black buttoned boots felt tight suddenly, so she loosened them. Perhaps today is the day, she thought. Her mind wandered. She tried to control her daydreams, but lately they seemed to have a life of their own. Oddly, her memories had become more vivid with the years, the endless waiting.

Clara tried to relax. She closed her eyes. A vision of herself appeared as the ten-year-old child. She was walking up the hill to her house, the very same hill she had just walked in her tight boots. Her hair was in braids and she wore a light cotton frock. She was singing to herself, on her way home for dinner.

Suddenly, images of her parents flashed before her eyes, appearing and disappearing in the blink of an eye. For a moment, she thought she heard her mother's voice. Disturbed by the images and sound, Clara stood up and brushed herself off. Perhaps the last light was playing tricks between the windswept branches of the trees. She knew better than to be out near the woods after sundown. Hibernation season was over.

She leaned over to tie up her boots for the walk back to Mrs. Riley's, the place she had called home for seven years. Through the love and care of Mrs. Riley and Anna, she had learned to laugh again. She had learned to care for the chickens and horses, to build a fire in the hearth, to cook and sew, recite her prayers, and even read a little. Clara stood up and glanced at the path down the hill. She heard the wind rustling through the trees behind her.

Then she heard another sound. It was not the wind. Clara's heart pounded wildly. She had waited too long, she thought. Her eyes darted around looking for the animal to show itself. She turned and backed up to the road. Out of the corner of her eye, Clara saw something moving. It was on the road. It was quite a distance from her, but approaching quickly.

She held her hand to her forehead, shading her eyes, peering, listening. She thought she recognized the sound of a horse and wagon. Was it her imagination? Was someone coming down the road? The panic grabbing her heart loosened its grip. She could breathe.

From a distance, the man driving the wagon could see a young woman standing in the road. He pulled up the reins to slow his mare. He did not know who she was, but he knew the house on the hill just ahead. His brother and his family had lived there once. The last time he had been in this country seven springs ago, he had come to bury his only kin. He had not wanted to return. The weight of his guilt had led him back down this road to find the niece he had left behind.

"Whoa, Belle, easy there." He slowed his horse to a walk, approaching the girl. Seeing the figure of the shapely young woman, he could not determine her age. Her light skin glowed in the orange sunset, her dark hair blew in the breeze.

Clara saw a man dressed in a brown suede jacket and cowboy hat driving an old wagon as it came within yards of her. His hair was a sandy brown mop. He was unshaven and wore half a smile, but she could see there was a handsome man behind this scruffy exterior. His horse, a black mare, was obviously well cared for, even though the dusty road bore its mark upon her.

"Evening, ma'am," said the man as he stopped his wagon. "What's a lovely young lady, like yourself, doing out here on the road this time of evening?" He winked and grunted a laugh.

His distinctive laugh jarred Clara's memory. She looked at him intently, trying to find the reason for her sense of familiarity.

"I know you," she whispered.

"What's that, Miss?" His mischievous eyes twinkled.

"Uncle Kyle? Is that you?" She could hardly believe the words she heard coming from her own mouth. Could this be the uncle she had been waiting for all these years? He was hardly the young man she remembered.

Kyle looked at the young woman who was walking closer toward him. "Clara? Clara—my God! Are you my niece, Clara?" Kyle jumped down from the wagon.

Clara ran to him and flung her arms around his neck. He caught her hug, startled to feel a woman's body against his. Could this ravaging beauty be the child he remembered? He released her and held her at arm's length. He laughed nervously. "Well, let me get a look at you, all grown up."

"Look," said Clara, spinning around in a circle. "It's me! This is the dress you sent me for Christmas, remember?"

Kyle had bought the dress in San Francisco a year ago and had sent it to Clara by way of fellow he'd met, a railroad man heading north on business. But he had never imagined the dress to look like this. Mrs. Riley had altered it to fit Clara when it arrived. Now, it fit tight against her small waist and full breasts.

"Oh, Kyle, I've waited so long for you to come. I almost gave up…" Clara knew she was acting like a child, but she could not hold back the mixture of pain and relief she felt.

"Don't cry," he said. Kyle picked up her chin, so she was looking into his eyes. He had never seen eyes like hers before. He could fall into them and be lost. He did not miss how she was looking at him, either. Her trust and innocence were intoxicating.

Clara felt happier than she could ever remember being. Now she knew her memory of her loving uncle had been real.

Kyle looked away. "Come, it's getting dark. We'll go to Mrs. Riley's and get your things." Kyle helped her into the wagon.

"You must be hungry," Clara said. "Shouldn't you rest? Where are we going? Are you going to take me back East?"

"So many questions," Kyle mused, noticing her change in mood, her childlike excitement. "If Mrs. Riley doesn't mind, I'd like to rest tonight. Then we could get started tomorrow, after breakfast. It might be a shock to her, you leaving with me so suddenly."

Clara thought about it. Although Mrs. Riley could never replace her real mother, she had treated Clara as if she were her own child. They had grown very close, especially during the past two years since Anna had married Thomas and moved in with his family. But Clara knew that Mrs. Riley wanted Anna, Thomas, and their new baby boy to move back to the farm. She had not stopped talking about it since Anna's pregnancy, which had been a difficult one.

"Thomas' younger brother and his new wife can help old Mr. Desell. Thomas wouldn't be missed that much," Mrs. Riley had coaxed Anna before the baby was born.

Clara knew that although Mrs. Riley would miss her too, leaving with Kyle might be a blessing for them all. Her departure might make it easier for Anna and Thomas to move back. "I think Mother Riley will be happy for me," Clara said to Kyle. "And I'm sure she'll be fine with you staying the night. There is plenty of room," she added. "Besides, she loves having a man around the house."

Mrs. Riley was surprised to see Clara drive up to the house with a strange man, one she didn't recognize. She came out of the house to meet the wagon. Clara jumped down and ran to Mrs. Riley. "It's Kyle, my Uncle Kyle. He came back, just like I said he would!" Clara bubbled.

Mrs. Riley had met Kyle once, at the Doyles' funeral. That was when she had agreed to take Clara for a year, until Kyle could find a suitable place. She loved Clara. She did not regret having had another daughter to care for all this time.

Mrs. Riley never told Clara of their one-year agreement. All Clara knew was that Kyle promised to return. Clara had been in shock, too traumatized at the beginning to understand much of anything. It had taken a year to nurse her back to health and several more before the nightmares had subsided. Mrs. Riley was glad Kyle had not come. She didn't think he could take proper care of Clara. From the looks of him, she wasn't too sure he could even now, but she kept quiet. He was Clara's only kin.

"Evening, Ma'am." Kyle took his hat off as he climbed down from the wagon.

"Evening, Mr. Doyle. You look like you've had a long trip." Mrs. Riley took closer stock of him. He was dusty. His well-worn clothes were those of Western city folk. While she still thought he was a rogue, he looked older and more handsome than she remembered. Perhaps he had matured. "The barn's out behind the house," she said, pointing. "Clara, show your uncle where the stall and hay are for his mare and bring some water." She looked at Kyle's hands. "Looks like you'll be needin' a wash before dinner, Mr. Doyle."

"Thank you, Mrs. Riley. I'd appreciate it."

Mrs. Riley went into the house and checked the bean soup. She had made extra, knowing Anna, Thomas, and little Ben would be visiting tomorrow. Then she took out another jar of pickled beets and warmed more bread pudding.

She felt both upset and relieved as she set an extra place for Kyle at the table. She didn't want Clara to leave, even though she knew her adopted daughter had waited a long time for this day. Clara was young and innocent, still pure. Mrs. Riley was afraid that a life with that uncle of hers might mean ruin and hardship. But Clara was getting older. She needed to meet a man and start a family of her own. Perhaps back East she would meet a suitable husband.

"Maybe Anna will come back home now," she said to herself.

"Mother Riley, can Kyle stay in the attic room tonight?" Clara came hurrying through the kitchen doorway, breaking Mrs. Riley's train of thought.

She looked up at Clara's hopeful face. Mrs. Riley had always appreciated how lovely Clara was. But it was more noticeable at this moment. She seemed radiant.

"He wants to take me with him. He wants to leave in the morning. Mother Riley, Mama, are you crying?"

Mrs. Riley couldn't help herself. Her eyes had welled up with tears. "It is all right now, honey. I've known this day would come." They put their arms around each other.

"I'm so happy and sad at the same time," Clara said through her tears.

"It's gonna be all right, dear child. Things will work out. You'll see, honey. God has a plan."

These were familiar words to both of them. Mrs. Riley's prayers to the Almighty had soothed Clara through many rough times. But Mrs. Riley worried. What did the future hold for her Clara? Envisioning her sitting in the wagon next to Kyle and waving goodbye, Mrs. Riley grew sad. Would she ever see Clara's sweet face again?

CHAPTER 5

Rita Kerner

QUEENS, NEW YORK, 1959

After Grandmother Pearl went to the nursing home, Rita dreamed about her often. In her dreams, it was summer. They were at the beach again, romping in the shallow ocean water. When the dream shifted, Pearl was in her cooking apron standing in their kitchen teaching Rita to make chicken soup.

"A *bissel salt*—a little salt, garlic, onions, celery, carrots." Pearl held up the parsnips. "This makes it *gut*—good." Grandmother poured some salt into the palm of her hand and tossed it into the boiling water. In a wooden bowl she chopped onions, her arms jiggling as she chopped. When she was done, she brushed a few loose strands of hair off of her forehead, rinsed her hands, and smiled at Rita. "You know *vas ist* next, *bubbie?*"

"You cut the parsnip, carrots, and celery," Rita's gleeful voice echoed in her dream.

"You will be a *gut balabuster*—a good wife." Pearl smiled through Rita's winding dream. Fleeting images of herself braiding Pearl's long hair drifted in and out. Before long, another dream scene found Rita sitting with someone else, who braided her hair. Rita looked over her shoulder to see a woman who resembled her mother, Lillian, combing and braiding. But Lillian looked different. Her skin was darker, her face gentler, clothes softer. Rita was not herself, either—not the Rita she knew herself to be. She was a young boy with long black hair.

35

"Chaske," the woman in the dream said. "You must do what your father asks."

Before the dream child answered, Rita awoke. She lay still for a moment trying to recapture the vision. Why had the woman called her by a boy's name, a name that sounded like, *Charlie*? What had the father in the dream asked her to do?

Rita reached for her art pad and pencil in the night table drawer. She drew a picture of herself as a young boy, but not with a woman combing his hair. She drew him on a horse with his hair blowing in the wind behind him.

"Rita, dear, are you up?" Lillian slowly opened her daughter's bedroom door. "Your father wants you to go visit Pearl with him, today. I have breakfast ready," she offered. "Irene and Tina wanted eggs, so I made scrambled."

Rita hid her pad under her pillow. "Okay, eggs are fine, Mom," she said, hoping Lillian would not ask about her drawings. She got out of bed and walked to the bathroom.

Lillian followed her with a fresh towel from the linen closet. "I'll make some toast. Will you do what your father asks?"

Rita turned and looked at Lillian. "What?" A memory flashed by her.

"Your father asked you last night if you would go to Lawn View Manor with him today, remember?" Lillian replied.

"Oh, yes, of course," Rita said, taking the towel from Lillian.

Rita closed the bathroom door. She could not stand the thought of visiting Grandma Pearl in the nursing home. But she did go with her father to visit Pearl that morning, as promised.

Rita and David walked down the sterile hallway past the sad eyes of many old people, who reached out for attention, for something as simple and familiar as a smile. Soon, Rita and David found Grandmother Pearl's room. She sat on a bed in a dark corner weeping.

"Mom?" David called out to her.

Grandmother Pearl looked up, but she didn't acknowledge Rita. She spoke only to her son.

"Oy, Gut in himmel! Oh, God in heaven!" she sobbed, covering her face with her hands.

Rita walked closer to her. There was something unrecognizable about Grandma Pearl. Something was obviously different, yet so inconceivable that Rita's mind could not accept what she saw. They had chopped off all of Grandmother's hair. Her long, beautiful, silver strands—gone! Rita gasped, tears welling up in her eyes. Her cheeks burned. She reached out to hug her grandmother, but Pearl pushed her away, still sobbing.

A few days later, Rita and David returned to the nursing home. Pearl was dying. Rita stood at her grandmother's bedside as the old woman floated in and out of consciousness, not recognizing Rita.

"Grandma, it's me," Rita whispered desperately. Rita wanted her to respond. She wanted Grandmother to know she loved her. Rita didn't want Pearl to die without forgiving her, for what must surely have been Rita's fault. She had not taken good care of her, helped her dial the phone enough, or found a way to take her back to see her brother and friends. Was Grandma Pearl dying of loneliness, of sadness? Rita blamed herself for being so intolerant toward the end. "Grandma," she pleaded.

The old woman whimpered. Then Grandma Pearl's glazed eyes closed. She slept.

Shortly after Rita and David returned home, the nursing home doctor phoned. Rita answered the phone.

"Your mother, Pearl, has passed away," he said. "She went peacefully," he continued, seemingly unaware he was talking to her grandchild, not an adult.

"She's dead? Peacefully!" Rita cried, aghast. How dare this strange man, who didn't know Grandmother's suffering and courage, use such a word! Rita called out for her father to pick up the phone. She ran into her room and slammed the door.

At the funeral, David sat next to Lillian, who held Tina on her lap. Irene and Rita sat by their father's side. David wiped tears from his eyes. Rita put her arm around Irene, who sobbed quietly. But Rita could not cry. She was numb. It was not her Grandma Pearl lying in that casket. Pearl did not have short hair. She did not wear make-up, nor did she dress in white lace. Rita could not weep for a dead bride dressed in white, with short-cropped hair framing her painted face, cold in her open casket. Rita turned cold, too. All she could think of was that it was her fault. Had Grandmother died because she had betrayed her?

That night Rita slept alone in the big bed in Grandmother Pearl's room. It took her a long time to fall asleep. In her dream, Rita climbed out the bedroom window onto the three-foot ledge that framed the dormer on the sloping roof. She sat there for a long time looking up at the stars. Then she stood up and jumped off the ledge.

But something caught Rita as she fell. It was like a great wind and suddenly, Rita was flying over tree-lined streets and rooftops. *"Don't be afraid,"* a voice whispered. A flutter of white feathers appeared in her peripheral vision, a sensation of soft goose down. Rita began to rise and swoop like a bird. Then a young man with long dark hair, dressed in deerskin pants appeared on horseback. Aglow, he was almost transparent, yet visible. *"Remember,"* he said softly. *"You are the one who must remember us."*

Momentarily, Rita had the sensation of knowing, of understanding, of recognizing the voice, the horse. But it all vanished in an instant. Her dream evaporated as quickly as it had come. What remained was the desire to fly, to be an eagle soaring into the starry sky. She didn't want the feeling to ever end.

But a chill woke her. She felt her body's weight in the pull of gravity. Semi-conscious and with her eyes still closed, she groped near her feet for a blanket. Not locating her cover, Rita peeked down at her legs, squinting in the light of a bright sunrise. Then her eyes opened wide. With a gasp, she sat up. She was perched precariously on the edge of the roof.

Carefully she moved, swinging her legs back onto the roof's ledge, maneuvering away from danger. Rita crawled back through the open window into Grandmother's bedroom. She lay down in the feathered bed, still feeling the sensation of flying, still hearing familiar, comforting voices. Hearing voices was not new to Rita. They had called her name since she was very young, but she could never find their source.

She looked over at the picture on her grandmother's dresser of a young Grandma Pearl holding little David, a toddler in the photo. Perhaps now the voices would be soothing ones, Rita thought. Maybe Grandmother would talk to her from beyond, like the voice in her dream.

Rita's tears slid down to her chin. She turned over and covered her head with a pillow, leaving just enough room for air.

"*Gey Schluffen, Bubala,*" she heard, as she cried herself back to sleep.

CHAPTER 6

Bertha Abraham

PHILADELPHIA, PENNSYLVANIA, 1904

Ten-year-old Bertha sobbed in big gulps of air as she held little Dorothy's hand. The two sisters followed Mrs. Bea Jackson, the big choir lady they'd met at church, down the long, dark hallway, the floorboards creaking beneath their feet.

Soon they were outside in the gray light of a cold February afternoon. A few old men stood around the stoop of the rundown rooming house drinking corn whiskey and smoking. Their hot breath and smoke swirled into the frigid winter air. A scantily dressed young woman, with painted red lips, leaned against the side of the building next to overflowing trash cans. She held a cigarette in one hand and with the other, clasped closed her thin wool coat. She stared at the three of them. Bertha looked down at the sidewalk and wiped her wet cheeks with her sleeve.

Beatrice Jackson took each child by the hand and quickened her step. "You children gonna be all right. Don't you be worryin' none. You'll come live with me and my Ben now. Get you some warm clothes and food. Most our children be grown and moved. Only Louisa be left." Mrs. Bea went on, "She's smart. She see to it that you be learnin' to read and write, too. She got some books and magazines. She be waitin'…"

Bertha and Dorothy had met Mrs. Bea when Mama had taken them to the First African Baptist Church in October, when summer's heat

40

evaporated, replaced by a chilly autumn breeze. Bertha remembered how excited her mother had been to meet the church ladies. Now grief-stricken, Bertha let Mrs. Bea's babbling voice flow over her. She didn't try to keep up with the stream of words.

"Come along, child," Mrs. Bea coaxed.

Bertha walked slowly on the icy street, looking back every few steps. She did not want to leave her mother in their room alone. Perhaps she'll wake up, Bertha thought. Even though a day had passed, Bertha still had hope that her mother was just in a deep sleep, not dead. She looked back one last time at the old rooming house on Seventh Street that had been home since they had moved from South Carolina.

Only yesterday, Bertha and Dorothy sat in their cold damp room, dressed in threadbare dresses and worn-out sweaters, shivering. They sat close to their mother, Mayella, who lay in the bed laboring to breathe. Then her breathing stopped.

Bertha leaned over and shook her. "Mama, wake up," she whispered.

Mayella was cold to the touch—still and quiet, like Papa had been the day he died of typhoid from "bad" water, Bertha remembered. She tried not to cry. She waited and pleaded.

"Mama? Mama, please wake up!" Bertha begged. "We be hungry, Mama…be cold…"

Dorothy cried and trembled. Bertha was sacred. She remembered Mama being scared too, after Papa died.

"We be the only Negro Indians up here," Mama had cried. "Lord, help us. We got nowhere to go." Mayella put her face in her hands. With their light reddish-brown skin and thick Indian hair, they were noticeably different from that of their dark-skinned neighbors. They had no family in this strange place, no one to turn to for help.

Bertha's grandmother had come from the Seminole tribes in Florida. Her family, Seminole Freedmen, settled with her Negro kin the years after the Civil War and emancipation. Mayella had been born in South Carolina, same as Bertha's Papa, Nathan.

Bertha had slivers of memory—bits of her parents' conversations and arguments, the taste of foods, medicinal herbs, recipes her grandmother and Mama taught her to prepare. She remembered the birthing of her sister and sitting on her Grandmother's lap while she rocked her to the beat and sway of melodies Bertha could still hum. She remembered the time before they had headed north to Pennsylvania, for her father to find what he said would be a better life, away from the lynchings and poverty.

"Look here," Nathan said, pointing to the local newspaper. Bertha's father knew how to read. He had taught himself with the help of missionaries. Even with poor eyesight, he could read plain words.

"This here is a chance for our people. Says here this Negro man is gone to *Har-vard Un-i-ver-sit-y*," Papa read, underlining the words with his finger. "He be goin' to a job at the *Uni-ver-sity of Penn-syl-van-i-a*. Name be *Dr. W.E. Dubois*." Papa looked up beaming, his dark eyes shining in his round face. "You see, Mayella, there be a chance. Things be changin'. Negroes gettin' a chance to get educated, get jobs up North."

But moving to the North had not meant jobs or a better life. Like many families moving from the South, they had moved in haste, unprepared, unaccustomed to living in a city and to the harsh Northeastern winters. There was no work for Negroes with few skills. Immigrants from Europe brought competition for housing and jobs. Soon, they had no money for food or warm clothes, and no coal to heat the stove or boil water.

Illness struck Nathan first. Once a burly man, his face became narrow, eyes sunk into their sockets, cheekbones angled, brow furled. As he searched for work each day, the freezing wind blew through his light jacket to his thinning body. The snow and slush seeped into his worn-out old shoes. Icy flakes clung to his hair, whipped against his face and hands. Then the typhoid epidemic caught him in its grip. He vomited and convulsed with fever. Mayella tried as hard as she could to soothe his pain, feed him what little soup they had.

Bertha remembered the cold night her father's suffering ended. The health department came the next day. They reported his death and took him away to Potter's field. Mayella cried and cried. So did Bertha.

After Papa was gone, Mayella found work as a bathroom attendant downtown. Clothing and feeding her children was all she could manage. Her own coat grew threadbare, no match for the three-mile walk to her meager paying job in the freezing cold, then back after sunset. Help from Mrs. Bea and the church ladies, a warm wool coat and scarf came almost in time. Had it not been for the harsh winter, one of the coldest on record, Mayella might have survived pneumonia. She would have kept her promise to attend church every Sunday. A Sunday like today—a day that Mrs. Bea came to check on Mayella and the girls when they did not show up for the sermon.

Beatrice and Benjamin Jackson were better off than most in the community. They had lived in Philadelphia a long time. Ben had a steady waiter's job. He worked every day, except Sunday. So did Mrs. Bea. She did laundry for the Clarks, a white family that trusted her as a domestic.

The Jacksons gave Bertha and little Dorothy a cozy room in their house on Spruce Street. With renewed optimism and the admiration of all the ladies in the congregation, Bea took pride in her newly adopted children. She sent them to a recently opened public school in clean and pressed clothes. On Saturdays in the nice spring weather, Bea would let the girls walk a mile to Hester's chicken coops for fresh killed chicken and just-laid eggs. In the summer and fall, they picked vegetables and herbs from the small garden out back. Every Sunday was church and a big family dinner. The Jacksons' grown children would come by some Sundays with their own families, filling the house with music, laughter, and children's voices.

A year after her mother's death, Bertha turned eleven. By then, she'd learned to wash clothes, sew, garden, and help cook Sunday dinner. She watched carefully and learned the secrets of Mrs. Bea's roast pork, southern style chicken, orange squash, greens boiled with seasonings, pork fat, and vinegar, black-eyed peas, and sweet potato pie. She and Dorothy had never had a meal like Sunday dinner at the Jacksons' house. Bertha liked cooking and baking the best, especially when Mama Bea would let her make some of her grandmother's corn recipes—the ones she still remembered.

Meanwhile, Louisa taught the girls to read and write. The Jacksons' youngest child was a tall, pretty girl of fifteen with coffee and cream-colored skin. Louisa was as smart as Mrs. Bea had claimed.

"Pick any page and I'll read it to you," she offered Bertha when they'd first arrived, showing off her skills. She could indeed read any page of the Bible. In the evening, she would read her poems to her adopted sisters. She told them all she knew about Philadelphia, about the hotel where her father worked, the tall buildings, theaters, and markets she had seen, the trolley rides she'd taken with her father every Christmas, the famous boat-house hotels, and Fairmont Dam up along the river. Bertha and Dorothy listened intently as Louisa read current events from *The Philadelphia Tribune* and stories from *The Colored American Magazine*.

"Someday, I'm going to publish a book of poems," Louisa said to the girls. "I will be a famous Negro poet, like Phillis Wheatley or Francis Harper," she announced with a flick of her wrist.

Bertha and Dorothy giggled when Louisa pranced around the room, swaying her hips and pretending to be someone famous. "Maybe you be at the Standard Theater one day!" Bertha laughed, remembering Louisa readings about the actors and plays.

The next Christmas, Louisa bought each new sister a notebook and pencil of her own. They were no ordinary notebooks. Louisa had decorated them, gluing oilcloth to the outside to make fancy coverings. The inside cover was designed with cutout pictures from *Good Housekeeping Magazine* that Mrs. Clark gave them.

Mrs. Clark sent home used goods with Mrs. Bea, things she and her family no longer wanted or needed. Louisa had blouses, skirts, even hats and scarves that had belonged to Mrs. Clark, a woman about Louisa's size. Mrs. Bea had reservations about the used clothes, preferring that Mrs. Clark pay her more instead, but Louisa was happy to have the store-bought clothes.

"Next winter, you will be big enough to wear this dress," Louisa exclaimed, holding a navy blue and white dress against Bertha's blossoming figure.

Bertha smiled and her eyes twinkled. For the first time in a long time, she felt an old, familiar feeling. She was happy.

CHAPTER 7

Rita Kerner

Grandmother Pearl's death came in spring just before Passover and the Easter vacation from school. Rita missed Pearl more than ever at Passover, her favorite holiday—the one about Moses, Miriam, and freedom from slavery in Egypt. It would not be the same without Grandmother's prayers and delicious food.

Rita didn't want to go back to school after the holiday. Her fifth grade class was supposed to hand in book reports after the break. Rita couldn't concentrate. She daydreamed more, lost in her imaginary world of animals and people, who spoke to her in whispers. She drew pictures in her school notebook and drawing pad. She slept in Pearl's bed and convinced David to paint the room lavender for her. Lillian bought her a new bedspread and lamp to match her new room.

Lillian took the time to enroll Rita in a remedial reading program. She managed to persuade the school's principal to put Rita in a regular class, after her achievement test score came within the "normal" range. Rita noticed the change in her mother's attitude. She seemed to care more. It surprised Rita. However, she wasn't totally convinced. It was still unfamiliar territory, even when Lillian took her to an eye specialist, hoping that Rita's eyesight might be the cause of her problems.

"Your daughter says she sees double in both eyes," the eye doctor laughed. "She's definitely got some problems, but I'm not sure it's with her eyes." He raised his doubting eyebrows.

46

Mrs. Kerner knew Rita was a confused child, slow to catch on, but not crazy. Lillian knew what mental illness looked like. She had cared for her own mother through many serious bouts of depression until an untimely death. So, Lillian took Rita to a different eye doctor.

"Your daughter has astigmatism. I'll prescribe glasses and eye exercises," the new doctor said in matter of fact tone.

Rita was afraid to wear her new glasses at school though, afraid she would be teased anew. She kept the glasses under her mattress and only used them to read when she was at home. Still testing the waters of trust, she didn't tell Lillian.

She didn't tell her mother about Mr. Stein, either—her fifth grade teacher, who had recently begun keeping her after class. When he'd finally let her leave, he'd follow her into the coat closet and touch her chest. She tried to avoid Mr. Stein, giving him every excuse, any lie she could think of as to why she couldn't stay after dismissal. But, when Mr. Stein acted like he accidentally touched her breast right in front of the class, she was mortified.

"Mom, can you buy me a bra?"

"A bra? You're eleven years old, Rita."

"But I'll be twelve this summer. I heard you tell Dad I was an early bloomer." Rita tried to convince her new mother-friend. "Please, can't I have one? I'm getting big and…and…the boys at school are saying things about me," she added for good measure. It wasn't a lie, just not the whole truth.

Soon, Rita had picked out a white size-B bra that fit her perfectly. Rita thanked the salesgirl who helped her. Lillian sighed as they left the store, realizing it was time to talk to her daughter about womanhood, about menstruation. She did not look forward to the task.

Rita was delighted with her new bra. She was also excited about a new girl, Debbie, with bigger breasts than hers, who had been assigned to her class after vacation. The girls gravitated toward each other. They became friends, each careful not to stay after school without the other. Debbie was Rita's first "normal" friend. She was not another retarded child like Mimi Waldenberg, the adopted daughter of her parents' friends, who came every month for a visit.

By the time fifth grade was over, Rita not only had a real friend and wore a bra, but she had managed to read her first book, *Custer's Last Stand*. The night she finished the book, Rita had a dream. In the dream, she was the surviving horse of the horrific battle. The Indian man who had been riding her lay dead, like so many others. When Rita awoke, she realized that there was another world. Not just the world of her dreams, but a secret world where writers of books could weave pictures in her head. In books, she could live different lives.

In sixth grade, Rita got the nicest teacher in the whole school, according to reputation. Miss Maloney was old. She had wrinkles, gray hair, and wore thick Oxford shoes, but everyone liked her. Rita thought someone had made a big mistake putting her in Miss Maloney's "smart kids" class. When the grades on their first test came back, Rita thought her new teacher probably agreed. Then something strange happened. Miss Maloney asked Rita to stay after class to help her clean the blackboards. She had kind blue eyes and a sweet voice, so Rita was not afraid.

When the other children were gone, the elderly teacher closed the door and asked Rita to sit down with her near her desk. "Look here," she said, pointing to a fresh copy of the same test she had already handed back. "Can you read this question?" she asked Rita, pointing to the first question.

"Yes," Rita said hesitantly.

"What do you think it means? What answer would make sense to you?" Miss Maloney asked.

Rita thought about it and realized that her original answer had been completely wrong. "I am not sure," she whispered, embarrassed.

"Okay, let me show you. See here…" Miss Maloney explained the multiple choices until Rita figured out the correct answer. They repeated this process with each question on the test. To Rita's surprise, her kind teacher gave her a blank test to do again. This time Rita got a mark of eighty percent. "Much better. See? You can do it," Miss Maloney encouraged her.

Rita wasn't so sure. After all, the teacher had helped her. Just then, Rita's mother appeared at the door of the classroom. Rita looked up at the clock. It was 4:30. Miss Maloney waved to Rita's mother.

"I was wondering where she was since she didn't get off the bus with the other kids. She is such a daydreamer!" Lillian barreled into the classroom, apologizing for her daughter. Turning red with embarrassment, Rita packed up her books before her mother could say much more.

"Oh, I'm sorry I kept her. She just needs a little encouragement and some test-taking skills," Miss Maloney offered. "Perhaps I could work with her after school, one day a week."

"That's very kind of you. Thank you, Miss Maloney."

Rita smiled inside.

Every Friday thereafter, Rita stayed late and Miss Maloney would go over the week's tests, letting her take them over once Rita understood the questions. Patiently, Miss Maloney had Rita read and copy sentences from books into a notebook, practice spelling and penmanship.

Miss Maloney cares about me. School isn't so bad anymore, and I still have my friend, Debbie, Rita thought as she walked home.

Although Debbie was in a different class, Rita sometimes went to her house after school. One afternoon, Debbie pulled Rita into her bedroom and closed the door. Debbie's mom was not at home. "Rita, do you want to sleep over?" Debbie asked.

"Sure," Rita said excitedly. She had not had a sleepover with a friend before. "Let me call my mom. Is it okay with your mom?"

"Yes, I asked her this morning on the way to school," said Debbie.

That night after dinner, the girls watched TV with Debbie's family until bedtime. They brushed their teeth, put on their pajamas and climbed into Debbie's double bed. They stayed awake, talking and giggling in the dark. Suddenly, Debbie reached out and touched Rita, cupping a hand over her breast. Rita was startled, but she felt a surge of excitement run though her body. She moved closer to Debbie. Then slowly, Rita reached under Debbie's pajama top and felt one of Debbie's breasts too. Soon their pajama tops were off and their hands caressed each other's ripening young womanhood, hormones of puberty driving desire. They fell asleep together, entwined. By morning, they still lay together half-naked, unaware that Debbie's mom was eager to wake her family, especially Debbie and her little friend, for special banana pancakes.

It would be the first such lesson learned the hard way for Rita. Debbie was severely punished. Her family was Catholic and threatened her with burning in Hell. Debbie was forbidden to talk to Rita, *that dirty Jew*, ever again. Whenever Rita saw her in the schoolyard at recess, Debbie avoided eye contact and walked in the opposite direction.

Rita's mother never mentioned anything to Rita about it. Assuming Lillian hadn't found out, Rita kept the incident a secret. Turning twelve, Rita's private life, blooming with visions, dreams, and sexual desires, was grossly different from the reality of her family. Compared to everyone around her—Rita felt separate. Why did she have to be so different? Why couldn't she be normal?

David noticed how withdrawn Rita had become lately. "Why is she always alone?" he asked Lillian. "Why doesn't she have friends? She seems to be adjusting to school, doesn't she? She's reading."

Lillian just shrugged and shook her head. She knew more than she let on, though.

To cheer Rita up, on her twelfth birthday, David bought her an oil paint set. Lillian signed her up for some painting classes on Saturday morning at a local arts and crafts program. Rita was thrilled with the gift. She threw herself into painting, creating an imaginary landscape with a pink, purple, and orange sunset casting rays across hills covered with yellow wildflowers, horses, and an old farmhouse. When the painting was done, to Rita's delight, even her mother liked it. As if by magic, Rita had found something acceptable she could do well. She could hardly wait to show her favorite teacher, Miss Maloney, before the school year was over.

"Why, this is beautiful!" Miss Maloney exclaimed. "We have a real artist in our class. Look at this lovely painting Rita made." Miss

Maloney hung the painting on the bulletin board.

Rita felt proud, but also nervous. She was so accustomed to ridicule, it was uncomfortable to have everyone looking at her.

One of the smart girls smiled at Rita. "That's a nice painting," her classmate said.

Rita blushed. "Thanks," she barely whispered.

All summer Rita painted. She painted pictures of imaginary people and places—an Indian boy in a magical forest, a little girl with braids in a flowered frock, a grandmother resembling Pearl's nurse sitting in a garden, horses running across the plains. When September arrived, Rita went to a new junior high school determined to make normal friends. She chose girls who talked about boys, who were less likely to have a crush on her and vice versa. She paid attention in class and did her homework religiously.

"Rita's growing up," Lillian said to David one evening. "I think it would be okay if I go back to work full-time again. What do you think? We could use the money."

"Yes, I think Rita's adjusting well. She can watch the kids after school," Rita's father agreed.

Adding to her self-confidence, Rita made the honor roll. With her first report card full of A's and B's, Rita ran back to her elementary school. Miss Maloney was sitting at her desk, marking papers. "Look!" Rita said breathlessly.

Miss Maloney looked over Rita's report card and smiled. "I knew you could do it," she said, her kind, blue eyes twinkling.

Rita threw her arms around her former teacher and hugged her. When Rita got home, she showed her parents her report card.

"Very nice," Lillian offered.

"That's pretty good," said David.

Rita didn't understand their less than enthusiastic reaction. Why weren't they more excited? It didn't make sense to her. Rita did not know about the doctor's warnings of permanent brain damage from her seizures during infancy.

"Don't expect too much," he had warned her parents. The Kerners had accepted the label of *retarded* when Rita was young. They still struggled with guilt. In spite of signs to the contrary, they were always waiting for the worst.

"I'm not retarded anymore!" Rita shouted, waving her report card at her parents. "I'm not like Mimi Waldenberg, who I don't think is retarded, either. She just has a big head," said Rita boldly. She pictured Mimi's elongated head—from a difficult birth, her adoptive parents had informed everyone.

Regardless of her parents' lack of joy, Rita beamed. Proudly, she waved the report card at her sisters, who stood gaping at her from the kitchen doorway. It was the first taste of freedom Rita had ever known. And it was just the beginning of her independence.

* * * * *

By fourteen, Rita had grown taller than her mother. Her teeth had grown straighter and her nose finally fit her face. Looking in the mirror atop Grandmother's dresser—one that now belonged to her—she admired her high cheekbones, curved lips, and dark eyes. She had a slim figure with curves that turned heads. She had inherited Grandmother Pearl's genes and like her, Rita's prized possession was her luxurious, black, shiny hair that had easily grown waist length. Old enough to appreciate the power of a woman's beauty, she was more self-confident, now caring less about what people thought of her.

Tying her long hair back in a ponytail, she looked again at her image in Grandmother Pearl's mirror. She wanted to feel like the woman she saw in the mirror, but she felt confused. Did she want the attention of boys? She wasn't sure.

Rita put on her jeans and an old sweater, camouflaging her grown-up female figure. She picked up the photo of her Grandmother Pearl. *"Shalom Aleichem*—peace be with you, Grandma," she said.

Rita grabbed some change, her keys, and double-checked her paint box, making sure all her paint caps were on tightly, her brushes in order. She took her jacket from the hall closet, then grabbed an apple and some cookies from the kitchen pantry. She scribbled a note on a pad by the refrigerator. *I'm off to art school. Be back later.* Sneaking two Chesterfield cigarettes and matches from her father's special drawer, Rita tucked them carefully in her jacket along with her subway money.

Then Rita walked out of her parents' house into a world all her own. Bright colored oil paint, turpentine, canvas, and brushes awaited her. At the West 57th Street Art League, nude models posed for a new generation of artists—her generation. She wrapped herself wild and spellbound in her own brilliant visions and dreams. All day she painted.

"Hey, Rita, join us!" Some of her artist friends were sitting in the cafeteria during the models' break. Rita waved. She bought a Coke and sat down, enjoying the camaraderie of friends. They accepted her, looked like her with their hands and smocks smeared with oil paint. They spoke the same language, with thoughts, visions and dreams swirling along uncharted paths and into esoteric worlds. They were not the *retards*. They were the outcasts, the weirdos—the geniuses who were about to change the world.

In the early evening, Rita and her friends went to Greenwich Village where beatniks, writers, and other artists converged. In dimly lit coffeehouses, they drank black coffee, smoked French cigarettes, and listened to Ginsberg's poetry, the new sounds of Dylan and Motown. Rita's life was changing. She felt freedom blowing in the wind.

CHAPTER 8

Clara Doyle

"Be a proper lady, like I taught you. Don't trust everyone just 'cause they're nice to you," Mrs. Riley said as Clara packed. "You're a pretty girl, Clara. You got to be smart too." Mrs. Riley was nervous. She saw how Kyle had looked at Clara last night during dinner.

"I'll be fine, Ma. And I'll try to send word as soon as we get East."

Mrs. Riley promised herself she would not cry. "We'll be thinking of you always, child." She looked into Clara's deep green eyes. "We will meet again." She hugged her second daughter, holding back tears.

"I love you…and Anna." Clara could not imagine never seeing Mrs. Riley and Anna again. With her belongings piled on Kyle's wagon, she promised herself she would return one day. She would talk to Kyle about it during their journey.

Kyle and Clara set out on the only road at the edge of the farm, heading north. He aimed to get to Woodyville, some one-hundred mile northeast, in a few days. "It's a ways to Junction City, Clara. There is an inn I know where we can stay tonight."

But Clara wasn't paying attention. Instead, she was thinking about what she was leaving behind—leaving the place of nightmares that were always creeping around the edges of her mind, waiting up on the hill for her, day in and day out. She had learned to smother her fear by staying close to Mrs. Riley and Anna, but the last few years had been lonely ones, ever since Anna had left to marry Thomas. Her memories had become harder to suppress. Kyle's promise to return was the one thing that had held her to life when she was the saddest. Now, her life would begin anew.

"Clara? You hear me?"

"Oh, how fine, yes, an inn. What is that like?" she asked, turning her attention to Kyle.

"Well," Kyle laughed, "it's a house with rooms where people who are just passin' through can spend the night. A man can get a bit of whiskey and, uh…" He cleared his throat. He had to remember to treat his niece like the young lady she was. "We'll rest there. We can get somethin' to eat and be on our way again in the mornin'," he said.

"Oh, Kyle, I'm so happy!" Clara cuddled closer and hugged him.

Kyle thought she smelled like violets. He glanced at her warmly as her softness pressed close. Still holding the reins in both hands, his right arm was pinned against his side, nestled between her breasts in her embrace. He had never anticipated that she would be this womanly or this beautiful when he'd set out to keep his promise. He snapped the reins and clicked to his horse, releasing himself from her affectionate gesture and his unsettling thoughts about her. He concentrated instead on an important money matter—a decision he had to make in the next few days.

They traveled in silence for some time. Clara breathed in the fragrant spring air and watched the rolling hills go by.

"I can't wait until we get to the East," she said after a while. "I will cook and clean your house. I won't be in the way, Uncle Kyle. I'll help you when you have company and go to the market like mother…"

Clara put her head down. She suddenly felt an overwhelming sadness thinking about her mother. Mother had talked a lot about the East when Clara was little. Clara had heard all about the markets, the fine houses, the library, the theater, and store-bought clothes—all the lovely things and the people her mother had missed after reluctantly leaving Philadelphia, for Oregon. Clara did not mean to talk about her mother, though. She did not know how Kyle would react.

"It's natural for you to think of her," Kyle said, sensing her hesitation. He took Clara's hand. "It'll be all right."

Clara felt instantly relieved by his gesture. And she liked that he was holding her hand. It had a calming effect on her, she noticed. His hand was big, but not coarse and thick, like a farm boy's hand. It was strong yet soft at the same time. She didn't want to let go.

But Kyle did let go. "Whoa, easy Belle..." He pulled back on the reins with both hands. He was glad he had the reins—a way of removing his hand from Clara's. There was an energy that shook him when he held her warm hand. "We'd better stop awhile and rest. Mrs. Riley made some food for our trip. Ain't you hungry, Clara?"

"Oh, I am," she said, realizing the day was half gone. Breakfast seemed far away.

Kyle pulled the wagon to a stop by the edge of the road near the shade of a large tree. Kneeling on the seat, he reached into the wagon to get their supplies.

Clara turned around, leaning over the seat of the wagon.

In such close proximity, Kyle was keenly aware of her movements, of her small waist, and of the way her thin wool skirt cascaded over her hips. He climbed down from the wagon and tied Belle to the tree. He took the bundle from Clara, placing it on the ground. Holding out his hand, Kyle helped her down from the wagon.

Clara's legs felt stiff after sitting for so long. She stumbled when her foot hit the step of the wagon. Kyle grabbed her before she could fall. He reached for her waist catching the weight of her body against his.

"Oh, oh, I'm sorry," she stammered.

Kyle noticed that she was blushing profusely before she regained her balance.

Clara unpacked the goods that Mrs. Riley had prepared. On the blanket that Kyle spread out in the shade of the tree, they sat and ate. "Uncle Kyle," she said, "how long will our trip take? Where will we stay along the way? Will there be danger from Indians, do you think?"

Kyle could not answer all her questions. Her child-like enthusiasm overwhelmed him. Had he made a mistake coming back for her? The enormity of the responsibility he faced was beginning to make him nervous. Would she be completely dependent on him? Had she really counted on him to come back all this time?

He shifted uncomfortably. He looked directly at Clara, trying to sum up his next move. Her dark emerald eyes mesmerized him when she returned his attention. What was it in her gaze that held him spellbound? He had been with many women, but she was so young, so alluring. Was it her adoration of him that made her so appealing? He shook his head to stop his train of thought. He knew he should not be thinking about her like this. After all, she was his niece.

"Uncle Kyle?" Clara had moved closer to him. "Thank you for coming back for me," she whispered.

Kyle couldn't find the strength to speak. Instead, he took her face in his hands and kissed her forehead. He held back his overwhelming desire to hold her, to kiss her full lips, to press her body next to his. He looked away from her gaze and stole a glance at her elegant neck and her ample curves.

Clara was no longer a child. She could feel the surge between them. Her entire body seemed to vibrate with his touch. She took a deep breath, her bodice brushing up gently to touch Kyle's arms. The heat of his hands against her face made Clara want to kiss him. She raised her head and closed her eyes in anticipation.

"Come, we should go. We don't have much time before dark," Kyle said, suddenly finding his voice. He let his hands slip from her face and stood up abruptly to regain some composure.

Clara's face flushed. She thought Kyle wanted to kiss her as much as she wanted him to. Now, she felt she had been foolish. He was her uncle. Of course, he didn't want to be with her the way a man wanted to be with a woman. Her need to be loved, to be held and touched had clouded her judgment. She would be more careful. She did not want Kyle to be upset with her.

When they were on their way again, Clara made sure she sat with enough space between them. She was careful not to touch Kyle again until they reached the inn and he helped her down from the wagon. This time she knew to stretch her legs before descending.

It was dark, but the inn was lit up. Voices and laughter emanated from the open windows. Clara took her time walking up the path behind Kyle. She could smell smoke, stale ale and whiskey even before they got to the door.

Kyle turned around when they approached the front door. "Wait here a minute," he said and went in.

Clara stood obediently until curiosity got the better of her. She moved close enough to the entrance to peer inside. Men and women sat at tables in a smoke-filled room, laughing and drinking ale from large glass mugs. The women, Clara noticed, wore thin, low-cut blouses with no buttons, so the tops of their breasts were visible. Some of them sat on men's laps. One man had his face smothered in the bosom of the woman on his lap, his arms around her waist. The woman laughed and tossed her head back, as if the man were tickling her. The man picked up his head briefly. He reached into his pocket with one hand and pulled out what looked like a coin. He put the coin between his teeth and resumed his position, nestling his face between her breasts. Clara felt excited and disgusted at the same time. She was staring so hard, she didn't notice Kyle until he was standing in front of her.

"Clara, sorry you had to see this. Come, we'll go 'round back to the rooms for guests. You have your own room. No one to bother you," Kyle reassured her. "I'll be next door."

But Kyle wouldn't be next door. He planned to go back to the saloon and drink. Maybe, he would even have a woman tonight. It had been awhile and he needed to release some of his pent-up energy. Perhaps that was why he'd felt his needs so strongly being close to Clara. He kissed Clara on the forehead again and left her in her room. He wandered down to the saloon.

A woman with bright red hair and blue eyes met him at the door. She walked with him to a table and after a few drinks Kyle was feeling himself again—relaxed and confident. When she brought him his fourth drink, she leaned over him deliberately brushing his cheek with one small, firm breast. Kyle drank in her rose-colored lips and long neck. He could see down her blouse to her nipples protruding into the flimsy fabric. He knew he would have her tonight and his loins throbbed with the thought.

Smiling, she took both his hands and slid them up her body. She leaned into his arms, her mouth finding his, in a wet whiskey kiss. She lifted her heavy skirt slightly and straddled his lap, rubbing against his groin with just enough pressure to drive him to desire. Kyle thought he would burst. He kissed her again, then stood up abruptly, lifting her off the chair with him, setting her down gently. "Wait," he said. "I'll be right back. I've got to step outside a minute."

Kyle stepped out into the crisp night air. His head cleared slightly. He wandered to the side of the saloon and relieved his bladder with a pleasurable sigh. As he headed back toward the saloon, a man staggered past him. He acknowledged Kyle with a grunt. Before he entered the saloon, Kyle noticed the drunk heading in the direction of the guest rooms. He knew exactly how the fellow would feel in the morning, having been that drunk himself too many times to count.

Kyle stood in the doorway a moment, scanning the saloon for the redhead. He caught sight of her leaning against the far end of the bar, smiling and talking to a man sitting on a stool next to her. He was leaning over her shoulder with his arm around her waist. Kyle watched for a minute trying to decide whether he wanted to interrupt. What trouble was he willing to go through to have her tonight?

He had made up his mind it was worth a fight, when he heard a woman screaming. The screams came from the direction of the guest rooms. Kyle swung around, suddenly remembering Clara. He ran the short distance to the extension of guest rooms, bolting up the stairs and barging through the main door. In the dimly lit hallway, he could see Clara's door was open.

"Clara! Clara!" he yelled, running. Enough moonlight illuminated the room that he could see a man standing near the bed. He grabbed wildly, throwing punches until the old drunk lay in a heap on the floor. Kyle pushed him out of the room and down the front steps.

When he returned, Clara stood in a corner of the room shaking violently. Her hair hung in her face and her cotton nightgown was ripped from the neckline to her waist. Kyle tried to soothe her. He lit the candle on the table and wrapped her night shawl around her. "Tell me what happened, Clara. I will kill him if he…"

"No," she trembled. "He tried to take off my nightgown. He was ripping it," she cried. Clara held her shawl tightly over her nightgown. She held onto Kyle's arm with the other hand.

Kyle smoothed her hair out of her face and kissed her forehead. "I won't let no one hurt you." Kyle felt responsible. He should have stayed with her. "Look, get your things and we'll go to my room down the hall. I'll sleep in the chair. You can get some sleep in that bed. I won't let nothing happen again, Clara. We'll leave here at dawn."

Kyle helped Clara get her belongings together, walked her down the hall, and tucked her into his bed. He moved the old armchair between the door and the bed. Then he took off his boots, loosened his leather, silver-buckled belt, and sat in the chair. He was close enough to Clara to hear her breathing, see the moonlight cast its light across her covered figure.

In the darkness, Clara reached for Kyle's hand. "Hold me," he heard her whisper.

CHAPTER 9

Bertha Abraham

Dorothy turned fourteen before Bertha's eighteenth birthday. Bertha had grown big and gregarious, while Dorothy remained shy and small for her age. Although they looked different, they loved the same things, especially reading and writing. They both treasured the diaries Louisa made for them every Christmas, even after Louisa got married and moved away. Together, the girls wrote in them every evening before bedtime.

Bertha wrote to keep the memory of her parents alive. She wrote down the things she could remember about Mayella and Nathan— recipes for food and herbal medicines, stories from her Indian heritage, wise words about freedom and equality. She felt overcome by grief and guilt one day, when she realized that while she could still remember her mother's voice, she could no longer picture Mayella's face. Her father's image had also faded from memory. She had no photos to retrieve them.

"Dorothy, do you think we look like our Mama?" Bertha looked at herself in the mirror trying to see a resemblance that would jar her memory.

Dorothy looked up from her writing for a moment, surprised by her sister's question. "I think *you* remind me of her." For Dorothy, only a sense of Mayella existed, not a visual memory. Her sister had replaced her mother, caring for her while under Mrs. Bea's protective wings. Dorothy turned back to her writing.

Bertha looked at the reflection of her own well-rounded figure. Her curves had filled in, and she felt herself almost pretty. Her hair was thick and wavy, her skin a dark, creamy brown. She wished Mayella could see how she had grown, how she had become a woman. "

Louisa's going to give me a new dress for my birthday," she tried to engage Dorothy again.

Dorothy looked up to see Bertha admiring herself.

Bertha held her hands above her hips, pulled her cotton nightgown in at the waist, and arched her back slightly. Her firm breasts rose, her rounded derrière accentuated by her exaggerated pose. Bertha's thoughts turned to romance. She yearned for love, for adventure. An energy flowed through her—an excitement she could feel, but not name.

A different kind of adventure would come as a birthday present from Louisa. "We're going to see the first Negro orchestra in the nation perform downtown!" Louisa exclaimed. "Happy Birthday, Bertha!"

Bertha was thrilled. She was grown up and going places.

At Christmas, Ben brought home an Edison phonograph. The house filled with spirituals of "Swing Low, Sweet Chariot" and "Go Down Moses" by Rowland Hayes and the Jubilee singers. Jazz and Ragtime records soon followed. Bertha sang along, dreaming again—this time of a handsome man who might love her like the ones in poems and stories she had read. He would take her to hear the music of Harlem, see plays on Broadway. But her daydreams were not to be.

At the end of the year, Benjamin lost his job at the hotel. Bertha could no longer daydream about the theater, travel, or romance. She had to help Mama Bea with her regular domestic work.

"Eighteen be plenty old enough to have your own work," said Mrs. Bea. "There be a new family movin' in the house next door to the Clarks, name of Waldenberg." She looked over at Bertha."They be needin' a maid for laundry and cookin'."

Bertha tried to look calm. "Thanks, Mama Bea," she said quietly. The thought of being in a strange white woman's home, saying "yes ma'am" all day long made her stomach ache.

"The Clarks' oldest be gettin' married to that Doyle fella, up from near the Alley neighborhood, too." She grimaced. "Don't know how he take to colored folks. Them Irish think we be takin' too many their jobs." Mrs. Bea remembered the violence that had erupted—a Negro man had been beaten to death near that area. "Guess, I just be askin' after Miss Clark, 'bout the Waldenbergs," she said. "Could be 'nuff work for you *and* Dorothy…" Bea's voice trailed off. She watched Bertha sink lower in her chair. She walked over to her daughter and put her hand on Bertha's shoulder. "I know you be wantin' to go up to New York, live with Louisa in Harlem." Her voice softened. "Maybe, someday."

Bertha was quiet. The Jacksons had saved her and Dorothy after their mother died. How could she let them down when they needed her? "Benjamin's more important than New York," Bertha said finally. She looked lovingly at Mama Bea. "You and Papa Ben helped me and Dorothy. Now I need to be here with you." Bertha stood up and hugged Mama Bea. "I see how old he's getting, how he ain't feeling well these days. I be stayin' close, Mama." Bertha had never seen Mama Bea cry. Now, tears welled up in the old woman's eyes.

That Sunday the family went to church as usual, but it was not a usual day. There was talk of war—in the newspapers, at church, on the street. If the United States got into the war, were Negro men going to fight? The congregation was buzzing. There were so many families flooding into the city from the South, thousands of young men anxious for education and work. How many would want the opportunity to join the army and fight?

"The new NAACP is going to support our men for the front, if war comes," Ben said to his friends after church. They gathered round to wait for their wives and children.

"I'd think about goin'," said a young man, who stood within earshot. He walked over to the group of older men on the church steps. Ben had never seen him before.

"You new here, son?" Ben asked.

"Yes, sir. I come up by way of Iowa. I worked at the Mills plant for a few years—a machinist. Just got a job at Midvale Steel over in the Nicetown plant—North Philly is…"

"They hirin' again, son?"

"Yes, sir. I think we be goin' to war soon. We got over fifteen hundred Negroes there now. Looks like more be needed, if war comes."

"What's your name, son?" Ben was impressed with the young man.

"Name's James. James Washington," he said, holding out his hand.

"Welcome," said Ben. "You got kin in town?"

"No, sir."

"Well then, I guess you be comin' to my house for Sunday dinner. My wife and daughters be happy to share what we have."

"Why, thank you, Mr.—"

"Benjamin Jackson, but you can call me Ben."

"Thank you kindly, Ben. I sure could use some home cookin'." James smiled broadly.

Bertha had noticed James, too. "Would you like a cool drink before dinner, Mr. Washington?" Bertha held a glass of cold lemonade.

"Thank you, kindly. Bertha, isn't it? Please, call me James. Your father's been so nice to invite me." James' white teeth flashed a smile, his deep brown eyes twinkled. "He's blessed to have such fine daughters."

Bertha noticed James' smooth skin, his long fingers, clean hands. His Sunday clothes were pressed. A light scent of peppermint and musk filled her nostrils as she handed him the glass. He touched her hand momentarily, accepting the cool drink. She felt her cheeks burn.

"Looks like it might be nice evening for a walk when the sun goes down a bit," James said, facing the sunset's orange sky. "Might you like to walk after dinner, Miss Bertha?"

"Oh," she said. "Yes, I might." She was startled by his directness. Had he heard her thoughts? Heard her heart beating faster?

Bertha sat next to James at the dinner table. His deep, melodic voice and his alluring smile made her feel dizzy. She had never felt like this with any of the young men who smiled at her in church. She had longed for a young man, like James—someone with ambition and skills. She had dreamed of such a gentle and handsome man, who would sweep her off her feet. Was James interested in her? Was he the one? Her stomach fluttered.

Bea and Dorothy noticed Bertha's attention to James. After dinner, Ben invited James into the parlor and turned on the phonograph. Soft blues filled the room. He offered James a cigar. Bertha's interest in James was not lost on Ben, either. They would make a fine couple, he thought. Ben puffed his cigar. "War is hell, son. No place for a man with a future like yours," he said.

CHAPTER 10

Rita Kerner

Rita walked beneath the shade of the blossoming maples and birches, but she still felt hot and exhausted by the time she turned down her block. The one-mile walk from high school with heavy books felt like ten.

When she arrived home Sammy, the new family dog, greeted her. He wagged his tail and shook with excitement. "Hi, Sammy, yeah, yeah—good dog." Rita dropped her books on the hallway table and pet the beagle. "Hellooo!" she yelled into the air out of habit. The house was quiet. Where was everyone? She hated coming home to an empty house, but didn't know why.

I should be used to it by now, she thought. She checked the dining room where Lillian might be buried in some newspaper articles or typing eighty words a minute at her typewriter, but to no avail. Everything was tidy and empty. She instinctively looked for Grandma Pearl even though the old woman had died four years ago—or was it five years? Rita still felt her presence when it was quiet.

"Helllloooo?" she called again, cocking her head to one side like the dog. Rita hoped someone would ease the inexplicable tightness in the pit of her stomach, that someone would burst into the room and greet her. But no one did.

Rita headed for the fridge to ease the anxiety of coming home to an empty house. She poured her usual after-school milk and grabbed some chocolate chip cookies from the cupboard. There were no signs of the evening meal in transit from the freezer to the fridge. In fact, there didn't seem to be much food around, except for the canned string beans and corn in the pantry. Who was making dinner tonight? She hoped it would not be her. But, with nothing in the works it would probably be Mom's burnt, shoe-leather hamburgers—that is, if someone remembered to shop. She thought about a long walk to Harry's Market. They'd let her buy on credit today, almost Friday, Dad's payday.

I'm too tired to schlep out again, she thought, plopping down on a kitchen chair. Rita finished the last bit of milk in her glass. The sweetness of the cookies lingered. She wished she had one more sip of milk, but there was only a drop left in the container, just enough to save for her parents' coffee. Rita rinsed the glass in the sink and went to her bedroom.

She didn't remember making her bed with the bedspread, the new one dotted with little lavender flowers that made patterns on her cheeks when she fell asleep on it face-down or sideways. Now her bed looked different. It was neat, corners tucked in, the bedspread smoothed out evenly.

Rita opened the closet to hang her jacket on the hook and change clothes. She pulled her dress off over her head, momentarily noticing how sore her breasts felt as the waistband squeezed over them. She threw her sweaty dress on the floor of the closet. It doubled for a perfectly good hamper, she thought, even if it did annoy her mother no end. She put on some shorts, a short-sleeved shirt, and peered at her bed again. Something was missing from its usual spot propped up against her pillow. Where was Suzy? "Where the hell is Suzy?" she said aloud, uninhibited by the sudden realization.

Rita looked back in the closet, then under the bed. She searched the living room. She found nothing. Sammy mirrored her movements, then he sat still at her feet. She pondered, "Where could I have left that miserable excuse for a doll?" Suzy was the doll that Grandma Pearl had picked out for Rita, on her seventh birthday. Rita had managed to save its soft plastic skin by bandaging it with white tape, mummifying it to save its body from her cuddling, singing and sobbing through nine long winters.

Suddenly, Sammy jumped up and ran to the back door. Rita heard the door open too.

"Mom?" she called.

"Hi, dear." Lillian's voice was not relaxed, not her high-pitched tone trailing off like a wisp of a cloud evaporating into the blue—the "Lillian in a good mood" voice. Today, Rita could hear the edge in her mother's tone. She walked to the kitchen.

"Rita, dear. Help Irene with the groceries. Where were you? Tina had to go to the dentist. When did you get home? I tried to call you to go up to Harry's for chopped meat. I had to make an extra trip." Lillian sighed. "Any good news in school, today? Did your dad call? When will he be home? Did you feed the dog?" Lillian rattled on. "Oh, shoot!" she said. "I forgot dog food…"

"Mom," Rita interrupted. "Where is Suzy?"

"I guess Sammy can have some…. What? Suzy who?" Lillian looked distracted. "Irene, could you put the butter and milk in the fridge, dear."

"Mommy, I'm hungry," Tina whined.

"SUZY!" Rita said louder trying to get Lillian's fleeting attention. "You know, Suzy, my doll!"

Where have you been for nine years? Rita wanted to say, but restrained herself. "Suzy, my only doll. You know, that soft, life-size baby wrapped in a pink blanket from Grandma Pearl on my seventh birthday. She was that *sick in bed on my birthday doll.*"

Rita's frustration at Lillian's lack of attention was boiling over in spite of herself. Was her mother that oblivious? Maybe, it was Lillian's new job, or worrying about Dad's union planning a strike, or Irene's parent-teacher meeting, or Tina trip to the dentist. Maybe it was exhaustion from their recent trip to Washington for the civil rights march or more terrible news on TV. But Rita still wanted to scream.

Didn't you see me take Suzy shopping with us every Saturday to the grocery store for all those years? Remember that lady came by and almost had a heart attack 'cause she thought it was a real baby? I was eight and I dressed Suzy in real baby clothes. Those clothes that I bought with my quarter a week, I saved and saved. Remember? I told you about the lady at Woolworth's Five and Dime, who asked me who the clothes were for and I said my little sister, who was two years old. And she said I had the wrong size, that they couldn't be returned, and that my mother would be mad. And you yelled at me, "What's the matter with you? How could you waste money on real baby clothes for a doll!"

"Suzy?" Lillian said abstractly. "Oh, that filthy thing." Lillian made a tsk-tsk sound. "It was falling apart. I threw it away this morning when I made your bed, which incidentally, you left a big mess." Lillian poured a glass of milk for Tina. "You're too old to play with it anyway, dear. Didn't you have it long enough, dear?" Lillian took a small package wrapped in white butcher paper from the grocery bag. "Rita, honey," she continued, "would you put this chopped meat in a bowl and I'll prepare hamburgers, okay? Rita? Where are you going? Rita…"

Rita ran out the front door. She ran to where the big metal trash cans stood by the side of the house. The cans were planted on the gravel, upside-down. They were empty. The pick-up had been made while she had been at school. Rita burst into tears. Then embarrassed, she covered her face with her hands in case anyone might see. "Stop crying! You're sixteen years old!" she reprimanded herself. Rita wiped her tears with a sleeve. *Mom is right. I am too old for dolls*, she thought. *I am all grown up.*

Rita touched her stomach. She was old enough to have a real baby. Old enough to sleep with her boyfriend, Marvin, a senior at her school. She had not told her parents about him yet. He was a tall, black eighteen-year-old. His good looks made him very popular with all the girls, but he liked her. They had almost gone all the way once, at his house.

Suddenly, another image floated into Rita's mind. She saw real babies lying dead. Real little ones killed in a church, not wrapped in white tape, or with white skin. The TV had blared, *"Negro children…*

*in a church in Birmingham, Alabama...*The front page of the newspaper printed a school picture of the little girls.

Rita felt scared and angry. People are killing children? Because of the color of their skin? she thought. What would happen to a child like she might have with Marvin someday, a black child. Then in what seemed like a sudden daydream, Rita saw herself standing on a street corner with two little black girls—daughters. She was pregnant, her big stomach protruding in front of her. She felt exhausted. The image vanished as fast as it had appeared.

Rita stood motionless next to the empty trash cans where Suzy, Grandma Pearl's precious gift of love and childhood memories, had been thrown away. The world is a cruel place, she thought. Tears streamed down her face, mixing with the light rain that had begun to fall.

CHAPTER 11

Clara Doyle

NEAR FLORENCE, OREGON, 1859

Morning light streamed into Kyle's face, waking him from a sound sleep. He breathed deeply, slowly aware of the cramp in his right arm. Suddenly, he realized Clara's head was resting on his shoulder, his arm wrapped underneath her. Kyle's heart pounded. He lay in bed with Clara. He tried to comprehend what had happened, but could only recall bringing Clara to his room and sitting in the chair near the bed.

Now, he looked at her in his arms. Barely breathing, he started to slide his arm out from under her. Clara stirred slightly, rolling away from him onto her back. His hand and forearm were still pinned under her, between her shoulder blades. Her torn nightgown was open, her breasts and belly lay bare, exposed to the slivers of golden light that glimmered through the frayed curtains.

Kyle had never been so close to such a young, naked virgin before. She slept on her back in calm repose. Her nightgown covered her body below the gentle curve of her navel, clinging to her shape, dipping delicately between her rounded thighs. His eyes devoured her. He leaned toward her slightly.

Kyle looked at Clara's face. Her soft lips were puffy, her checks rosy. Dark hair draped her sweet sculptured face, long neck, and silky shoulders, flowing out over the pillows. He wanted to touch her, feel her soft skin, caress the curve of her breasts, gently squeeze her ample ripeness. Breathing in the sweet scent of her warm body, he was more aroused than he could ever remember being.

Stop! a voice inside him commanded. Guilt swept over him. He pulled his arm free carefully and reached for the blanket that lay at Clara's knees. He covered her nakedness, then rolled quietly off the bed hoping she would not awaken.

Clara turned on her side, pulling her knees up like an innocent child. She lay undisturbed, still fast asleep.

Relieved, but still feeling his passion, Kyle walked to the open window to get some air. Pouring some cold water from the pitcher into the washbowl, he wiped his face with a washcloth. He parted the curtain to peer out the open window.

The day was cloudless and a warm breeze was blowing. Across the courtyard, some of the girls from the saloon were hanging wash on the line. Kyle caught sight of the redhead from the night before, stretching a sheet across the clothesline above her. With arms still raised, she pinned up her hair. Kyle gazed at her thin body, her long sculptured legs, small breasts, and light freckled skin. She was not young, but still pretty he thought. He tucked his shirt into his pants and walked quietly to the door. He slipped out of the room, careful not to wake Clara.

When Kyle got to the courtyard, the redhead was the only one still there. "Good morning," she said to Kyle. "I thought you had left. I waited for you, you know."

Kyle knew she hadn't.

She walked up to him, slowly. "You must have been tired, huh?" she teased, moving close enough to Kyle that her lips were a whisper away from his.

"I was," he said, bending his head toward her. "But I'm not too tired now." He kissed her lightly on the mouth. With his hands on her hips, he drew her to him, and whispered in her ear. She flashed her eyes seductively at Kyle and laughed.

"Now?"

"Are you busy?" Kyle asked.

She laughed again. "Never for you, honey." She took his hand and led him into a small cabin at the end of the courtyard, closing the door securely behind them.

Kyle came up behind her, wrapping his big arms around her small waist and kissing her neck. She smelled like lavender and smoke. He moved his large hands over her breasts, holding them as he had last night, feeling her nipples rise in his palms. She moaned. Still caressing one breast, he slid his other hand down to her belly, then further, reaching between her thighs. Thrusting her pelvis back and forth, she pushed her buttocks harder against his lust. He wanted to take her right there where they stood, but she took his hands from her body and walked him to her bed.

"You want me?" She stood in front of him, removing the lacing that tied her blouse.

Kyle watched her. He unbuckled his belt hastily. She removed her blouse revealing her lightly freckled breasts. In seconds, his hands and his mouth were upon her. He lifted her skirt, feeling his way to the warm place between her thighs. Pulling her down on top of him, he grabbed her soft buttocks. She pressed her pelvis into his groin. He was hard, ready. She whispered into his ear, unbuttoned his pants and touched him with firm, experienced hands. Skillfully she removed her own undergarments. Time disintegrated for Kyle, as she carried him into oblivion.

He did not recover for a while, lying spent, face down across the bed. The redhead was dressed and standing in front of a small mirror fixing her hair, when he finally stirred.

"Damn!" he gasped, jumping out of bed. He dressed quickly and pulled out two gold pieces from his pocket, placing them in the redhead's hand. Kyle kissed her cheek, then headed out the door. He had to get back to Clara.

What have I done? I'm no good at this, he thought. He ran into the room without knocking. Clara startled momentarily.

"Oh, it's you, Uncle Kyle," Clara exhaled, her hand over her heart.

"I'm sorry. I should have knocked," Kyle said, out of breath.

Clara noticed his heavy breathing. "What's the matter, Kyle?" She was fully dressed and packed. She had been standing near the window when Kyle had come in. "I'd been waiting only a few minutes here by the window, when I saw you running across the courtyard," Clara explained.

"Nothing," Kyle tried to hide his embarrassment. He was not used to being questioned. He felt awkward with his young niece. "Didn't want to get a late start, is all," he recovered. "You're ready. Good. We can go now."

"I'm definitely ready to leave," Clara said, still wondering where Kyle had come from in such a hurry. Before he could walk out the door, she reached for Kyle's arm. "Thank you for last night," she said.

Kyle's felt his stomach lurch. His pulse skipped, his face flushed. "Last night?" he said. His voice came out higher pitched than normal.

"For protecting me from that awful man," Clara said.

"Oh…" Kyle cleared his throat. "I'm sorry about that. It shouldn't have happened," he said. He still blamed himself. Kyle hesitated, then put an arm around Clara's shoulder. "Are you feelin' any better now?"

Clara caught Kyle's eye and smiled at him.

He didn't miss the way she looked at him, dreamy-eyed, like a woman who wanted love. He was not used to such strong emotions, not from someone so young. He was not accustomed to worrying or caring about someone else, not accustomed to the feelings he had for Clara. Responsibility and guilt gnawed at him.

"I'm glad you held me. It made me feel safe. I slept well."

Kyle was relieved that Clara didn't know he'd seen her, almost touched her sensuous young body. He managed a smile, picked up Clara's belongings and walked quickly out the door. She followed him down the steps and out to the stables.

"Mr. Doyle!" shouted the stable boy. "I have your wagon ready."

Belle was tied to the post at the trough. She was ready—brushed, fed, and watered.

"Thank you kindly, young fella," said Kyle. "Old Belle looks good this morning." Kyle stuffed something into the young man's hand. Then he helped Clara up to her seat on the wagon.

"Mr. Rudolph has some provisions for your journey like you asked, Mr. Doyle," said the boy. "He said for me to tell you to pick 'em up in the saloon."

"Thanks again, young fella," Kyle waved. He climbed up to his seat beside Clara, picked up Belle's reins, and headed toward the saloon. Clara held on to her seat, as the wagon jerked forward.

Kyle pulled up in front of the saloon. "I'll just be a minute, Clara," he said.

Clara watched him disappear through the door. She felt nervous. It was getting cloudy. The wind was blowing like it often did before rain.

Kyle walked inside, trying to see his way in the darkened saloon. Before he located the innkeeper, someone was beside him.

"Back for more, honey?" The redhead slipped out of the shadows.

"Mr. Doyle!" bellowed the innkeeper. He came out of the storeroom with a bundle. He slapped Kyle on his back. "Here are your provisions, son. Come back again with that pretty little gal of yours," he chuckled.

"Thanks kindly," Kyle said. He turned to his brief lover. "Day, ma'am."

She leaned toward him, kissing his cheek. "Come back this way without your gal," she whispered in his ear.

Kyle was still smiling when he threw the provisions in the back of the wagon. Clara thought he was glad to be leaving with her. "How long 'till we get east to the junction, Uncle Kyle?"

"Hmm, I don't know, Clara." He glanced up at the gray sky, squinting.

Clara noticed a sudden change in his demeanor, his expression.

"I reckon it all depends on the weather," Kyle said, climbing onto the wagon. He leaned forward and clicked to the mare. "Get-up there, Belle."

CHAPTER 12

Bertha Abraham/Washington

"Hold your breath for a minute," Dorothy advised, tightening Bertha's corset. "It has to be tighter, so your dress fits right, sister."

Bertha's wedding dress, a cream white, cotton batiste with a lace overdress and sash, lay neatly across the bed. Small silk buttons down the back of the bodice and lace trim at the neckline and sleeves added a touch of elegance to the special garment.

At first, Mrs. Bea had thought about altering the blue velvet dress she had made for Louisa's wedding, but changed her mind. Bertha needed her very own dress. Once determined on a course of action, Bea took great care to find just the right pattern. She looked in the magazines that Mrs. Clark had given her for the latest Edwardian fashions from stylish Philadelphia and New York designers. She wrote to Louisa, and talked to some of her friends at the First Baptist Church to get their opinions about what would look the best on Bertha. Fabric was expensive with the war in full swing, the right buttons harder to find, but the results were worth it. Bertha would be a lovely bride. With handsome James Washington in his dark suit, they'd make a fine-looking couple.

"Oh, it's beautiful!" Bertha cried when she saw her dress. "I never imagined I would have a wedding dress like this," she exclaimed, tears welling up in her eyes. "It looks like one from a magazine!" She threw her arms around Mama Bea.

"You sure 'nuff deserve it," Bea beamed. "You made me and Ben real happy, child."

Bea did not hide her tears or her joy that Sunday. Bertha, a beautiful bride in the stunning wedding dress, floated down the church aisle toward James Washington, her husband to be. After a big dinner celebration, the newlyweds were left undisturbed. They would consummate their union in the heat of the warm summer night.

The following day, Mrs. Bea knocked gently on the newlyweds' door. She had seen James go off to work just before dawn, as he did every weekday. "Bertha," she called softly. "Are you awake, child?"

Bertha straightened her love bed and opened the door. She was still in her nightgown. "I'm awake Mama. Good morning." She ran her hands over her disheveled hair. "Well, almost," she said shyly.

"No matter 'bout that. Come sit with me. I got somethin' special for you."

Bertha noticed Bea had a small tin box tucked under her arm. It looked familiar, but she could not remember where she had seen it before. "Now, I been waitin' for you to be grown, to be givin' you this here box. It belongs to you." Bea held the tin box in her hands. "I took it from your Mama's clothes bureau, when…" she paused. "I know Mayella be wantin' you to have it now."

Bertha's heart skipped a beat. She had not thought about the day her mother died, in many years. Now it all came flooding back, like the rush of wind before a rainstorm. "Mama had that box," Bertha whispered. "She used to tell me that when I grew up, she'd give it to me. I was to pass it on to my…" Bertha wept for the first time in a long time.

"It be all right, Bertha," Mrs. Bea comforted her. "Your Mama, Mayella in Heaven, be happy this day come. You grown up a fine, married woman." Mrs. Bea hugged Bertha. "Now take your time. I got breakfast waitin' when you be ready. I don't be goin' to work for a while yet."

Bertha held the box in her hand, turning it over and over, as bits of memory floated before her eyes. Then she slowly opened the box. She took a deep breath. The smell of sage filled her nostrils, spinning her through time. A thin, very worn piece of deerskin, with something inside, fit perfectly in the tin. Bertha unwrapped the treasure slowly. She found a little homemade book of yellowed papers bound with weaving yarn. Bertha fingered it lovingly, feeling the texture of her past, her mother, father, grandmother...the South.

Bertha instinctively held it to her cheek. She breathed in its essence, connecting her heart and mind to the inanimate object, until it came alive. Visions danced before her eyes. She saw her grandmother making cornmeal bread, helping Mayella bring baby Dorothy into the world, gathering plants and berries to make her medicines. She saw her father, Nathan reading and helping grandmother write words on pages—these very pages she now held in her hand.

Bertha opened the book. In her father's handwriting, the words of her grandmother were faded but still visible.

From my Grandmother
The Medicine of the Great Mother
For my daughters and 7 generations
Remember us

Bertha's eyes focused on the last words, which appeared to jump off the page. Unlike the others, the letters were unaffected by time. The ink was darker and vibrant. Why? How did that happen? Where had she heard those words before? Bertha closed her eyes, shutting out all distractions. Suddenly, she was flying over the treetops in an unfamiliar landscape of houses. In her peripheral vision, white down feathered wings surrounded her. Bertha looked at her arms stretched out in front of her. Her skin was white, too, like the wings that held her. She felt startled.

"Don't be afraid..." a voice called out to her. *"Grandmother is here. Remember. It is you who must remember us."*

Bertha opened her eyes. She did not know what to think, but was relieved to see her dark skin, her own hands that she recognized, holding the silvery tin box. She turned the pages of the little book. On each page was a recipe of herbs and plants for ailments of broken bones, coughs, sore, rashes, nervousness, menstrual bleeding, bleeding after childbirth, and more. The last two pages had recipes for using ground corn, the ones that Bertha's grandmother and Mayella had used. There were more recipes than just the ones Bertha remembered—the ones she had taught Dorothy and Mrs. Bea to make for Sunday dinner.

Bertha closed the book, tucked it in the deerskin and placed it back into the little tin. She opened the bottom drawer of her bureau. Wrapping it in an undergarment, she hid her precious magical box away. She promised herself to learn all its secrets. Smiling, she thought how someday, if she had a daughter, she would pass this sacred book to her.

* * * * *

It was only a year, before Bertha's wish for a daughter came true. Her first child, Belinda, was born in 1915. Lucille was born two years later. Now in the summer of 1922, eight years since her marriage to James, she was pregnant again. She hoped the new baby would come on time or even a little early, maybe the beginning of September in about two months. She prayed that Bea and the midwife were wrong, that her bigger size did not mean twins.

On the first Saturday in July, Bertha walked home from work, slowly with her two daughters in tow. Her back ached. It had become difficult for her to do her job at the Waldenbergs' place. She had agreed to take on some of Dorothy's work at the Doyles' home, too. It was something she had not planned. Dorothy had moved back to the warmth of South Carolina. Northern extremes of weather, especially the freezing cold winters, had been difficult for her delicate system. Before the new pregnancy, Bertha was happy to have the extra income for the family, to help James worry less about his job at the plant. Now, she just missed Dorothy's company. Bertha came to the corner of their street and waited to catch her breath.

"Mama, you want me to carry some of your bags?" Belinda asked, letting go of five-year-old Lucille's hand. Her big brown eyes looked up at her mother, her soft brown skin highlighted by the light blue cotton sundress Bertha had made for her. Only seven, she was built strong, like Bertha. Her braided hair was thick with red highlights, its texture reflecting her mixed heritage.

The summer humidity had made the afternoon unbearably hot. Sweat poured off Bertha's brow. She wiped her neck with a handkerchief. "We sure be happy for this heat come winter," she said to her daughters. "No use complaining over something we can't do nothin' 'bout."

"You need to rest more, Mama?" Belinda asked.

"You bein' a sweet child, Belinda." Bertha smiled at her oldest daughter. She handed Belinda one of the bags that Mrs. Waldenberg had given her containing a few used blouses for the children. Bertha gave a smaller bag to five-year-old Lucille.

Bertha did need more rest. A pain tightened in her chest, moved between her shoulder blades and up one side of her neck. She waited. She had felt it once before. In a moment it would subside. Bertha breathed deeply, thinking about her book of remedies from her own mother. The concoctions had kept her, James, and the girls healthy, so far. She tried to recall. Wasn't there something in that magical book for heart congestion?

A strange feeling suddenly came over her. As she stood on the corner two blocks from home, Belinda and Lucille by her side, her big belly protruding in front of her, she breathed away her discomfort. But the fleeting sensation of being trapped in a woman's body, in a life she had never envisioned—never wanted—lingered. She felt exhausted.

She looked at her daughters. "Maybe someday you girls goin' to have a chance," she said. Bertha looked directly at Belinda. "I don't want you to grow up and do laundry for white folks, Belinda. You hear me, child? You and Lucille…promise me you try to do better than your mama."

CHAPTER 13

Clara Doyle

Outskirts of Franklin, Oregon, 1859

The rain was cold, the wind bitter, when Kyle and Clara finally reached a small town. Cobblestones were barely visible under the thick mud dredged up by the torrential rain. Large, puddle-filled potholes made the wagon jar unmercifully. Clara could barely hold onto her seat. Through the pouring rain, she could see a soggy, little town come into view. She was relieved that they'd be stopping for the night.

Kyle pulled Belle into the stable, at the far end of a long row of buildings. He helped Clara down. She waited outside, under the overhanging roof of what appeared to be a general store. Clara was chilled to the bone. Her hair, skirt, and shawl were dripping wet. She stood shivering in the dismal gray light of the late afternoon.

Kyle stood in the rain, unhitching Belle from the wagon. He brought his mare into the stable, handing her reins to the stable hand. He grabbed Clara's drenched belongings and his pack from the wagon.

"Let's find the inn," Kyle shouted over the pouring rain. He took Clara's arm and pointed to a building at the end of the row of wooden structures. It was the tallest of the buildings, with two stories and a balcony facing the street.

Inside the inn's saloon, the warmth of the hearth, and the smell of stew, beer, sweaty men and perfumed women was a sharp contrast to the howling storm.

Kyle walked up to the bar. He arranged for accommodations with

Sam and Matt, the innkeepers. Matt, the older of the two brothers, directed Kyle upstairs to the landing and hallway where he would find two available guest rooms.

Clara's teeth chattered uncontrollably. She dragged herself up the stairs behind Kyle, weighed down by her wet clothes. On the second floor were rooms for the bar girls and for miners, fur trappers, and loggers traveling the rugged routes through Oregon, as well as railroad men traveling the West, with plans for railroad expansion.

Kyle opened the door to one of the unoccupied rooms and set Clara's damp satchel on the floor. "I'll go down and have a whiskey to warm up, Clara. You get settled." Kyle said. "Take off those wet clothes. There's a girl coming up with an extra blanket. I'll bring you some hot food," Kyle instructed her. He took off his wet buckskin jacket and hat, hanging them on the hooks by the door.

Before long, a young woman dressed in a blue skirt and a corseted blouse came into the room. She carried a wool blanket, a heavy cotton nightgown, an old dress, and a shawl. "You been out too long in that weather," she said, her brown eyes looking Clara over. "Best you get out of those wet things 'fore you catch your death," she said, as she turned down the bed. "Looks like you 'ready caught yourself a fever."

Clara felt dizzy. She did not resist the strange girl's help getting out of her wet garments, into the nightgown, and under the bed covers. "Thank you," Clara murmured. Her head felt hot, but even with the heavy blanket over her, Clara could not get warm.

"How is she?" Kyle asked the young woman. He walked into the room carrying a bowl of stew.

"She ain't goin' to eat no stew, handsome. She's too sick for that. Maybe some broth. I'll make her up some," the girl said. "She got herself a bad fever."

Kyle frowned. He moved closer to the bed. "Clara?"

Clara turned her head. She saw Kyle and stretched out her hand.

Kyle put the bowl of stew on the table near the window and walked back to her side. He took her hand. "Clara, you're burning up!" he exclaimed, touching her forehead. He poured some cool water from the pitcher onto a washing cloth and placed it across Clara's forehead.

"That feels good," Clara sighed quietly. "I'm sorry."

"It's all right, Clara. Being sick ain't planned. You just rest now. There'll be some soup coming soon," Kyle said.

But Clara did not hear him. She had drifted into a feverish sleep, her head soothed by the cool cloth. Kyle left the room and headed down to the saloon for more whiskey. He motioned to Sam, who obliged with half a bottle of his best drink.

The next morning brought a clearer sky. Clouds hung low only over the hills in the distance. Maybe, the worst of the storm has passed, Kyle thought. He went to check on Clara. Betsy, one of the bar girls, was tending to her. "How's she doin' this mornin'?" Kyle asked. "Her fever broke yet?"

"Afraid not, Mr. Doyle. She's still bad. She got a cough, too. Sam says we should get Miss Martha over to see her." She continued, "Miss Martha got a way with sick folk. The doc won't be back for a couple of days, tendin' folks up river country." Betsy cleared the broth bowl. She smiled at Kyle.

Kyle put his hand on her soft shoulder. "Thanks," he said. "Appreciate you lookin' after my Clara."

"Hope your gal gets better," Betsy said sincerely. "I will go get Miss Martha. Won't be but a few minutes."

Kyle pulled a chair up beside Clara's bed. He took her hand closest to him. It was still hot.

Clara's eyes opened for a moment. "Kyle," she whispered. Then she began to cough.

"Shhh," Kyle said. "Don't try to talk, Clara." He brought her some water. "Here, drink this." He lifted her head, so she could drink. "You're goin' to have to rest a while, Clara. Just take it slow. Don't you be worrying 'bout nothin'. You just get well now," Kyle said.

Clara's eyes closed. Her breathing came hard. But soon she slept again.

"What do you say, Miss Martha?" Kyle asked the stout old healing woman.

Miss Martha walked down the saloon stairs with slow, careful steps. She was sweating. Her bun-wrapped hair was half undone. "Mr. Doyle," Miss Martha shook her head. "I'm sorry to tell you this, but that child's goin' to be down for some time. With care, she might pull through, 'specially if Doc gets back soon. I'll tend to her with my remedies, but she got pneumonia, I figure."

Kyle frowned. He wiped his brow. He felt a sinking feeling in the pit of his stomach. "Thank you, Miss Martha," he said. "I'm grateful for you takin' the trouble. She's my only kin."

Miss Martha patted Kyle's shoulder. "You'd better get yourself settled for a bit," she reassured him. "I'll be back soon with some herbal tonic and soup." Miss Martha put on her shawl and bonnet. She nodded to Sam, who was wiping glasses behind the bar. Then she left.

Kyle walked out into the early afternoon light, too. An unfamiliar wave of emotion hit him. There was a lump in his throat. He swallowed hard. He took off his hat momentarily, pushing brown strands of hair back from his brow. He took a deep breath and clenched his jaw, intent on shaking off his doubts. He turned toward the stable.

"You come for your mare and wagon?" the stable hand asked Kyle.

"Uh, no, son. Why don't you saddle up Belle. I'll be riding her later this afternoon. I got some business down the road a piece. Won't need the wagon today," said Kyle, handing over a coin to the young man.

"Yes, sir!" grinned the stable boy, pocketing the shiny gold coin.

Kyle patted the boy on the back and walked back to the saloon.

Miss Martha returned with her herbal remedies and hot soup. She washed Clara's face and neck with a cool wet cloth. She placed it across Clara's hot forehead and sat down by the bedside to pray. Shortly someone knocked at the door. The sound woke Clara.

"Oh, come in, Mr. Doyle." Miss Martha whispered. "I was just getting ready to leave."

"Kyle? Is that you?" Clara whispered. She tried to lift her head, but could not.

"Shh, child," Miss Martha said. "The coughing will start again." She took the wet cloth from Clara's forehead and rearranged the pillows under her head. "Lie quiet now, dear," she said sweetly. She gave Kyle a sad look and pulled him aside. "There was a little blood in the cough," she said, covering her mouth slightly with her hand. "I wouldn't make her talk now. She needs to stay real quiet, Mr. Doyle. The doc should be getting back tomorrow."

Blood! The word echoed in Kyle's ears. Was she dying? She was fine just a few days ago. He pictured her sparkling eyes, her bubbling voice filled with hope, her beautiful body alive with longing.

"She'll recover won't she?" he asked.

"You best be here to talk to the Doc when he comes back—should be soon, Mr. Doyle."

"Yes, I see. Thank you for all you done, Miss Martha." Kyle sat down, keeping vigil in the chair next to Clara's bed.

Clara slept fitfully, her breathing difficult. After awhile, Kyle put his head down on the edge of the bed. He wanted to crawl in next to her and hold her. He wanted to run away too. Torn, Kyle dozed off, only to be awakened by a light knock at the door. Betsy glanced into the room.

"Oh, excuse me, Mr. Doyle," she said. "I just wanted to see if Clara was needin' anything before I went downstairs."

"Thank you, Miss Betsy. I was just leaving. I'll be heading out on business for a few days. I appreciate it kindly if you'd look after my Clara for me until I get back," Kyle said quietly.

Betsy looked at Kyle hard. "The doc will be comin' soon. Will you be back to speak with him?" she asked.

"I won't be gone long," replied Kyle, taking his hat and jacket off the door hook.

"I see," Betsy nodded and walked out, leaving the door ajar.

Kyle bent over Clara. He kissed her cheek softly, so not to wake her. His eyes burned. "Goodbye, Clara." Kyle's voice was barely audible. He closed the door quietly, walked down the stairs and out of the saloon. He did not stop to speak to Sam or anyone else. Kyle headed straight for the stable.

Within minutes he was in the saddle, reins in hand. He walked

Belle slowly to the town's main street. A misty drizzle had begun to fall from the cloudy gray sky. Light from the saloon shone across the wet cobblestones beneath Belle's hooves. Pulling the horse to a halt, Kyle looked north. He hesitated for a moment longer, then turned Belle's reins to the left and headed swiftly south.

* * * * *

A few days later, Betsy opened the faded curtains to let the sunshine into Clara's room. Doc's medicine and Miss Martha's tonic had worked. Clara had taken her first solid food the evening before. "Good Morning, Clara," Betsy said cheerfully. "You look a world better this morning, child. How you feeling, honey?"

Clara still coughed when she tried to talk in a regular tone, so she whispered. "A little better," she managed. She could sit up a bit with the pillows propped behind her. "Is Kyle back yet, Miss Betsy?"

"No, honey, he ain't, but don't you worry now. You just get well. He'll be back soon as he finishes his business." Betsy tried to reassure Clara, even though she was not sure Kyle would be coming back any time soon. She had seen something in him. She knew men well enough to know when they were lying. "Now, just you rest. I'll get you some porridge to take your medicine."

Betsy walked downstairs. She heard Sam and Matt arguing.

"We can't keep her here much longer, Sam. Her kin up and left her without paying beyond week's end. He ain't comin' back for her. We got a business to run. This ain't no sick house." Matt stamped off to the back room.

Sam looked up to see Betsy coming toward him. "How is she?" he asked. Sam had been a sickly child. He had compassion for Clara.

"Well, it's slow, but looks like she's goin' to get better, Sam. Maybe, she could stay with us, if she gets well and…"

"Stay? Thought you said her kin was comin' back for her?" Sam eyes widened.

"I did. But I have a feeling, that's all," Betsy said, shrugging a shoulder.

CHAPTER 14

Bertha Washington

Bertha wiped her face with a cold damp washcloth. The children had finally gone to sleep. The rain and thunder had kept them up past their usual bedtime. Bertha was thankful for the cloudburst. At least it would clear the air for a while. It had been a hot, muggy day, and the high humidity bothered her these days. The downpour had brought some relief, even if it was only temporary.

Bertha went into her bedroom. Her husband, James, was not ready for bed yet. She was glad. Maybe, she would have a few minutes to write to her sister. Bertha looked in the dresser drawer, then walked into the kitchen. "James, you see the letter I got from Dorothy yesterday? You know, the one I read to the children last night?"

James looked up from his work. He was tinkering with another new invention for the furnace system, sure his invention would change the way furnaces were built. "With coal and steel mills right here in Pennsylvania, couldn't be a better place to make a better furnace," he had a habit of saying. James looked at Bertha. "No, I didn't see the letter," he said. Then, because he knew Bertha so well, he added, "Wait awhile, Bertie. I'll help you look for it."

Bertha just sighed. She had been misplacing things lately. Since the birth of the twins three years ago and then Denise, her fifth child born last year, Bertha had steadily gotten worse, losing track of items more and more often. Although her children were in good health,

Bertha never regained her energy. Her former strength and stamina had vanished and with it, her memory.

It irritated her even more because she had always prided herself on being well-organized, a perfectionist of sorts. No matter how much work she had or how tired she was, Bertha's house was always neat and her children always groomed. Even though the children's clothes bore much use, handed down from one daughter to the next, they never dressed in anything unwashed or wrinkled. "Everything has a place," she had taught her girls. She taught them to cook and clean as soon as each grew tall enough to reach the sink and table with the help of a small stool. Except for the baby, she gave each of her children chores they could do every week.

Now, baby Denise slept soundly in her crib. She was big for a one-year-old. Soon they would have to add another bed for her. Bertha's other four daughters were fast asleep, too. Belinda, the oldest at ten, and eight-year-old Lucille slept in a large bed near the window. The three-year-old twins, Michelle and Daniella slept in cots near the door.

Bertha walked around to each of her beautiful children, covering them with the flowered cotton quilts she had washed the day before. Tomorrow morning, she would leave the youngest children with old Mrs. Bea, while she dragged Belinda and Lucille with her to pick up the laundry at the Waldenbergs and the Doyles, her regular Saturday route.

Bertha listened to the children breathing, unaware that James had come into the room, until he put his arms around her waist. Bertha leaned back against him, letting him support her a little. They watched their children sleep for a while. Finally, James took some folded papers from his shirt pocket.

"Here, Bertha." Bertha turned toward him. "Here is your sister's letter. It was on the shelf in the kitchen," he said, kissing her forehead.

Bertha took the letter and tucked it safely in her bosom, beneath her summer blouse. James' hands moved toward his wife's blouse, too. He whispered in her ear, his hands roaming.

"James!" Bertha scolded. She did not want to wake the children.

Bertha knew what James wanted. He was her husband, after all. It was not that she didn't like the attention, but lately she felt too exhausted to really enjoy their intimacy. But his pleasure, his need mattered to her. It was what had made her miscalculate her time and end up pregnant with their fifth child. She loved Denise no less than the other children, but Bertha could not bear another. She knew it would kill her. She felt ill often these days, but she didn't complain. James had enough to think about, just holding on to his job at the furnace company.

Bertha undressed and washed herself slowly, trying to remember when she had last bled. If this was a safe time, she would let James take his pleasure. She counted aloud, recalling how her mother had taught her women's wisdom. Realizing that she was seven days beyond her fertile time, she added some rosewater to her bath. James liked the way it smelled, and it was her way of letting him know she desired his affection.

Bertha changed into her white nightgown, carefully putting her blouse with her sister's letter near the sink, so she could find it in the morning. After Denise was born, she had written a letter to Dorothy, just in case her health failed. Hesitant to send it, she put it in a drawer by her bed, where it still remained. More recently, Bertha had decided to write Dorothy a new letter, asking her to come for a visit. It had only been two weeks since she mailed that new letter. She was glad to have received a response from Dorothy so soon.

Combing her hair back away from her face and putting some powder under her arms, Bertha relaxed. She walked into the bedroom where James was already in bed. Only a lit candle on the dresser illuminated the room. She extinguished the flame, then climbed into bed under the quilt, next to her husband. Resting on her side facing him, Bertha knew he smelled her perfume.

Jame turned, reaching for her in the darkness. Moaning, he grasped her soft hips and pulled her to him. Bertha could feel his large, swollen hardness at the base of her belly. James reached down to the hem of Bertha's nightgown. He pulled it all the way up over her belly and large breasts, so he could feel her nakedness against his.

He kissed and caressed her, until her breathing turned heavy. Then, feeling her desire, he caressed her soft thighs, searching for her moist center. Bertha moaned and kissed his neck. James entered her with a slow, thick thrust. He felt Bertha scratch his back and her pelvis rise. He felt her passion, smelled her sweet sweat, and their love-making grew deeper. It was only then, after his pleasure was complete, that he heard Bertha gasping for air.

Bertha had always liked the way James touched her, but recently she could not wait for James to finish. Tonight, as his large body lay on top of her and he pressed into her, her whole body heaved. A wrenching pain gripped her chest and her neck. She felt like she was drowning. She could not call out. She could hardly breathe. Terrified, Bertha had tried to pound on his back, scratching him in distress, but he did not stop.

"Bertha!" James felt panic rising in his throat. "Bertha!" he yelled.

Bertha couldn't catch her breath. She was holding both hands across her chest, grimacing in pain. James moved off her quickly, propping the pillows up, and lifting her into a half-sitting position. He instinctively massaged her chest, desperate to soothe her, help her breathe. He turned on the light, poured some water onto his discarded nightshirt, and wiped her brow. She was sweating profusely.

"Bertha!" he called again. Her eyes rolled upward and fluttered. He didn't know what was happening or what to do for her. It frightened him.

"Belinda," James yelled out. When Belinda didn't respond, he got up, threw on his pants, and ran to the children's room. He woke his oldest daughter.

"Get up, honey. Hurry! Your mother is very ill. Go fetch Mrs. Bea. Tell her to get Doc Porter right away."

Belinda got dressed and put on her shoes. James ran back to Bertha. Bertha lay motionless, but he could hear her breathing laboriously. He talked to her gently while he sponged her forehead with a cool, wet towel. He put her nightgown back on her.

It took every ounce of Bertha's energy just to breathe. She did not speak. She felt like the house had fallen on her. Time seemed to crawl by, until Belinda returned with Mrs. Bea and the doctor.

Doc Porter examined Bertha, then took James and Bea aside. "It's her heart, James. I wish I could say it will be better in a few days. She's resting now. I gave her something that should help, for now," he said, handing James a bottle filled with dark liquid. "Give her a spoonful of this when she wakes up, and then only when she is uncomfortable. I'll stop back tomorrow to check on her."

"Thank you for coming out in the middle of the night, Doc." James held back the tears. His voice cracked.

"Take it easy, James. Your children need you now, son." Doc put a hand on James' shoulder. He picked up his black bag and left.

Bea took Belinda into the children's room to comfort her. James sat down at the table. He put his face in his hands and wept. He loved Bertha more than he had ever loved anyone. She was part of him.

"Please God, don't take her from us," he cried.

"Don't let them children see you goin' on that way, James Washington," Mrs. Bea said firmly. She walked into the kitchen carrying several bundles. "I'll be takin' the younger children with me, but Belinda here, she wants to stay with you and Bertha. I told her maybe by morning Bertha be feelin' better." She was quiet for a minute.

James wiped his eyes and looked up at Mrs. Bea.

"I'm awfully sorry, James," Bea said compassionately. "I love Bertha like she be my natural-born child. God knows, her children need her." She shook her head. "The good Lord must have His reasons."

"Belinda can stay," James nodded. "I'm thankful you takin' the children for a while. I don't know what I'll do…" James eyes watered again. How could life go on without Bertha?

"You best send Belinda to me, later in the mornin'. I'll have her run Bertha's route. Let them folks know she's taken ill." Bea took the children in tow. She walked toward the door. "We be goin' now."

"Yes, yes." James got up. He kissed each of his daughters on the head. "You mind Mrs. Bea, now," he said sadly. He opened the door and watched them make their way down the street. A hint of dawn spread over the city rooftops, the hazy pink mist foreshadowing another steamy summer day.

James went into the washroom and splashed some water on his face, then dried himself. As he put the towel down, he noticed Bertha's blouse folded near the basin. Her sister's letter lay next to it. James picked it up, tears filling his eyes. He walked back into the bedroom to check on his beloved.

Bertha's breathing was more regular and she was sleeping. James sat near the window's light and opened Dorothy's letter.

My Dearest Sister,

How wonderful it was to hear from you after so many months. I'd been so worried about you. I saved the fare to take the train to Philadelphia. I asked Cousin Nell to help me get my ticket for a seat. She was happy to help me and asks about you. I look forward to meet the children. The only one I ever met, Belinda, she is a big girl by now. And doesn't remember me at all, I bet. But I remember her and James too. Some days I get so sorry that I never met a good man to marry. One that wouldn't mind about me not having babies. I guess I am too old now. But I could be a good aunt. And sounds like you could use some help. I hope you have gone down to a doctor if one of mama's remedies failed you. Tell them children I'm coming soon.

Sister, I wait to hear from you. Just let me know when to come. I miss you and Mrs. Bea. But you most of all.

Love, Your Sister Dorothy

James folded the letter and put it back into the envelope, which he tucked into his back pocket. He walked into the children's room and shook Belinda gently to wake her. "Belinda, child. I need you to stay here and help your mother," James said, lifting his daughter's chin up gently. "I got to run downtown, but I'll be back real soon, child."

Belinda rubbed her eyes and sat up. "Mama's better now, Papa?"

she asked. "Mrs. Bea still want me to go to Mama's job, tell them she be ill?" Belinda suddenly remembered.

"You wait awhile, Belinda. Stay here and take care of your Mama." He showed Belinda where the medicine was and left the instructions with her. He knew she could give Bertha her medicine. Then he left the house and headed for the telegraph office.

Bertha awoke, her chest and back tightening in pain. Belinda, still dressed in yesterday's frock and a worn sweater, stood by her bed. In her hand, Belinda held the bottle of medicine the doctor had given Bertha the night before.

"You need this now, Mama?" she asked. Belinda had not realized how sick her mother was, until this moment. She was scared.

Bertha nodded and tried to smile, so her beautiful first-born child would not be afraid. After she had taken the medicine, Bertha took Belinda's hand and closed her eyes. She felt sad that she would not get to see her daughters grow up, but something inside her told her that they would be all right.

Bertha longed to see James' face, to hear his voice. He had been so good to her. He had made her life bearable, made her feel safe and loved. She did not want to die. It was too soon. She had planned carefully this past year, knowing her heart was weak, but now that the time approached, she was scared. Bertha prayed silently to Jesus. A vision of herself and her sister, Dorothy, appeared. She saw them, as the children they had been, sitting with Bea, Ben, and Louisa in the old Baptist Church. Then she heard Dorothy calling to her. Suddenly, she remembered the letter to Dorothy that lay in her dresser drawer. Bertha opened her eyes.

"Belinda..." Bertha's voice was barely audible.

Belinda looked at her mother, eyes watering.

"Before I go," gasped Bertha, "promise me..." Bertha stopped to catch her breath.

Tears streamed down Belinda's smooth brown cheeks.

"Don't cry, honey child. I...love...you. Promise you remember... that I...always...be with you." Bertha raised her arms, reaching out to hold Belinda. "We…will…meet again," she said, stopping to gasp for air. "Promise me, Belinda." Bertha whispered. "Promise to give…the letter…to your aunt." Bertha pointed to her dresser.

Belinda walked to her mother's bureau. She opened all the drawers, until she found an old, wrinkled envelope, still sealed with her Aunt Dorothy's name printed on it. Next to the envelope was a small metal box. Belinda picked up the letter and returned to her mother's side, but Bertha had dozed off. Belinda crawled onto the bed and curled up next to her mother. She held the letter tightly in her hand and cried herself to sleep.

Before long, Belinda awoke to Mrs. Bea lifting her from the bed. She took Belinda, still groggy from sleep, into the kitchen to wait for James. "You drink this now," she said, handing Belinda some cool water.

"Don't Mama need some water, too?" Belinda asked.

"No, honey child. Your Mama Bertha has everything she need now. She be with Jesus."

Belinda looked up at Bea seeing the old woman's eyes fill with tears. Belinda could not breathe. For a moment, there was no air, no sound except for the pounding of her heart. Gasping, she held out her arms to Bea. She buried her face in Bea's apron and sobbed.

Two days later Aunt Dorothy arrived. Belinda had not forgotten her promise. After the church service, Dorothy read Bertha's last letter.

My Dearest Sister,

I be knowing for a long time that the end maybe come this year. I have nothing more valuable to show for my short life but my beautiful children and the best man I ever known. My children in your care I know will grow up safe and have families of their own. I ask of you only two things, my dear sister. That you pass to them your love and our mama's remedies and recipes that help me stay alive these past few years. With them and Jesus I be able to survive when Denise been born. Our mother's sacred tin box, please give to Belinda when she is grown up. Please take care of my best man in his heartbreak.

I am sorry we be living far apart these many years and I could not come see you. But I pray for you. I think if you wait awhile, my dear sister, your dreams will come true.

One day, we be meeting again in God's Kingdom.

I love you forever,

Bertha

CHAPTER 15

Rita Kerner

NEW YORK CITY, 1965-1969

Before graduation from high school, Rita was accepted into Hunter College. She was not sure she wanted to go to college, though. She wanted to go to art school. David advised her to be practical.

"You can paint to your heart's content when you're married."

"It wouldn't hurt you to marry a man with a good future," Lillian added. Happy that Rita had good enough grades to go to college, their plan for her still had marriage at the top of the list.

In her first year at college, Rita followed her father's advice. She took English, history, and art history classes. But by her second year of school, Rita spent less and less time at home. She didn't like school. Soon, she was thinking about moving out, getting her own place, spending more time with friends after classes.

"There's a great studio apartment on West 18th Street, two blocks from me." Marla, Rita's new best friend from school, encouraged her. "You could probably manage the rent with your job in the Village, if your folks could help you with the security deposit."

It was a good plan. Although David protested her decision, Rita convinced Lillian she could handle her own place. And the studio was perfect. Rita couldn't believe her luck at being able to afford her first apartment, with only a few extra hours a week at her job. Friday dinners were now only two blocks away, at Marla's place.

On Fridays, Rita had only one early class in art history. After her

96

afternoon shift at work, she was off to the market for Italian bread and wine for what had become a regular weekly event—spaghetti dinner at Marla's.

Arnie, an old friend of Rita's from her earlier Village days, began joining her at Marla's too. Rita had invited him, with Marla's approval, when they had met one day at Arnie's job at the Tenth Street coffeehouse. Rita's part-time job at the bookstore on Broadway was a short hop from the coffeehouse. Rita had begun spending her life there it seemed, when she wasn't in school or at work. She needed more coffee than normal to get through all the reading required for her degree in art history.

Rita thought she knew Arnie well. But lately, he'd been acting oddly. It became more obvious when they talked on the phone Thursday evening. He wanted to go somewhere special, just the two of them. He was excited about something he wanted to share with her. Rita thought it was strange that Arnie was being so secretive. She figured it must be a promotion at work, or maybe his band got a better gig than the one at The Dugout.

Besides, Rita liked being at Marla's on Friday nights. She and Arnie could go out together on Saturday night if he insisted, she thought. It wasn't as if they didn't spend a lot of time together. She was at his workplace at least five times a week, reading, studying. Sometimes, they spent nights sitting in Rita's new studio apartment, drinking, smoking and talking until the sun came up. She went to hear Arnie's band, and to midnight movies, dinners and breakfasts with him. They shared their treasured, common experiences, like the March on Washington to hear Dr. King give his most famous speech.

Although some of Arnie's black friends didn't get their friendship, Rita cherished her platonic relationship with Arnie. She liked that they could be good friends, that romance had not entered the picture. Neither of them ever felt the desire to be anything other than friends. There was something so familiar and comfortable about their connection. Now, she wondered if something had changed. Rita had noticed him hesitating lately, as if he wanted to say something, but wasn't sure how to say it. Whatever made him overly cautious these past weeks, Rita didn't have a clue.

On Friday evening, Rita had some news to share, too. An unusual letter had arrived from her sister, Irene, that afternoon. She couldn't wait to share it with Arnie and Marla. Rita hurried to shower and dress.

"I thought Arnie was coming with you." Marla opened the door and gave Rita a kiss on each cheek in her French tradition. She smelled like *Jean Nate* and *Ivory* soap, Rita noticed. "Well, come in, come in. I'm not finished getting dressed, anyway. You're a little early, *mon cheri.*"

Marla, wearing just her slip and bra, walked into her bedroom while she talked. "Sit," she said to Rita, pointing to her low double bed. The bed, draped in a white cotton lace spread, fit perfectly into the little alcove next to the door. Rita sat down, as Marla walked over to her dresser and picked up her make-up bag. She leaned forward to get a good look in the mirror perched atop the dresser, her breasts pressing into the dresser's top drawer.

Rita hated it when Marla was not dressed. She didn't know if Marla just enjoyed torturing her, or if she was oblivious to Rita's adoration. Was she really so innocent that she hadn't any awareness of Rita's lustful feelings toward her? Almost twenty years of age, Rita knew her feelings toward Marla were no teenage crush. She wanted to make love to Marla, the way men and women made love. Lately, those feelings had intensified. Rita was sure her feelings were obvious. But what if Marla thought it was a disgusting idea? What if she thought Rita needed help with her *problem?* What if Marla accused Rita of being a man inside a woman's body, like Rita felt she was sometimes? If Marla didn't realize it, then telling her might destroy their friendship. That was the last thing Rita wanted. She had kept her desire tightly under wraps for over a year. Only recently, had it come bubbling to the surface again with pressure-cooker intensity.

Rita tried to avoid staring, but she could not take her eyes off Marla. Looking at Marla half-dressed made Rita feel both excited and terrified. Marla's French good looks even made strangers turn their heads. Her luscious, long legs, slim waist, and full breasts that pushed up out of her low-cut lace bra made Rita hot.

"You look hot," Marla said, turning toward Rita, interrupting Rita's thoughts.

"Hot?" Rita's cheeks burned, her face flushed.

"Yeah, it's hot in here. I'll turn on the fan." She left the room and headed down the hall toward the kitchen. "You want some lemonade?" she yelled.

"Sure!" Rita was disappointed in herself. She'd had a chance to tell Marla that she was hot for *her*, not lemonade, but she'd been a big chicken. She got up to follow Marla into the kitchen.

Marla stood in front of an ironing board at the end of the hall near the kitchen. She slipped into a light silky dress. Rita stood still, watching Marla while she unbuttoned the front of the dress to expose some cleavage. Rita caught her breath. Marla walked toward her carrying two tall glasses of lemonade, her hips swaying beneath the flowing fabric.

"Could you help me close the clasp of my chain?" Marla asked, after they finished their drinks. She turned her back to Rita and held her long hair up, so Rita could fasten the thin gold chain.

Rita thought if she were brave, she'd wrap her arms around Marla and kiss her neck. But, Rita wasn't and there was no time left to build up her courage. The doorbell was ringing. Arnie had arrived.

Marla opened the front door. Arnie was standing there holding an armful of flowers and champagne, not the usual Friday fare. "Oh!" Marla squealed with delight, "Champagne! You shouldn't have," she said, kissing each of his cheeks.

Arnie looked a little embarrassed by the fuss she made over him. Rita understood. Everyone felt flustered being close to Marla.

"What are we celebrating, Arnie?" she asked, turning to Rita to see if she had any idea.

"Arnie has a big secret," Rita smiled. "He won't say anything except—"

"WAIT AWHILE!" Marla and Rita said in unison. They laughed.

Arnie chuckled, too, thinking Rita had probably guessed by now. Hadn't it been obvious for some time?

"What is your surprise?" Marla put a hand-cupped ear close to Arnie, so he could whisper to her. "Tell me, *mon cheri!*"

"Wait awhile," he smiled, handing Marla the flowers. "Let's sit and have some wine and dinner. This will be dessert," he said, holding up the champagne.

Arnie followed Marla to the kitchen and put the champagne in the fridge. Marla flirted with him, while she arranged the flowers in a water-filled vase and checked the pot of sauce, still simmering on the stove. She turned off the oven where a sweet, almond bread-pudding had finished baking, one that Marla had invented by combining a recipe for bread-pudding with her Aunt Nicolette's French pastry recipe.

Rita made herself comfortable on the couch. Unaware of the conversation in the kitchen, she opened her sister's letter to re-read it.

Meanwhile, Arnie confided in Marla. He pulled a small, red velvet box out of his pocket and beckoned Marla to come to the window. He whispered something in her ear. Marla gasped, peering into the little box he held open. She kissed Arnie on the cheek.

"Oh! This is so beautiful, so romantic!" she said softly. Marla loved romantic stories. She poured some wine into four goblets. Smiling, they both walked into the living room.

Rita was absorbed in reading. She hardly noticed when Arnie set the flowers down on the end table next to her. Marla placed the four glasses of wine on the coffee table, just when Rita looked up from her letter.

"Four glasses? An extra glass for Elijah?" Rita joked.

Marla laughed. "With a name like Brian? My Jewish parents would be happier if it were for Elijah."

"Oh, is your boyfriend coming tonight?" Rita asked, acting nonchalant. She glanced at Arnie. He said nothing. Neither of them cared for Brian, but they didn't want to hurt Marla's feelings.

"He said he might stop by, but he's working late, so he'll probably be too tired." Marla picked up a glass of wine and raised it. "To life! *L'chaim!*" she laughed.

They all clinked glasses and drank. Arnie liked their ethnic bantering, even if some of his black friends didn't get it. He'd had Jewish friends, before. He often said that racism and anti-Semitism were two sides of the same coin.

Rita felt a warm glow, as the wine and familiar comfort of her friends enveloped her. She loved Arnie and Marla. The three of them had a bond that would last a lifetime, she was sure.

"Listen to this," Rita said. "My sister wrote me this incredible letter. Should I read it while the spaghetti's cooking?"

"Let's hear it, *mon cheri*," Arnie mimicked, winking at Marla.

"The letter is dated May 30, 1967—four days ago," She cleared her throat and read aloud.

Dear Rita,

I was going to call, but I decided to write to you about something that happened last week. It's so amazing that I still can hardly believe it. If I hadn't been with my boyfriend Gregory at his place, I probably would think it was my imagination.

We were sitting on the couch, watching TV, fooling around. We had the blinds partly closed. He lives on the tenth floor. As you look out, there is a building only about five stories high, so there is a view of the roof.

Anyway, last Tuesday we saw a bunch of flashing lights outside through the blinds. So, we assumed it was a fire truck or police car on the street below with its lights flashing. When Gregory got up to go to the bathroom, I decided to go have a look out the window.

I walked to the window and opened the blinds. I couldn't believe what I saw. I could barely scream. There, above the roof across from me, was a thing...a saucer...a spaceship with lights, red and green and all around the middle there were like little windows or something and it was silver and making no sound but hovering. I screamed for Gregory. He must have thought someone was attacking me. He came flying out of the bathroom with his pants still around his ankles. "What the hell!" he yelled, then he saw it, too. I asked him to tell me what he saw. He could hardly speak. Then he said..."A...a flying saucer...oh, shit!"

We watched. Then it just took off toward the river and disappeared so fast that you would have thought you imagined it. But we didn't. Other people in the building saw it and the phone lines were jammed to the police and Gregory even tried to call the National Guard. Finally, when our neighbor got through, the police told her that it was just the sunset playing light tricks! Imagine that—light tricks. I didn't believe that. This thing was as real as can be.

Anyway, I've been feeling a bit shaky lately about the whole thing. I keep thinking about all the "Twilight Zone" programs we watched. What if "they" are really coming after us? I had to tell someone. I can't tell the folks...so what do you think? It is something, isn't it? Call me soon. Are you coming to Queens for a visit, soon?

Love, Irene

Rita looked up at Arnie and Marla. Arnie had an amused expression on his face. Marla, though, was as white as a sheet. Her eyes were red. Rita's excitement transformed into concern.

"What's the matter, Marla?"

Marla got up, walked into her bathroom, and closed the door behind her. Rita looked at Arnie. He shrugged, not understanding Marla's reaction either.

After a few moments, Marla came out of the bathroom. She looked a little better. "I'm sorry," she said. "I had a brother once. It's hard to talk about this. He used to have nightmares about spaceships and creatures. He was put in a home for the mentally disturbed. He died there...when he was eight-years-old." Her eyes watered.

"Oh, my God! I'm so sorry!" Rita felt awful. She'd had no idea that Marla ever had a brother. "I'm so sorry," Rita said again, walking over to comfort Marla.

But Marla turned away and walked into the kitchen. Rita turned to Arnie.

"It's okay. You didn't know. Come on," Arnie said, putting an arm around Rita's shoulder to soothe her.

Marla walked back into the living room with a big bowl of spaghetti. "Dinner's ready!" she announced, like nothing had happened. She placed the bowl on the dinner table. Marla had a gift for shutting off her emotions, at least outwardly.

"I'll get the sauce," Arnie said. Rita followed him into the kitchen, grabbing the bread, butter, and Parmesan cheese.

Just then the doorbell rang. It was Brian. For once, everyone was glad to see him. Brian was overwhelmed by their welcome. A conservative business student, he was not prone to great shows of emotion.

"It's good to see you, Brian" Arnie slapped him on the back gently. "C'mon let's eat while it's hot." Then, with uncommon chivalry, Arnie pulled out a chair for each of the girls.

"Who are you? And what have you done with Arnie?" Rita said to him half-jokingly.

Arnie's eyes twinkled.

After their hearty meal, Arnie excused himself. Rita thought he was going to the bathroom. Instead, he returned with the champagne. Marla leaned over and whispered something to Brian.

"Well," Arnie said, "I've waited a long time for this."

"For what? Champagne?" Rita laughed. It struck her funny.

Suddenly, Arnie was next to her chair. He dropped down on one knee, removing something from his pocket. "Rita," he said slowly.

Rita's heart jumped into her mouth. Arnie looked vulnerable and sincere. This wasn't funny. What the hell was he doing?

"Will you...will you marry me?" Arnie was holding a little, red velvet box with a thin, gold band nestled inside. "It belonged to my Grandmother Bertha…"

But Rita could barely hear him. He sounded like he was under water. Something had happened to the air. It was as thick as mud. Rita was gasping, choking. Then everything went black.

At first Arnie, Marla, and Brian thought Rita was overjoyed, until they finally realized she had fainted. When she came to, they were hovering over her like mother hens. Marla put a cool washcloth on Rita's head. When Rita felt steady enough to walk, Arnie took her home. They drank coffee and talked.

"I had no idea you were in love with me. Of course, I love you, too. I need a little time, that's all," Rita said. She did not want to hurt his feelings.

"I want to stay with you tonight," Arnie said quietly.

Rita tried to stay calm. A metallic taste filled her mouth. Her stomach churned. Still, she did not want to hurt her dear friend. "Okay," she agreed. "Why not? We should at least do it before…"

A big smile spread across Arnie's face. He stood up and walked toward her. He pulled her up, drew her to his large frame. He wrapped his arms around her waist. He kissed her deeply. Rita felt nothing, except a knot in the pit of her stomach.

"I need to get ready, you know," she said, wriggling out of his grasp. She went to the bathroom to brush her teeth. A big glob of mint toothpaste didn't feel like enough. "Okay, relax, you can do this, nothing new. Pretend you like it." Rita talked herself into a tough, whore-like stance that felt vaguely familiar.

"Be *Gunsmoke's,* Miss Kitty. C'mon you can handle any man, honey," she said to her reflection in the mirror. Rita could identify with the TV character—or was it lust she had felt toward her? It didn't matter now. It was too late for wondering which side to choose. She dabbed some perfume behind each ear and between her breasts. Putting on fresh panties and a T-shirt, she glanced in the mirror and tried a seductive smile. A chill ran up her spine, a sudden *deja vu.*

Arnie was already in bed under the heavy quilt. He had shut off the lights. Rita felt around for the edge of the bed and climbed in. He moved toward her. He kissed her, holding her hips tight to his body. Gliding his hands under her T-shirt, Arnie pulled it up and off her, pressing his bare skin to her nakedness. He rolled her over slightly, his mouth finding hers. He kissed her neck, his hands fondling her breasts. Rita tried not to bolt. She felt his sex pressing against her thighs, his body almost on top of her.

"Wait!" Rita panicked. "Wait, Arnie, I can't breathe!" He was heavy. She needed more time. "I need to get a drink." She jumped out of bed as soon as he rolled off her, his patience waning, his need throbbing.

"I'll have some, too." Arnie came up behind her.

The water ran from the faucet in the kitchen. He flicked on the light above the sink with one hand, holding her around the waist with the other. He pushed himself between her soft buttocks moving his pelvis slightly back and forth.

She still had her underpants on. Thank goodness, she thought. She filled two glasses with water.

"I can't wait too much longer," he moaned into her neck.

Rita squirmed free. She turned around. "Here's your water, Arnie."

He took the water and drank it down. Rita looked at his chest. Then she looked at the rest of his naked body. Her eyes fixated on his semi-erect penis. She froze. She stared, riveted to the spot. She couldn't speak. She could barely breathe. Her chest felt tight.

Arnie looked at her eyes fixated on him. She was gasping, choking as she stared at him. Am I that repulsive to her? He frowned.

Rita started to faint. Before her head hit the floor, he caught her. When Rita came to, Arnie was standing over her. She lay in her own bed, under the quilt. Arnie was fully clothed. The orange glow of dawn crept along the edges of the room.

"You'll be okay, now," he said kindly. "Wait awhile." He glanced at her one more time before leaving. The apartment door closed firmly behind him.

Rita sat up in bed. She tried to recall what had happened. The last thing she remembered was standing by the kitchen sink. "Water!" she said aloud, suddenly very thirsty. As she walked into the kitchen, it all came back to her. But why had she had such a severe reaction? She had been with men, even one she had not cared for much. But she didn't want a man anymore. She wanted Marla, not Arnie. She had to face who she was, what she was. She could not say the word...*lesbian*. How would she have the courage to tell either of her best friends?

* * * * *

Rita decided not to tell them. She pretended that she was too busy with her school work for socializing. The possibility of rejection was too painful. A few months later, Rita simply walked away and into the arms of a woman named, Beth. She was a lesbian who lived in the apartment above Rita's. A breath of fresh air, Beth was self-assured and experienced. Rita didn't look back. She thought she'd never see Marla or Arnie again. After all, it was a big city.

Then one day, when she was riding with Beth on her motorcycle on Eighth Avenue, she spotted Arnie on his bicycle. She hoped he would not see her. What would she say? Would it be obvious that they were lesbians?

When Beth stopped at the traffic light, Arnie did see her. He pedaled up next to them. He looked at Rita and nodded. "Well," he said, "How are you? It's been a while." He eyed Beth.

"Hi!" Rita said. "I'm okay. How are you doing?" A wave of guilt engulfed her. What else could she say? She wanted to say she was sorry, but she couldn't.

"I'm good," he replied. He looked at Rita, then again at Beth. Beth was wearing her leather jacket and boots. Rita could see him putting two and two together. An awkward pause hung in the air. Beth revved in neutral when the traffic light turned green.

"Well," Rita said. The driver behind them tapped his horn. "Uh... sorry, we gotta go. Maybe I'll run into you again and we can..."

"Yeah, I'll see you. Take care of yourself." He put a leg on one of the pedals and hoisted himself onto the bike's seat.

"You too..." Rita said sadly. Somehow, she knew they would

not meet again. As they pulled out into traffic, she squeezed Beth's waist tightly.

"So, who's Arnie?' Beth asked her later.

"It's a long story," Rita sighed. "I'll tell you sometime." Even Rita did not know how long a story it was. Beth would be a distant memory by the time she did.

CHAPTER 16

Chaske

NORTHERN GREAT PLAINS, 1801

"Chaske, where have you been? Your father has been looking for you. Why are you not with the other boys practicing your hunting skills?"

"Oh, Mother, it is so beautiful in the forest," Chaske's high-pitched voice cracked just slightly, his dark eyes full of excitement. "There are many more fish in the pools this summer. So much is growing."

"There you are, Chaske! I have looked for you all afternoon." The voice of Chaske's father was stern. He entered the family's lodge and frowned, the lines in his brown brow deepening, his eyes penetrating. "Where have you been?" he repeated.

"I am sorry, Father. I was in the forest."

The gangly, twelve-year-old boy looked down at his feet and squirmed slightly. He knew his father was angry.

"I am disappointed in you, my son. I have told you not to go into the forest alone. The council is preparing you for a great honor, and you are out wandering about the woods where you can get hurt. What would you do if you came across the path of a great mother bear? You are not prepared. You are to be a great warrior, but you must learn, practice, and follow the lead of your elders."

"But father, I saw a great eagle perched high in the rocks above the waterfalls. It was…"

"That is a very good sign, my son. The Great Spirit is watching over you, protecting you. Perhaps Wambleeska, White Eagle, will be your name when you become a man. But you still need to do your work and learn. For now, the horses need to be taken to the creek before dark."

"Yes, Father," the boy said obediently. He slowly walked out of the hut.

Chetan Lootah shook his head.

"Give him time," Mother Takchawee said, touching her husband's arm gently. "He is still young. He will grow up very soon and take his place. I think he has a little of your father in him," she added gently.

"My father, Wahkanda, was a great dreamer. His vision medicine helped our people. But the boy must learn the ways of a great warrior, now." He frowned again and walked out into the late afternoon sun.

Takchawee continued mending her son's blanket before joining her daughter, and the other girls and women to prepare the late meal. As she stitched, she thought about her only son. Perhaps he would settle down soon, stop running all over the woods, avoiding work and the skills he needed to learn. But some part of her was not sure. Chaske had inner sight. He used to tell her his dreams when he was just a little one. He seemed different from the other boys his age—with a faraway look in his eyes. She had wondered more than once, if the child were *winktes*, a two-spirit child. A few more months would tell. His vision quest was approaching. A sign would come. If Chaske took his place as a warrior, perhaps a leader one day, his depth of vision would be valuable to their people. But for now, she would say nothing to her husband.

"Mother, can I tell you…" Chaske began the next morning, when his father had left the hut. "The colors of the trees are especially green this summer. They make the water darker than I have ever seen it. Yesterday an eagle came and talked to me. He knew my name. Then, he swooped down, snatched a big silver fish from the dark, green water, and flew back up to his nest in the rocks. Mother, are you listening to me?"

"Yes, Chaske." She finished braiding his hair. "Now finish dressing and go help your father and cousins with their chores. Your sister and

I have much to do to prepare for the Sun Dance ceremony soon."

The boy finished dressing, put on his moccasins, and tied his belt strap around his waist. "I will go now, Mother," he said, leaving the comforting fold of her warmth and love. He walked out into the bright morning sun. He saw his father, his uncles, his cousins, and the other men preparing for the day's hunt. He wanted to roam off into the land of enchantment again, down a secret path he had discovered where waterfalls fell over the rock cliffs into deep pools of icy cold water, where ferns grew taller than him, and the smell of wild flowers and damp moss filled his nostrils. He wanted to take off his clothes, let his hair free down his back, feel the warm sun against his skin, and step stealthily among the rocks behind the falls, letting its wild spray splash his face. He'd sit alongside the edge of the pool, drying in the hot sun, as the fish made rainbows in the air, jumping out of the water in perfect arcs. He wanted to be where the birds called to him, fluttered, and glided back and forth from tree to tree, and where vines draped along the tall tree trunks, beckoning him to climb up to the lofty heights of their branches.

But Chaske knew better than to risk his father's wrath. Chetan Lootah was a patient man, but the boy felt his father growing agitated these days. Ever since the raid by their enemies, the loss of some of their horses and the news of the white skins, his father had grown less patient. So the boy turned away from the woods, toward the hill of low grass, where he would ready his horse and weapons for the day's hunt. Soon, his entry into manhood would be complete and with his rite of passage would come great changes.

It would not be long before Chaske spent less time exploring by himself. Instead, he would listen intently to the stories of his uncle, his father's oldest brother, Matoskah, White Bear. A man honored by the tribe, he had a short, wide stature with hands larger than average. His brown skin was wrinkled, but his dark eyes shined brightly. It was his expressive eyes that drew Chaske to his stories of the Great Spirit, and magical tales of animals, insects and birds, the history of their people, lessons of the seasons. Passed down from their ancestors as far back as time itself, stories of magic, humor, and tragedy unfolded, spilling out into the warm evening air during his uncle's storytelling time.

Chaske's favorite stories were the *White Buffalo Calf Woman* and *Eagle Flying Man*. He would listen to his uncle tell them to family and friends who gathered in his tipi in the evenings, during festive summer gatherings, or after successful hunts.

"Once there were two young warrior scouts out looking for buffalo," Chaske's uncle obliged his nephew. "Soon, they came across a young woman dressed in white buffalo skins standing near a bluff, above the valley. One of the two wanted to make her his wife and approached her with desire in his eyes. The other scout felt afraid and stood at a distance, knowing somehow that this was a sacred sign. As the first scout came close to the woman, a white mist enveloped them. Suddenly, the cloud vanished. Only White Buffalo Woman stood there. The first scout had disappeared. She called to the remaining scout to come and pick up the bones of the vanquished man. As he came close, she whispered to him in the voice of spirit. She gave him sacred symbols, the sacred pipe with twelve eagle feathers, and ceremonial words to call to the buffalo for a plentiful hunt. She told him to help his people and bring them the gift of plenty."

Uncle Matoskah passed the pipe to his brother, Chetan Lootah. The smell of the smoke filled Chaske's nostrils.

"We are a proud eagle nation," Matoskah added. "It is told when the earth was created, a great thundercloud appeared on the horizon. Flashing lightning and thundering descended toward the treetops. As the mists cleared, there was an eagle perched on the highest branches. He took flight and flew slowly down to the ground. As he approached the earth, he put forward his foot, and as he stepped upon the ground, he became a man."

Except for his time alone in the forest, it was during storytelling time that Chaske felt most happy. His spirit soared along with the birds in the stories of his ancestors. He was transported to places and times just like in his own dreams and visions. Sometimes, it was very hard to understand his place in all that was. As Chaske began to grow into his manhood, he clung to the stories even more, not wanting to lose his imagination in the harsh rules dictated by a warrior's life and the responsibility that awaited him.

Chaske was reluctant. Even the great hunt for buffalo was difficult for him. The only part he relished was riding. He camouflaged his dislike of killing by allowing his beloved horse to take flight beyond the hunt, out over the plains to the edge of the roaming buffalo herds, until his father reprimanded him. But the faster and longer he rode his brown and white pony—given to him by his oldest cousin, Napayshni, to mark his entrance into manhood—the more he felt himself to be part horse—majestic, strong, and able to run as fast as the wind. When he rode, his imagination took him soaring like a great eagle over the land, where he could hear the Great Spirit calling his name.

Even as his growing male stature took form, he still maintained his childlike good nature and generous spirit. He still clung to his mother's nurturing and found ways to daydream in solace for another whole season. Then, as his people returned again to their summer hunting grounds, something changed. Chaske felt something stir in him that he could not describe.

He felt a fluttering in his stomach, similar to the sensation he felt when he unexpectedly came across a snake—a sudden quickening of the heart and turning of the gut. No teasing from other young men, his own cousins, or cajoling from his mother, sister, or aunts could make him feel more uneasy. It had begun, he remembered, when he had noticed a girl from a nearby clan walking near the creek with her mother, picking long reeds and dead branches. Chaske had been watering his family's horses.

"Did you notice how distracted Chaske is today?" Takchawee asked her husband.

The elder snorted in disgust. "What more can I do? It soon will be a matter for the council," Chetan Lootah said, shaking his head.

"Oh, you old fool! Have you no eyes to see?" She bowed her head and bent down where she was sweeping. She had spoken from her anguished heart, but knew immediately that her words were too harsh.

She stood up and looked in the surprised face of her husband. Her voice turned soft and seductive. She spoke to him like she had when she was a young wife. "My beloved, our son has discovered his manhood. He has found passion in his heart and manly body, for a woman! Now he will change." Her eyes twinkled. "Our boy is becoming a man, you shall see. A new name like Wambleeska may fit all he sees with his new eyes."

Chaske's father looked at the old woman. Her hair, streaked with silver at the edges of her brow and her skin, once so smooth, showed its age. He looked into her deep brown eyes and took her work-worn hands in his, remembering the joy at their only son's birth, so late in their lives. "Yes, we will call him Wambleeska, now that he is coming of age." Chetan Lootah stood up taller and breathed deeper than he had in a long time.

Takchawee looked at her husband and smiled a rare, knowing smile. Chetan Lootah's heart softened, his eyes brightened. He took his wife in his arms and kissed her. For a few precious moments, they melted into the young lovers they had been, long ago.

CHAPTER 17

Rita Kerner

Rita didn't tell her parents when she dropped her classes at Hunter and started taking painting classes at the Art Students' League instead. She would handle the cost herself. Nor did she tell them about her relationship with Beth. They would be appalled, she thought, particularly her father. David had made such a scene about Marvin, the boy she had dated in high school, as she remembered.

＊ ＊ ＊ ＊ ＊

"Is he on something?" David asked. "His eyes are glazed. He's not Jewish, that's for sure! Is he still in high school?"

"No, he's not on something. He's an artist, a songwriter, Dad." Rita lied, knowing pot and pills were part of her boyfriend's scene. Risking igniting a firestorm, she added, "Why? Just 'cause he's black? Not like it's important, but if you must know—his mom's white, and Jewish! Since when is race or religion important to you, anyway?" Rita could almost see the steam coming out of her father's ears, but couldn't stop herself. "I can date who I want. And it's pretty hypocritical," she added. "You and Mom have always had all kinds friends. You have your union buddies. Mom goes to the all the civil rights marches. I should only go out with someone white and Jewish?" Rita was ready for a fight, but David stormed off without another word.

Had her parents become a stereotype? Did they really hope for her to marry a nice Jewish boy with plans for medical school? *It's just as easy to marry a rich man as a poor man* —Wasn't that just an expression they used, or was it a serious indoctrination into womanhood?

* * * * *

The memory made Rita slightly nauseous. Recently, the arguing and disagreements with her parents had become increasingly common. She has tried broaching the subject of the women's movement once, but it brought only a grunt of contempt from David. Lillian had listened at first, but Rita could tell she was hesitant to rock the boat. Telling them about Beth was out of the question.

Besides, things had been on and off with Beth lately. Rita had found some underwear in her lover's bathroom that didn't belong to either of them. Beth said they were hers, but Rita knew Beth wouldn't be caught dead in lace. Not even black lace. So they had fought. The yelling and tears were not a pretty sight. Rita was hurt, staying away from Beth, licking her wounds for a while. She'd recuperate, though—maybe try again.

Rita decided to immerse herself in her art for now. She liked that her teacher at the art school took an interest in her work. It meant a lot to her. Mr. Roberts was the top instructor in the painting department. She had been lucky to get into his class.

"The drawing is excellent. You have a real gift for realism." Mr. Roberts said, admiring Rita's most recent painting. "Now, I want to see you really make your portraits come alive, like the old masters."

Rita laughed nervously. She was a good artist—but the old masters? Not quite, she thought.

Mr. Roberts could see the self-doubt in her eyes. He was used to his students' lack of confidence. Having taught for so many years, he knew artists. Some had overinflated egos. But the majority, the truly gifted ones, were meeker, holding on to their brilliance, their sanity, by a thread. They arrived in his class having battled through childhood trauma, filled with mean or even well-meaning adults belittling them for claiming an artistic nature, badgering them into conformity or worse. He saw Rita's shoulders slump. He knew using the words "paint like the old masters" was like asking her to climb Mount Everest.

"Look, there is a trick to it. Well, it's more of a tried and true method," he said. Taking the varnish bottle, the one she only used after a painting was finished and well-dried, he mixed a little of its contents with some clean turpentine. "It's called *glazing*," Mr. Roberts continued. "You combine some turpentine and varnish and a little paint. Use a color that is darker or lighter than what is on your canvas already. In this case, a little yellow will work." He continued, "Let's concentrate on the face, the skin color." He tested the area of the canvas with a finger to judge its dryness. "It's dry enough." He picked up a paintbrush, mixing a small bit of yellow with the varnish-turpentine blend.

Rita watched him like a hawk.

"What you're after here is what we call a *bleed through* effect," he said. "The color beneath, the beige skin tone of this portrait, will *bleed through* the yellow glaze placed over it." He began to paint as he spoke. "You won't lose either color. You'll be able to see both at the same time—and more."

With light strokes, he brushed the glaze over the painting. Rita watched the canvas' metamorphosis. The skin tone Rita used for the model's face suddenly became radiant. Subtle undertones of beige turned a light pink and orange, bringing the image to life, as if caught in that splendid moment of light that reflects the glow of a brilliant sunset. "*Voila*—bleed through!" Mr. Roberts smiled.

If he had been a woman, Rita would have thrown her arms around him and kissed him passionately. With a simple stroke of a brush, he had changed her whole outlook on life. Maybe there was nothing she couldn't try, nothing beyond her ability. All one needed was knowledge. It was like each person had a key, their very own unique key that opened doors. She felt elated with the realization, the discovery of the hidden, yet logical nature of the world. Why hadn't she seen what was now so obvious? One had to find the right people, the right keys—one had to look beneath the surface, through layers of what appeared to be reality.

Rita flew home on the wings of pure inspiration. She intended to paint into the wee hours of the morning all the people and places she had seen, all the visions, dreams, and stories, using glazing. "Bleed through," she repeated, feeling the words roll off her tongue.

When she reached her apartment, she found a note tucked under the door. Still exuberant, she didn't hesitate to open it. She recognized Beth's handwriting. Perhaps a love note—an apology, she figured.

Listen kiddo, I'm really sorry. Things aren't working out. I've met someone and I'm leaving town. She lives out in the Hamptons— always did have fantasies of a Sugar Mama. She's got dough, but that's not it. I mean, it's great and all, but...Anyway, take whatever you want from my place. If you want to have dinner before I leave, let me know. I'm moving this weekend.

I'll always love you, Beth.

* * * * *

Rita came out of her liquor-induced comatose state long enough to answer the phone.

"Where have you been?" Lillian's voice was sharp, jarring. "Are you okay? We have been calling you for three days!" Lillian's voice softened. "Really Rita, your father and I were worried. Irene tried to reach you, too. She was going to come to your place on Monday, after she turned in her application for Hunter College."

Jeez! Have I been out of it that long? Rita thought. Her mouth felt dry and pasty. She walked by the mirror, trailing the phone cord. Disgusted by her reflection, she sat down on the bed again. "Sorry Ma, I had a touch of the flu. I wasn't answering the phone." Rita couldn't tell Lillian the real reason. "How about I come out to Queens this weekend—to catch up?"

"That would be very nice, honey." Rita could hear something different in her mother's voice—a mellowness almost. Lillian was turning fifty soon. Irene was starting college soon. In just three more years, Tina would be ready to fly the coop, too.

Rita shook her head. What the hell? She'd go make an obligatory visit, try like hell to stay out of trouble. For the first time ever, she wished they could have a day together, just mother and daughter—go somewhere away from both their lives, just be adults, be friends. Rita could use a good friend about now.

Rita showered and dressed. No time to straighten up. It was nine-thirty. She might make her ten o'clock painting class if she hurried. As she closed the door, the phone in the apartment rang. "Okay, Mom, what now?" she said aloud before she picked up the receiver.

"Hello? Yes, this is Rita Kerner. Who's calling?" She didn't recognize the woman's voice on the other end of the phone.

"A job, illustrating? Uh, yes, I guess so. I see," Rita said, hesitating. "Oh, Mr. Roberts recommended me? Yes, I know him. That was very nice of…sure tomorrow. Nine o'clock. Yes, I'll bring a portfolio."

Rita hung up the phone and rushed out the door, excited and anxious at the same time. Could she illustrate a book? Did Mr. Roberts think so highly of her skills? She skipped the elevator and ran down the stairs. If she got a good-paying freelance job, she would have enough money to move. She had been thinking about giving up her apartment, sharing a place with Beth. Now, that was not a possibility.

The thought of Beth was painful. I should have known, Rita thought. There were signs, lots of them when she considered it maturely, not with her child-like persona of optimistic naiveté. Beth hardly conversed lately, wasn't interested in intimacy, said she was tired all the time. There were the times she wasn't home when she said she was. One time, when Beth said she was sick, Rita went upstairs to surprise her with some chicken soup, only to find no one there. Rita shook her head realizing her wounds had still not healed from that fiasco.

But that was then and this was now. She had a class, a job interview, and next weekend, a trip to see her folks. "Focus," Rita said to herself as she hopped on the subway.

* * * * *

118

Rita was relieved that the painting she had covered with plastic remained dry on her rainy train trip to Queens.

"I brought this for you and Dad." She turned the medium-size canvas around to show Lillian, who sat at the kitchen table with her coffee and newspaper.

"Oh, that is lovely, Rita. Such nice colors. Your father will like it very much," Lillian said. "What do you call it?"

Rita didn't usually paint abstract images with political themes. But since she had learned glazing, she was trying it out, experimenting with multi-colored glazes on a variety of shapes and forms. "I call it *Make Love, Not War*," said Rita.

"Oh, like that slogan they used at the Fifth Ave anti-war demonstration last month? That's an interesting title for it."

"I know, it's not very original, but I thought it fit," Rita replied. "Don't you think?"

"Yes, I see what you mean," Lillian agreed.

"This would go great in your bedroom. Replace that depressing painting over your bed of the black carriage going down a road near a stormy gray sea."

Lillian looked surprised. "Maybe...we'll see," she said in a noncommittal tone. She looked at Rita's painting again. There were soft greens of an abstract forest, pale yellow flowers, blue patches of sky—the natural world on one side. Dark grays, blacks, and distorted images of war were on the other side, a tank between them, with its front end torn and burnt, but with the back section greening with what appeared to be vines and flowers growing from crevices and cracks.

It's like magic, Lillian thought. "You must get your talent from your father."

"Really?" Rita asked.

David had encouraged her artistically. He loved looking at art. But except for his love of collecting and fixing broken gold watches, his only other creative endeavor was tending their small terrace garden of roses.

"When he was stationed in England during the war...another

lifetime ago it seems like, he had a little sketch pad." Lillian paused, a faraway look in her eyes. "There was some unwritten code that the army men shouldn't get too friendly with the airmen, the *fly boys*. That's what they called them. They didn't always come back from missions over Germany."

Rita listened, spellbound. Why had she never heard this story?

Lillian continued. "Your father would sit and draw some of the fly boys in the barracks or pubs. He'd sometimes get their names, where they were from. After the war he sent some of those drawing to their families—the few he found, anyway."

"How come he never told us?" Rita asked. Was Lillian talking about her father? The father Rita knew?

"He never really talked much about the war. So much death with the bombing of London…" Lillian changed the subject suddenly. "Well, what else is new with you, dear? How's school?"

Rita was still absorbing the image of a father she didn't know. Now, she looked at her mother with new eyes. But she was still not sure if she should confide in Lillian. At some point though, Rita would have to explain. "I'm thinking of moving this summer," she took a chance.

"Where? Why?" Lillian looked directly at her daughter.

"The rent's going up, for one thing." Rita took a breath. "I'm thinking of moving to California."

"California!" Lillian's voice reverberated around the small kitchen.

"I know it's far away, Mom, but I need a change."

"A change! A change from what? What about school? What about Irene? She'll be going to Hunter. She could share the apartment with you." Lillian looked upset now.

"It's a studio, Mom. Besides, Irene can live at home the first year, like I did." Rita paused. Why stop now? She might as well spill the beans. "Mom, I guess I should tell you. I've been taking a painting class. I took a leave from school." Before Lillian could respond, Rita blurted out, "I can go back to college later. I got a new freelance job. I'll make enough money to move."

Lillian looked at Rita as if seeing her for the first time. "You took a leave from school?" she exclaimed. What isn't she telling me? Lillian thought. "Who do you know in California? What kind of job?" There was more to this story. "Did something happen, dear?" Lillian voice turned sincere, compassionate. "Are you okay?"

Her soft tone pulled on Rita's vulnerable heartstrings, cutting through her defenses. "Well, I've had a bit of a heartbreak, sort of." Rita looked at the floor.

"I didn't know you had a new boyfriend. You haven't mentioned anyone recently." Lillian got up, poured a cup of coffee for Rita, and refilled her cup. She glanced at the clock to see when David would be arriving home. She was glad to have her oldest all to herself, to be a confidant.

"Well," Rita took a deep breath and exhaled slowly. "It's not about a boy, Mom." The words hung in the air.

"What do mean?" Lillian asked.

"I've been seeing a...woman." For a moment, Rita could not believe what she had done. She waited for the earth-shattering hysteria to follow.

"I see," Lillian said quietly.

"You see?" Rita nearly fell off her chair. How could she see? What did she see? What did she know?

"I knew you were going through a phase. I mean you and that little girl, what was her name—Debbie, wasn't it? And that journal you brought home a year ago, the last time you were here."

"What? You knew about that? You read my journal?" Rita screeched.

"You left it out on the bed and I only glanced at it, dear." Lillian looked momentarily sheepish. "I'm not that surprised. Some girls go through a phase like this." Her tone softened again. "When I was a girl, I had a friend like that. But she married and then I met your father." Lillian paused. "Maybe you should read *The Well of Loneliness*, Rita."

"Jeez," Rita shook her head in disbelief. She didn't know whether to just be relieved that Lillian wasn't that upset, or that she had known all this time, or had invaded her privacy and said nothing. "I don't think it's a phase," Rita said wondering what "friend" Lillian once had.

And why had she read that book? "Please don't mention this to Dad, okay?" Rita pleaded. "You haven't told him anything yet, have you?"

Rita remembered when she had first menstruated and had asked her mother not to tell him. The minute David had come home though, she told him. As was some custom, unbeknown to Rita, she got slapped across the face with a big, *"Congratulations, you're a woman!"* She doubted there would be any congratulations this time.

"No, I won't," promised Lillian. "Maybe when you move to California you'll meet a nice man," she said, patting Rita's shoulder.

Rita wanted to tell her not to hold her breath, but let the idea go.

"Why don't you get washed up from your trip? Dad and the girls will be coming home soon. I am going to heat up the roasted chicken I bought and make a salad. Dad's picking up some dessert. We'll have a nice dinner." Lillian mustered a smile. "You can ask Tina about her honors classes. She got all A's."

"She's the smart one," Rita nodded, heading to the kitchen door.

"Wait," said Lillian. She handed Rita's painting to her. "Go put this painting in our bedroom, so your father will see it there. Maybe he'll exchange it for the other one."

"Thanks, Mom."

Rita walked into her parents' bedroom carrying her canvas. She looked at the old, haunting painting on the wall over the queen size bed. She stared at the horse-drawn carriage and the gray sea. For a moment, she saw herself as a small girl sitting inside the carriage, with a fur blanket on her lap. *"Clara, Clara…" Rita* thought she heard someone whisper. She felt a chill run up her spine. She shook her head to rid herself of the voices.

Clear and present again, Rita propped her *Make Love, Not War* painting up on the pillows against the wood headboard. She stood back and admired it. It was going to look so much better on the wall above the bed.

Then she heard her father's voice. David was home. He was yelling loudly, angrily, in Yiddish. So was Lillian. Rita heard doors slamming.

"Shit!" she spat. She ran into her old room—Pearl's room. She locked the door. Voices surrounded her immediately, but they weren't her parents' voices. They weren't angry voices. They were soft, comforting ones.

"Remember, remember...you are the one who remembers ..." One voice was audible over all others.

"Grandma Pearl?" Rita whispered. "Is that you?"

CHAPTER 18

Clara Doyle

MATT'S SALOON, FRANKLIN, OREGON, 1862

"She ain't no better 'en us. She ain't no damn wallflower," whined Rebecca.

"No, she ain't," said Sam. "Just have to ease her into it is all. She come up here with her kin and he done dumped her here like a sack of old potatoes. Shame, nice girl like that. Looks well-bred, if you ask me."

"Well, no one's askin' you," Matt grumbled as he walked by. "Just get her workin' and they can all stop fussin'. Let her earn her keep like the rest of the girls. Been almost four years already, and all she's done is cookin' and washin'. Hell, all the girls can do that. It ain't helpin' us make no money. She eats, don't she?" Matt spat. "We need to think about the future. Ain't no telling if Lincoln's damn war goin' to break the country in two, for good."

Matt walked into the back room behind the bar. Sam turned to Rebecca. "Look, just take it easy on her. I'll talk to her later."

Sam didn't like the idea of Clara being just another whore in the brothel. She was different, special. But he knew there was no way to save her any longer. He'd thought about marrying her more than once. But she was so stuck on her uncle coming back for her, she'd never given him a second look. Besides, he was still young. Matt wouldn't want him to marry, anyway. Sam resigned himself to the task and knocked on Clara's bedroom door.

"Uh, Miss Clara, I be needin' to talk to you," Sam said to the closed door.

Clara opened the door. "Good morning, Sam," she said, surprised by the early morning call. "You need me for something this morning?" she asked.

"Well, that's what I c-c-come to talk to you about," Sam stammered. "Can I come in? I be needin' to talk kinda private."

"Why, yes, I guess. Just let me get my shawl." Clara left the door ajar, took her shawl from the chair, and wrapped it around herself.

Sam walked in the room and closed the door.

Clara felt nervous, but didn't know why. "What's wrong, Sam?" she asked.

"Look, Clara, you ain't goina be able to stay here less you…you do what all the girls do to earn their room and board," Sam said. "I'm sorry to be, be, be tellin' you." Sam stuttered. He looked down at his boots.

"What do you mean, Sam? You want me to entertain the men that come in here? You don't mean…" She stared in disbelief.

"Yes, Miss Clara. Matt and the other girls, they don't want you here less you stop actin' like you're different, better 'en them. You gotta pull your weight, pay your way, just like the rest of 'em." Sam summoned the courage to look directly at Clara. He wished he had the guts to marry her, to save her. He started to turn toward the door.

"But my Uncle Kyle will be coming for me any day, Sam. He'll be so upset if…he'd be furious with you and Matt. He never meant for me to be here to become a…a prostitute. I can't do that, Sam. Please, Sam, don't ask me to do that." Clara began to cry.

Sam perspired. He wiped his forehead with the back of his sleeve. "Look, it ain't so bad. Just try it for a while—'till Kyle comes back. Nobody's gonna tell him. I'll see to it the girls don't tell him," Sam promised. "You just ease into it. The girls'll show you how it's done, how to please the customers. You know, just downstairs in the saloon. You can take your time getting used to the saloon first." Sam paused. "Then if you see what you like, it'll be your choice. It ain't bad, Clara.

The girls'll help you." Sam pleaded between Clara's sobs. "Matt won't keep you if you don't, Clara. And you ain't got nobody. Where will you go? It's comin' into winter, Clara." Sam turned to the door and walked out without waiting for her to speak.

Clara threw herself on her bed and cried. She held a pillow over her face and screamed Kyle's name until she was out of breath. Then she sat up, feeling suddenly defiant. "I'll show him," she said. "Wait 'till Kyle comes back and finds me all undone. He'll feel really bad for leaving me then." She wiped away the tears with her hands.

Clara painted a picture in her mind. Kyle would find her with the dirty men of the saloon and tear her away. He'd fight them off, take her away from this place. He'd beg her forgiveness for being gone so long and take her back East to start a new life, like he'd promised. She still believed in him. Clara knew it was only a matter of time. Kyle had important business, that's all. He was away preparing a life for them both. She just needed to be patient. She had to stay here where he could find her, where he had left her, where he knew she'd be waiting for him.

Clara stood up and walked to her little table that held a small mirror. One of the girls had given her some lip and cheek rouge, teasing and taunting her just the other day. Clara opened the little tin and rubbed some on her cheeks as she peered in the reflecting glass. She added some of the rosy color to her lips. She combed her hair and put it up more loosely, softening its style, framing her face. Putting on the black and white muslin dress that Kyle had given her, she smoothed the wrinkles away with her hands. The dress was thread bare in places and very tight, but still fit. She unbuttoned the bodice at the neck, just enough to show flesh beneath her graceful neck, but not enough to show the cleavage of her virgin breasts.

There, now let's see what they think about me, Clara thought. She opened the door and walked down the stairs to the saloon. Matt was wiping glasses on the bar, getting ready for the afternoon crowd.

"Whoa…look at you, Clara! I see Sam talked some sense into you. You're goin' to be the best gal at the place tonight! Betsy! Hey, Betsy! C'mon down here and take a look at Clara."

Betsy came wandering out onto the balcony. Her eyes widened when she saw Clara. "Well, don't you be lookin' just like one of us, now. 'Bout time you come outta that shell, Clara."

Matt looked up at Betsy leaning over the balcony, her nightgown half-unbuttoned. "Betsy, give some, uh, you know, instructions. And get her the right clothes."

"Go on, Clara. The girls will fix you up right. They'll show you what to do. You gonna be fine," Matt said, looking pleased.

Clara tried on a seductive smile. She walked up the stairs, moving her hips like the other girls. Betsy took her hand and they disappeared down the hall.

Matt was proud of Sam. "You done a good job, brother." Matt slapped Sam on the back when he came in from hauling the last of the empty beer kegs out back.

"Done a good job 'bout what?" Sam asked.

"With Clara, of course. She be prettying herself all up for the customers just like the other girls." Matt laughed. "She sure is somethin'."

Sam needed a drink. He poured a whiskey and drank it down.

Matt shook his head. "You're too soft, brother. She got a roof, food. That uncle ain't never comin' for her. You know that."

Sam just nodded. He cleaned the tables and tucked the chairs up close, trying to put the whole thing out of his mind. What's done is done, he thought. It wasn't his place to question it. Matt was his older brother and only kin. He was like a father, raising him after their folks died. He knew what was best. They had the saloon and the inn. They had food and drink. They wanted for nothing. Matt had seen to it they survived, prospered. Sam was facing the bar, his back to the staircase, when Betsy and Clara started down the steps.

"Hello, Sam," said Betsy.

Rebecca stood watching on the balcony and stifled a giggle.

"Sam, I want you to meet the new girl." Betsy's lustful voice echoed in the empty saloon.

Sam turned around to see Clara and Betsy standing together

on the bottom step. His cheeks turned red. His mouth was dry. He stammered. "Oh, that…is that Clara? I mean Clara, is that you? You look—you're lookin' good." Sam barely recognized Clara in a low cut blouse, flowing skirt, her face made up like the other painted ladies. The transformation caught him off guard. "I got to finish my chores, sweep out front 'fore noon." Sam walked out briskly.

In late afternoon, Clara had her first taste of her new life. She was surprised how easy it was to flirt and pretend to like it. She laughed and threw her head back, mimicking the other girls' movements. She sat on a man's lap and let him hold her around the waist, his gaze glued to her breasts which protruded slightly from the blouse Betsy chose for her. She swayed her hips as she walked from the counter to the table, beer mugs or shots of whiskey in hand.

It wasn't so bad, Clara thought. Then she thought of Kyle. He'd understand that she had no other choice. He'd come in one day soon, be glad she had the sense to wait for him. He'd buy her new clothes, the kind the proper women wore on their way to the little church at the far end of town or to the general goods store down the street.

"Clara." Matt came over to Clara as she returned an empty glass to Sam and waited for a refill. "There's a man here that would like your company later this evenin'. Since this being your first day, I told him I'd ask you myself."

Clara looked at Matt as she waited. "Am I serving drinks all evening too, Matt?" She sighed, feeling tired suddenly.

"No, Clara. Not drinks. Didn't Betsy show you?" Matt looked over at Betsy. He motioned to her. Betsy smoothed her skirt when she stood up from her bar stool and walked over to Matt and Clara. "Clara has a paying customer, Betsy. Will you talk to her?" Matt said gruffly and walked off.

"He wants me to go upstairs with that man?" Clara whispered. "I never did that before. I thought I was serving drinks. Sam said I didn't have to…" Clara was almost in tears.

"I'll take him tonight, but you're goin' to have to start sometime. I gave you all them oils and lotions to help you. I told you how. Take a shot of whiskey, close your eyes, put that perfume on under your nostrils." Betsy paused. "If you feel like vomiting afterward, eat the honey from the jar I gave you." Betsy saw Matt looking impatiently in her direction. She whispered her last bit of advice to Clara. "It don't hurt after the first time, 'less they're trouble. Matt's careful 'bout that though. He don't let that kind up here." Betsy sashayed over to a tall fellow who was eyeing Clara. She took him by the arm to a table in the corner.

A week later, Clara sat in her room, tears streaming down her cheeks. Her first time had been bad. Servicing the next two men, not any better. Betsy, Rebecca, and the other girls tried to comfort her. They helped her bathe. They poured her whiskey until she was too dizzy to walk, too drunk to feel any pain.

Today, she was sober and empty. She felt soiled. What would become of her? She thought of Mrs. Riley and Anna for the first time in a long time. Shame swept over her. Was this what it meant to be a woman? It was certainly not the way a proper young lady behaved, like Mrs. Riley had expected her to behave. Clara knew that for sure. "Kyle," she whispered. "Where are you?"

Clara changed her sheets. She washed and powdered, before putting on a clean nightgown. She climbed back into bed, too tired to go downstairs for breakfast. Instead, she dozed. In a fitful sleep, she dreamed of a young Indian boy on his horse running across an open plain. The dream vanished with a loud knock on her door.

"Clara!" Rebecca's voice called through the closed door. "It's almost noon. Sam is askin' for you."

"I'm coming," Clara managed. She did not open the door. She got up and opened the little tin at her mirror. With her face painted, she combed her hair and donned an outfit befitting her new life. "You'll be fine," she said to herself. "Make the money." She placed her hands under her firm young breasts, lifting them to enhance her cleavage. "Just pretend you like it."

CHAPTER 19

Rita Kerner

Rita landed at the San Francisco Airport on a Saturday afternoon in July. It was foggy and cooler than she thought California would be in the summer. She pulled a jacket from her suitcase and headed into San Francisco, to a place called Peg's. It was a club she'd heard about from the bartender at her regular hangout in New York. With suitcase, camera, and map in hand she was the epitome of a tourist. Except for her short-cropped hair, Rita thought she looked pretty normal.

By the time she reached Peg's, it was happy hour. Rita was happy to have a beer. The cool foam was just right. She watched the people entering the bar, a steady stream of women, all ages, sizes, colors and shapes—just like the bars at home. She relaxed. It wasn't going to be that hard meeting someone.

Rita sat at the edge of her barstool listening to Joplin's "Me and Bobbie McGee." Rita sang along like all the regulars at the bar and waited for the DJ to play some disco with a good dance beat. She noticed a young woman across the room, at the pool table, staring in her direction. Before the night was over, Rita knew they would be dancing.

"Hi," the young woman said, making her way to the bar. "Sue," she called, motioning to the bartender. "Give us two beers here, will ya?" Then turning to Rita, "Hey," she said, holding out her hand. "My name's Andrea. You just get into town?" She glanced at Rita's suitcase.

"It's that obvious, I guess. Jeez, and I was trying to play it cool," Rita laughed.

"Lots of folks moving here lately. You from New York? Me too!" Andreas didn't wait for an answer. "Us East Coast girls gotta stick together out here in Hippie Land. 'Specially New Yorkers, if you know what I mean."

Rita guessed she meant the New York accent thing, or maybe the Jewish thing, but she wasn't sure. By the third beer though, it didn't matter.

* * * * *

Andrea and Rita had a fast romance. Andrea showed Rita the ropes "in the life" by the Bay, introduced her to friends, and gave her a place to sleep—with her. But the romance was short-lived.

Rita liked Andrea, but after three months she knew her feelings weren't strong enough for a lasting relationship "Let's be friends," Rita said. "We can still enjoy doing things together. I'm cramping your style in this tiny place, anyway."

Andrea's style was being a slob. Her place was always a mess. Her cat didn't help. The big gray feline was the master of his domain with permission to lick any dish he pleased, even if a human was still eating from it. He made a habit of hissing at Rita. But she didn't complain about any of it. Andrea had been kind to her.

Rita hoped Andrea would understand. "Claire and Evelyn are looking for a roommate for their three-bedroom apartment just down the block, on Sanchez. I can afford that with my new job at the print shop." Rita paused. "I'll be close-by."

"Yeah, I guess you're right." Andrea shrugged. "It's been tight in a studio, but I really like you." Tears welled up in her eyes.

Rita hugged her lover's lean, wiry body, and gently swept the frizzy auburn locks off her forehead. Andrea pulled away slightly, wiping the tears away with her sleeve. "Hey, I'll be fine. Can we still go for bagels in Noe Valley, on Sunday?"

"Any Sunday you'd like," Rita reassured her. And don't forget movies at the Castro and walking at the beach, playing pool at the bar. Friends do stuff, right?"

Rita moved in with fifty-year-old Claire and her younger lover, Evelyn. They were an odd couple, but adorable. Claire was what Rita hoped to look like when she got older—skin still radiant and tanned, silver-streaked hair cut short, wavy. Her curves apparent even in tight jeans and a tailored shirt.

Evelyn was tall and thin, with long flowing blond hair, bangs in her face most of the time. She dressed in loose gauzy shirts and bell-bottom pants. In her thirties, she looked more like a teenager, a hippie flower child.

But the "opposites attract" theory was working for them. The partners were generous with one another. Rita appreciated their lack of drama, their steadfastness and honesty. She felt lucky to have found such good roommates. Claire and Evelyn even joined Andrea and Rita for bagels on Sunday.

"So, how's the job going?" Andrea asked. Having seen a copy of the book Rita had illustrated, and some recent sketches, Andrea knew Rita had too much talent to be making signs at a print shop.

"It pays okay. I like some of the guys I work with. The boss is a jerk though." She shrugged. "Can't have everything. It's a stepping stone," Rita said. "I'm looking for something more artistic, creative, but for now, it's okay."

To Rita's surprise, an unexpected opportunity presented itself the following Monday.

"Rita, I have a guy who wants to meet you, to see your art portfolio. He works over at Lehman's Department Store, downtown," Rita's boss, Mr. Clark, said. "There may be some freelance artwork for you, if you play your cards right," he announced.

Rita put down the twenty-pound drum of blue ink she'd just mixed and stared at Mr. Clark. He was about ten years older than her, but as arrogant as a teenage boy. Today, she ignored his bravado. The extra money for the holidays would come in handy. Maybe she might have a chance in commercial art doing something that matched her skills, after all. Could this be just the break she needed?

"Sounds great! When do you want me to meet him? What's his name?"

"Paul Leahy, an old buddy of mine. He heads up the display department at Lehman's. I told him you're an artist and you're looking for some freelance work."

"Thank you, Mr. Clark. That was really nice of you." Rita didn't expect him to be so nice. She wondered if he was trying to make amends for yelling at her, because she wouldn't make a union label dye for the Franzley campaign posters. "We're not a union shop," she had protested.

"Wear something nice. Get cleaned up like a girl." Mr. Clark looked down at Rita's jeans and sweatshirt. Her sleeves were frayed and damp from the screen washer. Her shop apron was smeared with the day's ink mixtures. Her hands were stained with photo chemicals, calloused by the manual work.

"You have a twelve o'clock appointment tomorrow down at Ralph's, the restaurant on the ground floor of Lehman's. Paul will meet you there," he said. "Oh, and come see me in my office when you finish with that ink. I have a job I want you to do as the new shop manager."

"New shop manager?" Rita was excited. Things were really happening.

She looked over at Enrico, who had been standing at the big electric printer, clearly within earshot of the boss's conversation. Enrico and Rita had become friends. He was very cautious, but had slowly opened up, sensing Rita's trustworthiness. Enrico had escaped a South American prison with only one leg intact. To strangers, his soft voice, and thin frame masked his intensity and intelligence. Now, he gave Rita a furtive look like a hyper-vigilant animal attuned to the slightest movement of a predator. She felt suddenly on guard.

Rita looked over at another of her co-workers, Victor, at the cutter. He was a delightful queen. She wished she had his bravery and flamboyance. "I'm gay, sweetie!" he'd said when he introduced himself. "I'm as queer as a three dollar bill. What you see is what you get, hon!"

Over at the screen wash area, a wild mop of red hair appeared over the side of the large wood frame. Terry, Rita's ethereal young friend and co-worker, waved as he washed. They often ate lunch together. A lot of the kids in Rita's high school had been drafted, like Terry, but he had gotten lucky. He was on the transport to Vietnam, out of Seattle, when his unit was called back. He'd been transferred to New Mexico—never got called up again, before he got out.

"I'm telling you Rita, some of them old dudes at that base been near a place called Roswell, about fifteen years before I got to New Mexico. You know that UFO crash that happened there. Hell, they talked about it like it was yesterday, like it had just happened. This one guy said he flew a reconnaissance plane." Terry's eyes lit up. "Said there were bodies. He saw 'em—said, no way they were human. I never told no one about this before," Terry admitted. "I think people just think it's bogus believing in little green men from Mars." He looked directly at Rita. "But you, hey, I don't know. You're different, Rita."

"Gee, thanks, I think," Rita smiled. A memory slid by her of Irene's letter about a flying saucer...of Marla and Arnie—another lifetime, it seemed.

Just then George, another co-worker, leaned over the rail of the loft where the drying racks stood and yelled, "Hey, Rita, you want these prints? 'Cause they're dry now."

Rita hoped George was not as drunk today as he'd been the last few days. God, how he even made it into work was a mystery to Rita. But he'd been an old friend of Mr. Clark's father, so he was part of the place, drunk or drunker.

Rita didn't know if it was the liquor talking when George gave Rita a heads-up a week earlier. "Watch out for him. He ain't his old man. Old Clark and me were friends, since coming from Philly. That young Clark's a spoiled son of a bitch...a scoundrel like his granddaddy was."

Rita walked toward Mr. Clark's office. "Come in Rita, I have a job for you as the new shop manager. This is not going to be pleasant, but it is your job now. I want you to fire that fruitcake, Victor."

"Excuse me?" Rita exclaimed.

"You heard me. I don't want him here. I want that faggot outta here, today."

"On what grounds?" Rita thought quickly, her head spinning. "Vic does a good job. He's great at the cutter. He's fast and accurate. Who will—"

"You'll learn it. I don't need an extra worker to cut. You can do it in a quarter of the time. I've seen you. You're fast. George will show you. Fire that cock-sucking faggot!" Mr. Clark raised his voice. "Fire him today. He can have one week's severance pay."

Rita was shocked. She could not listen to him rant. George was right, Mr. Clark was a pig. She was not going to fire Victor, because he was gay. She was too. Go to hell! she almost yelled.

"I'm sorry, I can't, Mr. Clark. I can't fire Victor for no reason, except you don't like him. You fire him if you want him to leave." Rita turned to leave.

"Rita! You fire him or you're fired! And I'll call Paul, tell him your work isn't worth seeing."

Rita couldn't believe her ears. This bastard is threatening me, she thought. He knew she needed the job to pay her rent, just like Victor did.

"This is a pretty awful thing you're doing. Don't you have a conscience?" Suddenly Rita was back in fourth grade, defending little Maryanne. Only Tim was not Maryanne, nor were they handicapped children. She and Tim could do some damage if they had a mind to, Rita raged.

Mr. Clark leaned back in his chair and laughed. He was getting a kick out of this. Rita walked out of his office.

Victor was having his lunch and reading the paper. He was sitting on one of the crates near the cutter like a soldier guarding his post. "Vic, I have to tell you something."

"What's up, kiddo? Saw you fighting with the boss man, again. He sure lets you talk back. Why honey, I swear I think he just loves to see you get mad."

"Yeah, well, now it's your turn to get mad, Victor. He wants me to fire you. He's prejudiced, Vic. A damn redneck. He's firing you because you're gay. He said if I didn't fire you, he'd fire me." Rita's eyes flashed angrily as she stared in the direction of the office. "Why don't we just both leave? Let's just walk out together."

"Shit! What a fucking son of a bitch! What a piece of shit! So, he had to get you to do his dirty work. Maybe he should walk over here near the cutter and see if a sex change might help his attitude!" Victor yelled loud enough for everyone in the place to hear.

"Let's just go," Rita said.

"No, Rita. Don't both of us need to lose an income." He took a deep breath. "Hey, kiddo, you stay. I know you need the job. He'll wear you down in no time the way it's goin', though." Victor packed up the rest of his lunch. "I'll leave. I hate the jerk, anyway. Hey, will you just make sure my last check gets to me?"

"Are you sure, Vic? I'll leave, too." Rita started to remove her apron and follow Victor toward the door

"No, Rita. I won't get my check if you're not here. Just send it to me, will ya?"

"God! Of course, please call me, okay?"

Rita looked over at Enrico. He looked away. Reaching over to the press, he fed printing paper into the enormous mouth of the feeder tray, then pulled the "on" switch. His silence was as loud as the giant machine cranking out the printed signs.

Rita no longer looked forward to the appointment with Paul Leahy. She had that "sold my soul to the devil" feeling. No one spoke above a whisper for the rest of the day.

The next day, Rita tried to muster some enthusiasm for her future. In spite of everything, she dressed in the only nice outfit she owned— navy blue slacks, a light blue blouse, and a cream-colored blazer and met Mr. Leahy at Ralph's, as planned. The place turned out to be more of a pub than a restaurant.

"What'll you have?" Paul Leahy asked.

"Oh, ginger ale will be fine, thanks."

"Have a real drink, honey. Your boss won't mind." Mr. Leahy

was a middle-aged, well-groomed businessman-type in a gray suit, a light shirt, and tie. His mischievous smile and blue eyes caught Rita's cautious attention. She brushed off her reservations, thinking about the art job she might get—a job that might mean a step toward a rewarding career away from the sign shop.

"Do you want to see my portfolio?" Rita asked.

"Let's talk a little about you. I mean, I'd like to get to know you a little first," Paul said. "Tell me about yourself."

"Well, I studied art history, but mostly I'm a painter and an illustrator." Rita pulled out her art resume. "I am very interested in finding artistic work," she added.

"That's nice. Are you married?"

"Uh, no, I'm not."

"Do you have a boyfriend?" His eyes smiled lustfully.

"No," Rita said, annoyed by the personal questions. She maintained a cool professional manner, though, hoping her art would sway him. "Would you like to see my work?" Rita opened her art portfolio, redirecting the conversation.

"Sure, sure." Paul Leahy finished his first drink, then ordered another. "This is your work?" Mr. Leahy seemed surprised. "It's real artwork. I mean, it's quite good." He looked at the pages in earnest. "This is quite good," he said again. He stared at Rita. "Look," he said almost whispering now. "I have to apologize to you. You seem like a nice girl—genuine, I mean." He took another gulp of his drink. "My friend, John Clark, he's not a bad guy, but he's not always such a nice guy. You know what I mean?"

Rita knew what she experienced. But what was this guy talking about? "What do you mean?" she asked.

"Look, Miss, uh, Rita. He set you up, kid." Paul looked embarrassed.

"Set me up, how?" Rita squinted.

"He wants to get you in the sack. He asked me to see if I could find out something about you, you know, maybe get you to pose for a film." Paul Leahy downed the rest of his scotch.

"What! Is this a joke? You mean you're not...this isn't a real interview?" How could I be such an idiot? Rita's adrenalin pumped. "What a fucking pig! He's married. Ugh, this is so revolting!" Rita yelled. She jumped up from the table and grabbed her resume out of her "interviewer's" hand.

"Look, I'm really sorry." Paul Leahy reached out. "Hey, let me buy you lunch at least…"

Rita was already halfway out the door.

* * * * *

"How did the interview go?" Mr. Clark chortled, as he looked Rita up and down.

"Fine, thanks." Rita said in her sweetest voice. Now, she thought, I will be better than that Sarah Bernhardt my mother used to call me. This guy isn't going to know what hit him.

"Oh, by the way, Mr. Clark, since I fired Tim, can I get his paycheck when I get mine later? I'll mail it out to him. With all the excitement about Paul Leahy, I forget to ask you before," she said, her sugary sweet tone disguising venom.

"Okay, sure, you did good. Come by for the checks before you leave. I'll get together with Leahy tomorrow evening, talk over your fee." He smiled, his eyes gleaming with delusional fantasy.

The next day at lunch hour, Rita grabbed Enrico and Terry. "C'mon, we're going to meet with the Printers' Union representative and the Franzley people. Want to help me blow Mr. Clark's business out of the water?" Rita whispered. "Remember the other day, he asked us to make phony union label dyes for the Franzley campaign job? Are you with me?"

Enrico smiled broadly. He nodded.

"Yeah," said Terry. "We got skills. We'll find other work." Then with a smirk on his face, he added, "Wish I could be a fly on the wall to see the bastard's face when he loses that gig."

* * * * *

A month later, Rita had a new job. She was up early on Monday morning to plan her after-school classes for the Haight Street Children's Center. Evelyn was sitting at the kitchen table licking stamps for her party invitations when Rita came in for her morning coffee.

"We're having a Halloween party," Evelyn said, pushing back strands of blond hair with the back of her wrist. "Do you want to invite Andrea? Or anyone from your new job?" she asked.

"Oh, cool! Yeah, I'll invite Andrea and her new partner, Janice," Rita said, looking over Evelyn's shoulder at the orange, pumpkin-shaped invitations. "Can I invite Joel and Susan from my new job at the kids' center? Are men invited?"

"Yeah, some of my gay male friends are coming. And I think Claire invited her two sons and their girlfriends. The more the merrier! But costumes are mandatory." Evelyn grinned. "Are Susan and Joel a couple?"

"Oh, no. Susan's a lesbian." A sly smile crossed Rita's face. "I'm kinda interested in her. She's sort of my type," she admitted. "Joel's straight, but he's really mellow. He's great with the kids at the program. And he's cool with gay folks."

"Susan, huh?" Evelyn noticed Rita's coyness. "Good for you. I can't wait to meet her—see your type," Evelyn teased, licking another stamp ever so slowly.

CHAPTER 20

Bertha's Family

"Push, c'mon, push now! You know how. That's it!"

Belinda wiped Mrs. Wigsby's brow. She was sweating profusely and cursing at Belinda under her breath as the contraction slowed. Belinda looked at Dr. Nelson. At the same moment, he looked up from the draping that hung over Mrs. Wigsby's legs, which were immobilized by leather straps and metal stirrups. Belinda moved quickly to his side. He waved her away and reached past her for the instrument tray bearing the forceps. Nurse Felice left the room momentarily. She returned with another doctor and a white nurse. She motioned to Belinda to stand back.

"The doctor is giving you something to help you, so the baby can come out now," the blond-haired nurse said.

Mrs. Wigsby lay flat on her back, arms strapped to the bed. Her face grimaced in agony, but soon she was motionless. Her glazed eyes just stared blankly at Belinda, who was in her line of sight on the side of the room. The medication entwined the laboring woman's brain in twilight, obliterating her ability to identify or react to the bone-wrenching pain.

Belinda felt sorry for this mother, but her heart went out to the baby, pulled into life with a cold iron grip. Its little head, dented by metal prongs, was unusually elongated. Poor little baby girl, thought Belinda. She accompanied Nurse Felice to the nursery, where they

140

cleaned, then swaddled the crying newborn in a blanket, placing her in a bassinet. Belinda attached a little name tag to the front of her crib and wheeled her over to the row of other newborns. Then, she left her in the care of the day nurse, who had just come on duty.

When her shift was over, Belinda walked out of Philadelphia General into the warm dawn. Streetcars were beginning early morning routes with people on their way to work. Belinda walked to the corner of 34th Street, to the small diner where once a week she treated herself to a muffin and a cup of tea. Selma's son was sweeping the floor. He smiled at Belinda. Selma was behind the counter.

"Hi, Miss Belinda. Sure is nice to see you this mornin'. You be wantin' your usual?" Selma was a middle-aged black woman, mother of three. Her eyes lit up when she saw Belinda. "You should be mighty proud, Miss Belinda," she'd always say. "Not many Negro girls be graduatin' high school and becomin' nurses. Maybe, things be changin' when the war's over," she told Belinda.

Would a new day be dawning for their people? She watched Belinda sip her tea. Maybe, it would just take one person—a person like Belinda—to change white people's minds, change laws, change colored folks' lives for real. Belinda was brave, Selma thought, getting a job at a white hospital rather than Mercy or Frederick Douglass.

"How's the job at the hospital goin', Miss Belinda?" Selma asked. She wiped the far end of the counter with a damp cloth.

"Oh, it is just fine, Miss Selma," Belinda said. It was hard to tell anyone her feelings. Belinda was overwhelmed herself.

"You all right, sugar?" Selma could read people, though she usually didn't let on about her gift. "What's botherin' you, child? Some folks in that white hospital not like havin' an educated colored girl 'round?"

"Well, I get my share of nastiness, you know," Belinda sighed. "But they need nurses now, what with the war on—it's a chance for us. There are three Negro doctors and two nurses there now. Maybe, things will change," she said. After what she'd seen today though, Belinda hoped for more than a change for her people, for herself. Something had to change for women, for mothers, she thought.

Although unsure about talking to Selma, Belinda felt like she would burst if she didn't confide in someone. She could never complain to her father or Dorothy. They had sacrificed everything, so she could go to the Nurses Training School at Frederick Douglass Hospital. Denise was still too young to talk with about such things. Her other sisters had their own lives, their own troubles. Besides, Belinda was her family's hero.

She looked around the diner to make sure no one was close enough to overhear her. She spoke quietly to Selma. "It's just the way they treat the mothers—and some of them babies." Belinda shook her head while she stirred her tea with a spoon. "All the pain the mothers are havin', tied down, doped-up—takin' those babies out with forceps," Belinda blurted out. She looked up at Selma. She immediately regretted her words. Selma's anguished expression was enough to silence her.

"White women be tied down? What do you mean takin' babies out with faucets?" Selma looked at Belinda in disbelief.

"Forrccepps," Belinda pronounced it slowly for Selma. She looked around again and lowered her voice. "When the baby won't come out, they pull it out with big, metal instruments." Belinda used her hands to demonstrate. "I guess seeing that poor baby, it really upset me today," she added. "I'm sorry, Miss Selma, I shouldn't be saying nothing about it. I have a good job. I should just thank Jesus and be grateful. Please forgive me." Belinda fidgeted, wiping her mouth with a napkin. She searched in her bag for some change to pay for her breakfast.

"God, have mercy!" Selma exclaimed, still shocked by what she had just heard. "God have mercy!" she repeated. "My daughter, Bessie, be due any day. She be wantin' to go to Frederick Douglass Hospital to have her baby. 'What do men know about birthin' babies?' I ask her." Selma put her hand on Belinda's to catch her attention. Before her young customer could leave, she leaned toward Belinda. There was fear in her eyes.

"My daughter says it be old-fashioned to have a baby at home." Selma shook her head. "My babies all be born at home. Not saying having babies ain't hard, but they come out fine. Labor in my own bed and my sister, God bless her soul, and the midwife help me. I remind my daughter she be born at home." Selma's voice softened. "The last one, that child right there," Selma pointed to her son, who was wiping down the tables. "I get to the bed just in time, for that one." Selma smiled, but only momentarily. She looked pleadingly at Belinda. "Miss Belinda, could I ask you? Could you talk to my daughter?"

Belinda hesitated. She and her sisters had been born at home, too. But, she was a nurse now. She could not talk to Selma's daughter about what she witnessed. "I will talk to her, Miss Selma, but I don't want to lose my job. I mean, I can't say nothin' bad about the hospital."

"It be between you and me, Miss Belinda. I do appreciate it." Selma whispered.

Belinda felt a pang of regret. She saw Selma's anxious expression. "Don't think you got to worry, Miss Selma. Lots of our folks go to Frederick Douglass Hospital. It's a good hospital." Then she added, "I'll stop by tomorrow afternoon, if Bessie be around." Belinda paid Selma.

"Thank you, Miss Belinda. Bessie be here, for sure."

Belinda walked to the streetcar stop on Chestnut Street and waited. When the streetcar arrived, she and an elderly man boarded the trolley, after two white women ahead of them. Finding a seat, Belinda stared out the window, but didn't see much. Lost in thought, she almost missed her stop.

When she got home she put her job, the last twelve hours, behind her. All Belinda wanted was a hot bath and the comfortable bed that awaited her. Opening the front door, she smelled the sweet aroma of Dorothy's freshly-baked cornbread wafting through the air. Its familiar smell reminded her of Bertha, instantly soothing her frayed nerves. She walked into the kitchen expecting to see her Aunt Dorothy. She wasn't there. Hearing Dorothy's melodic voice, Belinda peered out the open kitchen window. Dorothy was in the garden, tending to her herbs, singing her beloved hymns.

"Dorothy! Hi, Auntie!" Belinda waved from the window. Dorothy started to get up. "Don't get up, I'm just goin' to bathe and rest. Will you wake me for dinner?"

"All right, honey child. How you be?" Dorothy called back, looking up at Belinda, shading her eyes from the sun with one hand.

"Fine, fine, just very tired, Auntie." Belinda waved again.

Belinda moved in slow motion. She poured water into the basin and stripped off her clothes down to her cotton slip. She washed her hands and face. Suddenly, too exhausted to do more, she lay down on her bed. She was sleeping soundly when Dorothy came into the bedroom a few minutes later and covered her with the light cotton quilt, one that Bertha had made for her, long ago.

By sundown, with Denise home from school and James back from work, she woke Belinda for supper. Dorothy had prepared a festive dinner of roast pork, greens, sweet potatoes, peas, and her grandmother's traditional recipe of flat cornbread.

"What are we celebrating?" James grinned. His second wife sure could cook, he thought. Denise and Belinda waited to hear what special event it might be, too.

"We are celebrating Belinda's first year anniversary as a practical nurse!" Dorothy beamed.

"Oh! Aunt Dorothy!" Belinda got teary all of the sudden. She had not realized a year had come and gone, since she began her job at the hospital. She got up and hugged Dorothy. "Thank you so much!" Belinda turned to her father. "I owe this to both of you."

Dorothy beamed. James' eyes watered.

"I wish Bertha could see you, now." Dorothy voiced what James and the girls were thinking.

"Something tells me she is smiling down from Heaven," whispered Belinda. Her voice cracked a little. I am so lucky, she thought. But her heart ached. She had been missing her mother, Bertha, lately. Belinda had been old enough to help Mrs. Bea during Denise's birth. Recently, she had been having dreams about that day. She had wiped Bertha's forehead with cool, wet cloth as Bertha labored and witnessed Denise finally being born. Belinda had even helped Mrs. Bea wrap her new sister, bringing her to Bertha for nursing.

Belinda looked across the table at Denise and Dorothy. She

wondered if her aunt had sensed her mood lately. Had she made this beautiful meal to raise her spirits? There was no way she could ever tell Dorothy about the horrible things she had seen at work.

"Thank you, Lord Jesus, for your gracious gifts. Amen." Dorothy finished the prayer and smiled at James. She passed around the plates of food, waiting until everyone had been served before she took some for herself.

"Wait awhile now," James said before everyone ate. "I got something to say." He looked at Dorothy. "Thank you for all the care you given us, Dorothy." Their loving gaze across the table needed no other words. Then bowing his head, James added, "Thank you, Lord, for all my kin and for protecting our men on the front lines. Amen."

After dinner, Belinda helped Denise with the dishes, then pressed a clean uniform for herself. Bathing and retiring early, she'd be rested for work by morning. She climbed into bed and took her small journal from the nightstand drawer. Belinda wrote in it every chance she got. Her rambling thoughts, events of her day, hopes and sorrows filled its pages. In this way, she strengthened herself to face the days to come. Sometimes, if she remembered her dreams, she would write them down, too.

Tonight though, Belinda did not want to end her day writing the gruesome details of the tortuous birth she had seen. Instead, she decided to read her last entry.

April 17, 1942

Dear Diary,

Last night I had a strange and wonderful dream. In my dream, I was surrounded by children. They called me Grandma. There was a big family and a bakery. Denise and I were making cakes and the children kept coming in and out to look and taste. I felt so good as we worked together. There was a beautiful painting on the wall. It was a painting of my mother, Bertha.

I think I dreamed about Mama more, but then I had a nightmare about the hospital, so I don't remember now about that one.

The war still is bad. Papa listens to the reports on the radio and to President Roosevelt's speeches. Lucille's husband wants to enlist and fight with the Negro brigade, but Lucille doesn't want him to enlist.

I'll write again tomorrow. Belinda

Belinda tried to recapture the lovely dream of Bertha, savor its remaining essence. Then she placed the journal in her drawer and turned out the lamp. She pulled her handmade quilt up to her chin. "Goodnight, Mama," she whispered. "Jesus, thank you for all I have." Before Belinda fell asleep, she thought about Selma and her daughter Bessie, reminding herself to stop by to see them tomorrow.

Dawn had barely disturbed the sky's dark slumber, when the streetcar arrived the next morning at Belinda's stop. Still sleepy, Belinda sat down in a rear seat as usual. A very handsome, dark-skinned young man, whom she had seen daily for several weeks, sat across from her on his regular morning trip to work. He smiled politely at Belinda this morning. She smiled back, wondering who he was and where he went to work each morning. She had hoped he might notice her.

At the next stop, a mature, heavy-set woman with gray hair boarded the streetcar. She was dressed neatly, and carried a brown handbag and matching umbrella. She passed by the young man Belinda admired. "Hello, Mr. Williams," the woman said. "Looks like we might be havin' some rain today."

"Morning, ma'am. Yes, sure does look like it," he said and smiled. Then he looked over at Belinda one more time and winked.

Belinda felt a sudden flush of heat in her cheeks.

The young man stood up and walked over to Belinda. "Is this seat taken?" he asked.

"Why, no," she said. She was nervous and excited all at the same time. She squeezed a little closer to the window, so he could sit down on the seat next to her.

"I'm Jeremiah Williams," he introduced himself. "I've seen you ride this route everyday. You work over at General, don't you?"

"Yes, I do." Belinda said shyly. "Pleased to meet you. I'm Belinda Washington." She smiled, looking directly into his kind brown eyes. She sensed a vibration flowing between them.

Suddenly, the street car jerked to a stop. Belinda looked out the window to see that they were already at her destination. Quickly, she gathered up her belongings.

Jeremiah stood up to let her pass. "Maybe, I'll see you again, tomorrow?"

Exiting the streetcar, Belinda felt giddy. She walked briskly, fully awake, energized by flirtation and unexpected romantic possibilities. By the time she got to her station, she was ready to tackle her busy day. "Good mornin', Nurse Felice." Belinda smiled at the familiar sight of the head nurse exiting a patient's room.

"Morning, Belinda. You seem cheery this morning." Nurse Felice observed. A woman of few words, she did not like small talk. Her comment was not an invitation for Belinda to share how she was doing, but rather a subtle way of saying, "Let's get down to work." Her conversation was strictly about the patients, the job, and Belinda's responsibilities. Nurse Felice was permanently poker-faced, unemotional.

Belinda respected Nurse Felice, though. She was careful in her work, considerate to the patients, and knew how to talk to the doctors. When a doctor made a mistake, Nurse Felice could correct it without anyone being the wiser. Belinda had watched her save a patient's life once, without a word to anyone. Nurse Felice never let the suffering, the pain she saw around her get in the way of her duties.

"Mrs. Lourdy is due today. Dr. Peterson's patient, Mrs. Ward, is coming in today. Maybe twins. Dr. Gordon and Dr. Nelson should be here by 10 o'clock."

Belinda listened to the day's schedule, knowing that any emergency delivery would cancel routine visits and normal timetables. She noted the information on her chart, then checked the clock. Most of the patients were just waking. That meant breakfast trays, mixing formula for the newborns, and linen changes for the beds on the ward.

Belinda walked down the hall, past the nursery, to begin her rounds. She glanced in at the sleeping angels. She was good at keeping track of the births. By the end of each week, Belinda had held every newborn at least twice, cooing and singing to the tiny babies. The day nurse, Miss Carson, was busy mixing formula when Belinda came in.

"How are my babies this morning?" Belinda asked.

Nurse Carson didn't turn around to talk to Belinda. "All the ones that are still here are doin' fine, Miss Belinda. A few went home, a few left on the evening shift, you know." She kept on mixing and measuring.

A few babies were fussing. Belinda walked over to soothe them. She sang and cooed. Then she noticed one bassinet empty that should not have been. The Wigsby baby was missing.

"S'cuse me, Nurse Carson." Belinda tried to get Nurse Carson's attention. "Mrs. Wigsby got her baby in her room?" Belinda knew this was unusual, not at all the policy.

"Oh, no, she's gone, picked up last night." Nurse Carson said, her back still to Belinda. "The agency came for her—took her to that Jewish hospital. I don't know the particulars. I wasn't on duty when they came." Then, slowly, she looked over at Belinda knowingly and shrugged her shoulders. "Poor little thing. But maybe it's for the best. A child with an elongated head like that…"

"Maybe what's for the best?" Belinda asked, not comprehending what had happened.

"She's being adopted out. They took her last night," Nurse Carson repeated. "I didn't get the details, Belinda. Just the agency had the paperwork. They came and got her. That's all I know."

"Where's Mrs. Wigsby?" Belinda asked, suddenly realizing she was stepping over the line of protocol.

Nurse Carson looked at Belinda over the rim of her glasses. "She's been transferred to a different floor, Belinda." Nurse Carson's tone turned impatient. "You best forget about it and attend to making the beds for the patients you have today. Go on, now. I've got to tend to these babies."

Chapter 21

Rita Kerner

San Francisco, California, 1977

Rita poured grape juice into Susan's glass, then into hers. She passed the juice to Joel and his girlfriend. The bottle went around the table to Evelyn, Claire, and Claire's oldest son, Fred, and his pregnant wife, Pam. Andrea and Janice had beer, as usual.

"A toast!" Rita held up her glass.

Glasses hoisted, the dining room table at Evelyn and Claire's new house on Clipper Street was set for a celebration.

Rita began. "First, to Fred and Pam's wonderful journey—and a healthy new baby!" Rita continued as the cheers subsided. "And to Claire and Evelyn—many happy years in this lovely home!" Rita tapped her glass with a fork to quiet the rowdy crowd. "And as you all know, I have been trying to get pregnant. So, on the cutting edge of this radical endeavor, I want to thank Joel and Susan." Rita winked at Susan, her lover of several years. "And announce that we have a touchdown! It's official today—I'm pregnant!"

"Congratulations! That's so wonderful!" Everyone talked excitedly, at once. Glasses clinked, toasts were made. Pam, already six months along, hugged Rita.

"So, when? How many months?" she asked, suddenly bonded by their imminent initiation into motherhood.

"I'm due in seven months—in July!" Rita smiled.

She was relieved. The hard part of convincing Susan to go along

150

with her decision was over. Susan had been in an "on again, off again" relationship when they'd met at work. First friends, Susan had been overly wary about relationships, slightly depressed. Her drinking didn't help. It had taken a while for Rita to convince her to go to AA. A year after Susan got sober, they started a romantic relationship in earnest. But having a child was a huge step. Rita remembered that conversation.

* * * * *

"We've only been a couple for a few years. Now you want to have a child?" Susan's eyes widened.

"Hey, it's not like this is new information. I told you about my idea before we got involved. I showed you my sketches of the kids from the center. Don't you remember? I said I was going to research it, how to do it…"

"I guess I didn't realize you were that serious. Does that mean I also have to be a mother? 'Cause I'm not sure about that," Susan declared.

"Well, will you support me being a mother?" Rita asked. She was determined, no matter what the answer. Luckily, love prevailed. The answer Rita wanted to hear came in an anniversary present—a nursing bra wrapped in heart-print wrapping paper and a bow.

The commitment from Joel to help Rita conceive had been much less complicated. He simply agreed not to interfere, not be involved unless she asked, and to respect Rita's relationship with Susan. He'd been so easy to talk to about it. "Sure, I could donate to the cause," Joel said. "Why not? That would be cool."

No sooner had everything been planned, than Susan threw a wrench into the works.

"I want to go back to school," Susan complained. The children's center job had paid poorly, so Susan had been working at an insurance company for a year and hated it. "What if I apply to college? Rita honey, listen," she bargained. "We could go back to the East Coast. You could see your family in New York, and I could see mine in Maine. If I apply to a college in Massachusetts, we would be halfway between each of our families."

Rita thought about it. She liked the idea of being closer to her family now that a baby was coming. Although Massachusetts sounded good, Rhode Island along the Atlantic Ocean might work nicely, too. That night, Rita dreamed of a little house along the ocean's edge. The house had a porch and vegetable garden, the smell of the salt water and chicken soup—a good place to raise a child.

* * * * *

Everything that Rita could think of she had done before the big announcement. She planned it out. It would go relatively smoothly from now on, she was sure. She smiled at her friends, at Susan. They were happy for her. It's like a miracle, Rita thought. She had no doubts that she could count on Susan's promise of sobriety and Joel's promise to be a hand-off donor. Her friends and family would support her decision.

"I have one more important announcement!" Rita stood up. "This one is bittersweet, I'm afraid." She looked over at Susan. "Do you want to tell them, honey?"

Susan stood up reluctantly. She looked at Rita for reassurance.

"Well," Susan began. She avoided looking directly at anyone. "The good news is that I was accepted to Boston University. It means," she paused nervously, "we are moving back to the East Coast."

Susan sat down. Rita winked at her.

Claire patted Susan on the back. "Wow, congratulations! That's an accomplishment."

"Wow!" seemed to be the majority's unsure response. Only Joel had no response. His mouth just hung open.

Later, after everyone had returned home, Rita called her parents to tell them about the baby. She thought their desire for grandchildren, and the fact that she was going to move back East, closer to them, would be welcome news. David answered the phone.

"You're what?" David yelled into the phone. "Are you crazy?"

"Listen, Dad, I'm almost thirty years old. This is what I'm doing. If you don't want to be a grandfather to my child, so be it. Put Mom on the phone, will ya?" Rita hoped Lillian would be more sympathetic.

"Well, how will you afford to live if one of you is in school, and you're having a baby?" Lillian asked, silent on the more obvious "how" question.

"I'll work until the baby comes, and Susan will get financial aid. We've arranged for insurance, so I can have the baby at the Beth Israel Hospital in Boston. Don't worry."

* * * * *

The reality turned out to be a small, one-bedroom walk-up near Inman Square in Somerville—not exactly what Rita had in mind. More problematic, Susan had only enough financial aid for tuition and books. Rita would have to use her small amount of savings for them to make the rent until she could find work.

"Look, it's okay, just take it easy," Rita tried to reassure Susan. "When the baby comes, I'll stop working for just a few weeks. Then I go back to work and be able to afford daycare. My mom can come once a month for a few days to babysit, now that she's retired. That's why we planned to come here, for family, right? For now, we can manage on what we have." She gave Susan a squeeze.

Susan patted Rita's big pregnant belly. "Okay," she said. "We'll make it work."

Just then, the phone rang. Rita picked it up.

"Hi, dear." Rita recognized Lillian's tone of voice immediately. It was Lillian's, *not good news coated with sugar,* voice.

Rita covered the phone receiver with her hand and whispered to Susan. "It's my mom calling from New York." She resumed talking to Lillian.

"Hi, Mom. Are you coming up to Boston, soon?"

"I have some news that you might not like, but…"Lillian started. "Your father and I have decided to move to Florida for our retirement, after the baby's born. We need to move before another cold winter in the city. You know how your Dad hates the cold." Lillian was silent, waiting for a response. When none came, she continued. "I told him I absolutely would not think of leaving before you have the baby, though," Lillian added the sugar. "I told him he can leave earlier if he wants to. I'm thinking of staying through September, so I can help out if you need me."

Rita was stunned. She didn't know what to say.

"You, the baby, and Susan can come visit us in Miami. Tina and her new fellow will visit and so will Irene, Gregory, Julius…he's seven already, can you believe it? Did Irene send you his school pictures?" Lillian had it all planned. "Your father and I discussed coming back for July or August. The Waldenbergs invited us to spend a month next summer at their Brattleboro cottage. Isn't that nice, dear? Rita?"

"Yes, nice, I guess." Rita listened, her own plans unraveling.

"Their daughter, Mimi, will be visiting too," Lillian continued encouragingly. "You remember her? Mimi, their adopted daughter, who we thought had problems? Well, she's all grown up now. Maybe, you'd like to see her…Rita?"

"Yes, sure Mom." Rita didn't know how to respond. Hormones were making her weepy instead of angry.

"So, how are you feeling? Is the baby kicking a lot? What did the doctor say?" Lillian went on.

Rita's dreams of a happy extended family evaporated. She began to laugh, wiping away the tears trickling down her cheeks.

"What's so funny?" Lillian asked.

"The best laid plans of mice and men…" Rita said.

"What? Rita, are you okay? Are you getting enough rest, enough water? You know you have to drink more water when you're pregnant, dear," Lillian advised.

"Thanks, Mom." Rita composed herself. "I'm sorry you and Dad won't get to be a regular part of my child's life." Only now was there a moment of silence on the other end of the phone.

"I'm sorry too, Rita." Lillian finally said, her voice somber. "Maybe we can make up for some lost time in the summers. It's not as far as California."

* * * * *

Rita woke up in a stark hospital room in Beth Israel Hospital. She felt too heavy to move her body. Instead she turned her head, from side to side surveying her surroundings. The room, with its bare metal tables, looked like a place for autopsies, not an operating room. Rita's memory filtered through the medication that still made her groggy. Hadn't it only been minutes ago that her pale, exhausted midwife was standing in the doorway of a labor room talking to a young doctor, a resident, about Rita's contractions.

"The baby is too big. The mom's narrow. I told her it would probably be a C-section, so she knows. She signed the papers," the midwife said. "Mom's been pushing for almost three hours, while you were in surgery."

"We've been inundated with women going into labor, tonight. We'd better hurry." The doctor said. He looked over at a nurse standing next to Rita. "The baby's monitor on? Distress level?"

The nurse nodded. Another nurse came in and gave Rita a shot. An orderly wheeled her to the operating room. The contractions relentless, Rita thought she might explode along the way. Like an angel from heaven, an the anesthesiologist administered an epidural. A giant wave of relief engulfed Rita eradicating her agony.

Now, coming out of her medically induced fog, Rita remembered. The C-section had not gone as planned. She had felt the doctor cutting her. She had screamed through her oxygen mask.

"Put her out," were the last words she heard the doctor say, before general anesthesia poured into her bloodstream, rendering her unconscious. She never heard the baby cry.

"The baby! Oh my God, where is my baby?" Rita suddenly cried out. "Hellooo? Is anyone here?" she yelled, trying to get up. She was shocked to find herself tied down and unable to move. Panic rose in her throat. Where's the baby? What if they think I died? Is the baby okay? Her mind raced.

"Where is my baby? What's happened to my baby?" Rita screamed.

She thrashed her head and chest side to side like a wild animal, tethered. Tubes, IV stand, metal bars on the bed rattled. "Help!" she screamed.

Meanwhile, Lillian and Susan sat nervously in the waiting room, waiting for the doctor. Finally, he came out to greet them. "It's a boy. Mom and baby are fine," he assured them.

"A boy!" they said in unison. It was Lillian's second grandson. She was pleased. Susan had hoped for a girl, even though Rita had been sure it would be a boy. Today, she was just happy to be the "other mom" of a healthy baby.

"The baby will be in the nursery once he's been cleaned and checked. Mom's still asleep from the anesthesia. She'll be in recovery for about an hour or so," the doctor said.

But Rita wasn't asleep. And she wasn't exactly fine.

"Can you move your legs, yet?" It was a woman's voice.

A blur of white, a nurse's uniform, seemed to be just barely in Rita's peripheral vision. She could not move enough to get a clear view. "When your epidural wears off, someone will take you back to your room," the emotionless voice said.

"Is my baby okay? A boy? A girl? Is the baby okay?"

"Yes, the baby's okay."

Rita heard a door close. "Damn!" she said. "I hope Susan didn't say anything to the hospital staff about being lesbians or two mothers." She tried to relax. She focused on moving her legs. They were like dead tree stumps.

Although exhausted, Rita was determined to stay awake. She would count the minutes on the clock directly on the wall she could see. It was ten-fifteen. Is it morning or night? she wondered. With no windows and only the glare of fluorescent lights above, she could not tell. Rita closed her eyes to rest them for a minute. Suddenly, she was floating. She floated up and over a familiar farmhouse. Voices and people she thought she knew surrounded her.

A sweet old woman's face appeared before her. She was smiling and holding a pan of bread-pudding. "Anna's had her second child, after you left. A boy. His name is Noah," said the old woman, beaming.

Rita saw a young woman sitting in a rocking chair nursing a baby. She was thin and pale. But the baby was a healthy boy with dark curls and big brown eyes. In her dream, Rita saw the child laugh when he looked up at her.

Her vision vanished with the clanking of metal. Rita opened her eyes. The clock in her line of vision read eleven o'clock. The gurney on which Rita lay, was being jarred by a middle-aged nurse rearranging her IV and a hospital attendant unlocking the wheels.

"Okay," he said, "hold on. We're goin' up to you room, Mom. Baby's waitin'."

"A boy, right?" Rita looked at the nurse.

"Yes. A healthy, eight pound boy. Congratulations!" the new nurse said with a Spanish accent. Her dark, smiling eyes were kind. Rita thought she saw the nurse wink at her.

When Rita got to her room, Susan and Lillian were not there. Nor, was there a patient in the next bed yet. She was glad. A red-headed, maternity ward nurse came in to make Rita comfortable. "I'd like to see my baby," Rita said firmly.

"Of course, I'll bring him." A few minutes later, the nurse came back wheeling a bassinet up to the side of Rita's bed. She smiled. "Here he is, all safe and sound." She helped Rita sit up, checked her IV and moved her IV stand. She picked the baby up and gently put him in Rita's arms. "There you are, Mom—your beautiful baby. I'll be back in a little while to check on you," the nurse said.

Rita looked down at the sleeping newborn in her arms and melted into an altered state of consciousness, a euphoric bliss. She cooed to her dark-haired baby boy, counting toes and fingers, feeling his soft skin next to hers. "I will call you my little Noah," she whispered, breathing in his sweet smell. She kissed him, rocked him, and sang him a lullaby—oblivious to any time before this moment.

CHAPTER 22

Chaske/Wambleeska (White Eagle)

GREAT PLAINS, 1812-1816

"Hurry, my son," Chetan Lootah called. He put on the last of his warrior clothing, preparing for the battle ahead. "Now you will have an opportunity to use your new name and bring pride to our people. I am proud of you already, Wambleeska. You have hunted well and fought well against our enemies in the past. But, this war will be harder with many guns against us. You will have to use more than guns and arrows to fight. You will also have to use your wisdom."

Wambleeska was not eager to take on the enormity of fighting in the 1812 war on the side of the British. The elders, the chiefs of many of their people to the North and East had agreed to ally with the Shawnee, though. The British had encouraged them, promised them protection against the American government's expansion into their territory, and fulfillment of Tecumseh's plan for an Indian Confederacy–a sovereign state.

"This fight is important for all our people, "Chetan Lootah told Wambleeska and his cousin, Napayshni. "We must join Tecumseh, so our people will have a protected land, a nation that cannot be taken from us."

Wambleeska understood. Trying to resolve his fear, he asked the Great Spirit to protect him and his family. He remembered his rite of passage to manhood, his solitary vision quest into the mountains. A great eagle had appeared to him, a sign. But was his faith powerful enough against the guns that had already killed many of his people. Were his arrows, his shooting skills enough?

Supplied with British weapons, he and Napayshni practiced riding and shooting, with arrows and guns. Still, Wambleeska had a bad feeling. There had been much division among his people about the war. Doubt spread like the epidemics that had decimated the tribes not long ago. Treaties and agreements had been broken and lands divided by those who claimed to be honest. His people were still a strong nation, but the threats to their land, their way of life had increased and there seemed no end in sight.

Wambleeska dressed in his war paint and feathered headdress and climbed onto his horse. Along with the other warriors, he was prepared for battle. He quieted his trepidation, thinking about how he might prove himself a worthy warrior. Should he come back victorious, his marriage to Dowanhowee would be assured. He longed to see her look in his eyes, with the love and pride he knew was in her heart.

The war turned out to be as hard as Wambleeska had imagined. But within a year, victory was near, their warriors and British soldiers capturing and maintaining land from the border of Canada and the Great Lakes, westward. Before long though, the tide turned. A new, less experienced British commander took control and with him came defeat. At the end of what was to be the path of glory, lay Napayshni—killed by a bullet through his heart. At great risk to himself, Wambleeska recovered his beloved cousin's body for a proper burial ceremony. Grief-stricken from their devastating loss, the family pulled together.

By 1815, the war was over. As the winter months ended and spring waters ran free again, healing began. With new treaties signed, the people prepared for their summer Sun Dance, and the gathering of the Seven Council Fires. While the death of his cousin solidified Wambleeskah's abhorrence of war, his status as a warrior had won him a place as a leader. Before the summer festivities, Wambleeska's and Dowanhowee's families prepared for a late spring marriage ceremony.

Dowanhowee's grandmother, mother, and two sisters fussed over her, finishing the stitches with the last red and gold seed beads and blue glass beads on her white deerskin dress. Her mother braided her hair in tight braids wrapped in bands of crimson skins. Her youngest sister helped their grandmother and aunt with elaborately sewn and beaded moccasins for the special day.

At seventeen, Dowanhowee had been longing for marriage, and the match was a good one for their families. "I am happy today, Mother," the young woman exclaimed. "I have liked Wambleeska and his family since last year's summer hunting season. He is a strong hunter and now a great warrior." She remembered how he had looked on his way to a summer hunt before the war, when she first began to sneak glances at him. Dowanhowee thought she had not been noticed, but Wambleeska and his sister, Chumani, had noticed. At last, both families had given their approval.

Wambleeska combed his hair and braided it into one thick braid. He put on the new shirt his mother made for him from the finest skins and sinew. She had adorned it with the best beads traded for at the tribal festival before the war—when bone, horn, bear teeth and multi-colored glass beads were plentiful. His new leggings and moccasins she also decorated appropriately for a young warrior about to take a wife for the first time.

Before nightfall, a great meal had been prepared. The drummers and dancers had assembled to celebrate, and the council elders sat and smoked the pipe of Chetan Lootah. Wambleeska's uncles, Wachinksapa and Matoskah, told stories of Ikto's antics, amusing themselves and passing on story-wisdom to the young warriors. The women served the great feast.

"I am now your wife," whispered Dowanhowee. The new husband and wife stood inside the circle of feathered, beaded, and colorfully adorned dancers swirling around them to the beat of drums and songs. Wambleeska took Dowanhowee's hand, feeling as nervous as his young, new wife. In the fire circles, flames licked the cool night air as the ritual and merriment continued. Before long, the new couple was led away to their marriage tipi to consummate their union.

The young lovers moved cautiously closer to each other kissing tentatively at first. "You are all I have wanted for a long time. I have thought of you often," Wambleeska said softly, drawing Dowanhowee close to him. He felt her sensuous body against his. As passion met desire, they lay down on the soft mats prepared for them and disrobed under thick fur blankets. The feel of their soft, supple skin pressed together swept them along a river of sexual exploration and pleasure. Having been taught the nature and needs of their bodies, they moved in unison respectful of their inexperience and awkwardness. The excitement and ecstasy of lovemaking drenched them in heat, blankets fell from their bodies.

Late into the night, the embers of the fire circles continued to illuminate the remaining drummers. The soft hooting of owls echoed between drumbeats. Wambleeska awoke and reached for the blankets to cover himself and his sleeping young wife—but not until he looked at her naked body in a sliver of moonlight that peeked through the tipi from above. His lust rose and he reached out to touch her. Waking, she rolled into his strong arms and kissed him.

"I want to show you something," Wambleeska said quietly. "Will you come with me?"

"Where?" Dowanhowee asked.

"I'll show you. Let's take our blankets," he said. He stood up, put on his breech-cloth and moccasins, and wrapped himself in a warm fur.

Dowanhowee sleepily threw her dress over her bare skin and wrapped a blanket around herself. "Where are we going?" she repeated innocently, putting on her own moccasins.

"You'll see," her new husband said. "Don't be afraid." He took his hunting knife and then her hand, leading her out into the night.

They walked behind their marriage tipi, which was set apart from all the other tribal lodges. The full moon lit their path through the trees to a moss-covered clearing by the creek. Looking up, they could see a sky full of stars.

"Here," said Wambleeska, laying his thick buffalo fur down on the mossy bed. He reached over and removed Dowanhowee's blanket from her shoulders. He held her for a minute, kissing her, running his hands down her body.

She lifted her dress over her thighs, her hips, her breasts, until she stood bare and glistening in the moonlight. Desire flaming, she lay down on the fur and held out her hand, beckoning her beloved.

Wambleeska lay down next to her, covering them both with her blanket. There in the moonlight, they made love, while drums beat in the distance and the owls sang their haunting mating call into the soft spring breeze.

CHAPTER 23

Rita Kerner

BOSTON, MASSACHUSETTS, 1982

"Susan, can you take Noah to nursery school?" Rita asked. "I'm running late. I have to return this gift to Filene's before I get to work— it should be worth at least $50. We certainly could use the money."

You would think a Christmas bonus would be more than a glass vase, Rita thought, shoving it back into the Styrofoam peanut-filled box. The flower shop made a ton of money, thanks to me, she fumed silently. But the business had been sold, so Rita received a pink slip and this gift just in time for the holidays.

She didn't know who she resented more, the job or Susan. She was tired of supporting Susan, especially since Noah's daycare expenses had increased. Susan didn't seem to care about anyone except herself, spending all her time cramming for tests and writing papers, obsessed with getting straight A's.

"Susan?" Rita asked again. Can you take Noah this morning?"

"Okay, but I may be late getting him there. I have to finish some work for school," Susan said nonchalantly.

"Can you take him first? They usually take his group to the park in the morning. You might miss them," Rita pleaded. Why did she have to beg Susan to put Noah and her first? How was it that Susan had become so self-involved? Maybe she had always been that way.

Susan was no longer a partner. Had she ever been? Rita wondered. There were no more hugs or conversations at the end of a long day.

Polite and not so polite scheduling replaced affection. Affordable entertainment was television and romps at the playground for Noah. Vacations were out of the question. Rita's constant nagging for Susan to get some part-time work was useless. Rita felt stuck, frustrated. She and Noah deserved more, she thought, as she finished packing Noah's lunch box.

"Okay, Mommy's going now, sweetie." Rita kissed Noah goodbye. "Susan will take you to school. I will pick you up, honey. Have fun today!"

Noah kissed Rita. "Bye, Mommy."

Susan placed a bowl of cereal in front of him then sat down at the table with her tea. "See you later," she said. "I'll be home late, so don't wait on dinner for me. I have to get some library work done before I come home. Do you want me to take the chicken out of the freezer?"

"Oh, yeah, I almost forgot. Could you also pick up some more juice on your way home? I used the last of it for Noah's lunch." Rita rummaged in her wallet. "Here's some money," she said, handing Susan a five-dollar bill.

Susan put the money in her pocket without a word. She continued drinking her tea. There was no guarantee Susan would buy the juice, Rita knew, but she continued to give her the benefit of the doubt. Rita hoped Susan's love for Noah would override her selfish behavior.

Rita put on her coat and scarf. Adjusting the shoulder strap of her bag, she tucked the Filene's box tightly under one arm and headed out toward the bus stop. As she neared the corner, where recent construction had meant temporary traffic lights with no "walk" and "don't walk" signs, thoughts of losing her job rattled her again. With Susan not willing to work, with no serious communication between them, how would they manage?

At the corner, Rita absentmindedly checked the temporary light. The one facing oncoming traffic was red. Hurrying to cross, she paid little attention to the van parked near the intersection, blocking her view of the street.

Suddenly, as she stepped out into the street, it began to snow. Rita looked at the white snowflakes that seemed to come out of nowhere without warning. Although the day had been cold and gray, snow had not been in the forecast, especially a snowfall of this magnitude.

Another thought occurred to Rita. She could not feel the pavement under her feet. As hard as she tried to determine where she was, Rita had no sense of gravity. "I'm not walking anymore," she heard herself say. Then everything went black.

When Rita came to, she lay in the street. White Styrofoam peanuts and glass were scattered around her, but she did not see any of it. Blood gushed into her eyes. Searing pain in her leg was all she knew.

Rita screamed in agony. A man talked to her, trying to calm her. She heard other people's voices, too. A woman's voice whispered in her ear. "Rita, it's Janice. Do you recognize my voice? I'm Andrea's friend."

Rita remembered Janice. But how did she end up here? Andrea and Janice had moved back to New York, but then they had broken up.

"Lie still, help is coming. There's an ambulance…"

"My son!" Rita whispered to Janice's voice.

Janice leaned down to hear her.

Rita could feel her presence close. "Stop my partner, Susan, from passing by here with my son," Rita managed. "I live up the street. She will be taking him to school. Don't let him see me," Rita cried, her tears mixing with blood. All she could think of was how scared Noah would be. "Please stop them," Rita pleaded into the darkness.

"Okay," said Janice. "I'll tell her. Don't worry. Stay calm. Help is coming." Janice tried to soothe her. Rita heard ambulance sirens in the distance.

Pain ripped through her body, but she prayed for Noah. By some miracle, he had not been out in front of her in his stroller, she thought. Had she not been late, had Susan not agreed to take him, what would have happened? Rita cried. Still in shock, she trembled.

"Stay still!" warned the emergency room doctor.

Rita could not see him. Something had been placed over her face. She lay on the gurney, struggling to get enough air.

"I can't stitch up your forehead, if you don't hold still."

Rita tried to remove the facial covering. "I can't breathe. I was hit by a car. What kind of a doctor are you?" she cried.

The doctor did not respond. He stopped suturing, throwing bandages in the trash with a grunt of disgust. "You're done," he said, and walked out of the room.

Rita was alone. "Pigs!" she spat. She really hated doctors and hospitals. She waited for someone to come in, give her some painkillers and finish sewing her up. Removing the dry gauze from across her eyes, she propped herself up on her elbows and looked around the filthy county hospital room. "So much for a sterile environment," she said to the walls.

Rita scanned the room for some new bandages. On the counter next to her, she saw one. She managed to reach over and grab it. Unwrapping it, she placed it over the half-stitched gash in her forehead, a deep cut made by the flying glass of a broken vase. She looked down at her leg. Blood stained bandages were still wrapped around her left leg under the slacks the nurse had cut open.

"Time to go," Rita told herself. Grimacing from pain, she stood up, leaned against the gurney, then the counter and chair. She hobbled into the hall. After a bit, she was able to manage the dizziness. She sat down in the emergency room unnoticed among the many other sick, injured people. Unexpectedly, Andrea appeared.

Andrea's name, not Susan's was in Rita's wallet on the *in case of emergency* card. But it was a New York number. How had they reached her? How had she gotten here so fast?

"What are you doing here? I thought you were in New York." Rita was disoriented.

"I was. I just arrived last night, for a surprise visit to see you and Janice. But I wasn't expecting this kind of surprise. My God! You're a mess. Haven't you been seen yet?" Andrea said.

"Oh, please, let's just get out of here," Rita whispered.

"But you can't even walk on that leg," Andrea exclaimed, looking down at Rita's blood-soaked bandages and ripped pants leg. "Did they at least stitch up your forehead?" she asked, moving Rita's hand-held bandage away from her head wound. "Geez! What a lousy job! Did they give you a prescription for pain or anything—antibiotics? Crutches?"

"No, no, and they won't, so let's just go, okay? This is a county hospital, one of the worst. I'll have to go to a real doctor." She took Andrea's hand. "I just want to go home and lie down," Rita said, suddenly exhausted from her ordeal. "I got hit by a car and I lived. So, let's just get out of here before they kill me with neglect or a million damn germs."

"Okay, lean on me. Easy, go slow." Andrea put her arm around her friend's waist and held her up as best she could. "Sit on the steps when we get outside. I'll hail a cab."

"You know I never saw it coming," said Rita. "I never felt a thing, until I woke up on the street."

"You blacked out, thank God!" said Andrea. "And thank God, Noah wasn't with you."

"I know," Rita replied, not wanting to think about such a horrible scenario anymore. "What's weird," Rita said, focusing on the blackout, "is that I was awake the whole time, until just before I hit the pavement. I remember it all so distinctly. I was flying through the air. It was snowing. I was above the street and I remember thinking that I couldn't feel myself walking." Rita babbled, "And it was snowing, beautiful big flakes of snow. All the while, I was thinking it wasn't cold enough and…"

"Okay, sit down here, *Snow White*. Let me get a cab. Don't move," Andrea said, pointing an index finger at Rita.

Rita obeyed. She watched Andrea wave her arms and whistle when she saw a potential taxi. Safe in her friend's care, Rita's mind wandered.

Something had happened, Rita thought. In the grip of death, she had been awake, but not in a dimension where she could feel gravity or pain. Suddenly, like a revelation, she remembered the Styrofoam peanuts—white peanuts and broken glass that had flown everywhere, not snow. But why did she not feel the impact of the car? How was it that time had stopped or slowed down in that moment of flight? Was that the way it was when you died? Rita wondered. Did you fly away and time and pain ceased to exist? She was determined to find the answer.

The following week, Rita still lay in her bed. Her head hurt, but her heart felt worse. A heavy blanket of sadness suffocated her, weighing her down more than the new cast on her leg. Now immobilized, she had plenty of time to obsess about the accident. What had happened in that moment of impact she never saw coming or felt? And what about all that time floating, flying through the air? It could not have been more than a few seconds, yet it felt much longer. She had had time to question the weather and gravity.

Suddenly, Rita remembered a sensation of flying above the trees, after Grandma Pearl died. Was death just another kind of consciousness? Did I leave my body, but still have awareness? How did it happen that Janice appeared out of nowhere? Susan said Janice had indeed knocked on the apartment door to warn her of the accident. Was it just a coincidence that Andrea was in Boston for a surprise visit? Rita didn't understand what had happened. It was more than an accident, she thought.

* * * * *

"The cast is doing well. The swelling is going down." Rita's new doctor said reassuringly. "Your concussion is why you're depressed, though. It's common with this type of head injury. Didn't they tell you that at the hospital?" she inquired, writing in Rita's medical chart. It is okay to keep resting, but make sure you move around when you are awake, as best you can. Have someone with you if you get dizzy, especially on those crutches."

Rita listened and nodded. It was a relief to have finally found a good doctor. Damn hospitals, Rita thought. But she was glad to know she was not crazy for feeling so overwhelmed and that her guilt and sadness would end when she healed.

Meanwhile, Susan's care of Noah would suffice, Rita thought. Andrea said she could stay for a few days, too. But unbeknown to Rita and Susan, Andrea had called Joel in California. When he heard about the accident, he offered to come to help with Noah. Rita was not thrilled that Andrea had called him without asking her. After some thought though, she resigned herself to accepting Joel's help, since Noah had been asking about having a father, lately.

Surprisingly, Lillian and David sent her a small check to help with extra medical expenses. David even offered to call a couple of his old union buddies to see if anyone knew of job openings in Boston for her after she recovered. Tina and Irene sent get well cards, while Lillian called to check up on her and Noah every few days. Susan checked into insurance to see if Rita had a claim against the uninsured driver who hit her. Slowly, Rita would pick up the pieces of her life. However, she knew things would never be the same. A major change was coming.

* * * * *

The change would come the following summer, when the Kerner family came together in August to the Waldenbergs' cottage in Vermont. It had been twenty-five years since Rita had seen Mimi, the Waldenberg's adopted daughter, when their paths crossed again. Their mothers had remained friends for years, but until recently, neither had revealed that their daughters were lesbians.

"You're little Mimi Waldenberg?" Rita gasped, as if caught in a sudden, strong wind. "Oh, sorry, it's been a while," she said to hide her shock. But she was bowled over. Mimi was stunning. She was not at all the strange-looking, "retarded" child with a large head who Rita remembered. She was a grown woman—a handsome, beautiful lesbian.

"Ah," she laughed, "no one calls me Mimi anymore, except my folks."

Mimi's sexy, raspy laugh made Rita's heart stir. Waters of desire, waves of a visceral memory caught Rita by surprise. Where had she heard such a laugh before?

"I don't use Miriam, either," she smiled. "I changed my name to Toby some years ago. And this is my partner, Kim."

"It's really nice to meet you." Rita smiled politely at Kim. "I'm sorry my girlfriend, Susan, isn't here to meet you both. She's at home studying for her exams."

Just then, five-year-old Noah peeked out from behind Rita's legs. "This is Noah." Rita coaxed him to say hello.

Toby smiled and winked at Noah. Rita liked that Toby did not demand a response from her sometimes shy child. Kim smiled too, then gave Toby a look Rita recognized. Biological clocks were ticking.

For months after the reunion with Toby, Rita tried to control the fantasy of being with her. The magnetism was intense, palpable, so familiar. It was as if they had known each other forever, not just as kids. Rita saw Toby a few more times that summer, the last time just the two of them. It was clear by then, that neither of them wanted to deny what was about to happen.

"I have never seen you fall this hard," Andrea said. "What do you plan on doing? You're with Susan and Toby's with someone too, right?"

"I don't know. She wants to see me next weekend. I was going to see if we could meet in New York, stay at your place?"

"You can—Joel's not coming until the following week. Did he call you?"

"Yes, he said something about graduate school, about seeing a woman he met here the last time he was in town. A doctor, I think. A psychiatrist, someone he's interested in dating—ugh." She frowned. "Well, to each their own. I guess they've been in touch."

"How would you feel if he moved here?" Andrea asked.

"I guess okay, if he doesn't interfere too much." Rita replied. "It would be nice for Noah to have a man in his life, since my plans for my father being around didn't pan out so well."

Andrea sighed. "I hope you know what you're doing—with Toby, I mean. What are you going to tell Susan?"

"The truth," Rita said pointblank. "She's not interested in me anymore. I'm just convenient for her, so she doesn't have to get a real job. She does love Noah though. She'll take good care of him for the weekend. They might go up to see her family in Maine."

"Didn't you tell me her folks are drinkers?"

"Yes, but Susan's been sober for years." Rita said. She was sure it would be okay.

CHAPTER 24

Clara Doyle

Clara woke up early. The sky was barely light, the air still cool after an unusually chilly night. There was no rain for a change. Although it had been a wet spring, the roads would be not be so muddy, she thought.

Still, she was nervous. She had planned this day repeatedly in her mind for a long time. The decision to leave, to run away, loomed. She did not want the life of a "painted lady" any longer. She had learned to drink, learned to pleasure men, and had not gotten pregnant using all the tricks the other girls had shown her. But she longed for a child, for a husband, a family.

Clara took her flowered satchel from under her bed. The girls would just assume she was going to buy some yarn for knitting, a skill she had taught herself over the last few years. Matt would be going up to Corvallis today on his monthly route to buy goods for the house and liquor for the saloon. She planned to hide in the back of the wagon. She would be able to go with him if she could hide away for at least a day. By then they would be too far along the way to turn back, she planned. He would have to take her along.

Clara packed her satchel with a robe, undergarments, an extra shawl, blouse, and stockings. She dressed in the only long skirt and blouse she had that covered her completely, not the usual clothes she wore for the men. She would not show any bosom or legs, and would

172

wear little make-up. She braided her hair tightly, putting it up in a neat bun the same way the proper ladies in town fixed their hair.

While hatching her plan, she had questioned the men she serviced. "Do you go north from here? Is Portland a big city?"

"Portland! That's a long ways off. I go up to Corvallis, 50 miles, 'bout three days if the roads aren't too muddy. There's a mill, stores. You ever been outta this town?" asked one miner. "Ever been to Junction City, east of here? The biggest town round these parts—and Eugene, south not even two days."

One of her regular customers showed her a hand-drawn map. Clara didn't read well, but she knew some words. "What's over here?" she said, pointing.

"That there is Florence. This? Coos Bay. Over there—the Pacific Ocean."

The names were familiar. Clara thought that some were close to where she had lived with Anna and Mrs. Riley, her home. A wave of sadness and regret washed over her. She wondered if Anna and Mrs. Riley remembered her. They would be so disappointed, ashamed of what she had become. She could never go back.

"How far is that?" Clara asked, pointing farther north.

"That's Roseburg—south. The Oregon Trail is north." The fellow looked at Clara. He didn't look directly in her eyes, but at the top of her breasts, pushed up by her corset along the edge of her low cut blouse. "You can't go across the Trail alone, dangerous up along Columbia River way. Besides, you'll need more money that this." He handed her a coin and pulled her onto his lap.

I got some gold pieces, she thought. Kyle had given them to her.

"Your a good-looking gal," he said, tracing the edge of her blouse with his fingers. "Maybe someone will want to take up with you."

Clara had heard it before. All the girls hoped for a man who would come to marry them. But Clara had waited for Kyle so long, it had been hard to imagine someone else. If she ran off with another man, how would he find her? This very thought had stopped her from running away for the last few years.

But now, something had changed. She couldn't wait any longer. Soon no one would want her. She would be too old.

Sure that her plan to escape would work, Clara opened her door, looked down the hall and over the banister to the saloon. All was quiet. She stole outside before the sun was up and went to the stable. The stable boy was still asleep. One of the horses snorted. Several of the others stirred. She hurried to Matt's wagon to check the coverings. She would need a thick muslin cover big enough to hide her as she lay flat on the bottom boards. She would have to time everything just right.

She went back into the kitchen and put some berry preserves on several pieces of bread. Wrapping the treat in a cloth, she hurried to her room. Clara leaned against her closed door and took a deep breath to calm herself. A few minutes later, she heard Jean call her for morning tea and porridge.

Matt and Sam were in the store room doing a final inventory. "You gals need anything from the city?" Matt directed his question toward Clara. "Sam'll be handlin' things when I'm gone, so don't go givin' him no trouble."

"We could use some cotton cloth for some new clothes, Matt," Clara pleaded. "We're lookin' a fright in these old threads. Do you think we can get something nicer than what Mac got down the general store?" She knew what Matt wanted. "We can get more customers, more money if we look good," she flirted.

Matt grumbled. "I'll see what I can do." He didn't like spending money, unless it was stock for the business. Ladies' wear was something he counted on the girls to do for themselves. He gave them a small amount of money every month to spend at Mac's for personal needs, lip color, soap, fabric and thread. Should do, he thought.

Clara took the opportunity to get her satchel, make a obvious exit. "I'll be headin' down to Mac's to see what they have then," she said. "Maybe, Mac and his wife got some new fabric for skirts."

Matt looked over at Sam, who was cleaning the bar. He nodded to his younger brother, relieved.

"That there's a good idea, Clara," Sam said. The other girls agreed, reluctantly.

Clara took her cue. She walked out quickly. Once in the stable, she spotted the stable hand. "Mornin' Daniel, I brought you some bread and jam."

Daniel brightened. "Thanks, Miss Clara," the boy said.

Clara had practiced bringing him a piece of jam and bread, a piece of pie or honey biscuit every few days for the last few weeks, in preparation for this day. So it was not unusual for him to see her today. She knew he would not tell anyone about the treats.

"This is just between you and me," she whispered. "No one has to know. I might get into trouble, see?" she plotted. Daniel nodded.

Clara had planned it well, she thought. Daniel ate, unaware of Clara's exit. She walked toward the open doors, along the line of stalls, and ducked into the alcove where Matt's wagon stood already loaded with supplies for his trip. She maneuvered into the wagon, and covered herself with a sheet of muslin, tucking herself in tightly. Then she pulled the heavy wagon covering over her. If someone looked under the wagon cover, Clara thought, she would look like a sack of potatoes.

Suddenly, the wagon shifted. She heard Daniel attaching the horses. Horse bridles, harnesses, metal and leather slapped against the front of the wagon. Soon, she heard Matt's voice.

"All set, Daniel? Horses fed? Watered?"

Clara felt the wagon shake as feed bags were loaded behind the seat. "All set, Mr. Matt."

"Here you go." Coins clinked in Daniel's hand. "Give some to your ma, you hear?"

"Thank you kindly, Mr. Matt. Sure will."

The wagon lurched forward. Clara's heart pounded so hard, she thought Matt would hear it. She was suddenly terrified. Matt would be furious when he found her. What if he just threw her out in the middle of the road? In the middle of nowhere? Would he think her so ungrateful? He had let her have a room, food, a place to live, so she wouldn't starve...or worse.

Clara tried to stay calm. But as the reality of the risk she was taking sank in, thoughts of doom persisted. She had to be resourceful, think through each scenario. If she got to Corvallis, could she get to the Oregon Trail from there? Might she find a kind man traveling further north or east? Would the gold coins she had pay for a coach from Corvallis? Were there any coaches? What about the railroad? She had forgotten to ask about trains. Maybe, she could find work doing laundry or cooking. She would only sell herself if she had to, if that was what it would take to go back East. Clara thought of Kyle. Would he be upset that she had left? Would she ever see him again? Maybe, she should have gone south to California, she thought. Clara wiped silent tears from her eyes.

The wagon bumped along for hours. It was a rougher ride than she had imagined. Her body hurt. Clara closed her eyes. Tired, she dozed fitfully keeping one hand over her mouth to muffle any noise she might make accidentally, when the wagon hit a big bump. Suddenly, she heard Matt call to the horses. The wagon slowed, then stopped. Her heart leaped. She listened.

Matt got down from his seat. His back and legs were stiff. He climbed down, then tied the horses to a tree trunk. At the edge of the rode Matt emptied his bladder. He stretched, surveying the road ahead. All was quiet.

Peeking out from her covering, Clara saw nothing but trees and sky. She had not thought about having to urinate. Now she had to go badly. Perhaps Matt was doing just that. This might be her only chance.

With that thought though, she felt the wagon jar again. Matt climbed back onto the seat and snapped the reins. "Get up there," he clicked to the horses. The wagon bolted forward.

Clara would have to hold her bladder until the next time the wagon stopped. By then, she figured, even if Matt caught her, they'd be too far to go back. She would plead with him to take her. She would tell him she was sorry, beg for forgiveness. Once they got to Corvallis, she could run away.

By the time they stopped, Clara was feeling sick. She had not eaten or drank any water all day. She waited until Matt got down from the wagon. She heard him feed and water the horses, then heard him walk away. Lifting the wagon cover, Clara peered out. The wagon had stopped at the post of a small, rundown shack a short distance off the road. Quickly, she tried to get out of the wagon, grabbing her bag. Her legs stiff, back aching from the long, grueling ride, she hurried. She ran behind some trees, down a small embankment. Hidden by thick vegetation, she squatted and emptied her bladder fully, contracting her pelvic muscles hard, shuttering involuntarily.

Cleaning, adjusting her garments, she crouched slightly to remain unseen. For a moment, she thought she heard the sound of water. She walked carefully just a few yards through the trees, and to her great relief found a small creek. The water ran clear over the rocks, moss and ferns grew along its edge. Clara fell to her knees, cupped her hands, and drank quickly. She kept alert, listening for Matt and any movement of the horses. She did not want to be left behind

With her thirst abated, Clara climbed up the embankment careful to stay hidden, just out of sight. From her vantage point, she could see the wagon and the shack. She looked up at the sky to see if she could determine the time. The sun had gone down, but the sky was still light enough to see clearly. It would be dusk very soon.

She remembered the trader who told her it was about three days to Corvallis. Clara figured that they had completed one full day. Would Matt stay here for the night? Could she sleep in the wagon, hide under the covering all night? Would she be safe? Suddenly, Clara realized she had not thought of wolves or bears. She had no shotgun, no one to protect her. Frightening as the thought was, she would have to take a chance. She settled in and waited to see if Matt would return. When he did not, Clara found the extra bread she had packed in her satchel and gobbled it ravenously. Exhausted from her ordeal, it wasn't long before she fell into a deep sleep.

In what seemed like only moments, the sun woke her, its inviting warmth spreading over her face and hands. She had slept through the night in spite of the damp cold and her fears of wild animals. Now the sun was shining. Clara opened her eyes, squinting in the bright light.

A sudden cramp in her back thrust her awake in a panic. But it was too late. Matt was staring down at her in disbelief.

Matt moved closer, his big frame casting a shadow over her. "What the hell you doin' in there?" He boomed. "Are you crazy?"

An old man came lumbering out of the shack. He craned his neck, peering around at the wagon bed. "Damn," he said. "You left that gal out here all night?"

Matt fumed, "I should just leave you here! You givin' me more trouble than you're worth!" He stormed back to the shack.

The old miner just stared at Clara. "You need somethin' to eat, ma'am?"

Clara looked down, ashamed. Another feeling lurked beneath the surface, though. She felt angry, defiant. It was an unfamiliar feeling. She looked at the old miner. His gnarled hands were stained, his back hunched, his gray hair wild. "No, thanks," she said.

Clara got out of the wagon and brushed herself off. She smoothed her hair, her dress, stood up straight. She refolded the garments in her bag she had used for a pillow and ate the remaining bread.

The miner reappeared with some hot liquid. "Try this," he said. "They call it *Arbuckels*. Traveler give it to me, from Portland. I sugared it." The old man grinned. His few teeth were brown.

Clara took the hot black drink. It smelled appealing. She was thirsty. She sipped the rich, sweet liquid. "Thank you," she managed a smile. When Matt returned, she felt alert, more awake than she had in days.

"You done wasted two days of my time. I gotta bring you back. Start over again! No telling the weather." His voice was sharp.

"You can take me with you. I won't give you no more trouble. I could do the dress fabric shopping," she pleaded.

Matt frowned. He fed and watered the horses, ignoring her. When he finished, he threw his jacket up on the seat.

The old man came out and handed Matt a bag. "Here some vittles. You fixin' to leave the gal?" he asked.

"Be back for her in four days," Matt said.

CHAPTER 25

Rita Kerner

NEW YORK CITY, 1984

Rita reached for the pack of cigarettes on the nightstand. She had started smoking again after years of abstinence.

"You know I hate it when you smoke in bed," Toby said softly. She stroked Rita's bare back.

Rita ignored Toby's gentle plea. She lit her first cigarette of the day, taking a deep drag. She propped up the pillows behind her head and exhaled. Waving one arm in the air, Rita tried to disperse the foul-smelling smoke. "I'm sorry, Toby. I know I should stop, but now is…" Rita did not finish her sentence. Why rationalize? she thought. Her life was in turmoil, painful goodbyes were imminent. These were the facts. Smoking was not going to change anything or help her in the long run. But today, Rita didn't care about the long run. For Toby's sake though, she took only one more drag, then extinguished the half-smoked cigarette in the ashtray. Rita started to get out of bed.

"Hey, where are you going?" Toby reached for her arm and pulled Rita toward her. There was desire in her eyes.

Rita smiled. "I'll be right back, love. I'm just going to brush my teeth." She saw the look on Toby's face. Rita loved the unabashed, raw desire between them. For a few precious days each month, they were swallowed in passion that overwhelmed rational thought. Their intensity had turned their lives upside down. "Cosmic" was the word Toby used to describe it. Rita liked that. It defined perfectly the way

179

they transported each other to a place beyond time and words, where the essence of their beings lived, drenched in love and light. It was a place where the sweet brine of their female earthly bodies and the ethereal energy of their androgynous spirits met and merged into one.

There was very little Rita did not love about Toby—how her eyes twinkled mischievously when she laughed in her low raspy voice, how her tough, controlled exterior melted from Rita's touch, and how her lean athletic body erupted in ecstasy when they made love. Rita found Toby's dry humor and depth of intellect alluring. She could be funny and boisterous or cool and silent.

Toby felt a new sense of freedom too—an openness she had never experienced before. Magnetism overpowered them, changing a friendship into a sexual odyssey. Neither of them could attribute the depth of their intimacy to friendship or family history. How could it be explained by their recent friendship since reuniting at adults? How could such passion have arisen in a such a short time?

Lost in thought, Rita moved slowly out of bed.

"Come right back," Toby whispered seductively.

Rita stretched her arms in the air, arching her back. Her smooth, olive skin and dark hair caught the sunlight through the partially-drawn blinds. She stood just out of Toby's reach. Toby lay in bed absorbing Rita's curves. Rita could still feel Toby's gaze as she walked out of the room.

Toby stretched and yawned, rousing herself slightly. She reached for her glasses and looked at her watch on the nightstand. It was ten-fifteen. They had to make it to the airport by four o'clock to see Andrea off, she thought. Her mind resisted focusing on a time schedule. The last thing she wanted to do today was go to the airport. She had just come in from Philadelphia two days ago and had to fly back tomorrow. Next time she would drive, she thought. Everything felt so rushed. There was barely time to relax. She was tired of traveling, tired of the guilt she felt every time she left Kim, tired of the heartache every time she left Rita.

"What time is it?" Rita asked, noticing Toby staring at her watch.

Rita climbed into bed next to her and pressed her cool body against Toby's side. Toby removed her glasses. She turned to face Rita. Her lover smelled like peppermint toothpaste and musk.

"We have time," Toby said softly as she rolled Rita onto her back. Toby bent over, kissing Rita first on her minty lips, then on her neck and shoulders. Taking Rita's breasts in her hands, she caressed them until Rita moaned. Lust slowly devoured and liquefied them. They moved in perfect unison, the heat of their bodies rising, their energies entwined. The air got light, their breath quickened. Time slowed down then ceased to exist at all, evaporating into the fire of their passion.

They had barely cooled down when Rita heard the key turn in the front door lock. "Anyone for bagels?" Rita heard Andrea's voice trailing off toward the kitchen. She looked at Toby, who lay in her arms semi-conscious.

"Honey, Andrea's home," Rita said, nudging Toby awake. Rita reached down, ungluing their bodies. She pulled up the sheet and blanket that had fallen off the bed. Rita covered Toby's still damp body. Andrea walked in just as Rita was pulling the sheet over herself.

Andrea smiled at Rita. "Nothing I haven't seen before, Ms. Modesty," she said knowingly.

Toby, half-awake, grunted a laugh. Rita acknowledged the amusement her present lover and a former flame were enjoying over her embarrassment.

"Sorry to intrude on your privacy, but I've got to see if I packed everything before we leave," Andrea said, heading to check her dresser on the far side of her bed. She let Toby and Rita use her apartment for one weekend a month. Rita stole time alone with Toby, bringing Noah with her to New York for visits with Joel and his fiancée, the doctor. Susan had started drinking again, so Rita had moved out with Noah and rented a small place in Cambridge, a temporary solution until there could be rational discussion of finality. Meanwhile, Rita and Toby had continued their long distance affair.

Andrea had met someone too, on a business trip to Seattle. She was on her way to live with her new love. The *u-haul syndrome*, as it was known among their peers, had ensued. It was a plane that would take Andrea to start a new life, departing at four o'clock from La Guardia.

For Andrea, the future was clear. For Rita, there were more complications than she wished to think about. She tried to fool herself into believing Toby's love would conquer all. If only Toby would end her relationship with Kim, Rita thought. Hadn't Toby kept telling her to be patient, that it was just a matter of time? Rita continued to wait for Toby's reassuring words of devotion to manifest into a tangible commitment.

"Oh, shit! What time is it?" Rita sat up in bed.

"It's twelve-thirty. I think we should leave here about two o'clock." Andrea suggested. She was taking a few remaining items from the top drawer when the front doorbell rang.

"That's got to be my neighbor. I told her to come by for a set of keys to give the landlord, after the weekend." Andrea walked out and closed the bedroom door behind her.

Rita got out of bed. She handed Toby her robe. "Do you think we have time to go to the shop on 72nd Street? I really wanted to get your birthday present today. The store will be closed later and tomorrow is Sunday." By Monday, Toby would be home celebrating her birthday with Kim. Birthdays and holidays were bittersweet for Rita.

"I guess if we hurry. But you don't have to buy me anything, spend more money now."

"I know, but I'd like to get you that vest you wanted."

Toby moved close to Rita. She put her robed arms around Rita's bare waist, pulling Rita gently to her. Rita felt Toby's warm hands move over her hips, then caress her back. "I always think about you. I don't have to have that vest or anything else to have you on my mind," Toby whispered into Rita's ear.

Rita's eyes filled with tears. She pulled away from Toby, not wanting to cry, not now. She walked out of the room and into the bathroom. Rita turned on the shower and got in, letting the warm water rinse away the sweat and tears. She closed her eyes, breathing in the steam. Soon, she felt Toby's soap-filled hands sliding slippery over her body.

Andrea had coffee made, the bagels cut and buttered, when the two lovers got to the kitchen, dressed and ready to go. "We're just going down to pick up Toby's present. Are you all set?" Rita asked.

"Yes, I'm just about ready. Keep an eye on the time, though. It's after one already." Andrea smiled, rechecking all the drawers and cabinets for forgotten items.

Toby checked her watch. "Don't worry. We'll definitely be back by two o'clock," she assured Andrea.

Rita and Toby walked down four flights of stairs and out into the hot, hazy light of the afternoon. Rita put on her sunglasses. On the street, they were just friends.

The store was only a five-minute walk. The desired vest was displayed in the window.

"Look, there's your favorite!"

Inside the store, Toby found two colors she liked in her size and went to the fitting room. The fitting room was near the lingerie department. Rita looked inquisitively through the racks of sheer nightwear. She waited for Toby. Never owning any lingerie, she wondered what it would be like to wear something sleek and sexy—a straight girl thing. She held up a deep red silk-and-lace negligee that was low cut and very short. Holding it against her body, she tried to imagine it on without clothes underneath.

A deep, raspy laugh, then a quiet moan caught Rita's attention. Toby was standing a few feet away looking at her in awe, an expression on her face that Rita had never seen before. Or had she?

"What do you think?" Rita flirted, feeling a sudden déjà vu.

"Ah, it's incredible!" Toby had an odd sensation, as if time had momentarily spun backward. She saw herself standing in front of a much younger version of Rita, whose sheer nightgown was torn open, breasts exposed. Lust pulsed through Toby's veins. Chills ran up her spine.

With not one, but two purchases made, they dashed back to Andrea's place. Andrea was still checking off her "do before I leave" list.

"Have a good time?" Andrea smiled, observing their flushed faces. She handed Rita a set of keys. "Leave these in the kitchen. It's an extra set." Andrea walked around in circles. "I took care of the lights. Ugh! I forgot to call the phone company back. I think it will still be on tomorrow though. You can leave the sheets and…"

"It will be fine. Don't worry, Andrea. You are done." Rita followed Andrea, double-checking all the closets and cupboards.

"C'mon, let's get the stuff in the car," Rita urged her nervous friend. She put an arm over Andrea's shoulder. "It's two o'clock. We should go, kiddo."

It wasn't until they got to the airport terminal that tears flowed. Rita continued crying, allowing her emotions to escape, even after Andrea had boarded the plane. She let Toby hold her in public. For once, Rita did not worry or care what anyone else thought.

As they left the airport, Toby stopped at the gift shop to buy some gum. She bought a card for Rita. *"Even when we are far apart, you are always in my heart,"* Rita read aloud. It was sappy, Rita knew, but she believed every word.

That night after dinner out, they went to Andrea's apartment for the last time. Toby took off her new vest and slacks while Rita put on the red silk negligee. They lit candles and put the flowers they bought in a glass of water next to the bed. They drank wine and ate chocolate ice cream. Their cold chocolate kisses turned hot. Holding each other close, they danced slowly to cool jazz on Rita's portable radio. Their night of romance electrified the air—their laughter, tears, and ecstasy making music of their magic together. Drenched by love and spent emotions, the two lovers fell asleep in each other's arms just before dawn. They slept soundly, drifting into the place where spirits live in the depth of dreams. There they parted.

Toby saw herself in a room she vaguely remembered. It was a woman's room, not her own. In her dream, she was no longer a woman. She was dressed in men's clothing. A white shirt, heavy pants, a leather belt with metal buckle and black leather boots were on the man she felt herself to be. In the dream, Toby peered out a window, down to the muddy cobblestone street. A horse unhitched from its wagon was saddled and ready. A stable boy looked up. "Mr. Doyle," he called and waved.

The dreamscape shifted and he gazed back across the room. A woman was sleeping in a bed against the wall. A low light emanated from a lantern on the table near the bed. The woman was young, not more than twenty or so. While she looked different, he suddenly recognized her. It was Rita. Her dark hair framed a sweet face. He could see the curves of her body under a cotton and lace nightgown, which he instantly knew he had bought for her. Now, she slept, like an angel. He felt a sad. A lingering sense of regret and guilt swept over him before he looked away from her beautiful sleeping figure.

Aware that his horse was saddled and waiting, he knew he might never see Rita again. He had not told her he was leaving. She would awake and find him gone in the morning. The ache inside his chest grew difficult to bear. Then suddenly, he was sitting in his saddle, reins in hand. He felt wind and rain hit his face. Cobblestones flashed beneath his horse's hooves.

Rita awoke, hearing Toby stir. She looked over at her. Tears at the edge of her lover's closed eyes slid down her temples. Was Toby crying in her sleep? Rita wanted to wake her, comfort her. But she didn't.

Rita looked around the desolate room left empty by Andrea's departure. The walls were bare. Holes gaped where pictures had recently hung. The flowers on the nightstand lay wilted in the glass. Rita heard rain tapping against the window. Anxiety gripped her heart. Where would she and Toby meet now, have their rendezvous? This place between Boston and Philadelphia, had been their halfway point, their sanctuary, a love nest where Andrea had been their nonjudgmental friend. Choking back tears, Rita reached for her cigarettes.

CHAPTER 26

Bertha's Family

QUEENS, NEW YORK, 1958

Belinda looked up from her seat on the subway as it rolled into the Penn Station stop, screeching to a halt at the 34th Street end of the underground. She had lost track of time since leaving Brooklyn. Grabbing her knitting, she quickly stuffed her needles and yarn into her bag. She rushed to the subway door just as it was about to close.

A white man in a dark suit held the door open and leered at her. Belinda squirmed past him and out onto the platform. She had to make her connection to Queens quickly. The private nursing job she was starting today began at nine o'clock sharp. The job meant she could send some extra money home to Aunt Dorothy now that Papa was gone.

Papa's heart had just given out from old age. Belinda was glad he had not suffered. She was glad also that he had lived to see her married to Jeremiah and the birth of her first son, Arnie. When her younger son was born two years later, she named him James Jr., after her father. She knew her mother, Bertha, would have liked that. Belinda still missed her family in Philadelphia, but when she was offered the job at the visiting nurses agency in New York, she was grateful Jeremiah and her boys had agreed to move.

Belinda hurried down the escalator and onto the platform for the train to Far Rockaway. She had only a few minutes to wait. She boarded the train and found a seat easily, taking out the directions

186

she had written down. She read them again carefully. The family she was to meet lived in a house a few blocks north of her stop. The elderly woman that she would be caring for had diabetes and was forgetful, her daughter had reported to the agency. She needed a nurse on weekdays from nine in the morning to three in the afternoon to make sure she took her medication and ate properly. No one else would be around during those hours, except the dog. The oldest grandchild, Rita, would be home from school by three, and Belinda could leave her in charge then.

It was drizzling as the train climbed out from underground onto the outdoor tracks. The clouds had looked foreboding this morning, so she'd taken her umbrella and sent her children to school in raincoats. As the train clattered along, Belinda relaxed and observed the scenery of a place she'd never been before. For Belinda, nothing could spoil the day. She was more content than she had been in a long time. She and Jeremiah had good jobs, a nice apartment in Brooklyn, and their two boys were doing well in school.

Belinda reached her destination at nine-fifteen. She walked up the few stairs to the attached row house and knocked, suddenly nervous about the time. A white woman with brown hair and blue eyes opened the door.

"Hello," she said. "You must be Mrs. Williams, the nurse. I'm Lillian Kerner. How do you do? Won't you come in?" She led Belinda into the foyer. "I'm so glad the weather didn't slow you down too much. I told my boss I'd be an hour late, since I wanted to get you acquainted with my mother-in-law," Lillian rattled on without taking a breath. "Please, let me take your coat and things. The front hall closet is right here." Lillian hung Belinda's coat in the closet and offered her a place for her scarf and other belongings on a bench in the front hall. "My mother-in-law's name is Mrs. Pearl Kerner. She is in the kitchen," the younger Mrs. Kerner said, pointing the way down the hall. "I hope you don't mind her ways. She can be a bit difficult at times."

Belinda finally was able to get a word in. "I'm used to taking care of all kind'a folks," she said. "I'm sure she won't be a problem, Mrs.

Kerner." Belinda followed the woman down a hall to a modern '50s style kitchen. The room was light even on such a cloudy day, thanks to a big picture window that faced a little terraced rose garden. Small ceramic figurines adorned the window's wide sill. They were like the kind Aunt Dorothy had, Belinda noticed, only these were white. She turned her attention to the elder Mrs. Kerner, who sat at the kitchen table nursing a glass of tea.

"Mom," Lillian spoke loudly. "This is Mrs. Williams, the nurse. She is going to stay with you during the day and help you with your medication and meals, until Rita gets home from school. Remember? We told you she was coming today."

The old woman looked up at her daughter-in-law with vague disgust. Then she looked at Belinda as if sizing her up. *"Kain ein horeh, a schvartze shiksa?"*—Protect us, a black Christian? She did not greet Belinda.

"I'm so sorry," Lillian Kerner apologized to Belinda. "She means no harm. She is just ignorant."

Lillian turned to her mother-in-law. "Mom, *macht nicht kain tsimmes fun dem! Farshtaist?*

"I told her to do what you say and not make any trouble." Lillian said to Belinda. She understands more than she lets on. English is not her language, but she can make herself understood when she tries."

Belinda nodded. "What does she like to eat? I can make her some food after her insulin."

"She likes to eat everything, sometimes too much. She forgets she's had a meal, and then she goes back to the refrigerator for more. You will have to remind her. She likes a cheese sandwich with tomatoes and lettuce or egg salad. There's some egg salad already made in the fridge." Lillian opened the refrigerator, pointing out the Tupperware container and vials of Pearl's insulin. "The bread is here, in this drawer. There is always fruit, too. Her other medication supplies are here." Lillian opened another kitchen drawer. "She likes to watch TV in the living room," Lillian continued. "Here is the receptionist's number at my job. If there is a problem someone will come get me. Our phone is in the front hall." The younger Mrs. Kerner put on her wool coat and finished her instructions. "My daughter, Rita, will be home by three, the younger two girls come home by school bus, around the same time. You can leave then, before rush hour." Lillian opened the front door. "Sorry I don't have more time today. If you have any questions, we can talk tomorrow morning." She paused. "Good luck and thank you for being on time," Lillian smiled. Without waiting for a response from Belinda, she left.

Lillian Kerner talked so fast, Belinda's head was spinning. She walked back into the kitchen to greet the old woman. Belinda noticed how well-dressed Pearl was—clean and pressed in her white blouse and dark green jumper, a small cameo brooch below her neck. Her silver hair was braided, wrapped up into a bun held with combs. Belinda thought of her own mother Bertha, who would have looked pressed and neat like Mrs. Kerner, even in her old age. "How you feeling today, Mrs. Kerner?" she asked.

The old woman looked up and sighed. "I ask God to come for me." Pearl returned to sipping her tea in silence.

Belinda understood the old woman's sentiment and her accent. She had worked with elderly clients before. Some, like Pearl, had come from other countries. Belinda made a cup of tea for herself, feeling Pearl eyeing her every move.

"Would you like to watch some TV, Mrs. Kerner?" asked Belinda, pointing toward the living room. "We can watch, *Queen For A Day,* if you like."

Mrs. Kerner drank the last of her tea. She got up slowly from the table and followed Belinda into the living room. Pearl sat down on the edge of the couch, so her heavy black shoes could touch the floor.

Belinda noticed how uncomfortable the old woman looked. She plumped up a throw pillow and placed it behind Pearl's back. "Sit back, Mrs. Kerner," she said. "You'll be more comfortable." Pearl understood and sat back. She appeared to relax a little. Belinda brought a hassock, so Pearl could put her legs up. "Good for your circulation," she coaxed her patiently.

They watched TV together for the next few hours. Pearl dozed off a few times. Belinda kept track of the time for her client's insulin and lunch.

The first day seemed to go by quickly. Belinda made Pearl her favorite cheese and tomato sandwich and some chicken noodle soup, with only minor interference. Pearl reminded Belinda to wash her hands. Belinda did not let her annoyance show. She put the food on the table and took the insulin out of the fridge. She swabbed alcohol on the old woman's arm. Pearl took her insulin shot without complaint and was happy to eat her lunch. Belinda knew from experience that meals were so often the highlight of the day for elderly folks.

Afterward, Pearl lay down for a nap. Belinda went into the kitchen to clean the dishes and counter. She hummed to herself softly while she finished, a habit she'd picked up from Aunt Dorothy. She sat down for a cup of tea when she was done, looking at the little figures on the windowsill. She was surprised by how easy her job was. She felt confident of her skills. Belinda had only a short time of reflection when she heard a key in the door.

"Hellooo!" a young voice called out.

Belinda stood up quickly and walked toward the front door. The Kerner's eleven-year-old daughter was hanging up her jacket on the wall hooks. Her school books lay scattered at her feet. She looked up at Belinda and stepped over them.

"Oh, hello! You must be my grandmother's nurse. I'm Rita." Rita held her hand out to Belinda.

"Why, yes, I am," she said, taking Rita's outstretched hand, noticing the girl's openness and big smile. There was not a hint of shyness, suspicion, or reservation in this child, unlike Belinda's experience with most white people, upon first meeting. "How was school, today?" she asked as if Rita were her own child.

"Oh, well, I'm not such a good student," said Rita. "I'm starting to like reading, but art is my favorite. The rest not that much." Rita shrugged her shoulders. "Where's my grandmother? Did she give you a hard time?" Rita asked without skipping a beat. "My sisters' school bus should be here any minute."

Belinda wondered why the family thought the old woman was so difficult. Perhaps, she thought, Mrs. Kerner was just on her best behavior this first day, and things would not be as easy as they seemed.

"She's taking a little nap," said Belinda.

"Oh, that's good." Rita walked into the kitchen. She took milk from the fridge and cookies from the cabinet. "Yeah, sometimes she gets tired in the afternoon. But, I usually wake her up when I come home, so she can sleep at night. She has sleep problems." Rita poured some milk in her glass. She took out two more glasses for her sisters. "Sometimes Grandma gets up, walks around, and eats meals she thinks she's missed. Sometimes she hides food in her bedroom dresser. You gotta watch out for that. She thinks people are going to steal our food."

Belinda was suddenly uncomfortable. "What people?" she asked.

"She grew up during a war in Russia, and people stole from her family," Rita explained. "They killed her whole family. She and her brother were the only survivors. Sometimes, she remembers that," Rita continued. "It's very hard, because she won't listen. She doesn't believe me or anyone else. My father can sometimes talk to her, but he doesn't have any patience." Rita talked between bites of chocolate chip cookies.

Belinda understood. She appreciated Rita's youthful honesty. "I see," said Belinda. "You know, child—God has plans we don't understand. Sometimes terrible things happen to innocent people."

Rita really didn't believe their was a God—or a Heaven or Hell—but she was polite about it anyway. She knew God and Jesus were very important to Christians, especially Negro Christians, like David's union buddy, Sam, and his family. Lillian had taught her to respect everyone's religion. "Freedom of religion is a right, like freedom of speech. Even not being religious is a right." Lillian had said. She taught Rita to respect everyone's race, too. But, Rita still didn't understand why white Christians hated Negro Christians if they all believed in the same God. Why would a God, a Christian God or a Jewish God have a plan for terrible things to happen to innocent people?

"I don't understand why some people are so dumb and mean," Rita said.

"My poor grandmother was just a child when that happened." Rita put her glass in the sink. "Well, I should go wake Grandma up before my sisters get home. Are you staying 'till my mother gets home?"

"Oh, no dear," said Belinda. "Your mother said you'd be okay if I left when you got home. My sons and husband will be waiting on dinner. I'll be going to the market on the way home."

"Okay, I'll be fine. My sisters will be home soon, then Mom. How old are your kids, Mrs. Williams?"

"My oldest is thirteen, my little one is ten." Belinda smiled at Rita. Maybe this new generation would be different, less prejudiced, she thought. She gathered her belongings together and headed for the door. "Well, I'll see you tomorrow," Belinda said.

Out on the street, Belinda breathed the cool air. She hurried to the train, thinking about her own children. They'd be home alone for a few hours before she got home. She was a little worried about her new day schedule. Belinda usually worked nights when Jeremiah would be home with the children. At thirteen though, Arnie was old enough now to take care of his younger brother, she decided.

Belinda's train came on time. She found a seat near the window. She settled in and looked out, not noticing as the landscape and buildings became a blur of shapes and colors. Belinda was lost in thought, allowing her feelings and perceptions to surface. Mrs. Kerner had not been the problematic client the younger Mrs. Kerner thought she would be. As a matter of fact, after her initial reaction to Belinda, Pearl seemed to like the attention. She was obviously lonely, thought Belinda. Now she would have someone to talk to. Her English was limited, but she'd been able to make herself understood well enough.

Poor thing, Belinda thought, remembering Rita's story of her grandmother's early years. How could she answer that child's question, her own children's questions too? Why was there so much hate in the world? Why did the color of a person's skin, a person's religion become something to fear, something so loathsome that people would resort to such violence? Sheer ignorance, she thought.

"There, but for the grace of God…please protect us…" Belinda said under her breath as the train pulled into 34th Street.

CHAPTER 27

Rita Kerner

BOSTON, MASSACHUSETTS, 1985

When her temporary apartment lease in Cambridge ended, Rita moved across the river to Boston. She found a small flat and what seemed a half-way decent elementary school for Noah. She was conflicted about Joel and his soon-to-be wife relocating to Newton, about twenty-five minutes away. But at least she would not have to depend solely on Susan, with Joel living close enough to help when she went to her second job a few evenings a week. Anxiety about more visitation was taking a toll. She wasn't sleeping well.

One night, Rita woke up from the same dream she'd had many times since childhood. She reached for the full glass of water on the nightstand and gulped down half of it to wash away the unsettling images.

Closing her eyes again and dozing, Rita surrendered to her dream's lasting impression, her vantage point as a passenger in a horse-drawn coach. She saw the back of a black horse pulling the carriage she rode in. Sounds of leather slapping against the horse's side and clicking of hooves filtered through her vision. The carriage shifted, reeling along a rocky dirt road on a cliff above a gray, stormy oceanfront. She looked out at the waves crashing against the large boulders, jagged rocks that jutted up from the sea floor. She felt chilled to the bone. The wind whipped against her face.

Just then, sensing the presence of someone near, a man appeared

194

sitting on the coach seat next to her. He smiled warmly and covered her lap with a fur blanket. He called her by a different name, and seemed to be trying to soothe her. His voice was barely audible over the crescendo of the angry sea. She looked in his direction, not recognizing anything in her line of sight, except the wind-whipped cypress trees and a church cemetery. She looked down at her hands, which lay motionless in her lap, numb and cold. They were the hands of a child.

Jarred awake again by the disturbing vision, Rita opened her eyes. She turned her head and looked at the green numerals glaring from the electric clock radio—3:05 a.m. It was dark in the apartment except for the stream of light from the corner streetlight, but she got out of bed anyway. She went instinctively to check on Noah, who was asleep in his room. Skippy, the new terrier she had gotten for Noah, raised himself from his little dog bed and moved slowly behind her.

Rita walked into the kitchen and helped herself to a small glass of milk, hoping the calcium would help her sleep. Skippy wagged his tail and gave a little yelp anticipating breakfast. "Shhh…" Rita whispered, giving him some biscuits, so he wouldn't wake Noah.

Swallowing the last drop of milk, her mind wandered back to the strange dream. Why did the painting that had hung above her parents' bed, the picture of a black horse pulling an old carriage along a road adjacent to a gray sea, still have such an effect on her? She pondered it for the umpteenth time. Even though Lillian and David lived in Miami now and had long since replaced the old painting with her colorful abstract one, its ghostly image still haunted her dreams.

Rita shrugged off further thoughts about it and headed back to bed. Skippy followed close behind. He curled up again in his dog bed. Three more hours until her radio alarm would go on should compensate for the disruption the dream had caused, she figured. She snuggled back into her soft pillow and fell asleep.

Not more than twenty minutes had passed when Rita awoke suddenly, hearing a radio playing. She checked her radio clock. It was not on. She listened. Not able to discern the words clearly, Rita was annoyed enough to get up to look out the window. Skippy picked up his head and watched her. What idiot is blasting his car radio at this hour, she thought. In the big city, their new corner apartment was great for natural light, but amplified noise from the street below.

Opening the window, Rita saw only unoccupied parked cars on the street below. She did not hear any radios. Satisfied that it must have been a passing car, she settled down to sleep once more.

There was nothing in Rita's experience to prepare her for what happened next. Within fifteen minutes, she awoke again to the sound of a blasting radio, this time with a list of random words screaming in her ear. "CHAIR! COUCH! CAT! TABLE! BOOK! DOG! ORANGE! PIANO!..."

Someone must be drunk or playing a joke in the apartment below, she thought. Irritated, Rita jumped out of bed. She walked to Noah's room to see if his sleep had been disrupted, too. Noah was fast asleep. His room was quiet. Thinking breakfast was soon, the dog wagged his tail and headed to his bowl in the kitchen.

Rita followed Skippy into the kitchen. Suddenly, the sound began again, a low hum at first. Then the volume increased. Rita was fully awake by now. She wandered from the kitchen, to the dining room, to the living room, trying to determine where the noise was coming from. She listened more carefully to the words to see if they meant anything..."HAT, BEANS, NOTEBOOK, DOOR, STOVE, HAMMER..." The words had a constant speed, but seemed to have no significant pattern. They were just a list of random objects. Rita decided it was more important to get sleep than try to investigate any further.

She went to the bathroom and stuffed some cotton in her ears. Noticing a slight headache coming on, she took some Tylenol from the medicine cabinet and downed two with the remaining water on her nightstand. Again, she nestled into her bed, this time with the dog at her side. She dozed off.

She woke up again about a half hour later and pulled the cotton from her ears. The list was no longer one list, one radio—but two. Two overlapping lists, each boomed louder, faster. The words were almost indistinguishable from one another.

"What the hell is going on?" Rita said angrily to herself. She felt feverish and exhausted. Again, she pushed herself out of bed and into the bathroom, nervously checking on Noah along the way. Satisfied he was not affected by whatever was going on, she got the thermometer out of the medicine cabinet and took her temperature. All the while, the harrowing lists of words invaded the apartment. The voices seemed to grow louder with each passing minute. Were the voices in her head? she wondered.

"PANTS, BOTTLE, BIRD, SINK, DINNER, LIBRARY, BALL, WATER…"

Rita turned on the bathroom light. "Shit!" she said, reading 101 degrees on the thermometer. "Damn, I'm going to miss work." Not being able to afford another sick day after the week off last month to take care of Noah's flu, Rita was worried. "Okay, just sleep," she advised herself aloud. Noticing that her own voice overrode the deafening lists, she crawled back into bed. Rita sang softly to herself. Soon she was in a deep sleep.

At 4:45, the alarm clock radio went on. The song, "Broken Wings" played softly this morning from her favorite pop music station. Exhausted and half-asleep, Rita listened. Rousing slightly, she breathed a sigh of relief. The voices were gone and everything was normal, she thought. Her night's ordeal was over. She reached to turn the alarm off glancing at the green digital numbers. "That can't be the right time," she startled.

Rita normally set her clock for 6:30 on weekday mornings. As she sat up in bed, the music went silent. Automatically, she reached to adjust the volume, to hear the end of the song, to reassure herself all was right with the world. But as she turned the volume dial, the incessant screaming lists began again.

"No, NO, NO!" Rita yelled, yanking the radio clock's electric cord from the socket. But it didn't help.

"BLANKET! LAMP! GARAGE! STEP! FISH! COMB! FOYER!

CANDLE!…" the words persisted, growing even louder. Rita turned on the light and got out of bed. She rummaged frantically through the nightstand drawer for her phone book. Finding her doctor's number, she dialed the phone.

"Hello, who is this?" a man's voice came through loudly. It was the doctor's husband.

"It's Rita Kerner. May I speak to Dr. Jordon." Rita whispered. She paced back and forth, dragging the phone cord with her until she heard the doctor's voice.

Dr. Jordon" Rita began to cry. "It's Rita. Please help me," she pleaded, trying to arrange her thoughts above the noise.

"What is it, Rita? It's 5:00 am. Is it an emergency? Did you call 911? What's wrong?"

"I…can't…voices…radios…lists of things…loud and I don't… know where…they are coming…from."

"Okay, take it easy, Rita. Take a deep breath. You are hearing things? Did you take any medication? You may be having an allergic reaction."

"No, just Tylenol."

"Any other symptoms? Did you take your temperature? Does your head or neck hurt? Do you have a fever?"

"Yes, it was 101 when I took it."

"All right. Just stay calm. It's probably just fever delirium. Take Tylenol every four hours, and put a cold washcloth on your head to bring the fever down. Drink fluids. Then rest," Dr. Jordon instructed. "Call me back if your fever gets higher. You can come into the office this morning."

Rita hung up and began humming again, warding off what now sounded like three radio lists. Fever delirium, she thought, recalling Lillian telling her about the fevers that had caused the seizures she'd had as a child. Rita walked into the bathroom, dampened a towel with cold water and wrapped it around her head like she remembered to do for a high fever. She could tell her temperature was getting higher. She had little strength to fight the radio lists that blasted in her ears.

Soon it would be time to get Noah up, make him breakfast and take him to school. "Okay," Rita said aloud, more confident that hearing her own voice helped quell the strange noise, if only momentarily. "I am going to make breakfast and pack a lunch now!" she said loudly, pretending to talk to someone. She proceeded to feed the dog, and make eggs and toast for Noah, all the while talking, chanting, humming. Each time she stopped vocalizing, the radio lists would pick up speed and volume like a cruel game.

"Noah, honey, Noah," Rita coaxed her son awake. "It's time for school, honey."

"No, Mommy, I don't want to go. I'm tired. Can I stay home, please?" Noah begged, not budging out of bed.

"No, honey, not today," Rita managed. "I'm sorry. You can sleep late tomorrow, Saturday. Come on, I have breakfast all ready. Wash up and get dressed, Bubbie. I'll call Estelle."

Rita's neighbor, Estelle, had kids that went to the same school as Noah. She usually drove them to school on Friday. Maybe, she could catch Estelle this morning before she left. "Please be home," Rita prayed as she dialed the phone.

"Oh, hi Estelle, glad I caught you...I was wondering..."

"You want me to pick-up Noah this morning?" Estelle asked before Rita could finish.

"Oh, could you? I'm not feeling well and..."

"No problem, we'll be leaving the apartment in about fifteen minutes. We'll meet you in front of your building."

"Thank you so much. You're a lifesaver," Rita said before the lists, the voices drowned out her ability to hear or think clearly. She hurried to help Noah get ready and out the door in time for his ride to school.

"Hi, Rita," Estelle greeted them when she arrived. "God, I mean no offense dear, but you look awful. Have you seen a doctor?"

"Not yet," Rita managed. "Thanks again for taking Noah this morning. I'm sure this will pass."

"PANEL, BOX, STAMP, CARD, STAPLE, KEY..."

"It's probably a twenty-four hour thing, you know," Rita added. She bent down to hug Noah goodbye. "I will see you after school, sweetie," she said softly.

Back in the building, the radio lists, no longer discernible words, blared loudly. Rita dialed Dr. Jordon. "I am not able to control what is happening!"

"How high is your fever?" the doctor inquired.

"I haven't taken my temperature in a few hours."

"Okay, take it and call me back. It sounds like fever delirium. It should pass as soon as the fever drops. Take some more Tylenol. Remember, every four hours. Drink plenty of cold fluids. If you're not feeling better by tomorrow, you'll have to come in."

Rita did not take her temperature or call Dr. Jordon back. She was too tired, too upset to do anything, except drink some cold water and crawl back into bed. Leaving enough space for air, she stuck her pillow over her head. She sang herself to sleep for twenty-minute intervals for the rest of the morning and into the early afternoon.

Resigned to the tumult, she managed to get through the weekend. She sent Noah to visit Joel. By Sunday night, the volume of the lists had subsided slightly like the doctor had predicted. Monday brought more relief. Rita stayed home from work again afraid she might appear insane if she had a bad relapse.

By mid-morning, Rita's fever was gone and the apartment was quiet. So quiet, that Rita decided to chance turning on the TV, but just then the phone rang. It was Irene. She was crying. Rita's heart jumped into her throat. "What's wrong?"

"It's Mom," Irene sobbed. "She had a heart attack...she's in the hospital."

"Oh, my God!" Rita started to cry too. It couldn't be. Mom's not old enough to die. She just retired. "Okay, I'll be on the next flight to Miami. Did you call Tina? How's Dad? What hospital?"

Rita wept while she scrambled to get her things together. She called Joel to make arrangements for Noah and the dog. She took a cab to the airport and prayed that the voices of lists would not return. She needed to see Lillian, help David.

By the time she got to the hospital, Lillian was being kept alive on a respirator. David could barely communicate with anyone except Tina. He was in shock. Rita kissed her mother and held her hand. She sat with her sisters and read to Lillian. David slept in a chair by her side for two days. Late into the third night while her family slept, Lillian slipped away.

Rita, Tina, and Irene made all the final arrangements. Rita kept her emotions under control. They spoke to the funeral director, called all of Lillian and David's friends, and checked with the cemetery. They comforted David, made food for him and took turns sitting with him as was the Jewish tradition. They packed Lillian's personal items away, leaving the things David wanted to keep close, taking mementos of remembrance for themselves.

It wasn't until Rita got back home that she could really cry. She cried with Noah and helped him understand what happens when someone dies. Rita had come to accept the possibility of life after death, even a place one could call heaven. "Grandma is in Heaven, a place that is so nice," She held Noah close.

Noah cried. He loved his Grandma even though he only got to see her every August. "Grandma's happy in Heaven and she can see you. You can say something to her any time you like." Rita reassured him. They lit a candle and Rita read him a story, one that Lillian had read to him on warm summer evenings when they had visited together in Vermont.

"Can I see Grandpa David?" Noah asked, wiping his tears.

"Yes, sweetie. He'll be up to visit soon and you can see Aunties Tina and Irene, Uncle Gregory and your cousins, too. We'll all get together like we do every summer. Grandma would like that. Would you like to talk to Grandpa David on the phone?" Noah brightened as Rita dialed the phone.

* * * * *

The apartment was quiet for a few weeks. No voices bothered Rita. She kept thinking about Toby's call to express her condolences. A phone call had been appropriate, though Rita waited for Toby to come see her. After all, Toby was the only one close to her who had known Lillian. Rita was still convinced that Toby would come back to her, even though Toby had made a promise to Kim to end their affair.

"I'm so sorry about your Mom," Andrea phoned Rita too. "How are you doing?"

"Thanks, Andrea. It's good to hear from you. I'm not doing great, but we're managing." Rita said. Andrea was the one in whom she could confide about feeling overwhelmed. Lillian's sudden death, long hours at work, single motherhood, the weird voices in her apartment that came and went, her cycles that had become longer with more blood loss, Susan's constant nagging about Noah not spending enough time with her—it was all too much. And then there was the unbearable waiting for Toby to return. Rita was sure it was just a matter of time.

Still, feelings of hopelessness made it a struggle to get out of bed in the morning. Vacillating between anxiety and depression, Rita pulled herself together each day to take care of Noah, her job, and the mundane chores of survival. She just put one foot in front of the other.

"I got laid off my part-time, evening job yesterday, so it's going to be a bit tight," she told Andrea. *Tight* was putting it mildly. While it had been hard making ends meet already, losing her supplemental income would mean further debt. Rita would not take money from Joel. Susan was a lost cause. Even if they would help, money would only make their relentless harassment for time and control over Noah more difficult.

"So sorry. Seems like when it rains it pours," Andrea offered.

"Yeah, on top of that something weird is happening in my place." Rita knew she had to get away. Getting out was the only way out. But how? she thought. Where would she get the money to leave, and how would Joel and Susan react? Where would she go? And how would Toby know where she was if she left?

"What's happening in your apartment?" Andrea's voice filled with concern.

Rita had begun to hear screaming late at night. Blood-curdling screams filled her ears. Like the endless radio lists that came and went, she could not discover the source of the screams. At first, they sounded like they were coming from Noah's room. But every time she would jump out of bed to check, he would be sleeping soundly.

As if that was not upsetting enough, on some days the windows were open when Rita came home from work, even though she had purposely closed them before leaving in the morning. Things would be disturbed in her closets, and she would have trouble finding things. In the evening, when she walked the dog for his last evening walk, odd things appeared to her on the dark street. Sometimes, she thought she was hallucinating. She trusted Andrea, sharing her stress.

"Maybe, someone's in your apartment when you're not there," Andrea suggested, alarmed at what Rita told her. "Does anyone else have a key?"

"Yes, Joel and Susan have keys, in case of emergency for Noah," said Rita. "But that would not explain it, would it?"

"Maybe it's haunted? You did say the apartment was lived in by a woman who died there, right?" offered Andrea. "I mean, it could happen."

"I don't know. I hope you don't think I'm totally nuts. I started to tell Joel, and he said I should see someone."

"That might be good advice," Andrea said. "Think about Noah. And stop thinking about Toby. You seem to be having enough problems without obsessing about her. I don't think she is coming back, Rita. You're just making yourself sick."

"Andrea, you don't understand. She loves me. She said it would just take some time." Rita was convinced that if Toby knew she was having trouble, if she knew how she needed to leave, get away from Susan, Joel and his know-it-all wife—she'd come. Toby had promised to come, take her and Noah away, make a life with them.

CHAPTER 28

Clara Doyle

MATT'S SALOON, FRANKLIN, OREGON, 1886

Clara sat at her vanity mirror, perfuming her neck and underarms, dabbing cake make-up on her cheeks. She carefully applied red rouge to her thinning lips along an invisible path remembered from the fullness of youth. She wiped off the excess, careful to have just enough—not too much or too little.

It was a balancing act that she had mastered, resigning herself to remaining at Matt's after her failed escape years ago. She shuddered at the remembrance of the strange old man, the four gruesome days of satisfying him and the other men, while she waited for Matt's return. Since then, she had learned to please her customers with only enough sensual stimulation to secure her room and board. Trying to hold onto the memory of innocence and purity for the possibility of Kyle's imminent return had become a tired delusion. Her fathomless hope had waned and shriveled like her thinning skin.

Walking a threadbare tightrope, Clara automatically adjusted her low-cut blouse. She eyed her sagging cleavage in the mirror and pulled her breasts up higher in her corset, one at a time. "I'm ready, now," she said aloud to her reflection.

Matt unloaded the last wooden beer keg from the wagon and hauled it into the saloon. Sam was already hoisting last night's empty keg from its stand on the counter at the end of the bar.

"Stacy starts tonight, Sam." Matt grunted and lifted the keg in place. "You'll be havin' that talk with Clara, like we said, won't ya? Wouldn't be right for the old gal to find out from the others." Matt looked directly at Sam. "You best be doin' it first thing this mornin'."

Sam grumbled. He didn't want the job, even though he knew it was his responsibility. He'd been the one who had taken Clara in, coming close to falling for her once upon a time.

"Look, Sam," Matt resumed, "no one wants her old bones no more. Besides, she can still keep the girls in line. No harm keepin' her on for that job and lettin' her hold onto the room. You'll see, brother, she won't take it so hard," Matt said reassuringly.

"I'm not much good at talkin'," Sam protested.

Matt gave Sam a stern look.

"Okay, okay," Sam responded. Wiping the bar down and setting the liquor bottles and glasses in order, Sam momentarily distracted himself from the impending, disagreeable task. It wasn't long before he heard the girls upstairs beginning their morning routine.

Clara appeared on the balcony overlooking the saloon. She was the first one, as usual, to be ready on Monday morning after the girls' night off. She eyed Matt and Sam talking at the bar as she came down the stairs. "Good morning there, boys," Clara said loudly. "The beer shipment in already? It's goin' to be busy soon with them railroad boys from Eugene and Junction City coming though."

"Morning, Miss Clara," Matt cleared his throat. "Yep, we're getting an early start." He didn't look directly at Clara. Matt walked past Sam, gave him a knowing glance and patted him on the shoulder. He headed toward the storeroom without another word.

Clara noticed Matt's attitude and abrupt departure. "What's wrong with Matt?" she asked Sam.

"Uh, nothin'," said Sam. "I guess he got a lot on his mind, is all."

Clara suddenly felt uneasy. The hair bristled on the back of her neck.

"Look," Sam began, "it's like this, Miss Clara. Now, don't take me wrong. I'm just goin' to say this plain and simple." Sam paused, his dark eyes looking at Clara's tense face. "We need to have some new girls here. We got a new one named Stacy, comin' in tonight."

Clara's eyes widened, pupils dilating into deep green. Her mouth felt cotton dry. Her throat tensed. "What are you saying, Sam?" Clara's voice cracked.

"I'm just sayin' we hired a new girl. We need you to keep an eye on the girls, now—kinda keep 'em in line and make sure the customers get what they come for, that's all." Sam picked up his counter rag and began wiping the bar again. He spoke without looking up at Clara. "Ain't gonna be all that different. You can take a rest from nights, is all...if you know what I mean."

For a moment, all Clara was aware of was the sudden pounding of her heart. She looked directly at Sam. "You think I'm all used up? Too old? Think the boys don't want me no more?" Clara yelled.

Sam shrugged. "It's just business, Clara. Just business."

Clara spun around, stomped briskly up the stairs and back into her room, slamming the door behind her. She sat down hard at her vanity. Burning tears streamed down her face making pale tracks on her painted cheeks. She buried her face in her hands and sobbed. "All these years," she cried. The years of trying to make this place her home, trying to run away, waiting and hoping it would all come to an end. She had never imagined she would be tossed out and replaced by a young girl—a girl just like she had once been. She had never really imagined growing old here.

Sam shrugged. Distracted by doubt, he picked up a broom and swept the floor. What else could he have said?

"How'd it go?" Matt's voice interrupted Sam's thoughts.

"Don't know. She ain't happy about it, that's for sure." Sam propped the broom against the wall and walked to the saloon doors. "I need some air," he mumbled.

Matt climbed the stairs and knocked gently on Clara's door. "Clara, Clara, you there?"

Clara wiped her eyes roughly with the hem of her blouse and smoothed her graying hair. She opened her door to see Matt standing with his hat in his hands.

"You all right?" Matt asked sheepishly.

"I'm fine. I'll keep the girls in line—do my job, Matt," Clara replied with no emotion.

"You can keep the room, Clara, no charge. You can stay here as long as it suits you. We won't never put you out, you hear? " Matt stood up straighter.

Clara could not look him in the eyes. She nodded. "Thank you, Matt."

"Okay, then. We got a deal. Now you get yourself cleaned up and help the girls get that extra room ready."

Clara nodded again and closed her door. She heard Matt's footsteps going downstairs. Clara felt a wave of exhaustion. She lay down on her bed and covered herself with her knitted shawl, the pain in her chest rising. "Kyle," she whispered, "where are you?"

Clara drifted in and out of a fitful sleep. She dreamed she was combing an old woman's hair, braiding long silver strands in neat, even sections. The woman sang a lullaby in a foreign language, but Clara could feel the sweet sadness in her voice.

A loud knocking woke Clara with a start. "Clara? Clara?" It was Matt. Clara sat up in bed trying to get her bearings.

"Just a minute!" she yelled and got out of bed. She straightened her dress and opened the door.

"This here is Stacy," Matt said.

A thin, pale young woman with blue eyes and wisps of straw-colored hair cascading from beneath her hat stood behind him. She wore a light green summer dress. Under her small bosom, a wide sash highlighted her narrow waist.

"Mind showin' her to her room, Clara?" Matt looked displeased.

"Oh, why yes. I must have dozed off," Clara apologized. "Nice to meet you, dear. Come this way." Clara took Stacy's small bag from Matt. "Please excuse me, I wasn't feeling so well. I meant to be ready for you when you came. How was your trip? Where did you say you were from?" Clara walked Stacy to her room.

"I'm from Portland, ma'am. I worked at Sweet Jane's on the river before I—" Stacy stopped in mid-sentence. "I had no place to go after what happened. Mr. Matt found me when he was traveling up the river last month and asked did I want to come work for him."

"Well, Matt's a good man and he treats his girls right," said Clara. "What happened to you up there, honey? Someone hurt you?" Clara felt a twinge of protectiveness. Stacy was just a kid, barely eighteen—skinny, with bruise marks on her arms. "We're gonna have to feed you, first thing," she said, starting to help Stacy unpack her small bag.

"I had some troubles, but it wasn't until an old gentleman, Mr. Doyle, came through town that things got really hard for me," Stacy confided, not looking up at Clara.

Clara stopped breathing, frozen to the spot where she stood. The room began to spin. She grabbed the edge of the bed frame to steady herself. Unable to speak, she endured Stacy's flood of words.

"I was so scared after my brother died and left me alone," Stacy went on, removing each stocking while she talked. "I went to stay with my aunt at her small boarding house, when Mr. Doyle came one day inquiring about a room." Stacy took off her remaining garments and put on her worn robe. "He said he was traveling up the coast on business. He seemed like a nice older gentleman, well-dressed and polite." She glanced up wistfully. "He made me feel very special." She paused, not taking notice of Clara. "After a few days he was supposed to leave, and well, I had become so fond of him—I asked if he might take me along. So he agreed." Stacy rummaged through her belongings looking for her comb. "My aunt was not pleased by my decision, though, 'cause she thought he was a gambler, old enough to be my father," Stacy rambled. "But he made me laugh. And he was gentle, always touching my face and kissing my forehead."

Clara's stomach lurched. Her whole body began to quake inside.

"He brought me to Sweet Jane's and we got a lovely room there," Stacy continued, unaware of Clara's reaction. "He was very patient with me and gentle. But after a few days, after I had given myself to him fully," Stacy emphasized, "he left! He told Madam Jane he had to get back to his wife and son—paid for my room for a whole month.

I was so distraught, I thought I might as well die. But Miss Jane, she filled me with liquor and comforted me." Stacy sighed. "Other men wanted my affections too, but they were cold and rough. So, I ran away." Stacy paused again. "I couldn't go back to my aunt after what I'd done. That's when Mr. Matt found me and offered me a job here," Stacy said smiling, slightly. Done with her story, she took her towel in hand. "May I wash up now, Miss Clara?" she asked, finally acknowledging Clara's presence.

Clara did not answer. She just stared into space.

"Miss Clara?" Stacy said, louder this time. "Can I use the tub now?"

Clara came through the fog long enough to point to the washroom down the hall. Stacy walked out of her room, leaving Clara rooted where she stood. Suddenly, Clara felt all the air in the room rush into her breathless lungs. Her delayed gasp reverberated in her ears. She began to salivate. The gaslight flickered, darkening the already dimly lit room. Clara's legs moved under her. Before she could slam the bedroom door, she vomited all over the floor.

CHAPTER 29

Rita Kerner

BOSTON, MASSACHUSETTS, 1986

The day was still sunny and mild when Rita left her new day job at Filene's Basement. She had enough time to stop at a near-by coffee shop for a cup of coffee before picking up Noah at his after-school program. Joel would be coming over, since he usually watched Noah when she went to her evening job on Tuesdays. "Oh, damn!" Rita suddenly realized she had not called him to cancel his visit. She looked at her watch. "I might be able to catch him," she said to herself.

Arriving at the coffee shop, she made a beeline to the pay phone, a quarter in hand. She dialed Joel's number.

"Hello," Joel's voice sounded harried.

"Hi, it's me, Rita," she said. "I don't…"

"I am running a little late, but I should be there very close to six," Joel interrupted.

"It's okay, slow down" said Rita. "I've been laid off my evening job, so I don't have to go anywhere tonight."

"Oh," replied Joel. There was an awkward pause. "Well, I'll come anyway. I want to see Noah, and I did want to talk to you about something, too."

"Okay, I guess. I am not feeling in much of a visiting mood. And there is no extra food," Rita tried to discourage him.

"We can go out. Noah likes to eat out. Melanie's Diner is just up the street. The Chinese take-out place is also okay. We do that sometimes,

210

anyway. You can join us if you want. But I don't want to talk in front of Noah."

Rita let Joel's condescending tone and comment go by. Eating out was a luxury she couldn't afford, especially now. "Yeah, okay, we'll see," she said. "See you later, then. I am out of change. I gotta go." Rita hung up and sat down at the counter. What was it he wanted to talk to her about? she thought.

Rita didn't like Joel's attitude of late. Ever since he had married Ms. High and Mighty, Dr. Karen Know-It-All, he had changed, become so disrespectful. He and Karen and Susan had become so demanding of time with Noah, the poor kid was exhausted from going from one place to another. Rita sighed. It was too hard. She was sorry she had ever used Joel to have a child. Bad mistake. Rita shook her head. She ordered a cup of decaf and tried to relax.

Later that evening, after Chinese take-out dinner, Rita suggested Noah finish his homework and get ready for bed. "I'm tired too, so let's call it a night," Rita said to Joel, attempting to maintain control of her life and get Joel to leave. "Noah, honey, get into your pajamas, brush your teeth. You can read the homework chapter for tomorrow in bed. I'll be there in a few minutes." Rita's voice was calm, but firm. "It's time to say goodbye to Joel now," she instructed.

Joel looked annoyed. Noah gave Joel a goodbye hug and went into his room without a fuss.

"Let's talk in the kitchen," Rita's tone cooled. "What is it you wanted to talk to me about, anyway?"

"Look, Rita—I want to know, what the hell is going on with you? Andrea called me. She's worried about you. Says you told her you were hearing voices in the apartment? You look a mess, too. Exhausted. Even Noah says you're acting strangely, not paying attention to things." Joel raised his voice. "And I had a dream last night," he continued. "It woke me up. I fell back asleep and the dream repeated, woke me up again. People in the dream said to tell you not to do something—but I don't know what."

Rita turned around, wide-eyed. Now he had her attention.

"They said you would know if I told you. How is it possible for this to be happening? What are you doing? What are you planning?" Joel was angry.

"I'm not planning anything," Rita said defensively. "And don't raise your voice at me. I'm not responsible for your dreams, and I'm sorry you are being disturbed."

Rita was startled, appalled by this turn of events, as well as Joel's accusations. She tried not to show it. What was going on? she thought. How did this happen?

"Look Joel, I'm going through a rough time now, so lay off."

"You ought to see someone, a shrink. You need to get some damn help," Joel retorted.

"I do not have money for a therapist, even if it would be something I'd consider. Besides, it's none of your damn business."

"You think it isn't? That's where you're wrong. Maybe, Noah should come stay with me and Karen until you get over your problems or stop whatever weirdness you're getting into," Joel threatened.

"I think you'd better leave now." Rita demanded, careful not to raise her voice. If she were younger, bigger, stronger, or a man, she'd physically throw him out. Rita kept her composure though, knowing any sign of hysteria would add fuel to the fire, give him further cause to threaten her. Were Joel and his new wife just waiting for any sign that she was crazy? she thought. Was it their underlying prejudice about her being a lesbian? What weirdness was he talking about? Did they think she was practicing some kind of witchcraft and had the power to influence other people's dreams?

"Please go," Rita said again, more softly. "We can talk about all this another time. I have to get up early. I have an employees' meeting at work early in the morning. And Noah has to go to sleep now."

Joel put on his jacket, took his briefcase, and walked to the front door. "Look, just go see someone," he said as he left.

Rita locked the door behind him immediately. It crossed her mind that maybe she needed to change the lock. Too bad she didn't have some magic powers like that *Oz* character, the good witch of the North.

"Poof, be gone!" she mimicked.

But this was serious. What had happened to Joel? Rita thought. He'd become so vindictive and paranoid since his relationship with that doctor. Goddamn dreams! "Damn them for talking to him in a dream," she muttered under her breath. She looked up as if someone were hovering above her. "Talk to me, damn it! Talk directly to me! In sentences, not lists of words! Tell me what the hell is going on, for God's sake!"

"Mommy?" Noah was standing in the hall in his pajamas. Skippy sat next to him. He looked at Rita, alone in the foyer by the closed front door. "Who are you talking to, Mommy?" he asked.

"Oh, sweetie!" Rita felt ashamed. "I'm just talking to myself. It's nothing important." She saw Noah's worried look. Rita wondered if Joel's attitude had affected Noah. "Don't worry, honey." She hurried to comfort him, explain away his confusion. "I was just trying to remember something. It's nothing. C'mon, let's go read that chapter together. Did you brush your teeth?"

Rita tucked Noah into bed and sat beside him as they read aloud. Skippy curled up at the foot of the bed. When they finished reading, Rita kissed Noah goodnight. She gave him a hug feeling the softness of her child's cheek. "I love you, honey. *Gey schluffen,* sleep well," she said.

"Good night, Mommy. Are you going to sleep now, too?"

"Yes, love. I think we all need a good night's sleep. Skippy can sleep with you, okay?"

Noah smiled, rolled over and hugged the dog. Then he fell asleep quickly.

Rita went into the bathroom, undressed, washed and got into her flannel pajamas. She looked at her weary face in the mirror. Brown eyes with dark circles underneath in a pale olive-skinned face stared back. Her once shiny hair hung dull and lifeless. Rita felt as exhausted as she looked. She crawled into her own bed leaving the night light on in the hall bathroom. She fell asleep quickly, too.

In a sound sleep, Rita dreamed of herself walking down a path to a cottage in what appeared to be an Irish countryside, long ago. Inside, there were people having a party. They were all in costumes. The outfits were all so different, she noticed. There was a Native American chief, a pale buxom waitress, a red-headed woman dressed in fine linen, a dark-skinned man in uniform, and a handsome young fellow with a cowboy hat and boots. She saw a young musician with sheet music, a gray-haired white woman in a long skirt and shawl, an old black man and woman in their Sunday best, and a finely dressed dark-haired gentleman with a gold watch and chain.

In her dream, Rita was eager to join the party, but the people eluded her. They seemed to float above her. Rita kept trying to jump up and join them, but to no avail. Then one of them spoke to her. "You cannot join us. You must stay where you are until it is time, until you have learned..." But when Rita awoke, she could not remember what it was she was supposed to learn. She lay awake for a while trying to piece the dream together. Then she fell back asleep.

When the screams began later that night, she awoke again with a start, her heart pounding. She ran to Noah's room, but found him sleeping soundly like always. Skippy picked up his head and looked at Rita, but did not get up. Rita walked slowly back to her bedroom.

"Enough!" she said to herself. She turned on the overhead light and the lamp on the night table, turning her room from night to day. She took off her pajamas, took a quick shower and dressed in the clothes she had ironed for work. Walking to the hall closet, she pulled out one large suitcase for her belongings, a medium-sized one for Noah's.

"We're done here," she whispered. "It's time to go."

She would not announce her decision to anyone. They would be gone before anyone could stop them or, for that matter, know where they were. They would simply leave. She would take what they needed and head out at dawn.

What Rita did not plan for was the decision Joel and Karen had made that evening after Joel arrived home from dinner with Noah. Phone calls had been made, and wheels put in motion by fear were already turning.

Rita would not get very far. She did not have enough money or energy to go farther than New Jersey. After 24 hours on the run, she returned to Boston. She asked Susan to watch Noah for the weekend and boarded the dog. Then she went to find help. She couldn't remember having slept or eaten.

* * * * *

Joel picked up his phone after two rings.

"Hello, I'm looking for Joel Peterson," a woman's voice said.

"This is Joel Peterson. Whose calling, please?"

"This is Massachusetts General Hospital. A Ms. Kerner listed you as her emergency number."

"What's wrong? Is she okay? Is there a child with her?"

"Well, no, no child. We don't know if she is okay. She was here for an evaluation with Dr. Wagner, but she left before we could treat her. Might you know where she is? The doctor was concerned with her condition."

"What was her condition?"

"I'm sorry we are not at liberty to say, but since you are listed as the emergency person, we just thought you should know that she's left. Perhaps you could encourage her to return or seek some further assistance."

"I see…thank you. What did you say your name was?"

"This is Mrs. Frank, Adele Frank. I'm a social worker here. I did her intake. She was evaluated by Dr. Wilhelm Wagner, our head psychiatrist."

"Well, thank you. I will see to it she gets some help. She's been going through a rough patch."

Joel hung up and walked to his desk. He took some papers from the desk drawer and signed them. Then he dialed his lawyer's number. "Hello, Ms. Noland. I have decided to go ahead with the restraining order and emergency custody papers we spoke about yesterday. Do you have any time first thing tomorrow morning? I know it's Sunday, but it's quite an immediate situation—an emergency."

CHAPTER 30

Wambleeska (White Eagle)

SOUTH DAKOTA, GREAT PLAINS, 1832; 1842-43

"In the beginning, the Gods resided in the sky, in the stars. The humans lived in a world inside the earth." Matoskah, Wambleeska's uncle, spoke slowly and deliberately, repeating the story he had told many times, for as long as he could remember.

"The chief Gods were Takushkanshkan, the Sun, his wife, Moon and Wohpe (Falling Star), their daughter. There was Old Man and Old Woman whose daughter, Ite, was married to Wind. Ite and Wind had four sons, the Four Winds. There was also Inktomi, the devious spider trickster.

"One day," Matoskah continued, "Inktomi convinced Old Man and Old Woman that they could raise their daughter's status by arranging an affair between Sun and Ite. Takushkanshkan punished Sun by separating him from his wife, Moon and so created Time." Matoskah's eyes grew wider.

"Soon, Old Man, Old Woman, and daughter Ite were sent down to earth. When Ite and her husband Wind were apart, he and their sons, the Four Winds, with the help of Wamniomni (Whirlwind), created Space. Then Wohpe also fell to earth.

Alone on the newly formed Earth, Ite asked Inktomi to find the people she called the Buffalo Nation. In the form of a wolf, Inktomi traveled beneath the earth and discovered a village of humans. Inktomi told them about the wonders of the earth and convinced one man, Tokahe, to accompany him to the surface. Tokahe came up to the earth's surface through a cave—the Wind Cave—in the Black Hills, Paha Sapa. He looked with wide eyes at the green grass and blue sky. Inktomi and Ite introduced Tokahe to buffalo meat and soup, showed him tipis, clothing, and hunting tools. Then Tokahe returned to the village beneath the earth. He invited other families to travel with him to the earth's surface."

Matoskah's arms pointed up as he spoke, his voice growing louder.

"When they arrived, they discovered that Inktomi had deceived them. The buffalo were scarce, the weather had turned bad, and they were soon hungry.

Suddenly, Wohpe appeared to the first people as a real woman, dressed in white buffalo skins. She was discovered by two warriors who were hunting for buffalo. One of them wanted to make her his wife. He did not respect her or understand who she was. As he came close to her, he was covered by a mist and reduced to bones. The other hunter was instructed to return and tell the people that she, White Buffalo Calf Woman, would appear to them the next day. He obeyed. He knew she was a sacred being to be respected. White Buffalo Calf Woman came and presented the people with a bundle containing the sacred pipe. 'In time of need,' she said, 'smoke from the pipe and pray to Wakantanka, Great Spirit, for help. The smoke from the pipe will carry your prayers upward. That is when she gave the seven sacred rites of our people." Matoskah took the red clay pipe from his brother, sharing the smoke with him.

The youngsters sat listening attentively to every detail of the creation story as the old man gestured, his arms drawing circles in the air. The smoldering embers of the fire illuminated his animated facial expressions. Kimimela's eyes grew wide as she listened to her great uncle. She glanced toward her mother, Dowanhowee, and her grandmother, Takchawee, every now and then, to see if they, too, were listening to the story. It was a story they had each heard since their own childhood, like their ancestors, for generations.

Kimimela did not tire from the listening and could have stayed up all night with the elders, but soon the big day was coming. The preparation for the anticipated Sun Dance and honoring ceremony, and the gathering of many families of the Oceti Sakowin, Seven Council Fires. There would be so much to do. Sleep was needed now for everyone. But Kimimela was thinking about other things. She turned around and maneuvered close to the matriarchs as the others prepared to leave the tipi for their own.

"How long will it be until I am a woman, mother?" Kimimela asked quietly.

Takchawee stroked her granddaughter's head and sighed. "You want to grow up so fast?"

"One or two more springs and you will be like a flower blossoming in the warm sun, my pretty daughter," said Dowanhowee.

She turned to Takchawee. "I had hoped my own mother might have survived to see my daughter's coming of womanhood ceremony. I am so glad to have you as my mother now, my family." Dowanhowee said warmly.

"Come now, Kimimela," Takchawee whispered. "Time to rest. Before you know it, you will be singing your own children to sleep. Do not hurry to grow. This is your time to be young."

* * * * *

Grandmother had been right. Now, ten years later, Kimimela prepared her own first son's mats and blankets, tucking her young child under the warm furs for a night's sleep. She sang her ancient lullabies to him, remembering all the stories and songs she had heard as a child, sitting by the fire with her own mother, father, grandmother, elders. It was comforting to her, especially this evening. She could bury her fear and sorrow in the memories. Her husband had been killed in battle not long ago. Kimimela still grieved, while her mother and father seemed more distressed than ever before.

War between their enemies had increased. They felt an ever-present danger now—their hunting grounds depleted, buffalo slaughtered by the soldiers, fierce fighting between nations, and impending surrender to the white man's settlements. The families spoke of devastating illness and war more with each passing season. They spoke of the white man breaking treaties for good, of their people losing everything they held sacred.

Kimimela lay close to her son, singing softly and watching his young sweet face, as his breathing slowed into a deep and peaceful rhythm. She choked back tears, thinking of the harm that might come to him in the years ahead.

Her father, Wambleeska, knew his daughter's fears. His visions had become more vivid with the passing years. As his resolve to fight his enemies wavered, so did his status as a leader. He had grown tired of conflict with the tribal elders and his wife. They did not share his views, or his decisions. He no longer trusted the treaties with white men who did not honor them, nor respect their great nation. While the answer of his people was to fight encroachment and broken promises, Wambleeska did not want to fight, either. He no longer sought out the wisdom of others about his dream and visions, because he saw no hope.

Not long ago, he had gone up to the high ridge above the camp where the view of the setting sun along the far hills cast a shadow across the valley. He'd let the reins of his horse drop, and sat in prayer to the Great Spirit for a long time before the visions appeared. He had been having such visions since he was a young boy, running along the waterfall's edge in the forest of his youth.

Now, in his mind's eye he saw the sacred Paha Sapa dismembered by white men greedy for gold metal. He saw the rivers and lakes, near and far, filled with black, thick, oily water destroying plants and birds, poisoning wolf, deer, beaver, bear, all the four-legged ones. Nowhere were there buffalo. The sky was dark and blood flowed from peoples' eyes and ears. He saw his people sick, dying, walking in long lines, cold and hungry, too ill to save themselves. He saw his family torn away from their sacred lands and stripped of their traditions. Hundreds of parched women and children waited for water, for food. His elders downed white man's medicine, ripping memory and language from them. In another vision, Wambleeska saw trees torn from the earth, whole forests cut down and dragged away by snorting, smoke-belching monsters. He smelled putrid air, his throat choked by pungent smoke from structures that towered up to the sky, the sky itself ablaze. Fish lay dead along the shores in great numbers. Mountains rumbled and spat great waves of fire. The whole of mother earth wailed, bucked, and split apart, water rushing into all the lands.

Sharp pain tore Wambleeska from his vision. He felt his heart being ripped from his body. Wambleeska trembled, watching the sun set behind the ridge, replaced by a turquoise twilight blanketing the landscape. A sliver of moonlight shone down on him. The air cooled. His horse, sensing his fear, shifted her position and headed home. Wambleeska did not need to use the rope reins, trusting his horse to take him back to his family. But, he would not know how to tell them what he'd seen. He could barely comprehend it all himself. How could he describe the death of their Mother Earth? Who would do such a thing to the Great Spirit's gift, the source of all life? No one would believe him. There were no words to make such visions understood.

That night, Wambleeska lay awake next to his wife, unable to sleep. Dowanhowee felt his uneasiness. She knew his quiet repose was not normal, as his night breathing was usually amplified by low snoring sounds.

"What is it?" Dowanhowee whispered. "What's troubling you that you don't sleep, husband? Are you sick?"

"I've had troubling visions," Wambleeska replied. He didn't want to say more.

"What have you seen?" Dowanhowee asked.

"I cannot say…I have no words for the visions. We must leave this land or we will be captives."

"Leave? What do you mean? Where will we go?" Dowanhowee raised her head, alarmed. "We are already fighting for land, for food. Haven't we been pushed far enough? I think you do not want to fight the white skins, isn't that so?" Dowanhowee had a tone of disappointment in her voice.

"I don't wish to talk now. You are a stubborn old woman. We have been talking with Wachinksapa about our disagreements, as man and wife for much time. You are displeased with me, like the others? You believe I am weak, a poor warrior, because I see things differently? I see that our people cannot win no matter how hard we fight, no matter how brave we are, no matter how many we kill. They have already killed so many. One day they will come and take our sacred land, our way of life." Wambleeska turned away from his wife. "I am going to sleep now."

Dowanhowee lay awake for a time. So much time had passed, so much had changed. Had her love for him changed because of the pressure of others? Her husband's stature as a warrior had been lost over the years. Since the death of their daughter's husband in a skirmish Wambleeska had reluctantly led, after enemies encroached on their land, stealing horses, Wambleeska seemed to have lost so much of himself, too. Now, his visions distracted him.

Lately, his jealousy of Kangee, a man Dowanhowee admired, had become a regular source of tension, as well. There was no reason for it, though. Kangee had always been respectful and his attention seemed innocent, like a friend who understood her disappointment. Wasn't he just being kind? Dowanhowee took a deep breath and tried to relax, so she could sleep.

The next morning when she awoke, Wambleeska was dressed and leaving their tipi. "I have decided to take some supplies and go meet our relations, our friends to the west and south. I will go alone and come back for you, our *Tiopaye*—our family. The others can decide if they will make camp further west, when I return." He finished gathering what he'd need for his journey. "We must leave, join others. I hope you will trust my visions, Dowanhowee. I am certain this is the only way out of danger. We are outnumbered by white men who will stop at nothing to destroy us and the land itself. If we go, there may be a chance we can survive.

Wambleeska came close and held Dowanhowee in his arms for the first time in a long time. "I will come back for you, soon," he said. "Wait here for me. You are my family and I will protect you." Wambleeska leaned to kiss his beloved wife.

She kissed him, her heart aching for him, for his unrest, his confusion. How could he leave on such a dangerous path alone? She would wait, though.

As days turned to weeks, she worried. Soon the season changed. The women of her family comforted her, but alone at night she cried. She spoke to Great Spirit and waited. Kangee comforted her too. He and the others encouraged her to forget. "Wambleeska will never return," they said.

The following spring, she married Kangee. But by then, the tribal elders had decided they were too few in number to fight the white soldiers and the government's relocation plans alone. They would have to move farther west and south to join larger, stronger tribes, members of the Oglala nation. Wambleeska had been right, after all.

Heart-break over the loss of Wambleeska had taken a toll on Dowanhowee's health. She was suffering with chills and fever as they left. Her daughter and the other women helped her walk. Loaded down with their tipis and belongings on a journey along ancient trading routes, they traveled. Soon Dowanhowee was too ill to walk, so Kangee held her on his horse. For three days their small band of women, children and old men walked, stopping to camp at night. Dowanhowee's fever grew worse.

"I am so thirsty," she whispered. Kangee soothed her. Kimimela held her mother's head up to drink cool water. "I will die in our new land," she said, looking up at her daughter's sad face. As she closed her eyes, a last tear slipped down her burning cheek.

CHAPTER 31

Rita Kerner

OUTSKIRTS OF NEWPORT, RHODE ISLAND, 1988

"You're not going to put up lights and decorate outside too, are you?" Noah complained. He looked at the gifts for their new neighbors and his teacher stacked on the coffee table. Rita had wrapped the gifts in shiny red and green paper.

"No, I wasn't planning on it," Rita replied.

"Why do we have to give people Christmas presents? Our neighbors don't give us Chanukah presents," Noah reasoned.

Rita looked at the tree and presents she bought to assimilate in this new land of Rhode Island. Maybe this was a bad idea. Noah had been through enough, lost enough—his grandmother Lillian, the break-up with Susan, the stress of the custody battle with Joel, her own problems coping. She had tried to protect him, keep him safe. Except for a short time, she had been able to keep him with her. But she'd had to surrender to joint custody. The last two years had been hard on both of them.

Rita blamed herself. But she knew, in spite of everything, finding a better place to live and getting a new start was the best thing she had done. She had stuck to her plan, negotiating it into the custody decision. But it had taken a while to finally move to Rhode Island.

Because the move was still new, maybe now was not a good time to ignore their traditional holidays, Rita realized. She decided to pick up some Chanukah decorations, wrap all Noah's gifts in Chanukah paper. She would hang the Chanukah cards that they received, put the Christmas cards away, take down the small tree.

For so many years, the idea of a Christmas tree had been objectionable to Rita, as well. The only time her family had ever had a tree, she was ten. Irene had whined so much, her parents reluctantly got one. Poor Grandmother Pearl stayed in her room for days, refusing to come out until it was gone. Rita tried to comfort her to no avail. She didn't know that for Pearl, the Christmas tree was a symbol of death—a memory of the tzar's soldiers inciting the Christain populace to kill the Jews, her family.

Then, came those little Christmas excursions to Christian households in their new neighborhood in Queens. Lillian made her and Irene visit people who didn't want their presents, and who didn't have any presents for them.

* * * * *

"Oy gevalt! A shandeh un a charpeh!"—Oh, such sorrow! A shame and a disgrace! *"Oy Vey, Goyem!"* Grandmother Pearl said, shaking her head as Rita's mother instructed Rita and Irene.

"Girls, take this cake to the O'Briens," Lillian said proudly, placing some plastic wrap over the angel food cake she made using a *Betty Crocker* recipe. "They don't know about Chanukah, so say 'Have a nice Christmas' when you give it to them. Don't forget and be polite."

* * * * *

When the memories faded, Rita set the menorah on the mantle placing a white Shamas candle in the center and picking a blue candle for the first night. She laid the rest of the box of candles beside the shiny brass menorah in readiness.

"Are we going to light the candles and make potato pancakes, Mom?" Noah walked over to Rita.

"Of course, Noah, honey. Come here, sweetie." Noah sat down on the sofa with Rita.

"I want to explain why it can be hard for Jewish people when

Christmas comes," she began. "There's a word, *as-sim-i-la-tion*—it means when people who are in a minority, fewer in number like us, try to fit into the society that has many more people, like those who are Christian. Sometimes the 'fitting in' is confusing, sometimes it makes no sense." She paused. "Sometimes the minority are not welcome. Remember when you were a little boy and you thought the streets were decorated in lights for Chanukah, not Christmas?"

"I hate holidays," Noah said. He got up and walked back to his room. Turning on the Saturday morning cartoons, he tuned out.

Rita sighed. "Yeah, I know what you mean." Rita hated them when she was his age too.

* * * * *

"Oh! Look at those blisters." Lillian was shaking her head in disgust.

"Is it my fault I can't walk in these stupid, white patent-leather shoes? I hate this stupid hat," Rita complained loudly, picking at the elastic band under her chin, attached to the strange flowered bonnet on her head. "Who asked us to come to Washington for Easter? Not me. I don't even know what Easter is. Grandmother said it's a *goyish* holiday. You said she couldn't come with us." Rita whined. "I want to go home and hear the story of Passover about Moses and the Red Sea." She looked at her father. "Why do we have to go all the way to the White House to roll the President's eggs on his lawn? Mom said you voted for a different president." Rita grumbled. "I want to eat hard-boiled eggs for Passover with Grandma."

"Listen here, young lady!" Lillian's tone was sharp-edged. "Your father worked many extra hours and saved so we could have our first family vacation—come to visit this beautiful city. It is the capital of our country. You picked out those shoes, so I don't want to hear any more complaining, understand? If we see a store, we'll get some band-aids."

* * * * *

Funny the things one remembers, Rita thought. She walked into the kitchen to make a mental note of what she needed to buy for *latkes,* potato pancakes.

"Noah!" she called. "I'm going out to the market. Do you want to go with me?"

"No, Mom. But could you get me some batteries, double A, okay?"

"No problem. I'll be back in about an hour. Don't forget to take the dog out." Rita walked to Noah's door to make sure he heard her. Chores and selective hearing went hand and hand for her preteen.

Outside a light snow had begun to fall. Oh, just great! A white Christmas, too! Rita thought it was ironic. It was hard to avoid a picture postcard Christmas in New England. It was also hard to avoid the Christmas music in all the stores. She scoured shelves for Chanukah paper, cards, dreidels, chocolate *gelt,* coins—finding only some of what she wanted while recordings of "Silent Night" and "Joy to the World" filtered through the store's sound system.

Finally, Rita got to the market for the potatoes, onions, eggs, sour cream, applesauce, and matzo meal. It was not Chanukah until the potato pancakes were frying in the pan. The thought always brought back memories of Grandma Pearl standing over the stove, frying the potato pancakes in chicken fat. The delicious, sweet smell filled the whole house, warming every chilly corner with heat and security.

Rita piled the groceries, batteries, and decorations in the car. She drove home to their one-bedroom apartment in a quaint old house, just outside of town. As she pulled up to the house, Noah came outside.

"Ma, someone from work is on the phone for you." Noah had come outside only in sweatpants and a sweatshirt. "Did you get the batteries, Ma?"

Rita pointed to the bag with his batteries. "Hurry, let's get inside. You'll catch a cold without a jacket."

Rita put down a bag of groceries on the kitchen table and picked up the phone receiver. "Hello? Oh, hi Tom! How are you?" Rita was surprised her boss was calling her. The shop was supposed to be closed on Monday for the holiday. Rita had taken a few extra vacation days afterward, since Noah's school was out for Christmas break. "Is anything wrong?" Rita asked, praying there'd be no change in her schedule.

"I know that this is going to sound strange, but I'm calling you because, well…" Tom paused. "Because of a dream I had last night. I can't put it out of my mind." Tom's voice trailed off.

"A dream?" Rita tensed.

"Yes, a bizarre dream. This is so weird. I'm pretty uncomfortable about it. Has this ever happened to you? Because it has never happened to me before. I'm supposed to give you, well, a message. Please tell me this makes sense to you or I'll feel pretty stupid," Tom said.

Shit! Rita thought. "It's okay, Tom," Rita said as calmly as she could. She couldn't believe this was happening again. Damn! She thought she had gotten away from all this. She was trying so hard. Why couldn't they just talk to her, instead of everyone else! "I'm really sorry, Tom. Yes, it has happened on occasion," she tried to sound nonchalant. "What was the dream?"

"Well, this guy comes to see me at work and he is really dressed funny. I mean, he's got on a purple velvet jacket covered with all these colored buttons and an odd hat. He tells me that he has a message for Rita, for you. He says that I must warn you of something that is going to happen. He didn't say what, but just for you to be careful."

"Oh," Rita said, not quite knowing how to respond. What the hell was going to happen now? she thought. "Well, thanks Tom, I think. I'll try to be careful."

"Do you have any idea what it is about?" Tom asked.

Rita knew he deserved an answer. After all, the dream had disturbed his sleep and clearly set him on edge. But she didn't know what to say. The only thing Rita could think of was her concern about her old car. It was in need of repair. Rita had been worrying about the added distance she would have to travel, since Joel had changed the planned meeting point to pick-up Noah for his holiday visit. That couldn't be it, she thought.

"Not really, Tom, except my car does need some repairs. Guess I'll have to have it looked at. Hey, I do appreciate you telling me, though." She liked him. The job he had given her had saved her life—allowed her to move here with Noah.

"I'm sure everything will be fine," Rita reassured him. "And don't worry. People usually don't have more than one dream about me." She laughed, trying to lighten the load for Tom's sake. And save her job.

The idea of meeting Joel much farther from their original planned designation had been worrying Rita. Their hostile history left her feeling vulnerable, even a hundred miles away. They were between battles temporarily. For Noah's sake, she could not go through another scrimmage now, especially not with Joel, a much scarier surrogate dreamer of impending doom.

"Well, then I'm glad I told you. So, take it easy, okay?" Tom sounded better. "Hey, and have a Merry Christmas!"

"I will, thanks. You too. Enjoy the holiday!" Rita hung up the phone slowly. She was not happy. Not only did she have no money to fix the car, but now she'd have to walk on eggshells again. Why did it always happen? Why the forebodings, the warnings? Couldn't she do anything right? Couldn't she have some peace? It had always been a catch-22, those invisible forces that made it seem like she was suffering from paranoid delusions, even when someone else had them for her.

Still wearing her jacket, Rita walked outside and lit a cigarette. She had almost kicked the habit again, but still had half a pack. Now, she was glad she had some smokes left. She sat down on the porch and looked out at the snow-covered landscape under the vast canopy of stars unobstructed by buildings. This was her favorite place to think. Small as the porch was, its expansive view of land and sky set her at peace, connecting her to the natural world, the universe.

"Please, Spirit, Angels, God, if you exist, protect us. Please, dream man in velvet, Mother, Grandmother... Can you hear me? I don't want to be afraid anymore."

CHAPTER 32

Bertha's Family

PHILADELPHIA, PENNSYLVANIA, 1993

James Williams Jr. walked up the well-shoveled steps of his mother's house with his ten-year-old daughter, Nakisha. It had begun to snow again, making this a white Christmas Eve, as predicted for the whole Northeast.

"Won't Nana Belinda be surprised by the present we got her?" chirped Nakisha. "I can't wait to see what she got me. When will Mama, Jay Jay, Camilla, and the baby come? Are we going to have turkey?"

"Hush, girl. Just wait awhile," James Jr. said, too tired to keep up with his daughter's incessant questions. "Mama and the kids are on their way—be a little while later. Just give Nana Belinda a hug and don't be asking her for your present now, you hear? She's got to have presents for all them nieces and nephews, not just you."

"Okay, Daddy," said Nakisha, trying to contain her excitement. She still wanted to know if Uncle Arnie, Aunt Katherine, and the cousins would come to Christmas dinner, but she dared not ask, not now anyway. She'd ask her Nana, who would be happy to answer all her questions, she thought.

James Jr. stood on the front stoop. He let go of Nakisha hand, holding his mother's large gift tucked under his other arm. He rang the bell.

Belinda opened the door with a big smile, happy as could be to see her younger son and her beautiful granddaughter. "Hello, come in, come in out of that nasty cold. Why look at you!" Belinda took off Nakisha's wool hat. "Why child, you are bigger than just two weeks ago! And pretty as ever. Look how nice your Mama done braided your hair." Belinda took Nakisha's coat and scarf.

She turned to James Jr. "Hello, son, how are you? You look tired. Here, let me take your coat, too. You want to put the package in the parlor near the tree?"

"Sure Mama, thanks," James Jr. handed his mother his coat to hang in the hall closet. Before he could say anything else, Nakisha burst her bubble of silence.

"Nana Belinda, we got you a big present, and it is in that package Daddy has. Do you want to see it? Are we having turkey or ham? It smells so good in here."

James Jr. gave Nakisha one of his "settle down or else" looks. "What did I tell you, Nakisha?" he said firmly.

"Oh, leave the child be, James. She's just excited. Ain't every day it's Christmas. You remember how you and Arnie were when you were her age?" Belinda said, holding Nakisha close to her.

"Are Uncle Arnie and Aunt Katherine and the cousins coming?" Nakisha blurted out. She looked up at her Nana, her protector.

"No, honey child, they can't come all the way from Vancouver to Philadelphia. That's too far. Costs too much nowadays." Belinda looked over at James Jr. with a twinge of sadness in her eyes. She had visited Arnie twice in the last ten years, but coming back to the States was still not possible for Arnie. Problems with amnesty still plagued his return all these years after the war.

Belinda was only thankful that he'd finally met Katherine, who had relocated from Eugene, Oregon to Vancouver. Although she was a white girl, Belinda felt happy for her oldest son. She turned out to be a faithful wife and good mother.

Belinda and Jeremiah had moved back to Philadelphia after James Jr. finished high school. She had wanted Arnie to move with the family, but he had stayed in New York. They moved into the house with Dorothy to take care of her until the end. Aunt Dorothy had been alone since Papa's death ten years before. So, Belinda wasn't in New York when Arnie said he had met someone special there. She had sent Arnie his Grandmother Bertha's wedding ring though, to propose. When things had fallen apart, Belinda tried to persuade Arnie to join them in Philadelphia. The draft ended those plans a year and a half later.

Now Belinda was happy for his safety, his marriage, and three wonderful grown sons. She only wished she could see them all more often. She wished Jeremiah had lived long enough to see them grown, too.

"Oh, but you know what?" Belinda's wrinkled face suddenly lit up, remembering the letter she received from Arnie just yesterday.

"What?" squealed Nakisha.

"I got some new pictures of your cousins in Canada for you to see, and some special cookies I made just for you!" Belinda clasped Nakisha's hands in hers and winked at James Jr.

James Jr. looked relieved to be done with the responsibility of his exuberant daughter. The new baby had come unexpectedly late in his marriage. He felt too old to be up at all hours. Exhaustion diminished his patience. He was glad just to take care of his mother's wrapped present, propping it up safely against a wall near the large, color-filled Christmas tree in the living room. Then he sat down on the couch and flipped on the TV. Christmas always made him irritable. It had been that way ever since Arnie had left.

"How come you like to make cakes and cookies, Nana?" Nakisha asked. She sat down at the kitchen table and took a big oatmeal cookie from the plate. "Oh, this one is warm, Nana!" she said, her dark eyes sparkling in anticipation. She bit into its sweet softness, closed her eyes, and savored its thick sugary taste. A big smile spread across the child's face.

"That's why," said Belinda. "'Cause I love to see your face when you eat 'em, sugar!"

"Noooo. C'mon, really Nana, why?" Nakisha took another bite.

"Well, I guess 'cause my mother, your great-grandma Bertha, and her mother before her, they loved to bake. They had their own secret recipes handed down to them from their people."

"Their people?" Nakisha asked.

"I mean, our people." Belinda thought for a moment, remembering her talks with her own sons when they were about Nakisha's age. "We all have mothers and fathers, and our mothers and fathers have mothers and fathers, and behind them are their mothers and fathers."

"Like when you stand in that funny mirror at Play Land and you can see lots of yourself behind you," Nakisha interrupted. "So my great, great, great, great, great grandmothers and grandfathers, right?"

Belinda laughed. Nakisha was a clever child, like her mother, Olivia. "Yes, just like that. Our people go way back, to slave days and Indian times, child—all the way back to Africa."

"Indians? We learned about Indians in our history books, Nana. My teacher calls them Native Americans." Nakisha finished her cookie. "Can I have some juice, Nana?"

Belinda's hands shook just a little as she poured apple juice into a glass for her prodigy. "That's where some of the recipes I use, come from. They are from the marriage of Indians and black folks—our people."

Nakisha looked at her Nana, narrowing her eyes, digesting the new information. "The recipes come from Indians? We have Indians in our family?" she finally said.

"Yes, when we were slaves, some Indians...Native Americans... helped us, so some recipes are part of Indian tradition." Belinda leaned over toward Nakisha. "Do you want to know the secret?" she whispered, enticing her inquisitive grandchild.

Nakisha's eyes opened wide. "Yes, Nana," she whispered, mimicking her Nana quietly.

"It's corn. The Indians called it maize," said Belinda.

"Maize? My teacher told us about maize! She brought in some maize to show us." Nakisha was delighted that she knew about Native American history. "You put that in your bread, Nana?"

"Yes, and in the cakes and cookies, too!" Belinda smiled, her whole face lighting up with the pleasure of surprising Nakisha.

"Do the people at your bakery know your secret?" Nakisha asked quietly again.

"No, they come to buy the bread at Bertha's Bakery because they love it. Only you and me and my sisters know the secret ingredient!"

"Did your mama know it?" asked Nakisha, her never-ending curiosity still aglow.

"Yes, she's the one who passed it to me. And now I'm passin' it to you, child," Belinda said, hugging her favorite grandchild.

"Oh, Nana, this is the best present for Christmas." Nakisha hugged her grandmother, feeling her softness. The smell of Nana's rosewater perfume and freshness of her bleached apron filled her with delight. "Oh Nana, wait till you see what we got for you!" Nakisha nearly burst holding her own secret.

Just then, the doorbell rang again. Nakisha jumped up from the chair and ran into the hall. Her father was already at the door. Nana slowly joined them. Olivia came in carrying baby James. The seventeen-year-old twins, Jay Jay and Camilla, hurried into the warm house. Behind them followed Belinda's sisters, Denise and Daniella, each with husbands, grown children, and grandchildren in tow. Belinda took note of all her relatives. Missing was Lucille, who was too ill to join them and was being cared for by her oldest daughter, and Michelle, who had passed away from complications of diabetes last spring.

Slowly, the house filled with family. Belinda hugged each of her sisters, grandchildren, nieces, and nephews in turn. Soon, they would sit down in the dining room and enjoy turkey, ham, and all the fixings that Belinda and her sisters had made. But first, Nakisha wanted to make an announcement. It took almost ten minutes to get everyone quiet enough to hear her. She finally stood up on a chair and rang the bell Belinda had for such occasions.

"I am the passer down of an important family recipe that Nana gave me, so I am going to give Nana her present for Christmas,"

Nakisha announced bravely, looking over at her parents.

James Jr. and Olivia looked at each other in surprise, then whispered to one another. Olivia finally nodded. "That would be just a perfect thing for you to do, Nakisha, but after dinner, honey."

Denise and her two daughters brought the food to the table and the young ones helped out with plates and napkins. The men carved the meats, while the young adults carried more chairs to the tables and helped serve everyone in turn. When they all sat down to eat, James Jr. led the family in prayer and celebration of the Lord's birth. He quoted scripture just like he'd done for many years, being Belinda's only son at home for the holidays. It was not long before the feast commenced with fanfare, laughter, and joy. Belinda's heart felt full, blessed with her family all around her. If only Bertha could see her now, she thought.

After the dinner, each of the children took turns cleaning dishes and the table, while the grown-ups sat in the living room talking and listening to Bessie Smith and Ella Fitzgerald on the cassette tape player. The men lit up cigars, poured glasses of whiskey and rum. Tea and coffee brewed to accompany dessert—Belinda's famous cakes and pies.

With the help of the younger children, Belinda took presents from the hall closet and set them under the tree. She changed the tape on the stereo player to her favorite old Christmas album, *The Magic of Christmas,* by Nat King Cole. The sweet melodies filled the house.

"Nana!" yelled Nakisha. "C'mon, it's time for your present." The child pulled her grandmother very gently by the hand to join the other adults in the living room. In her late 70s now, Belinda didn't rush anymore. James Jr. stood up and helped his mother sit down in her favorite reading chair. Jay Jay, James Jr.'s strapping young college-bound son, hoisted Nakisha up to sit on the piano.

"Okay everyone, it's time for presents!" announced Nakisha. All the younger kids came running into the room. "Everyone sit down, because it is Grandma Belinda's turn. She is the oldest."

James Jr. walked over to Nakisha motioning her to be quiet. "Mom, we all honor you. Thank you for having our family together for Christmas." He leaned over kissing Belinda's cheek. "We have somethin' special for you. Nakisha wants to tell you about the gift." He nodded to Nakisha.

"Nana, my mama found a wonderful gift. She brought it home on the train from Newport Island," Nakisha began.

Olivia whispered in her child's ear. "Oh, I mean from Newport, Rhode Island," Nakisha corrected herself. "She went to visit Granddaddy 'cause he was sick. She went by a store with paintings." She looked at Olivia for reassurance. "Oh, yeah, it was an art gallery."

"It was the strangest, most wonderful thing." Olivia took her cue. "In November, I was just taking a few hours off from caring for my Dad. I went into a gallery and met an artist who painted portraits from her imagination. She said that she rarely knew who they were, but she'd had a dream about a woman who owned a bakery. In the bakery, there was a painting of what appeared to the owner's mother or grandmother. So the artist painted what she saw in her dream." Olivia beamed. "The frame on the painting was most interesting, because there were Native American symbols painted along the edge," she said. Nakisha jumped down from the piano holding Olivia's hand, and they carried the wrapped painting to Belinda.

Belinda removed the wrapping. "Oh, Jesus, be praised!" She gasped, holding her hand to her heart. "Oh. praise the Lord!" she sighed, tears welling up in her eyes.

Her family members stared at the painting in awe. They looked from one to the other, recognizing the matriarch, Bertha. Tears flowed down Belinda's cheeks. Denise and Daniella grasped each other's hands. "Praise God!" they said.

"This is a sign from heaven," Belinda managed, choking back her tears. She looked down at the perfect portrait of her mother, Bertha, just as she remembered her.

Nakisha walked over to her grandmother and put her arms around her neck. "Don't cry, Nana," she said. "We love you." One by one, her children and all the little ones hugged her until her tears were dry and laughter again filled the house.

The next day Belinda, Denise and Daniella walked to Belinda's bakery. The sign above the doorway read *Bertha's Bakery Delights.* "I'm just sorry James and Dorothy aren't here to see this," said Daniella. She hammered a small nail into the wall just behind the pastry case and hung the perfect painting of Bertha.

Belinda looked at her sisters, then back at the painting. "I believe we are all here together now," she said softly.

CHAPTER 33

Rita Kerner

"Look I'm really sorry, but we are going to have to let you go," Tom mumbled. He had a hard time looking at Rita.

"Is this about that dream you had about me?" Rita was upset. She needed the job more than ever after the holidays. "I'm so sorry. I don't know how it happened—the dream, I mean. Your warning helped, though," Rita said, hoping he would understand she was grateful. "I had a terrible scene with my son's father and my car broke down on the way home. Things might have gotten a lot worse, if I had not been on guard, thanks to you."

Rita did not go into the details, but it had become a near disastrous fight, one that had gotten physical. Having been warned, she'd been able to grab Noah away before Joel could take him again, for what might have been a permanent holiday vacation.

"No," said Tom "It's not about that. Gail wants to set up a new department for handling incoming orders. It's about money. It's just business."

Rita wasn't buying it, but she accepted Tom's answer. She knew Gail, his business partner, would try to find a way to fire her. Gail's cousin, the delivery guy, had harassed Rita on three separate occasions. Rita had told him off the last time in not so polite terms. Hell, it wasn't the first time she'd been harassed at a job, Rita thought. Perhaps it wasn't the whole story, though. Had Gail found out she was doing

237

paperwork from home again? Rita considered Gail's arbitrary policy an abuse of her contract. What difference did it make where she filled out the reports, after she put in her eight hours?

There was no time to sulk about it. The next few days Rita posted tutoring signs around her neighborhood and checked the local paper's employment pages. Weeks went by. She kept busy looking for work, then painting—her art a calming, almost meditative experience. Lately, she painted mostly portraits, the faces of people that came from her imagination.

Rita did not tell Noah that she'd lost her job. She didn't want to worry him, or want Joel finding out she was unemployed. So, she painted in the morning after Noah left for school. She looked for work in the afternoons. She had managed to save a little money. They could get by a few more weeks.

Luckily, by the following week Rita had found a job at a bookstore not far away. The job did not pay well, but when they offered her the position after the interview she accepted. Accounts receivable was fairly mindless work and she could even afford one or two discounted, damaged books left for employees in the cafeteria, a few times a month. Not bad, she thought.

Feeling relieved, Rita shopped for a big roasting chicken, a bag of potatoes, carrots, onions, and a head of fresh broccoli. She splurged on a ready-made chocolate cake for dessert. While dinner cooked, Rita put the finishing touches on one of her paintings. She stood back and evaluated her work with a skeptical eye. Not usually satisfied, this time Rita was almost pleased with her painting of an elderly woman with violet-blue eyes and a mischievous smile. Her subject's white hair was swept up into a grandmotherly bun. She wore wire-rimmed glasses that hung low on her narrow, slightly turned-up nose. The old woman looked Irish, Rita thought. She had rosy cheeks, the ruddy glow of sensitive white skin susceptible to damp, cool weather. She wore a light blue-flowered frock, a shawl, and a cross around her neck. Rita had painted her sitting in an easy chair holding what appeared to be rosary beads. On the table, next to the seated woman was a vase of flowers and a small plaster statue of the Virgin Mary with three winged angels.

Rita was surprised by the painting's details. Where the hell had all the Catholic religious symbolism come from? Rita thought. Who was this person? For first time, Rita considered that her imagination might not be the only thing at work when she painted. Her writing had evolved the same way. Sometimes, she would reread a poem or prose passage not knowing where the information came from, as if someone else had helped her write it. Lately, her poems and stories had almost begun to write themselves.

She looked at the painting again. The woman who stared out from the canvas looked real. Rita liked her. There was something familiar about her, but the woman was not anyone she recognized.

"Who's that?" asked Noah when he walked into the house.

Rita gave him a hug. "I don't know, just a painting, I guess. How was school?"

"Okay." He sniffed. "What's cooking? It smells good, Mom! Is it a special occasion?" Noah walked into the kitchen.

"Well, I got a new job closer to home. Thought we'd celebrate a little," said Rita, glad that she didn't have to explain being laid off. "I'm making your favorite—roast chicken with potatoes and carrots."

"Wow, chocolate cake, too!" Noah exclaimed. He opened the refrigerator for his usual after-school juice box and grabbed two cookies from the cabinet before heading to his room.

"I'll call you when dinner's ready. Get your homework done. We can watch TV after dinner, honey." She had just started to put away her paints and clean up when the phone rang.

"Oh, hello Ms. McCarthy. Thank you for returning my call." Rita said, pleased to hear the melodic voice of Jane McCarthy. She'd recently seen an article in the paper about Jane, a local woman who did astrology readings. Rita had decided to give herself a gift for her upcoming birthday. It seemed like a good idea especially now having gotten a new job. Maybe a reading could shed some light on her future, or provide some direction about her art. "Yes, I can wait until Saturday morning. That would be fine, thank you," Rita said. "I have your office address. You want to meet elsewhere? Okay, let me get a pen to write down the new address."

This would be Rita's second astrology reading. She'd had one several years ago, when she'd been thinking of leaving Susan. Somehow, Rita felt her path was about to change again. She had already decided she would remain single for a time, just make friends—at least until Noah finished high school. It was not only for Noah sake, but also for hers. She was tired of complications, scaring people with her weird dreams, her visions and voices, tired of picking the wrong people to be in her life. It was time to get to know who she really was, to devote time to herself, her art.

Later that week, when Rita arrived for her appointment with the astrologer, she was greeted by a warm welcome. Jane made Rita feel like she was an old friend.

"Rita? Hello, please come in. I'm Jane." The tall, light-skinned woman with hazel eyes smiled. She shook Rita's hand. "So nice to see you."

"Sorry I'm a few minutes late," Rita said. She stepped into Jane's carpeted foyer.

"No problem. I appreciate you coming here instead of to my office. I'm glad to finally meet you after the delay in my schedule. My mother has some health problems, as I mentioned. I've been staying here with her this past month."

Jane walked down the hallway. Rita followed.

"We can do the reading in the study, so we'll have some privacy. Here, let me take your coat." Jane hung Rita's coat in the hall closet.

"Um, sure smells good in here." Rita breathed the sweet aroma coming from the kitchen. The delicious scent seemed familiar, but she couldn't quite place it. She relaxed into the inviting warmth of Jane's mother's apartment.

"My mother refuses to quit cooking, even though she's supposed to be taking it easy. That smell is her famous bread pudding baking in the oven," Jane said, leading Rita down a hall to the study.

"Hmm, bread pudding. That is unusual," Rita said. "I didn't know people really made that anymore."

"Yes, well, she's had an old family recipe from Ireland. I'm sure she'd be delighted to have you try some when we're finished, if you'd like."

"Oh, that would be nice," Rita said politely. She could not remember ever having eaten bread pudding, but feeling an intimate connection with the sweet aroma, she couldn't be sure.

"Here is your chart. I have adjusted the time just by a minute or two in each direction to account for birth time error. When we talk, it should become clearer."

Rita made herself comfortable in an overstuffed chair in the cozy, flower-carpeted study. Afternoon sunlight flooded the room. The peach-colored walls cast a warm glow on Jane's light creamy skin, as she sat down in a rocking chair across from Rita. Surrounded by shelves of books, pictures frames, knick knacks, and plants in small clay pots, Rita felt right at home.

"I've kind of taken over this room, since I've been staying here," Jane explained, noticing Rita observe her surroundings.

"It's nice, very inviting," Rita replied. She settled in to hear her reading.

"So, you seem to have a very creative mind," Jane began. "You are very talented, absolutely gifted."

Rita had never heard the word *gifted* applied to her before.

"But things have not been easy. You seem to have had a very difficult time a few years ago. See here in your house of relationships. And there seems to have been some illness, some disruption, like an obsessive problem. Have you ever had a near death experience? Do you know what I mean? Does this make sense to you?

Overwhelmed, Rita just nodded.

Jane continued. "And I see here loss in your house of careers, as well." Jane pointed at the chart filled with symbols and lines going in every direction.

"Yes , well all of that and…I had an experience with a haunting in my apartment that caused me terrible problems. Rita felt nervous. She had never discussed this with anyone since telling the doctor in that hospital."

"What happened?" Jane asked. She sensed Rita's fear and her need to talk about it.

"It was lists of words—voices. It went on for days." Rita waited to see Jane's response.

"Did you have a fever?" Jane asked gently.

"Yes! How did you know that?"

"Did you figure out what was happening?" Jane asked.

"No, not really. The doctor said it was delirium from the fever. It finally went away. I was glad to move eventually. It has always bothered me—that and other people having nightmares about me—warning me." Rita paused realizing she didn't even know this women she was confiding in. "Is that in my chart?" she laughed nervously.

Jane was quiet for a moment. Rita noticed a change in her manner.

"What is in your chart is that you have a gift, an ability." Jane explained. "Sometimes when we ignore who we are—our gifts that is, the universe has a way of waking us up." Jane continued. "It's kind of like dreams. They give you information with a little tap. If we ignore the message, the tap becomes a knock. If we still don't pay attention, the knock becomes louder until it is a nightmare." Jane paused. "For people with a gift like yours, it sometimes takes a fever, for the breakdown of reality to awaken you." Jane continued.

"A breakdown of reality?" Rita asked.

"Well, it's more a breakdown of a barrier, but with a purpose. It is a breaking through, shaking everything up, showing you another reality—that things are not always what they appear to be. It happens so *you can remember who you are.*"

The words echoed in Rita's ears. She had goosebumps. She tried to absorb what Jane was saying, wrap her mind around Jane's meaning, the truth of it. "It's another key," she whispered in a flash of recognition. Jane was a person with important keys, like her painting teacher, Mr. Roberts. Suddenly, as if all the synapses of her brain opened at once, Rita knew the keys were all connected somehow.

"Look here." Jane pointed to her chart again. "This is called a Grand Trine. A change is coming that will mean you will have to pay more attention to your creativity. There is success with this aspect of your life. There is also a change coming in your house of relationships." Jane motioned again. "Another few years…"

Rita was transfixed, elated, as this wise woman continued explaining her chart and its astrological meanings. Rita could not recall having ever felt so validated.

"Thank you, so much," Rita said when they finished an hour later. "This has been so informative, so helpful. I am so grateful for this experience."

"Excellent, I'm glad. Now, how about some bread pudding? My mom's probably been waiting to offer you some."

Rita gathered up her bag and followed Jane back down the hall toward the living room. "Mom," Jane raised her voice a little, leaning forward slightly. "This is Rita."

An old woman, with white hair swept up into a bun, looked up from her knitting. She sat comfortably in her easy chair, with her rosary beads laying in her lap. Her wire-rimmed glasses hung low on her small, narrow nose. She wore a blue flowered house-dress and a light beige shawl around her shoulders. A gold cross hung from a small chain around her neck. Beside her chair was a mahogany side table with a vase of silk flowers and a small plaster statue of the Virgin Mary surrounded by plastic angels. Rita stared into her violet-blue eyes. A mischievous smile spread across the old woman's face.

"I am happy to meet you, my dear. I'm Mrs. McCarthy," she said. She started to get up. "Would you like some bread pudding before you go?" she offered.

"I'll get it, Mom. Don't get up." Jane was already on her way into the kitchen.

No one noticed that Rita was silent. Stunned, she just stared at Mrs. McCarthy like she was seeing a ghost. Chills danced along Rita's spine. Her painting had come to life before her eyes.

"Come, sit here by me," said Mrs. McCarthy. "Tell me what you do.

Do you have children? Jane is my only daughter. She is so kind to take care of me, but I can still cook. I still have it up here!" The old woman pointed to her head.

Rita tried to compose herself. Just then, Jane came back into the room with plates of bread pudding for everyone. Rita ate a forkful of the sweet, warm treat. A wave of emotion washed over her. Her eyes filled with tears.

"Don't you like it? Is something wrong?" asked Mrs. McCarthy, noticing Rita's eyes watering.

"Oh, no," Rita shook off her turmoil. "It's delicious. I like it. I'm just a little tired. Perhaps I could come another time and talk to you." Rita stood up and thanked Mrs. McCarthy. She gave Jane a check and thanked her again. "I'm sorry I can't stay. I have to get home for my son's dinner. I'd love to come again, though."

"You will come back again, won't you Clara?" Mrs. McCarthy asked.

Rita turned around and stared at Mrs. McCarthy.

"Her name is Rita, Mom. This is Rita," Jane corrected her mother.

"Oh, Anna, don't be silly. Don't you recognize Clara?"

"I'm sorry, Rita," Jane motioned for Rita to come into the kitchen. "Mom has a little dementia, early Alzheimer's the doctors think." Jane spoke softly. "She calls me Anna sometimes and other people by different names. You'll have to forgive her."

"Uh, it's fine, really. I understand," said Rita, her mind reeling.

They both walked back to Mrs. McCarthy. "Mom, Rita would love to visit with us again. She is going home now." Jane pronounced her words loudly and distinctly.

"Anna, why are you talking like I'm deaf?" asked Mrs. McCarthy. "Clara, can you talk some sense into her?"

Jane smiled at Rita and shrugged. "Come on, I'll walk you out," she said, resigned to her mother's condition. She handed Rita her coat.

As Rita drove home, her whole body tingled. She couldn't wait to get back and look at her paintings stacked in the hall closet. Rita hurried, speeding along the road until she came within view of the new place, one she had found for her and Noah just months ago on the outskirts of town. It was a small, yellow house with a big porch, dormer windows, and a garage.

Rita remembered having first laid eyes on the house after the holidays, when she had driven a scenic stretch to her new job at the bookstore. The winding, two lane road was dotted with cottages giving way to a rocky beach, an expanse of sky and sea. Rita loved traveling this way, especially on gray days when the surf was wild, waves lapping violently against the shore, splashing salty spray onto the street and the vehicles. Somehow, the sky's dark clouds felt comforting in their familiarity. Was it the wide open space or the sense of danger and foreboding that was alluring? Rita wondered.

Closer to the village, trees and houses appeared once more, old Victorians and brick. A small bakery and post office were the first signs of the busy town ahead. Rita stopped at the bakery on occasion for a coffee and a warm roll before heading to work.

"It is a very old beach house, servants quarters really, built in the late 1800s," the landlady had told Rita. "The furnace is fairly new, so it works well. It will be warm in the winter. It's a cozy place for two." There was small backyard—space for a garden. Rita could smell the salt air, feel the sea breeze when she stood on the wrap-around porch.

Rita pulled into her driveway, waving to her neighbor, Ted. He stood next door by his car, his beer belly sticking out of his worn, white T-shirt. A cigar hung out the side of his mouth. He was talking to another potential buyer about his classic gold-colored Packard, his "baby." Rita knew he would never sell it, it being the only real tie he still had left to his deceased wife. Rita smiled at him, feeling a special closeness to this gruff, unkempt man. He had offered to help her put in a vegetable garden in her new backyard. Somehow, he was part of the magic of this strange little town, part of a dream she once had.

Rita climbed the few stairs to the porch where Skippy waited, tail wagging. She petted the dog and hurried into her quaint house. Taking her paintings from the hall closet, she laid them carefully on the dining room table. She looked through the many portraits. One was of a young Indian man and woman dressed in ceremonial garb. Another was a handsome, fair gentleman with a neat mustache and a gold pocket watch. There was a black woman dressed in a summer dress with two children, an older black woman holding a cake, a young fair-skinned farm girl and her horse, a cowboy sitting on a wagon, a barmaid with red hair, and several others.

Finally, Rita came across the painting she was looking for. There, at the bottom of the pile was the more recent painting of Mrs. McCarthy, exactly as Rita had seen her only thirty minutes ago. Her violet blue eyes looked out from the canvas and seemed to twinkle. Her mischievous smile beckoned.

Rita began to laugh. She howled with glee and twirled 'round and 'round like a kid, until she was out of breathe, dizzy. Then, she ran over to her computer on the desk near the double windows that overlooked Ted's yard. She clicked the mouse until she came to the story that she had begun one night, a long time ago. Since that time, the story had simply evolved every time she had returned to it. Staring out from the computer now was the beginning of a story of a girl named Clara, and her adopted family, Anna and Mrs. Riley.

Clara had gone to visit the Riley's that afternoon, before the evening meal. She had promised her mother she'd be back before sundown, when her father would be returning from his business trip. She would remember to tell Mrs. Riley, so she would not stuff Clara with her delicious bread pudding and spoil her appetite. Clara went into Mrs. Riley's house through the kitchen door as she always did.

"Hi, sugar," Mrs. Riley greeted her warmly. "You're just in time for bread pudding, hot out of the oven."

Clara's resolve wavered. The sweet aroma of sugar and cinnamon filled the air. "Oh, it smells really good! But, no thank you, Mrs. Riley. I can't. We're having dinner early tonight, because my father is returning from a trip..."

Rita began to cry. Tears of sadness and joy ran down her face. Then she burst out laughing again. Overwhelmed, a tidal wave of emotions, images, memories of places and people so long forgotten, flooded her consciousness.

"Remember" she heard a voice whisper. *"Remember..."* It was Grandma Pearl's voice. Suddenly, Rita was flying with a great white eagle, high above the treetops, soaring over great mountains and rivers, forests and deserts far, far away. She was not afraid anymore. She was free.

CHAPTER 34

Clara Doyle

MATT'S SALOON, FRANKLIN, OREGON, 1893

Cold winter winds rattled Clara's bedroom window, blowing a draft through the slight crevice along the old sill. She awoke feeling unusually chilled again as she had for the last few nights. She reached for her extra blanket from the foot of her bed and pulled it up to her neck. "I'll have to make a trip to the general store for some more yarn," she mumbled to herself sleepily.

She closed her eyes and thought about knitting a new shawl for herself and maybe some for the girls. She'd make an extra warm blanket for the child Stacy was carrying. The baby was sure to need it with the chill in the house. That is, if Sam would let her stay on through the winter. Shame on him if he'd throw her out after the years she had given the place, Clara thought. She'd come to care for Stacy like a daughter. She didn't want to lose her, especially now. The thought of the baby both excited and terrified Clara.

She tried to fall back asleep. A rainbow of yarn weaved its way through shifting images of flowered meadows, young women's faces, sounds of men's laughter, and a baby's happy gurgling. Clara's breath turned slow and heavy. A sense of contentment carried her along to a memory of the brightly-colored blankets she had made for the girls last year. The memory of their warm affection toward her at Christmas time when she presented them with her handiwork, seeped through her veins like sweet wine. Clara held a pillow close in her arms and

248

breathed away the tightness in her chest that always crept up on her just before slumber. She fell asleep before dawn cast a pink glow along the edges of her gingham curtains.

Later that morning, Clara dressed in her long dark skirt and jacket. She put her hat over her neatly combed hair, which she now wore pinned up in a tidy bun. She applied a small amount of lip rouge and a few dabs of make-up to her pale, wrinkled skin, before she walked down the stairs, into the morning light.

Sam was out at the wagon tending to the day's delivery and talking with a well-dressed young man, a stranger in town, who Clara had seen him with a few times recently. She walked by quietly, momentarily noticing a slight familiarity in the young man's mannerisms. Walking in her irregular, but determined gate, she continued down the cobblestone street to Mac's General Store.

"Good morning, Miss Clara. Why, you're out early. It is nice to see you," Mrs. Landers, Mac's wife, a plump woman with fading red hair and rosy cheeks, greeted Clara with a warm smile. Mrs. Landers hadn't always been so friendly. Once upon a time, she wanted nothing to do with any of those "painted ladies." She had treated Clara with disdain and loathing, Clara recalled.

"Now, she thinks I'm just a sad woman with no family to look out for me in my old age," Clara had told the girls after her last errand, some months ago. "Now that I am old, she don't worry about me *havin' a dance* with her husband!" Clara chuckled.

What had also changed the tide was their interest in yarn, their love of knitting. The common ground broke the ice between them. "We have some nice new colors, Miss Clara," Mrs. Landers offered. "I dyed them myself from the new colored dyes my husband brought from Portland," she said proudly.

The two rummaged through the skeins of colored sheep and goat yarn, chattering away like best friends about stitches and textures for Clara's intended project. Before long, Clara had found what she needed to purchase.

"I'm glad I could help you. Please do bring a shawl to show me when you finish," Mrs. Landers said. She wrapped Clara's chosen yarn in a large piece of muslin, secured with twine.

"Thank you for all your help, Mrs. Landers. I'll be on my way home, now. Good day," Clara said, smiling politely.

Strange, Clara thought as she walked out into the street again, that she should have called the saloon "home." She had finally grown accustomed to her place and tending to the girls over the years. Now, she found solace being alone in her own room, no longer working the floor, nor managing the girls. The brothel was the only life she had really known. Just a vague memory of her family remained, one that she visited mostly in her dreams.

The only one Clara still had a vivid image of was Kyle Doyle. She had kept Kyle's name and memory alive a long time. Bitterness replaced the pain and longing for him the day Stacy had come. She had given up waiting for Kyle after that day, referring to herself as Clara Riley from then on. Regardless, the damage had been done. His abandonment had torn a hole in the fabric of Clara's spirit that no yarn and knitting needles could repair.

Of late, Clara had sought help from the local preacher to ease a renewed wave of grief and sadness that threatened to engulf her. On her first foray into the newly built church at the edge of town, she froze—afraid of being ridiculed and shunned. Father Gaferty had kindly welcomed her. She found most parishioners too polite to say a negative word to her. After a while, some folks even acknowledged her presence with a nod, especially when the sermon's focus was forgiveness and salvation.

Clara found herself calmer, happier in church, especially when the preacher spoke of a new home. It was a home Clara tried to imagine. The thought of its possibility soothed her. He had called it the Kingdom of Heaven. It sounded wonderful to Clara. If she remembered correctly, Mrs. Riley had talked about Heaven, a long time ago.

Lost in thought, Clara carried her yarn package into the saloon and up to her room. Soon, Jean, Stacy, Rosie, and the newest girl, Alice—all still in their nightgowns, surrounded Clara, curious and excited to see what colors she had bought.

Hearing all the commotion, Sam came upstairs and stood at Clara's door. "You all best be gettin' yourselves cleaned up and dressed soon," Sam mustered a stern voice.

Sam was in charge, and had been since Matt's heart had given out a year before. "Too much whiskey, cigars and women," Doc Beardsley had reported, underlying the medical cause of death.

Sam was on his own. Clara and the others knew he was none too happy about it, either. In fact, he seemed downright tired of the business. The place needed fixing. Taxes, liquor prices, and fights were all on the rise. "I'm aiming to sell this old place," Clara had overheard Sam say recently. He'd been talking to the well-dressed young man she'd seen him with on occasion. The man—the son of a wealthy businessman—was up from San Francisco. From what Clara could surmise, he had offered Sam a good price for the property.

After years of stops and starts, the Southern Pacific had finally connected the tracks from the Sacramento Valley to Portland. Trains from San Francisco to Portland had begun to run more frequently. Libraries, schools and museums were springing up. There was even talk about women getting the right to vote, one day. Things were changing. There was pressure from town folks to close the brothel, build a proper hotel for travelers, visitors coming by train through Junction City and especially Eugene, with railroad tycoons building the big university there.

"All right, Sam. I'll see to it they are ready on time," Clara reassured him, putting away the yarn. She was careful now not to make Sam mad. Clara worried. She hoped she had not made a mistake talking to Sam about Stacy the other day. The girl was too far along to be working. Clara had gone as far to advise Sam to marry her, but she'd meant no harm. To her, Sam always seemed a lonely soul with a longing heart. And Stacy needed someone to look after her.

Sam eyed Clara and grunted. Then he walked back down the hall.

Clara brushed aside her concerns about the future. She picked up a skein of indigo yarn. With graceful movements she wound the yarn into a ball as her mind wandered. If only the railroad had been built sooner, she might have had a safe way to leave when she was younger. If Sam sold the place, could she take a chance and leave now, at her age? Could she take one of those fancy trains to California, Clara day-dreamed.

"Miss Clara, I'd just love a blue shawl, if you have a mind to make me one, too," Alice interrupted Clara's thoughts. "There's a young man visiting town who's been looking for me when he comes in for his beer," Alice smiled. "He's a refined gentleman, not like them miners. He's got money, too. I heard him talking to Sam 'bout how his father died, left him a fortune in gold—something about coming up here on railroad business. And you should see the fine gold watch and chain he said his father gave him, been in their family a long time. Says his name is Mr. Doyle, Jr." Alice brushed strands of blond hair from her forehead. "Sure would like to marry such a fine man, leave this old town—ride far away on one of them new trains." Alice's eyes sparkled in her waking dream. Her face glowed.

"You, said it, honey!" laughed Jean. "Marry him if you can, but we all could use some new blood around these parts!" She touched her own bosom, winking knowingly at Stacy. "Some big spenders would sure help us all."

Alice sat down on the bed across from Clara, the yarn spread out between them. "Don't know how long he'll be in town, but if I had me a pretty new shawl, maybe I could catch his eye, Miss Clara. Do you think I might? Never seen such a pretty boy before," she said, looking at Clara dreamily.

But Clara was miles away. She no longer heard Alice or the rest of the girls as they chattered away and got dressed. Oddly, she only heard Kyle's voice. Clara stood up slowly, her bones aching. Through a fog, she walked stiffly to the window and brushed the curtain aside. She peered down to the cobblestone street.

There, just below was Kyle. He was exactly as she remembered him sitting so tall and handsome in the wagon, holding his horse's reins, waving up to her. He was motioning to her, calling out her name, waiting for her. She noticed his bags, her belongings too, all tied up in the flowered satchel she had brought from Mrs. Riley's place. Clara raised a hand and waved back. Then all went black.

"Miss Clara?" a soft voice whispered. "Miss Clara, it's Stacy. Do you need some more tea now?" Stacy walked into Clara's dimly lit room and bent down near her bedside. "How are you feeling, Miss Clara?" she asked gently.

Clara opened her eyes and looked up at Stacy's sweet face. "Oh, my dear, I'm feeling much better, now. Thank you. I must have given you a fright, I'm sorry." She touched Stacy's face, running a frail hand down her smooth cheek. "Now don't you and the girls fret over me. I'll be fine. I'm just so tired now. I'll start those shawls and a little blanket for the baby soon. You run along and get some rest now, dear one." Clara's head felt heavy on her feather pillow.

Stacy slipped out of the room, closing Clara's door quietly. She turned and walked toward her room, just when Sam reached the landing. The house was quiet now. Everyone else was already asleep.

"How's she doin?" Sam half-whispered.

"Better, I think," Stacy replied quietly. "Maybe that new doc could come by tomorrow and check on her," she added.

"I'll go down and ask him, first thing in the mornin'," Sam said. He lowered his eyes, but remained fixed where he stood.

Stacy stood holding her robe closed over her pregnant belly.

"Stacy," Sam uttered her name softly. "I'd been meanin' to talk to you. I…well, maybe this ain't the right time, but…well, I'm thinkin' about sellin' the place." He paused. "I know you havin' the baby and all, that you might be needin' someone and I tho…tho…tho…" Sam began to studder. He took a deep breath. "I mean, would you consider me bein' someone?"

Stacy didn't move, except to cover her mouth and stifle a gasp.

"I know I'm an old fella. Well, you maybe can think about it then," Sam said. He turned to head down the stairs. Stacy let her robe go and gently grasped his shoulder. She reached out, pushed her body against his in a tight embrace, kissed his neck, and cried softly. Sam held her and smoothed her hair. He kissed her cheek, lifted her up gently and carried her to her room.

Clara slept soundly for some time, lost in a dream of a dark carriage creaking along a coast road pulled by a black horse. In her dream, she looked out the window of the carriage toward an angry, gray sea. Wind churned the ocean, whipping it against the jagged rocky shore. She felt terribly cold. Looking down at her black dress, she saw her soft child-size hands motionless in her lap. Then, Kyle was sitting next to her in the carriage. He covered her lap with a fur blanket.

Clara awoke suddenly, almost too cold to move. Shivering, she arose with a sense that she had forgotten something important. She took her shawl from the bedpost and draped it around her shoulders.

She walked toward the little table near her window where an oil lamp, still lit, cast a dim glow. Two knitting needles lay beside it. The yarn she had purchased was piled on one of the two chairs next to the table. She bent over slightly, fingered its fine texture, separating the colors that her old eyes could barely decipher in such low light. "Indigo for Alice...natural white for Stacy, her baby." She touched the madder red and yellow ochre yarn. "For Rosie and Jean," Clara carefully pronounced each name like a prayer. I must finish making the shawl for young Alice, the blanket for Stacy's baby, she thought.

Clara picked up the indigo blue and natural white balls of yarn. She sat down in the chair and began to knit. Despite the pain, her deft hands moved with the speed and accuracy of a master. Performing a marriage ritual of knit and pearl, she needed no extra light or spectacles. She needed only hope, faith that this magic shawl might bring her uncle's son closer to atoning for the sins of his father. She would leave it draped over the back of the chair, give it to Alice in the morning.

Clara knitted into the wee hours of the night until Alice's new shawl and a small blanket for Stacy's baby were complete. Having satisfied herself that everything was in order, Clara climbed back into bed, her back racked in pain, her teeth chattering uncontrollably. She pulled all her blankets about her, laying her head on the feather pillow once again. Soon, she heard a child crying, sobbing loudly. Her chest tightened, as it often did before sleep. This time though, her heart felt like it would burst and shatter into a hundred pieces.

"Don't cry, child," a voice called to her. "You are not alone. We are here. *Remember us.*" Clara heard her mother's voice.

"We are all here waiting for you, Clara. Come child. Let go now," Peter Doyle's voice beckoned.

"Papa?" Clara whispered. Clara felt hot tears on her face. The sobbing was coming from her own throat, the ache in her heart overflowing, breaking.

"Let go of the pain, let go now. God has a plan, sweet one," Clara felt Mrs. Riley's arms reaching out to her.

Suddenly, Clara was not cold. She felt warm and very light. Her chest, which she thought a moment ago might explode, was painless. Clara breathed a long, deep breath, waiting to see if the pain would return. She could not feel any pain. She could not feel her body at all. Light like a feather plucked from her pillow, she began to float weightlessly—as if on air, up, up, above her bed.

Clara opened her eyes and looked down from high above. She could see an old woman sleeping in the bed below. Her silvery gray hair framed a gentle, peaceful face. She could hear the voices of her mother and father, almost see Anna, Mrs. Riley, their presence so close to her. She floated toward them, down a pathway lit by all the colors of dawn, over the mountains of her home.

CHAPTER 35

Rita Kerner

Jane dialed Rita's number. "Hi Rita, it's Jane...Jane McCarthy."

Rita answered, "Oh, hi Jane. How are you? How's your mom doing?"

"She's feeling a lot better now that they got her pacemaker in and adjusted. That's actually one of the reasons I'm calling. She wants to see you."

"Oh, that would be nice. I have to take Noah to soccer practice at three. I'll stop over after I drop him off." Happy that she and the McCarthys had become close, Rita hurried to get ready for the change in her afternoon plans.

Mrs. McCarthy sat in her favorite chair. She told Rita about her hospital visit while Jane prepared the tea. "It was good they found out a pacemaker was all I needed," she said.

"I'll say. Your symptoms sure gave me scare," Jane added. She carried a tray with tea and cookies into the living room. She offered Rita a cookie and then poured the tea.

Mrs. McCarthy looked directly over at Rita. "I wanted to see you about your paintings, dear," she said, taking a teacup from Jane. "Jane and I would like to help you open a gallery."

Rita almost choked on her cookie. "Really?' she sputtered. "Oh, that would be incredible! I don't know what to say."

"I thought about it after you showed us the paintings last time

256

you came for dinner. I think you have something important to give people. I just want you to promise you'll get your work out—let people know what you do. You have a real gift." With a mischievous smile, she added, "You came back to us, so Anna and I want to help you, Clara."

Rita looked at Jane, waiting for her to correct Mrs. McCarthy. Rita expected *"Oh Mom, this is Rita, not Clara."* But Jane just smiled. "I went for a past-life reading myself. Turns out, I lived in the West during pioneer days, a homestead in Oregon." She raised one eyebrow, looking at Rita. "And I did vaguely remember being called Anna."

"She begged me to call her Anna when she was a little girl," chimed Mrs. McCarthy, winking at Rita.

Later that afternoon, Jane took Rita to see a gallery space belonging to a friend, not far from her regular office. It was in an old Victorian house on Rhode Island Avenue, built at the turn of the twentieth century. It had recently been renovated and turned into commercial space. The small, vacant gallery was a large room on the ground floor, its walls painted with a fresh coat of white paint. There was natural light from the old-fashioned, paned front windows. A side door to the new gallery space faced a grassy yard that boasted a pine tree and rose garden.

Rita could not believe her good fortune. Jane arranged and paid a reasonable rate, then co-signed the lease agreement.

"It's perfect!" Rita gleefully spun around the room. She hugged Jane. "Thank you so much for this opportunity. Words are really not enough."

"I'm really excited for you. Mom is, too. We can't wait for the opening. Mom says you should call the local paper. They have an art section. I haven't seen her so animated in a long time."

Rita painted through the cool New England autumn. She planned the gallery opening for early November, just as the holiday season approached. She lined the windows with small white lights and draped them each with a garland of fresh pine. In two corners, she put potted burgundy coleus on pedestals. A vase of dried eucalyptus, purple sage and silver dollars she placed on a small table along with her business cards. Rita looked around the gallery. "Sublime!" She beamed.

Before long Rita had brought her paintings from home, the ones that she had painted over the years since Noah and she had moved to Rhode Island. There were four paintings of Native Americans from the same tribe. One was a man on a horse looking out across the plains at sunset, another of two women, mother and daughter, then one of a young boy in the woods near a waterfall, and the last, a young woman in white deerskin ceremonial dress. Rita hung them together on one wall.

Across from those, she hung paintings of another family. A matriarch, an African American woman in a bakery, holding a cake. Another was a man and woman on their wedding day. There was a painting of a farmhouse with horses in a meadow and the painting she had done most recently of Mrs. Riley and Anna, along with several others. With these paintings hung, there was still a little bit of wall space to spare.

The following week Rita painted two more paintings, portraits of more people she did not know. One was a spry old man with red hair tinged with gray. He wore a purple velvet jacket with bright colored buttons and a crooked hat to match. He was a quirky-looking, but delightful character. As Rita added the last bit of glaze for the bleed through effect that she'd learned so many years ago, she heard voices and laughter. She couldn't quite decipher the words, only a distinct Irish accent. Rita knew from experience that the laughter was not from a voice outside, not a voice in her head, not like the radio lists that had tried to get her attention years ago. These were voices from a love-filled, peace-filled place. She called it the "no such thing as death place" that others called Heaven.

That was why the portrait glowed like a real person—the old man's image was telling a joke, then having a good hearty laugh. Rita was very pleased. She did not find it odd that her paintings would have some qualities of actual people they represented. It was comforting and joyful.

Her next painting was also a portrait. This one seemed like an imaginary fellow, a wizard, a Merlin. His face was remarkably kind, his eyes shone with great wisdom and depth. She painted his robe in deep blue, the color of the night sky when the stars become visible again, just before the blackness of night. Small silver stars randomly placed on the blue background and a sliver of silver paint along the collar of the robe, added a touch of elegance and magic. With the stroke of a brush Rita added a design of two lightning bolts to his wizard's hat. His hair and beard contrasted in stark white, while his dark eyes, fair skin, and rosy cheeks, complete with glazes, finished the picture. Rita closed her eyes for a sensation about him. There was the sound of excited, youthful voices.

Aside from these two paintings, Rita had two more at home she wanted to include in the gallery. But neither of these last two would be for sale. She opened the hall closet and removed two wrapped paintings taken from her parents' place in Miami. The painting that had hung over Lillian's and David's bed for years of the black horse and carriage on a road by a gray stormy sea belonged to her now. So did the one that replaced it—her painting, *Make Love Not War*, the one on which she had first practiced the bleed through technique. She would hang them in the gallery as a reminder to herself that she had come a long, long way. Looking at them anew, she knew the story was not over yet.

The night of the opening, Rita dressed in black slacks and a red silk shirt. She added a silver chain, and put on a white wool blazer. She checked on Noah. "Are you almost ready, honey? I'm going to let you drive over." She knew that would light a fire under her young man with his learner's permit.

"Really?" Noah stood up straighter, pace quickening. He finished combing his hair. "Okay, I'm ready," he said. "Do I look okay?"

"You look great!"

Noah was dressed in a shirt and tie with his jeans and belt. Even before he put on his shoes, he was taller than Rita by several inches. Where did the time go? How had he gotten so tall, so fast? It seemed like just yesterday he was taking training wheels off his bike and playing Little League baseball, Rita recalled.

At the gallery opening, Jane took charge of pouring champagne for the adults. Noah poured soda for the few kids that came with them. Mrs. McCarthy greeted people from her chair of honor near the refreshments, which she had helped to prepare. Bach played on a CD player as guests circulated, admiring the art. Rita's friends, neighbors, people she didn't know, and those who had seen the announcement in the arts section of the local paper dropped by—a better turnout than she had envisioned.

Halfway through the evening a little round, red-headed woman arrived. She made a bee-line for the painting of the quirky man with a purple velvet jacket and crooked hat. She began to laugh loudly. People noticed. Rita excused herself from a conversation and walked over to her.

"You like this one, too?" Rita asked. "I enjoyed painting him."

The woman laughed again. "You know, if I didn't know better, I would swear you copied this from a photo of my great grandfather. It's his spitting image. He was a pip—could make you laugh just to see him, never mind his joking around," the woman said. "He also had a sixth sense, you might say—a knack for warning people about the future." She laughed, hoping this would be a welcome detail for the artist. "Has it sold yet? I'd like to buy it."

Rita suddenly flashed on her old boss, Tom, and his dream. He had said a man dressed in a purple jacket had come to warn her to be careful. Rita shook her head.

"Oh, really? It's sold, already? That's too bad," the patron said, seeing Rita shake her head.

"Oh, no! It's not that—you just reminded me of something. Please—the painting is yours, Ms.—I didn't get your name." Rita held out her hand to shake.

"Gladys Doyle. So nice to meet you. I never expected this—just came in on a whim when I saw the gallery opening sign and balloons outside. My family will be so delighted with this." She turned back to the painting. "I'll give you a check this evening. Can I pick it up tomorrow, though?"

"Of course, Ms. Doyle," Rita said slowly, unbelievably. "By the way, I hope you don't mind my asking…was your grandfather from Ireland?"

"Yes, most of my family still lives in Ireland, except for a few that emigrated to America in the early 1800s. How did you know that?" Gladys peered more intently at Rita.

"Just a feeling. Sometimes I just get a sense of the portraits as real people, even though I don't know them, if you know what I mean." Rita hoped she wasn't driving Gladys away.

"Oh, I do. Just looking at your work, it's so life-like. They all look like people you might have met or seen in a family album."

"Thank you so much." Rita smiled. She motioned to Noah to bring her the sold tags. Before she could digest what had happened, another art patron came up to her.

"Are you the artist?" asked the middle-aged man. He was a handsome fellow with fair skin, a well-trimmed mustache, and beard. His blue eyes sparkled.

"Yes, I'm Rita Kerner," she shook his hand. "And you are?"

"I'm Donald Palmer…Don," he introduced himself. "I teach science at a high school over in Providence. My wife and I were visiting a friend here this weekend, thought we'd come in. I'm interested in purchasing the wizard painting."

"Oh, that would be just terrific. He has such a special quality, doesn't he? So wise and kind—a certain electric magnetism."

"Hence the title of the painting, *Lightning Strikes Twice?*" he laughed.

"Are you talking about my husband?" A woman suddenly appeared next to Don.

"My wife, Ruth," he said, taking her arm.

"How do you do? Your husband likes the wizard painting."

"Of course he does. He's just an old wizard himself," she smiled.

Somehow Rita knew she wasn't kidding.

The next Saturday, Rita opened the gallery at noon and by late afternoon, several people had come and gone. But she hadn't sold anything that day. Consoled by interesting conversations with those who stopped in, she was especially grateful for having met a reporter from the Newport Daily News. She hoped he would write a good review in the art section's profile page.

Then, out of the blue, Jane dropped by. "I just came by to see how things are going—see if you needed anything."

"They're going well, although no sales yet today. But I'm glad you're here. Would you mind very much giving me a little break to run down to the corner to get a sandwich?" Rita asked. "Do you want me to pick up something for you, too?"

"No thanks," Jane replied. "But you go get some air. I'm fine. You have the price list here, so who knows? Maybe, I'll even make a sale for you," she laughed. "Take your time."

"Oh, thanks so much," Rita was relieved. "I won't be too long."

But an hour whisked by. When she returned to the gallery, Jane was writing a note.

"How'd it go? Sorry, I forgot I had to mail a bill, so I stopped off at the post office," Rita apologized. She had not expected much action during the time she was gone.

"Not a problem. I sold two paintings!" Jane was gleeful. "Can you believe it? Five minutes after you left, a woman came in and bought two of the Native American paintings. The mother and daughter one and the woman in the ceremonial dress. I was just writing you a note. I got a phone number. Her name was Cleo...Cleo...Summers." Jane held up Cleo's check.

"Fabulous! Oh, thanks so much, Jane. I'll be able to make the rent myself this month!" Rita looked at the check. The name looked familiar. Hadn't a friend invited her to a lesbian potluck dinner at the home of a woman named Cleo, a few months ago? Rita had been unable to attend because Noah had been down with the flu. Rita wondered if it was the same person. How many Cleo's could there be? I should give her a call, Rita pondered momentarily.

The next day, Rita started another painting. The day went by quickly. At closing time, she cleaned up her paints, and decided she would call Cleo. At that moment, a pretty African American woman came into the gallery. She appeared to be middle-aged, with warm brown skin and light braided hair. Dressed in a wool cape and dark slacks, her turquoise jewelry matched the blues and greens in her dashiki-style blouse.

She browsed slowly, then suddenly fixated on one painting. Rita thought she saw tears in her eyes.

"Are you okay? Can I help you?" Rita asked. "I'm Rita Kerner, the artist." She held out her hand.

"Oh," The woman shook Rita's hand. "I'm Olivia Williams. This is your work? It's amazing how real the portraits look." She turned to the painting she liked, speaking to Rita while staring at it. "I'm visiting my father and some friends in town. They mentioned your new gallery, so I thought since I was in the area….how much are the paintings?"

"They range from three-hundred to about twelve hundred, for the larger ones. The one you're looking at, "Woman In A Bakery", is four hundred and fifty."

"Well, it is amazing." She shook her head. "God works in mysterious ways, you know?" She didn't wait for an answer. "I'll just have to buy it," Olivia said. She searched her purse, looking up at the painting again. "It's my mother-in-law's mother—my husband's grandmother, Bertha. My goodness, the likeness is just phenomenal. How did you manage this?" She looked Rita over, sizing up her age. "There is no way you could have known her, is there?"

"No," Rita smiled, "not in this lifetime, anyway. The faces just appear as I paint," Rita explained.

"You have a gift, don't you know…from God."

Rita knew something was certainly from a source greater than herself. The paintings were affecting other people, not just her. People she didn't know were recognizing their relatives and friends. Something was happening. Something big.

Olivia Williams walked out the door with the painting she bought. Rita cleared her desk, putting her receipt with her other paperwork in a file drawer folder. Distracted by thoughts of her just-made sale, she did not notice Jane's note with Cleo's number slipping into the file cabinet. Rita took her belongings and closed the lights. As she left she heard a voice whisper. *"Remember…You are the one who remembers…"*

Rita went home. She made dinner as usual while Noah fed the dog. After dishes and homework, she and Noah played Scrabble, as they had done dozens of times on chilly winter evenings. She picked her first seven letters, H A S N A M U, rearranging them randomly on the little wooden placard until she found a word made of six letters with one left over. Together, they caught her eye. S H A M A N and U. She picked up the dictionary.

Shaman, a noun; a member of certain tribal societies, who acts as a *medium* between the visible world and an invisible spirit world; one who practices magical arts.

"Medium," she said aloud, little chills at the back of her neck.

Noah looked up. He smiled broadly. He had taken his letters and gone first. He made the word COURAGE on the scrabble board, using all seven letters for a bonus score. "Medium?" he exclaimed. "I'd say that is better than *medium*. Let's see you beat that!"

CHAPTER 36

Bertha's Family

Nakisha reluctantly climbed the stairs of the New York Public Library dragging her suitcase behind her, hoping the wheels would survive the long haul up the mountain of steps. NYU had closed just yesterday for holiday break, and she hadn't made it to the stacks in time. She needed one more bit of research material for her report before she would be on her way home for Christmas. Well, she thought, trying to look on the bright side, at least I can catch the shuttle to Penn Station from here. She repositioned a strap of her backpack across her shoulder with one hand, tightening her grip on the suitcase handle with the other. The weather had turned wickedly cold. The wind whipped down the canyon walls of the concrete jungle chilling her to the bone. Nakisha was glad she had worn her scarf and gloves her mother, Olivia, had sent her.

She showed her college ID to the library clerk and checked her suitcase. On the library's computer, she found the book she wanted in the book catalog, the material she was researching on West Nigeria's Yoruba culture. Before her arranged time for research was finished, she located a copy of another rare book, *The Little Old Bookshop* by Nicolette M. Lécuyer. She copied the information she needed and returned to the first floor desk. She handed the librarian her school card.

"An unusual book, quite old, last reprint was 1949." The librarian checked Nakisha's materials. "You like history?" The librarian smiled, her perfunctory duties complete. "You might also try looking at the bookstore around the corner that carries out of print books, if you want an actual bound edition."

Nakisha noticed the change in her expression. "Yes, I love history. Oh, thanks for the information. I'm doing a report for school, and I came across this title in my research of obscure women writers from the 18th century." Nakisha looked at her watch. There might be time to look at that bookstore. Wouldn't it be cool if I could get an old copy, she thought.

"Ah, good for you! Well, enjoy reading the material. I hope it helps with your report. Come back again when school reopens. There's lots to explore here." She handed the card back to Nakisha. "Merry Christmas!"

"Same to you," Nakisha said politely. She put her notebook and research material carefully into her backpack, picked up her suitcase at the check-in, and walked out into the cold afternoon. At the corner, instead of ducking into the subway, Nakisha turned east and walked down the block looking for the used bookstore the librarian had mentioned.

It wasn't long before she found it and to her great surprise, the very book she wanted. *The Little Old Bookshop,* by N. M. Lécuyer was dusty, its pages thin and yellowed with age, its leather binding threadbare, but still intact. Although worn, the title was still visible, letters embossed across the front of the book. The cost was more of her Christmas money than Nakisha had intended to part with, but she was so thrilled to have found it that she didn't give it too much thought. She handed the clerk twenty-eight dollars. Then she ran to 42nd street, practically flying down the IRT stairs and onto the subway.

By the time she got to Penn Station, she was out of breath. Rushing had gained her ten extra minutes, though. She purchased her ticket for the Boston-bound train and still had time to get coffee before she'd have to board. Nakisha rolled her suitcase easily on the polished granite floor to the closest coffee shop near Track 17. Hungry, she ordered a bagel with cream cheese to go with her coffee. So far, Christmas break was turning out well.

* * * * *

Rita looked at the big clock in the center lobby of Grand Central. It was two o'clock. She had lost track of the time having lunch with Noah, meeting his new girlfriend, Kate, for the first time. The young woman was a blond, blue eyed, California girl, pretty and soft spoken. Underneath her sweet exterior, Rita could sense the assuredness carried by those born into money. Rita wondered if California was in her son's future. *Just as easy to marry a rich...*Rita heard Lillian's voice.

She rushed along thinking about what a nice few days' visit it had been. She loved seeing Noah. He had finished school, had a job. He was so grown up, she thought. They had taken in the exhibit at the Modern Museum of Art and eaten at her favorite Indian restaurant on 6th Street. This morning they had picked up bagels for the next leg of her trip.

Running late, she would have to hurry to catch the shuttle to Penn Station. Her train was leaving at three o'clock. If she missed that one, she would be getting to the first writing conference she had ever attended, too late for dinner. She wanted to be on time. Stuffed in her suitcase along with her clothes were bits and pieces of her journals, some sketches and the beginning of the story about Clara. She was looking forward to trying a craft in which she had only dabbled.

The shuttle pulled into Penn Station dispersing hundreds of passengers into the hubbub of the rapid-paced terminal. Rita squeezed onto the platform among the throngs and rode up the escalator. She checked her new cell phone. It was a quarter to three. With no time to wait in line at the ticket counter, she would have to pay for a ticket on the train.

Rita wheeled her suitcase along the smooth stone floor, wishing she had time to pick up coffee to have with one of her bagels. She checked the departure board, then walked as fast as she could to Track 17, where an already crowded train waited. Rita boarded and managed to find an unoccupied double seat with minutes to spare and purposefully put one of her bags down on the empty spot next to her. "I hope no one sits here," she muttered under her breath. The idea of striking up a conversation with a chatty stranger was not appealing. She had too much on her mind.

* * * * *

Nakisha didn't want to sit at the back of the train. Walking back and forth along the platform at Track 17, she could see that the train was packed, though. When she heard the conductor's "All Aboard" call, she gave up worrying about the long walk at her destination and climbed aboard a rear car. She perused the scene. There were several open seats, but none completely empty. She would have to sit next to someone. Nakisha finally settled on a middle-aged white woman sitting by the window in the fifth row. At least she would have an aisle seat.

Rita noticed the young black woman coming toward her. She smiled at her politely, hoping the she would just keep walking. But of course, she did not.

"Is this seat taken?" Nakisha asked.

Rita smiled and moved her bag. Nakisha set her backpack down on the seat next to Rita and lifted her suitcase into the overhead compartment. Rita noticed her lean, strong body.

"*Youth is wasted on the young...*" Rita heard Lillian's voice. Older and wiser, Rita understood the expression. Age had crept up on her seemingly overnight. Hadn't she just been a spry young woman herself? Now she had to ask the conductor for help with her bag, her back too fragile for lifting heavy objects above her head. Rita resented the desertion of her able body.

"Hi," said Nakisha. She settled herself into her chosen seat. "I think I just made it in time. The train is really crowded."

"Yes, holiday's coming soon. Such a busy time of year." Rita hoped that would be the end of the niceties and she could read her conference booklet. She took the brochure from her satchel.

Nakisha wrapped up her half-eaten bagel and put it in her bag. She pulled out her library book and glanced toward Rita, noticing the writers conference pamphlet. "Oh, are you a writer?" she asked.

Rita looked at the young woman. There was something familiar about her, she thought. "No, well, not yet—maybe someday. I am an artist. I am going to a conference to learn something about writing, though. It looks interesting."

"An artist? Wow, what kind of art do you do? Are you a painter?" Nakisha asked. "I love art. I was thinking about majoring in art at college."

"Are you in college?" Rita asked before she could stop herself.

"Yes, I'm at NYU—I'm a freshman. I'm going to major in women's studies with a minor in historical anthropology, after the basic liberal arts classes."

"That's very impressive. I was involved in the women's movement in the 70s." Rita found herself surrendering to conversation as the train lurched forward, proceeding slowly out of the tunnel, and into the late afternoon light.

"Oh, I would love to interview you about that time in history. I asked my mom, but she was too young to remember that."

It was bad enough that she couldn't lift her own luggage, Rita thought. Now this? Had she become a part of history already?

"I'm doing a report for English Lit about women writers. It's an overview of historical facts that influenced the ability of black women to write and get published—kind of like a time line. I'm concentrating on America and Europe, first." Nakisha turned the book over in her lap exposing the front cover. "I just got this book," she said beaming. "It's written by a French woman in the eighteenth century. I found it by accident, when I was researching."

Rita glanced at the title of the rather worn book—*The Little Old Bookshop.* "Looks interesting," she said.

"Yeah," said Nakisha, cradling the book like a precious jewel. "So, what kind of art do you do?"

"Well," Rita took a deep breath. What could she say to this young student? "I paint portraits," she said, deciding to keep things simple.

"Oh, portraits are wonderful!" exclaimed Nakisha.

Rita was surprised by the young woman's enthusiasm. "Yes, they can be rewarding."

"My family has a portrait painting that's really wonderful. It's kind of magical."

"Really?" Rita had chills, always a sign that something important was about to happen. Was it coincidence, or something more that this young woman had sat next to her? She had options of other seats on the train. *"God works in mysterious ways..."* Rita heard a voice in her head.

Nakisha began without hesitation. "When I was ten, almost eleven really, my mother was on a trip. She went to an art gallery while she was visiting in Rhode Island. In the gallery was a picture of my great-grandmother, painted by the artist, the owner." Nakisha paused momentarily for emphasis. "But here's the thing that's amazing. The artist had never met or seen a picture of my great-grandmother, but she had painted an exact portrait of her! Isn't that incredible?" Nakisha laughed in delight. "Not only that, she painted my great-grandmother in a kitchen, baking—and my great-grandmother loved to bake."

Rita's eyes watered. She felt like laughing and crying at the same time. She reached for a tissue.

Nakisha looked at Rita. "I'm sorry, are you okay? Maybe I'm talking too much—I do that sometimes."

"You can call me Rita. What's your name, dear?"

"Nakisha. Nakisha Williams."

"I am very pleased to meet you. I am the artist your mother met in Rhode Island. It's my little gallery in Newport."

Nakisha jumped up from her seat. "No way. No way! How can that be?" Her eyes were wide and wild.

Rita looked at this sweet girl, so full of life. This child was somehow connected to her, she thought.

Nakisha sat back down. "How did this all happen? You paint my great-grandmother who you don't know, my mother goes to your gallery and I sit next to you on a train?"

"Yes, it is pretty amazing. Most people wouldn't believe something like this could happen. It must be more than a coincidence," Rita said. "I have some kind of a gift when it comes to painting. I'm just starting to understand it myself."

"My family loves that portrait. It was like a sign from God for my grandmother. 'Till the day she died, she never stopped saying how it was the most wonderful blessing." Nakisha was tearful. "And us meeting like this on the train. That must be the angels, too."

"Yes, I'm sure of it." Rita said as the train slowed. They were coming to the first stop in New Haven. "What's your destination?" Rita asked. "I am getting off here in New Haven to make a connection."

"I'm going to Boston for Christmas break. My mom lives there now. God, she'll never believe I met you."

"I'll give you my email address and you can write to me, if you'd like," Rita offered.

"Oh, I'd like that!"

"Maybe someday, we'll meet again. I'll come hear a lecture on historical anthropology by the famous Nakisha Williams!"

"It was my grandmother's dream for me to go to college. Now I am in college. Who knows—maybe I will write a book someday, too." Nakisha glanced at the conference pamphlet in Rita's lap again. "Maybe someday, I'll go to that writers' conference also." She laughed.

"Nakisha, do you mind my asking, what was your great-grandmother's name?" Rita tried to remember. "I think the woman who bought the painting, ah, your mother—she may have told me. But I've forgotten."

"Bertha. Her name was Bertha Washington."

"Bertha…" Rita heard the name roll from her lips like a lullaby. "Bertha, of course. Now I remember."

"She was married to my great-grandfather, James Washington," Nakisha explained. "And one of her daughters was my grandmother, Belinda, who we gave the painting to."

"Sounds like a wonderful family," Rita said. The names all sounded familiar. She tried to focus, but the conductor had opened the door. The loud clacking of the wheels against the tracks distracted her. Cold air was rushing into the car. Rita pulled her coat closed and wrapped her scarf around her neck. They were close to her stop. She composed herself and stood up.

"It was really good to meet you, Nakisha. I will be thinking of you." Rita leaned forward to give the young woman a hug.

Nakisha hugged Rita. "Thank you, this was really awesome! I can't wait to tell Mom. And please do write to me, too."

When the train came to a stop at the New Haven station, Nakisha helped Rita with her suitcase. Rita stood on the platform waving to Nakisha as the Boston-bound train pulled away. "Wow!"she said to herself. She shook her head in amazement and walked down to the lower level, to the bus depot where the Greyhound bus would take her to Amherst.

"Amherst?" The driver took Rita's ticket. "Going to that conference? Have some other ladies on the bus going there, too. You a writer?" the driver asked.

"Yes, a writer," Rita said hoping a simple "yes" would suffice. She'd had enough excitement for one day.

CHAPTER 37

Rita Kerner

MIAMI, FLORIDA, 2000

Rita had only been home from the writers' conference for two days when Irene called.

"I have some bad news, sis," Irene's voice was subdued. "Dad's had a turn for the worse. The cancer's spread. He's resting, you'd better come, though."

Rita was in Miami by her father's bedside the next day. She found Irene and her husband Gregory sitting alongside David's hospital-style bed. It was set up in the guest room of the apartment their parents had chosen for their retirement.

"Don't talk to him about, you know…dying," Irene whispered to Rita. "It upsets him."

Rita knew Irene was the one who was upset by the idea of death. She didn't understand death, the hereafter. None of them had been raised religiously and certainly not with the idea of reincarnation. To Irene, death was just sad. It meant goodbye forever. Perhaps David was afraid, too. He didn't have a connection to spirit either, didn't believe in a soul, or have a deep faith in a god, for that matter.

Rita walked close enough to her feeble father to see his chest moving. He labored for breath.

"Hi, Dad," Rita said softly into his good ear.

David opened his eyes, squinting like he was in bright sunlight. In his half-sitting position, he reached for Rita's hand. "Rita," he said.

273

"You got here?" He made an effort to sit up a little more.

"Of course," Rita said.

"How's Noah?" David asked.

"He's okay. He's got a good job. He's working and taking some additional college credits this summer." Rita now wished she had encouraged Noah to come along. By the look of David's condition, there was not going to be another chance to say goodbye, not this time around.

"Dad, Rita's going to make dinner. Gregory and I are going out to the market. We'll be back soon." Irene reassured him, like he was a child. "I'll change your sheets when we get back."

David nodded. "Rita makes a good Jewish meal," he said. He laid his head back on the pillow and closed his eyes.

"He's not very happy with our cooking." She shrugged. "There is some chicken in the fridge, so make whatever else you can find with it. I'll get some more fruit at the market. He seems to like that."

Rita put the chicken in a pan and smothered it with onions and garlic. She found some white potatoes and a jar of applesauce in the pantry, so potato pancakes were a sure thing. A bag of frozen green beans, hiding in the back of the freezer, were still good. She remembered how one summer her father had grown green beans and tomatoes in their little terrace rose garden. He had let each daughter take turns picking the vegetables when they ripened. Where had that David gone? Rita thought sadly. At least Noah had helped to repair their connection a little during summers in Vermont. David loved all his grandkids, in spite of everything.

Searching further, Rita found a jar of half-sour pickles, and added those to the menu. One of David's stories floated into Rita's thoughts—his boyhood memory of the juicy pickles that sat in big, brine-filled wooden barrels on the sidewalk in front of the deli, where Grandmother Pearl and Rita's grandfather worked before the Great Depression.

For dessert, Rita found a little box of chocolate pudding among the lime, lemon, and raspberry flavored Jell-O packages in the pantry door—his favorite dessert, except for ice cream.

"Pop." Rita brought a dinner tray to her father.

David opened his eyes again. "I smelled it cooking. Mmm, so nice to have a good meal," he said. "You are still a good cook. Mom taught you well."

Rita knew he meant his mother, her Grandma Pearl, not Lillian. David savored each bite, but could only eat about half the meal. The chocolate pudding he devoured. He wiped his mouth and smiled slightly. *"Mecheieh!* Great pleasure! Irene and Gregory don't know from such a good meal." He lay back against his propped-up pillows with a satisfied little grin.

Rita started to clear his tray.

"Wait. Why don't you sit for a minute, Rita. I want to ask you something." David looked serious.

Rita sat on the love-seat near the window across from his bed. She glanced out at the palm trees and flowers lining the sidewalk that led up to the condo steps. It was getting dark outside. She wished it would cool off a little. The apartment had been oppressively warm and humid all day. Such hot weather in the middle of winter felt strange to Rita.

"You must have known people who died…I mean during the AIDS epidemic?"

"Yes, I knew a few people, why?" Rita asked. She looked at her father. She'd heard the question, but was taken by surprise. The topic of death was not on the menu, especially not the devastation of the gay population, in the '80s.

"Did anyone you know want to hasten their death, end their suffering?" David asked.

Rita could see his sincerity. Irene was wrong. Death was something he needed to talk about. Somehow, after all this time, he had finally realized that it was Rita with whom he could talk. Fifty-three years of history between them melted away. They were back where they had begun. Between her childhood and his imminent death, so much had been left unsaid. Anger had replaced the love and caring of the early years. But David was not angry anymore. Now he needed her. She was in his favor once again.

"Not that I know of, Pop. Most of them were young," Rita said sadly. "They wanted…wanted to live." The death of so many still painful, a reminder of terrible times. Even now, two of Rita's friends were surviving only by the grace of God and a triple medicine cocktail.

"I did know someone from work who had cancer, Dad. She was older. She fought for a long time." Rita knew what he wanted to hear. Somehow her experiences meant something, now. "She stopped eating, drinking, taking her medication. She was in a great deal of pain and stayed alive as long as she could. Then she decided to let go."

David put his head back and seemed to stare at the ceiling. For a moment, Rita wondered if he had heard her answer.

"Life is all gone now. There is nothing left—it's all over," he mumbled.

"Really, Dad, it's not. There is a whole other life beyond this one and then some."

David looked up. "How do you know? How are you so sure you know about death?"

It was not a mean question. He was not the old David, critical of her life, her choices, her looks. There was no hostility. He was transitioning. She knew how it would go—the fear, the resolve, then the letting go.

"I have a gift," Rita paused. Words that she'd never voiced to him before echoed in the room. "My work allows me to paint people I don't know. I don't have pictures of those who have died. They tell me how they look. I can talk to them and hear them."

David just looked at Rita. "Paint pretty pictures, like you did when you were little," he said.

Rita knew he could not accept her answer. But she let it be. She walked over to the small bookshelf that held his medication. A worn, hard-covered book was lying open on the top, next to the prescription bottles.

"Dad? Do you want me to read to you?" Rita picked up the book, holding it open.

"That book's for Noah," He said. "I want him to have it. It was my favorite book when I was young," he managed.

"I will be sure to give it to him, Dad."

David nodded. He repositioned himself, trying to get comfortable. Rita could tell he was in pain. She rearranged his pillows and covered him with a light cotton blanket.

"Do you want your pain medicine, Dad?"

"Later..." he mumbled. He closed his eyes and dozed.

As Rita prepared to let him rest, she placed the book he saved for Noah back on the shelf. She glanced at the title. *The Little Old Bookshop* was embossed in gold letters on the worn front leather cover. A wave of emotion swept over her. A recent memory on the edges of her mind, a ripple in time and space, dizzied her. Hadn't she seen that title before? Suddenly, she remembered the young black woman she'd met on the train going to Amherst. Were all the people she met, she knew, connected? Had she and David had more lives together than she remembered?

That night Rita fell asleep, exhausted. In a dream, she found herself peering around a corner, down a cobblestone street bustling with horses and horse-drawn wagons. It was a gloomy day. The street looked like old photographs of downtown San Francisco from a museum. She was looking for something, but she didn't know what.

Then the dream shifted to a small shop. It was a clock shop. The sign read *Fine Clocks and Watches*. There were two men standing in front of the store. It was her father and another younger man. She recognized them both. Her father was the person Rita knew—David Kerner, but he looked different, with dark hair combed back beneath a black cap, a long mustache, a fine leather jacket and riding britches. She recognized the younger man too, but was not sure how. She stood and watched them, as if she was observing an old Western movie.

Her father had his precious gold watch and chain in his hand. The other man was looking at it, then up at her father. Rita instinctively knew the two men were brothers. They began to argue.

"Don't be a fool, Kyle! You and those cowboys are gambling on that gold mine. The railroad is a better bet than that. I won't part with this gold watch for you to squander on your schemes and whiskey. I aim to meet with some wealthy men comin' from back East about building the railroad up through Oregon, now with statehood near. The railroad is goin' to make us rich. We can have all the gold we want."

"I ain't no fool, brother," Kyle said. "I know you made money up there at Rogues Bend in that gold claim even before I came west. And it ain't no secret old Pop giving you that watch."

"Look, Kyle, I gave you the money to come across the Trail, and I've earned most of what I have. You're a man now. Be smart. Get rid of those gamblers you been traveling with. They're outlaws. They'd knife you in the back, soon as look at you, if you cross them." Peter Doyle said. "Look Kyle, why don't you come up to see me? The railroad men are comin' through in a month to meet with me 'bout a railroad line between Portland and Sacramento." He put a hand on his younger brother's shoulder. "The railroad's coming west, brother. We're talkin' about progress and some real money, kid. You want gold? Well, just show up—alone. And don't be telling those criminals you drink with nothing about it."

Rita felt a searing pain in her shoulders and the weight of gravity pulling her down. Before she awoke, a fleeting vision of Kyle appeared. He was drinking whiskey and bragging to some men about his wealthy brother, with lots of gold up in Oregon. She saw them, his outlaw friends with guns in hand, riding up a hill to a familiar looking house on a hill. Wind swept cypress trees, a meadow of horses and the smell of sweet bread and cinnamon filled her nostrils. She woke up with a start. She lay flat on her back for a few minutes, feeling queasy. Then she sat up and drank some water from her glass on the night stand.

"Rita? Are you up?" Irene came in the room. "Dad won't take his medication." Panic laced her voice. "I gave him his regular toast and tea for breakfast, but he didn't eat. He only drank a little tea."

Rita grabbed some coffee in the kitchen and went into David's room. "Pop? Would you like some pain medication? It will be okay," she said, hoping he would understand.

David was having trouble breathing. He nodded. Rita gave him his morphine. She poured some ice water and moistened her father's lips.

"Dad, you have to eat," Irene said. "Tell him, Rita."

"It's okay, Irene. Maybe he will have something later. Let him rest."

Rita could feel her mother's presence and could hear Grandma Pearl's singing, *Sclof in zizzen ruh,* sleep in sweet repose. She could see Lillian holding out her arms. Rita could hear her voice "*...remind him of that time after the war...*"

"It's okay, Pop. We're here. You're going to be okay," Rita said softly. She put her hand on his crown chakra, the top of his head. "Try to sleep, Dad." Rita knew the word *sleep* would not be scary. "Dream of Mom, now. Can you picture how she looked when you married her? Remember that pink dress she wore?" Rita stroked his bald head. It was something her father had done—stroked her head when she was little to help her go to sleep. It had made her feel secure, the last sweetness of the once close bond she remembered.

Rita felt sad. What a waste, she thought—so many difficult years between then and now. For what? Her desire to be something other than someone's wife? Her loving women? Not wanting to remain near home, where he could control her? Maybe she was to blame, too. She went as far away as possible and didn't look back for so many years. It had been hurtful to her mother, she knew. Had David cared? Rita looked down at her father. He was very near the end.

It was time to call the rest of the family. Irene and Rita arranged for their sons to fly to Miami. Tina, her husband and oldest daughter were on the next flight out from La Guardia. They sat vigil. The hospice nurse came and went. Gregory cooked for them, but nobody was very hungry. Three days passed. David had brief wakings until the fourth day. He did not wake up again, but his breathing rattled loudly.

"Dad, we're right here." Rita leaned close to David. "Do you remember the time you and Mom went to that lodge after you got back from the war?"

"Why are you asking him that?" Tina whispered. She looked at Irene who shook her head. Only Rita remembered the pictures and love letters found in that forbidden closet that Lillian warned her not to open. A dare to the rebellious teenager Rita had been, she had looked in the closet when her mother was not home.

"Remember how you and Mom danced that night? And how the wine made her so tipsy? Remember the love letters you wrote, how she had saved them all in that shoe box?" Rita continued talking into Davids good ear.

Tina eyes widened like a child hearing a new story. Irene listened too, nervously tucking David's blanket around him. She began to take off his gold watch to make him more comfortable. David stirred, clenching his hand into a loose fist. He did not wake up. Irene looked at Rita with a glimmer of hope in her eyes. Rita shook her head.

"Leave it," Rita whispered gently. Watches had always been something David loved. He had more than one gold watch. They were his treasures. Now, he was still holding on, Rita understood. Even in his unconscious state, David held on to the material world by a thread. His gold watch was his badge of honor, his victory over the poverty of his parents immigrant roots, over the Great Depression. It was his claim to the America he had fought for, the land of freedom, safety and dreams—and the only thing preventing him from slipping away into the great unknown.

Gregory came in to check on things. "The kids can come in to say goodbye now," Rita said. Tears filled Irene's eyes and dripped down her face in silence. Gregory took her hand. Tina put a tissue to her own wet face.

The next morning, when Irene and Gregory work up, they found Rita asleep on the love-seat near David's bed.

"Wake up, Rita, wake up! Dad is not breathing!"

Rita stood up, still half asleep. She leaned over her father and felt for a pulse. There was none. "Mom has come for him," she said, putting an arm around Irene's shoulder. She looked at David. He was at peace. "Maybe, you should wake Tina and the rest of the family," Rita said. When her sister and brother-in-law left the room, Rita leaned over and kissed her father's cold forehead.

"Thank you for being my father," Rita said. "Next time, we'll do better."

After the funeral, Rita and Noah flew home. She comforted Noah. She encouraged him to take a few more days off from work, go camping with his friends. He agreed.

For the next few days, Rita could still feel David's presence, his shock at finding Lillian, his parents, and friends again. They were all there to meet him as he passed into bliss, the realm beyond incarnation. Rita laughed. "See Pop, I told you—the party's just beginning!" she said.

An odd feeling overcame her. She tried to tune into the sensation. Even though she had not been close to David for so many years, his passing made her feel alone. She was no one's daughter anymore, an orphan. Rita realized there was something else she felt. She was jealous. Some part of her wished to go home, too. Finally, she let her tears flow.

CHAPTER 38

Wambleeska

SOUTH DAKOTA, GREAT PLAINS, 1842

Wambleeska set off along the path of the buffalo hunt, heading south and then west along the tributaries of the great river. He knew some of the ancient trade routes beyond the hunting grounds of his people. The territories west to the Big Horn Mountains in Wyoming and south to the Platte River in Nebraska were still home to strong nations belonging to the Seven Council Fires. His kindred tribes had not succumbed to the white man.

He would head toward the Oglala camp along the North Platt River in Nebraska. He would meet with council elders, speak with them about relocating farther west, away from the encroaching white settlers and government threats. He would tell them about his visions of hardship to come, about the devastation of the Great Mother. He was determined to find a way to take his people to safety. Their imminent danger haunted his waking and sleeping dreams. A powerful nation, they could band together in greater numbers and remain safe longer, he was sure.

Wambleeska traveled until darkness. As night surrounded him and the sky filled with stars, he wrapped his fur around him snugly. He walked his horse, moving slowly in the moonlight through a clearing where a broad pine tree with low-hung branches provided a ladder. There he could reach a safe height and take cover from wolves and the night wind. Wambleeska secured his mare to a low tree limb and climbed into the strong, wide branches—his bow, arrows, knife, and satchel held close in case of bear or mountain lion. He covered his head with his warm fur, leaned into the trunk, and wrapped his legs around the branch under him. Secure in his nest, he fell asleep, exhausted from travel.

Soon he dreamed. In his dream world, he felt a great sadness. Wambleeska stood on a high cliff, looked down from a great height, and then without thought, he jumped. As he fell, a great winged bird suddenly caught him. An enormous bed of white feathers engulfed him, softer than flower petals, yet strong—strong enough to hold him, fly with him, soar and swoop high above the trees.

The bird spoke to him as it flapped its giant wings and soared gracefully through the night sky. The air felt warm against his cool skin. Out of his peripheral vision he saw the long black hair of his youth flowing from his head out into the wind. In his dream, Wambleeska looked at his hands buried in the bird's feathers, holding tightly, in the same way he clenched his horse's mane. For a second, he thought they looked like the hands of a child, a young girl. With that thought, the magnificent bird-being spoke to him. *"Grandmother is here with us now. Don't be afraid. You have chosen to be here. Remember...remember why...remember why you are here."*

Wambleeska awoke with a start. Abruptly conscious of his tree dwelling, he tightened his grip around the trunk, secured his seated position, and stretched each leg slowly, one at a time, so the blood flowed smoothly in each foot again. Had the wind blowing through the trees or an owl hooting into the night air awakened him? He listened carefully, attentive to the night sounds of the land and his horse. His mare, legs folded under her, rested on the soft pine-covered forest floor. Wambleeska looked about him, his eyes accustomed to the darkness. Seeing nothing, he slept again. When he awoke the next time, a golden dawn hugged the horizon.

Wambleeska climbed down from his safe perch and walked his horse through the woods. He was careful to watch for animal tracks—wolf, bear, mountain lion. But he was hungry, very hungry. Anything that moved would be his prey.

Soon, a rabbit appeared a short distance away, behind a small cluster of trees. He stopped in his tracks. His horse stopped too. They stood very still. Without telegraphing his movements and without a sound, Wambleeska gracefully raised his bow and let the arrow hit its mark. The rabbit fell.

Wambleeska moved quickly. The smell of blood would draw other prey. He thanked the rabbit for its sacrifice. Removing the arrow, he wiped it and his hands with damp leaves, and prepared his sack for carrying his meal undetected. Adeptly, he mounted his horse and rode quickly to an open expanse of grassland.

As he came to the edge of the woodlands, a great plateau spread out in front of him. Towering mountains loomed in the distance. The sky's pink and golden hues lit the vast landscape. He found a spot where he could see in all directions and could watch for danger. Keeping bow and arrow ready, he gathered twigs and prepared a small fire with the hands of a master fire-maker. He scraped away dirt and leaves from his kill, skinned it with his knife and placed it into the fire. He ate every bit ravenously while his horse grazed on moist grasses. He burned the blood-soaked leaves, then put out the fire with dirt. He cleaned his face and hands in the wet grass, pulling handfuls from the ground and piling the lush green shoots on the pile of dirt and ashes, thanking the Great Spirit for the four-legged ones who sustained his survival.

For the next few days, Wambleeska collected berries, mushrooms, wild onions, and seeds wherever he found them along his journey. He ate squirrel and pheasant, and drank from small streams. He followed along in the direction he remembered, moving at dawn, dusk and early evening in the light of the moon, careful to keep hidden from soldiers and scouts. He hoped to reach the camps of the Two Kettle or Brule before long. But he reached a curve in the North Platte River, still alone.

In the late afternoon, Wambleeska fell asleep in a cave along the low ledge near the river. He dreamed of his reunion with his wife, daughter and grandchild, his *Tiospaye,* family. He saw their smiling faces upon his return, how proud they were that he met with elders of other Oglala tribes, found a place for them where they could live in safety. He saw the procession they would make like they had each season, taking up their tipis, horses and dogs—moving the people to new hunting grounds, to their winter or summer lands.

The next day was dry, a hotter day than usual for late spring. He traveled farther west. In late afternoon, Wambleeska stopped along a tributary, so he and his horse could drink its cool, silty water. The tall grass along the nearby ridge blew in the wind like waves across a river. He listened to the chirping birds, to the rustling of small animals in the underbrush and the high-pitched song of tree frogs. He watched for snakes. For a moment, he thought he heard voices of people, but shook off the idea attributing it to his loneliness. It seemed like a long time that he'd been without the kind of restful sleep he'd once known, pushing himself further each day, enduring the elements and isolation. His visions were more frequent. Even in his waking hours, Wambleeska noticed that he saw and heard things that usually came only in his sleeping dreams. Now, he slowed his breathing. The quieter his breath, the more he was convinced that the sounds he heard were not his imagination. Perhaps, his people were just up ahead.

He took his horse's reins, pulling her up from thirst, walking to where the stream opened wider toward the great river, where the low-lying trees and bushes gave way to the sandy cliffs and where dust rolled up from the dry earth. There was so much sand in the air that Wambleeska's eyes burned. He rubbed them slowly. He bent his head slightly, hunched over, and put his arm across his forehead to shield the blowing dust from his eyes. He trudged forward in the dust storm, not seeing exactly where he was going. Knowing his horse would follow him, he loosened his grasp on her reins.

Suddenly, the mare stopped. She snorted, nostrils flared, her ears went back, eyes frightened. Instinctively, Wambleeska looked up to see what had spooked her. His heart jumped into his throat, pounding hard. Adrenalin pumped through his veins. He stood frozen as if in some horrific nightmare from which he could not wake. A massive wagon train had come to a halt just a few hundred yards from where he stood. Forty wagons filled with white settlers were making camp. Time slowed. Voices boomed loudly, only muffled by the thick dust-filled air spinning around Wambleeska. Before Wambleeska could move, a man aimed his gun at him.

Through a cloud of sand, he heard a woman scream. "Indians! Indians!"

A man came running toward her, pulling her to safety. Another aimed his shotgun in the direction she pointed. A bullet whistled by Wambleeska's head. White men on horseback were shooting.

Wambleeska turned to run, but pain seared his chest, his throat. A burning bullet had ripped through him. He fell forward. With great effort, he retrieved his knife from his belt. He would not die. "I will kill the white men and save myself," he whispered, as he lay on the ground. He waited.

"Hurry, Mr. Doyle, your wife will be safe with the other women. Take your firearm. Come with us to the ridge," the wagon master said. Several men mounted horses. "If there's one of them Indians, there's bound to be more. That one looks like it fell where we got him." He pointed to the ridge. "Better make sure, since we're settlin' in for the night. More wagons be coming soon too, so there will be plenty more of us than them," the wagon master surmised, wiping sweat and dust from his brow. "So many wagons and dust should scare 'em off."

He turned and looked at Peter Doyle with some disdain. "Good for you to get some practice killing Indians. You're gonna need to use that gun—you're not in Philadelphia no more. This here is the West," he laughed. "Indian country, just like I told all you folks. It's kill or be killed."

Peter Doyle picked up his rifle, reluctantly. He looked over at his young wife, Sarah. He could see she was afraid. "It will be okay. Stay with the others," he said to her, mimicking the cowboys and wagon master, men Doyle admired. They were fearless and rugged souls who'd taken others over the Trail before them. They knew danger and death. They knew how to protect themselves and the wagon trains on the treacherous journey across this magnificent and wild landscape. Peter Doyle's hesitancy evaporated. He held his gun with conviction and mounted one of his tired horses.

"There, by the bushes," a scout pointed, as the men came up the ridge. "He's crawled over there from the looks of the blood trail."

The men dismounted and stood near Wambleeska, who lay motionless on the ground.

"Hey, don't get too close, Doyle," the scout warned. "They play dead," he said, poking Wambleeska with the barrel of his rifle.

Wambleeska didn't hear them or feel the hard metal jab his ribs. His knife lay wrapped tight in his hand under his lifeless body. He was far away, flying up with the great white eagle over the mountaintops and trees. Voices, soft and calm, whispered and praised his name as he swooped and soared in the waning rays of dusk, light sweeping orange and purple over the peaks. He saw his mother, father, his uncles, cousins, his kin standing in a circle around a ceremonial fire, waving to him as he flew toward them. They showered him with songs and wrapped him in fur and beaded skins.

"You'd better make sure he's dead, Doyle."

Peter grimaced. He moved closer toward the Indian. He could already smell the urine and blood.

"Doyle, shoot him! Put another bullet in him for good measure. Just like you're putting down a horse, man. Do it quick. Now."

Peter Doyle raised his gun and cocked it. He hesitated, feeling his stomach churn. With the weight of expectation from the others bearing down on him, he aimed at the Indian's back, and pulled the trigger. More blood oozed out of the dead Indian. Peter knew he had shot a dead man. He had never killed a human being before, and regardless of the law of the wilderness, he knew that the Indian was a man, not an animal. A terrible chill grabbed him and would not let go. No amount of whiskey or wool could warm Peter Doyle that night.

CHAPTER 39

Rita Kerner

Rita cleaned off her desk at the gallery. She was thinking of closing the space since rents were rising. She wanted a change, too, but wasn't quite sure what she wanted to do. She rummaged through her old invoices, to purge the ones that were no longer needed for tax purposes, when she came across a small note. It was old and faded, having obviously been misplaced among her files. There was a phone number on it and a name, Cleo Summer. She tried to place it. She looked in her "paintings sold" file. There is was.

Sold/December, 1993:

Dowanhowee, (Lakota woman in ceremonial dress), oil on canvas

Mother and Daughter, (Lakota women), oil on canvas

Sold to Cleo Summers, Providence, Rhode Island. Ck#945

Now Rita remembered. This was the woman to whom Jane had sold two of Rita's favorite paintings after the gallery had opened a number of years ago. Having never gotten around to contacting her, Rita wondered if she should still call her. Curious, she didn't think about it for long. She dialed Cleo's number. A message directed callers to a new number with an area code Rita recognized as Northampton, Massachusetts. Throwing caution to the wind, Rita punched in the area code and number.

A woman answered.

"Hello," said Rita. "I'm Rita Kerner. We have never met, but you came into my gallery in Rhode Island, several years ago. You bought two paintings of…"

"Oh yes," Cleo's mellow voice said. "I just love your work. Of course, I still have them."

"Well, thanks you so much. I notice you have a new number. Do you get down to Rhode Island much any more? If you're ever nearby, please stop by the gallery sometime," Rita offered.

"Oh, you know, I'm so glad you called. I was just talking to a friend about these paintings. I found your website just the other day. I'd love to talk to you about your paintings," Cleo said. "Do you ever get up to Northampton?"

"Well, I guess I could. As a matter of fact, I was thinking I'd like to have a little change of scenery. Are you busy this coming weekend?"

Rita felt butterflies in her stomach. Was she asking a woman she never met, knew nothing about, for a weekend date? She couldn't believe it herself. But heck, she thought, why not take a risk? Noah was on his own. She no longer had the same responsibilities or restrictions of scheduling. With only two brief affairs in the last few years, Rita's imagination shifted into gear.

"So, I'll come up this weekend, maybe we can have a bite?"

"That sounds lovely. Do you like Japanese food?"

By the time Rita and Cleo had finished their conversation, Rita was more excited than she had been in a long time. She could barely contain herself dialing Jane's number.

"Hi Jane, do you have a minute?"

"Sure, Rita. How are things going? So sorry to hear about your Dad."

"Thanks, Jane. I'm okay. How are you doing? Did you get the paperwork for your Mom's estate worked out with probate?"

"Yes, I'm glad we are done with that. I'm thinking about a change of scenery for a little while. Maybe someplace warm for the winter."

"Yeah, that sounds great. It would do you some good to get away. How about that Caribbean cruise you wanted to take?"

"Might just do that. So, to what do I owe this call? Do you want to do lunch and catch up, one day soon?" Jane offered.

"I'd love to. I was wondering if you could check my chart real fast and see about a new connection. You know, a possible a relationship?" Rita inquired nervously.

"I have the computer on already…looks very positive at this point. Venus is definitely in a positive aspect for you now. Go for it! Hey, and let me know when you have some free time."

"Will do. And thanks, Jane. I'll call you after the weekend. I'm going for a little change of scenery too," she laughed.

Feeling more confident about an otherwise rash decision, Rita left for Massachusetts on Saturday afternoon, arriving at the planned location, a Japanese restaurant on Northampton's main street.

Cleo was waiting for her when she got there. She was a pretty woman about her own height, but slightly thinner. She wore a wine red sweater with a multicolored scarf and black jeans. Beautiful, Rita thought, aware of the fluttering in her stomach.

Through dinner, Rita watched Cleo closely. With an artist's eye, she traced the shape of Cleo's face, her dark hair with wisps of bangs, her perfectly-shaped lips. Mesmerized by how Cleo laughed as she threw her head back slightly, how her green eyes twinkled seductively, how she chewed her food slowly, sensually—Rita had barely been able to eat her meal.

"Would you like to come over to my place for tea?" Cleo asked. "I don't live far. Just across town near the park."

Rita laughed nervously. There was nothing she would have liked better than to go to Cleo's apartment. Yet she was surprised when Cleo asked. It took courage to initiate such an invitation. She had not pegged Cleo as the assertive type, so she was pleasantly surprised, though a bit disconcerted. Rita had not met anyone like Cleo before.

They had an instant rapport. Absorbed in each others stories of lives lived out loud, they laughed—the conversation easy, flirtatious. But, suddenly Rita felt awkward, even though it was she who had asked Cleo out to dinner, under the guise of thanking Cleo for her art purchase.

"So, would you like to come up for tea?" Cleo asked again, waiting patiently to see if Rita would take the sweet bait.

"Yes, that would be nice," said Rita, realizing a cup of tea might be more than tea.

Taking the plunge, Rita narrowly managed to squeeze her car into a parking spot on the side street next to Cleo's building. She followed Cleo up a flight of stairs to her second floor flat..

"Oh, hope you don't mind, I have a cat," Cleo said, "but he probably won't come out. He's not too friendly." She paused. "Actually, that is an understatement," Cleo added. "He has been known to bite occasionally." Cleo put the key in the lock. "You're okay with cats?"

"Sure, I have a dog, but we had a cat, too," Rita answered. "Didn't want my kid to be an only child," she laughed. "I like all animals," she said, following Cleo into the apartment.

On first impression, Rita felt immediately embraced by Cleo's warm, inviting space. It had a designer's touch and an artistic flair— not pretentious, just tasteful.

"Here, I'll take your jacket. Make yourself comfortable," Cleo said, pointing to the couch in the living room. "I'll put some water on the stove."

Rita sat down and tried to relax. She closed her eyes for just a moment and breathed deeply. Suddenly, she felt an animal's paws, a heavy weight in her lap. She opened her eyes. A huge orange cat was staring her in the face. "Oh, hi there," Rita said. "What's your name?"

"Oh, wow! That's Aries. I have never seen him do that with anyone before!" Cleo said, walking back into the room.

Aries purred. Rita pet him as he nestled into her lap. There was an awkward silence. Cats knew things.

"What kind of tea would you like?" Cleo asked, breaking the silence. "I have Earl Gray, Chamomile, Peppermint, Lemon Zinger."

"Lemon Zinger would be great," said Rita.

Cleo walked back to the kitchen and soon returned with a tray carrying two mugs of hot tea and a small plate of chocolate chip cookies.

"Oh, nice, thank you," said Rita. She moved slightly. Aries stretched and moved too, resettling on the couch next to Rita.

"This is a lovely apartment," Rita said, stirring her tea with a spoon.

"Thanks," said Cleo. "I'm glad to be settled, finally, after the break-up."

"How long has it been since you and your ex separated?"

"Patty and I broke up seven months ago. I went out to Los Angeles for a while to stay with friends, but my twins are still in college here, so I wasn't ready to move that far. Besides, now that I've finished school myself, I can concentrate on my second career. I have a new job starting in Amherst in a few weeks, so when this place came up, I grabbed it. Would you like to see the rest of the apartment?" Cleo suggested. "The tea's a little too hot, anyway."

"Oh, yes," said Rita. She wanted to get to know Cleo. This she was sure of, especially upon entering the bedroom.

Cleo's bedroom was an eclectic mix of elegant and comfortable. The bedspread—a tasteful pink, burgundy, and green floral—covered the queen-size bed with matching sham-covered pillows propped against an oak headboard. Careful attention had been given to the art prints that adorned the cream-colored walls, with their wine-toned matting and silver frames. Above the bed hung Rita's two paintings of Native American women. They seemed to be right at home.

A simple glass vase filled with pale pink roses sat on the antique, mirrored dresser. Small, lush throw rugs were scattered on the shiny, dark hardwood floor. A fresh candle was nestled in a little ceramic bowl on one of the two nightstands, with a matchbook waiting beside it. Lighting from a pink-shaded lamp on the opposite nightstand softened the edges of the space. Rita practically melted when Cleo lit a sage incense stick, its familiar aroma quickly filling the room.

"Don't your paintings look perfect here?" Cleo asked.

"They do, perfect." Rita's senses were overwhelmed, startled by the unexpected sensual allure, seduced by the room's femininity and symmetry. She could almost feel the clean, cotton sheets beneath the velvety quilt. With that thought, her cheeks flushed. Her body's heat rose. To be near a woman unlike any she had ever known, to be in

Cleo's bedroom where her paintings hung on the wall above the bed, drew Rita in. The bed called to Rita, enticing her to lie in its soft luxury.

Face flushed, Rita pushed hard against the remembering, the knowing, the desire long-buried. She could hear only the sound of her own heartbeat, the blood pumping through her veins as she turned away and walked into the adjacent kitchen. Embarrassed by an audible gasp she thought had escaped her lips, she covered her tracks and walked ahead of Cleo into the bathroom on her semi-guided tour of the apartment. She breathed deeply to calm herself.

Along the side of the tub near the window hung a large ornamental kite made of silver and turquoise fabric. "Did you make this lovely kite?" Rita asked, finally able to look directly at Cleo without blushing. She gazed at Cleo intently. Rita felt herself begin to let go, begin to accept whatever was about to happen. Attracted like a fish to the lure, like a fly to the spider's web, she could picture herself falling for this mysterious, beautiful woman.

"Oh, yes, I did," Cleo replied. She hadn't, but could have done so easily, being a woman of many talents and charms. It would only be later that she admitted wanting to impress Rita. And so she had.

In the moment, the answer seemed natural and wonderful to Rita. Cleo's next room contained a sewing machine and a poster with the words ARTIST in bright colored letters with a simple definition of the "Divine Nature of Creating Art." Shelves of fabric piled neatly in order of color and pattern sat next to a sewing table and chair. Rita felt more than interested, more than impressed. She felt a euphoric bliss. Possibilities swirled about her, images of desire danced in the periphery of her vision. To be falling for an artist like herself had only been a dream.

"What about your place? Your gallery? Do you live alone?" Cleo asked as they sat down again to have their tea.

"I still live near the gallery, a little house we have been in for some time now. My son has recently moved out on his own, so I'm just getting used to that."

"It's nice when they go off to school. You miss them, but it's also good to have more time for yourself, new things." She walked to the bookshelf along the wall near the kitchen. She returned with a book. "Have you ever seen this book?" she asked.

Rita looked at the cover and the title, *Intuition and Creativity: The Art of Marla Woods.* "That is similar to my artwork," Rita said as she looked through the book, again surprised by Cleo's perceptiveness and sincerity. Rita was flattered that Cleo had taken the time to find out more about her. She finished her cookie and put her cup of tea back down on the coffee table.

Cleo sat down, closer to Rita this time. Nervous and excited, Rita continued looking through the book. The sculptures were exquisite in detail and design. She read a few lines, skimming the captions beneath the pictures. "These are amazing," Rita said, feeling Cleo's gaze. She looked up.

Cleo was staring at her intensely. Her smile drew Rita toward her in slow motion. Cleo leaned forward, kissing Rita ever so gently on the lips. Aries, the cat, lay between them. He did not budge.

Rita's heart pounded. Electricity ran up and down her whole body. She pulled Cleo closer to her. She kissed her back with a long, deep kiss. The taste of chocolate cookies and lemon tea, the smell of lavender soap, the sensation of rose petal-soft lips filled all of Rita's senses. She knew it would not be too long before the dizziness of their intense desire would overtake them. Still, she wanted to go slowly, to make sure her heart would be safe.

"I usually have to work on Saturdays" Rita said. "Maybe we can get together again next weekend on Sunday? Spend some time getting to know each other?"

* * * * *

A few weeks later Rita sat in the gallery finishing a painting of a petite French woman. The outfit, color, and style looked like someone who might have lived in the 18th century. Rita stared at it. "So, who are you, dear one?" she asked the portrait. Just then Rita heard the gallery door open.

"So who is this woman?" Cleo's voice teased.

"Oh, hi! What a nice surprise."

She hugged Cleo. Cleo kissed Rita.

"Happy New Year! I missed you," she said seductively. "Did you get to see your son for New Year's?"

"Oh, yeah." Rita had a pang of empty-nest syndrome. "He's doing well, thanks. He and his girlfriend came up for the day."

Cleo read her easily. "Hey, it's not that far—you can see him often. My twins come home on holidays. It's a whole new life of freedom—except for the money. That never ends."

They both laughed. Cleo walked over to Rita and put her hands on her waist.

"Hey, how about if I take you to lunch? There's a new little place I saw that just opened up the street."

"Okay, let me clean up and close up." She held her latest painting up. "Do you like it?" Rita asked. "I'm not sure who she is yet. But I'm sure I'll find out soon enough!" Rita put her paints away and cleaned her brushes in turpentine.

"You really should write a book, too, "Cleo said. "The stories of your paintings are so amazing."

Rita looked at Cleo. She knew they were falling in love. As winter deepened, their romance grew stronger, their kisses more passionate, their conversations more intense. One chilly weekend when Rita visited Cleo their affection turned hot. Their bodies pressed close, hands caressing the curve of backs, soft breasts, voluptuous thighs. In the light of the moon, long deep kisses lit a firestorm in Cleo's romantic bedroom. Ablaze in love-making, drenched in bliss, they explored every part of their sensual womanhood. Skillfully teasing, penetrating desire climaxed in a flood of ecstasy. They lay entwined, exhausted, satisfied. They fell asleep, then woke, desire igniting their languid bodies. Their music grew louder once again.

Memory flooded back in waves of adoration, making sense of Rita's breathlessness. Rita knew that Cleo was someone from her past, another lifetime. She felt her very spirit in her heart and soul. Rita rolled over and kissed Cleo deeply. "I'm falling for you, you know," she smiled, looking into Cleo eyes, pools of green water in a pine forest. She looked at the radiant and dreamy look of satisfaction on Cleo's face. "Oh," Rita gasped, her heart skipping a beat. "I remember you! Dowanhowee," Rita said.

"That's the title of your painting, love," Cleo's voice lilted in Rita's ear. She pointed to the painting of the beautiful young woman in a white deerskin dress decorated elaborately with beads and feathers. "I love that one."

In Cleo's modern love nest, visions as clear as day danced in front of Rita's eyes. Rita saw her boyhood, in grassy lands and deep green forests where bright blue skies, clear waterfalls, and cold streams flowed. She listened to the calls of birds in the lush green brush of spring, felt long black hair flowing against a bare back. She saw her young boy-self dart quickly, gracefully through the woods. Then the visions that had come later, in the heat of summer sunsets that lit plateaus and valleys in hues of gold and crimson, appeared before her. Rita remembered being a man of great dream-scapes, his people not understanding or believing what he saw—the horrors that awaited them at the hand of the invading armies of white-skinned men. They could not imagine the devastation of the land and its animals by other humans, or fathom the destruction of the Great Mother upon which all their lives depended.

Rita looked up at the paintings on the wall above. There was beloved Dowanhowee, a beautiful young woman who once comforted and loved the person she had been, the man she had been. Together they had conceived a daughter. Rita looked at the other painting that she had named simply "Mother and Daughter." She knew them now.

It was not long before Cleo would remember too. One snowy night in February, during love-making, visions like holograms of the man and woman they had once been appeared vividly to both of them.

"I remember you," Cleo said softly as their bodies pressed close. "Now, I remember you," she repeated. Tears flowed as they kissed.

"I knew you would," said Rita. "It's like we are part of some fantastic journey, the journey our very cells are remembering. It's just a matter of unlocking our hearts—trusting."

Then, as if only seconds had passed from their life on the plains to the present one in Cleo's bedroom, memory's magic door opened. Drums began to beat. Rita heard them, the drums beating under Cleo's bed. She heard an owl hooting, though the windows were closed.

"Do you hear that?" Cleo whispered to Rita.

Startled, Rita sat up in bed. "You mean you hear that, too? The drums? The owl?"

"Yes," said Cleo quietly. "Are you making that happen?"

"I'm not doing anything," Rita said, feeling herself an innocent participant in this shift of reality—the lifting of the veil between the worlds, past and present colliding, overlapping, time disintegrating. She reached over to the night table and lit a candle.

Rita sensed Cleo's uneasiness. Familiar as Rita had become to the transformation of reality, there was something haunting, a warning in the sound of the drums beating loudly beneath the bed and owls hooting in the dead of a snowy New England winter. Rita could not stop them, but she was not afraid. "Come close, my love. Come with me," Rita said softly.

"Where are we going?" Cleo whispered.

"Don't be afraid. We're together again...I love you." She wrapped her arm around Cleo. In each other's naked feminine embrace, their deep kisses transported them across the mists of time. They became young and old lovers again, with all the joy of hearts on fire, of sexual appetites that knew no bounds. Their spirits soared around the steamy, candlelit room, ecstasy flamed anew.

Suddenly, under the vast starry skies of what once was, they lay together on soft, mossy grass at the edge of a creek, its waters flowing over rocks into dark green pools. A full moon peaked beneath the leaves and branches of the forest trees as warm breezes cooled their shimmering bodies. Dancing drums beat in the distance and spring owls hooted their mating calls into the balmy night air.

About The Author

Ayin Weaver began her career in New York City as an artist and illustrator. With a degree in art, she later became an educator with a flair for innovation, developing language arts curriculum using art and storytelling as a basis for teaching students with learning disabilities.

Inspired by travel, spirituality and a family tradition of storytelling, her writing gives voice to her commitment to human rights, peace and environmental protection. Her current work in fiction and poetry focuses on challenging the fear that promotes prejudice, while supporting civil rights for women, minorities, and the LGBT community.

Ms. Weaver lives in California. *Bleed Through* is her first novel.

Made in the USA
Middletown, DE
16 September 2021